SHOOT

Sharon turned the sh___ __ ___. And the bathroom was suddenly quiet. Her hair soaking wet, half-blind from the water in her eyes, Sharon gripped the edge of the shower curtain to yank it aside. She froze.

My God, she thought, is someone *out there*? She firmly shook her head. Anthony Perkins, right? she thought. She managed a throaty laugh as she pulled the curtain open and recoiled in terror as a flash of light filled the room, followed immediately by a second blinding flash. Sharon backed up to the wall and hugged her breasts. As the red haze cleared from her vision, she gasped.

Her tormentor sat on the counter beside the sink. He lowered his camera and let it dangle from the strap around his neck. He picked up a pistol from the counter and pointed it at her. He had a lot more shots to take—one way or another. . . .

IN
SELF-DEFENSE

IN SELF-DEFENSE

Sarah Gregory

A Signet Book

SIGNET
Published by the Penguin Group
Penguin Books USA Inc., 375 Hudson Street,
New York, New York 10014, U.S.A.
Penguin Books Ltd, 27 Wrights Lane,
London W8 5TZ, England
Penguin Books Australia Ltd, Ringwood,
Victoria, Australia
Penguin Books Canada Ltd, 10 Alcorn Avenue,
Toronto, Ontario, Canada M4V 3B2
Penguin Books (N.Z.) Ltd, 182–190 Wairau Road,
Auckland 10, New Zealand

Penguin Books Ltd, Registered Offices:
Harmondsworth, Middlesex, England

First published by Signet, an imprint of Dutton Signet, a division of Penguin Books
USA Inc.

First Printing, January, 1995
10   9   8   7   6   5   4   3   2   1

PUBLISHER'S NOTE
This is a work of fiction. Names, characters, places, and incidents either are the product
of the author's imagination or are used fictitiously, and any resemblance to actual persons, living or dead, events, or locales is entirely coincidental.

With special thanks to Ruth Kollman,
Who, tired of being Della Street,
Went back to school in a phone booth,
And came out as Perrietta Mason

AUTHOR'S NOTE

The examining trial depicted herein is, technically, contrary to Texas law. Under the statutes, examining trials are conducted only prior to indictment. Exceptions are made, however, one peculiar to Dallas County, where the procedure is permitted post-indictment when the arresting officer wasn't available for testimony prior to the convention of the grand jury. In the case of a minor certified to stand trial as an adult, such an exception might be possible because, prior to certification, the evidence against the minor is withheld by law. It's never been done, but it might be. Consider this as poetic license, whatever, or if you choose, courtroom purists may now gleefully point the finger. Writers' skins are thick.

Other than this one exception, legal events described here are pretty much as they'd probably come down.

"And so we hold that a defendant's right
to counsel in any criminal prosecution,
much more than a procedural right or an
instrument of orderly legal process, is
the very bedrock on which our system must
stand; and that anything other than the
unabridged granting of that right, no matter
the evil alleged to the accused, is an evil
far greater still."

> —*Tall Deer* v. *Oklahoma*,
> from the 1917 majority
> opinion by Justice
> Learned Hand

"Man, it's just like any other business,
they tell you all this shit just to get
your money. Then they go buddy around with
all them D.A.'s, and whatever the D.A. wants
to do to you is what gets did. After they
get our money and then get us in the courthouse, us guys just don't matter anymore."

> —Texas death row inmate
> John Earl Bandy, in
> interview prior to execution,
> November 11, 1988

Prologue

The woman cringed against the headboard in a robe of lime green silk, the folds parting to reveal tensed, flawless thighs. She clutched satin-covered pillows to her breast, her mouth twisting in sensuous disgust as flying droplets of blood spattered the quilted spread and smooth rose-patterned sheets. There was sudden wetness on her cheek. She touched the damp spot, then stared dumbly at the red smear across her fingertips.

The two teenage man-boys ignored the woman. One youth, a hulking, deep-chested redhead in jeans and a waist-length khaki jacket, stood with his back to the bed, hands on hips, his head inclined arrogantly as he watched the man on the floor writhe and twist in vain to dodge the blows. The man held out his hands in silent pleading. The husky redhead showed a toothy grin.

The other boy, tall and thin with hints of dark peach fuzz on his cheeks, raised the steel lug wrench to strike again. The man's eyes widened in agony. He raised his arms in a feeble attempt to ward off the blow. The wrench glanced off purple satin-covered forearm to land solidly against the man's lacerated forehead. There was a sound as if a bat had struck a ripe melon. More blood flew. A crimson flood drenched the redhead's jeans. His grin broadened.

In minutes it was over. The man's body lay twitching on its side, the purple robe soaked in redness, one foot bare, the other foot encased in a fur-lined slipper. The thin boy's chest rose and fell rapidly as he stood over his prey, *the steel wrench dangling loosely from his fingertips. As one the teenagers turned to face the woman.*

Long-lashed eyelids softly closed as she cast the pillows aside. A sob escaped her lips. She moved quickly, her robe riding up to expose one bare hip as she slid across the mattress to stand. The boys stared at her. They stood rooted in their tracks as she circled them, stepping carefully to avoid the dead man's outstretched hand as she made her way warily over to the bathroom door. One splotch of red clung to her honey blond hair. She reached behind her, grasped the knob to open the door, and started to go inside the bathroom. Only then did the tall, thin teenager move.

He took one long step and halted the closing door. The woman's eyes widened slightly as she faced him through the crack. She looked up at him, the top of her head on a level with his chin. Woman and man-boy stood speechless. The boy looked down at the blood-drenched tire tool as though seeing it for the first time.

Finally the woman stepped forward. She raised on the balls of her feet, slid both arms around the boy's neck, and planted a long, lingering kiss on his lips. He responded, their mouths twisting hungrily, their pelvises grinding together. They held the embrace for a full thirty seconds while the burly redhead stood by and shifted his weight nervously from foot to foot. She finally placed her hands on the thin boy's shoulders and pushed gently away from him. "You must hurry," she said. Then she stepped onto the bathroom carpet, pulled the door to behind her, and secured the lock with a soft click of tumblers.

1

Russell Black, firm of jaw and rugged of countenance, thoughtfully considered the resumé of applicant Sharon Jenifer Hays. The resumé, presented just that morning in bold letter-perfect format, exhibited the following highlights: U.T. School of Law, Class of '86. Six years as a Dallas County A.D.A., fifty-one felony trials. Seven capital cases, all won; three men dead by the needle, four more on appeal. A former Texas Lady Longhorn with a hang-'em-high attitude.

Finally Black set the resumé aside. His expression softened, deep leather creases around his eyes relaxing as he considered now the personal appearance and demeanor presented by the selfsame Sharon Hays: poised finishing-school posture in a high-backed leather chair, elbows on armrests, manicured nails showing a clear lacquer polish, dark hair short and razored at the neckline with fluffed-out, flippant bangs in front. Light blush makeup glowed on soft cheeks, lip rouge casting a faint rose tint, her mouth full, her nose slender. Showcase legs confidently crossed, her ankles delicate above gray high-heeled pumps. Homecoming queen candidate, dressed for the walk down the fifty-yard line with the Longhorn band playing "Eyes of Texas" in the background. Perhaps just a bit of uncertainty in her look, a woman with a whole lot more going for her than her beauty, but still not sure whether being female was a strike against her in Russell Black's eyes. She'd be hoping that her record spoke loudly for itself. Which, Black had to admit, it did.

Black gently closed the folder containing the resumé. "I never met you," he said. "But I make it my business to know who's who over at the D.A.'s office. You leavin' was kind of sudden, wadn't it?" His voice was deep, his accent straight from East Texas piney woods, same vibrant quality as a tree-stump evangelist.

She met Black's gaze with steady brown eyes. "Zero days' notice," Sharon said. "But I hope you won't hold that against me. The circumstances were pretty different." Her tone was soft and cultured, low notes on a xylophone.

Black swiveled in his chair to face away from her, concentrated fleetingly on his own framed law degree where it hung on the wall—University of Houston, Class of '69—then gazed out his first-floor window across Jackson Street, toward the rear entry to the George Allen Courts Building, formerly the main courthouse and renamed for a county commissioner. As Black watched, two young men in three-piece suits hustled side by side up the steps and disappeared through the revolving door with attaché cases banging against tailored dark pants legs. S.M.U. grads, Black thought, that or some Ivy League school. Since the criminal courts had relocated a couple of miles to the west, on the other side of the Stemmons Freeway underpasses, attorneys from white-collar civil firms were about all that frequented the old white brick courthouse anymore. Black had liked things more in the old days. Back then he could cross the street, go down to the George Allen building's basement cafeteria, and drink coffee and shoot the bull with other criminal lawyers like himself, guys in cowboy boots who knew what life on the streets was all about. Now it was two miles in traffic to the new Crowley Courts Building, not worth the drive just to sit around and shoot the bull.

"There's rumors goin' around, Sharon," Black said, his gaze out the window. "I guess you already know that." He went directly to a first-name basis, letting her know that his wasn't a formal operation. The D.A.'s people called each other "Mr." and "Ms." until the cows came home, which Black personally considered a lot of horseshit.

Sharon cleared her throat. "Since they're about me, I haven't heard any of them. Just ask me what you want to know, and I'll do my best to fill you in." If she minded his using her first name, you'd never know it from her tone of voice. Black liked her answer and manner of presenting it, and mentally placed two marks in the plus column for Sharon Hays.

He turned back around in his chair, lifted his leg to rest his ankle on his knee, and pressed his shin against the edge of his desk. His suit was blue with a tiny gray pinstripe, his boots gray hand-tooled lizard. "I'll do that before we're finished," Black said. "First I want to get a couple of other things out of the way. Why you quit the D.A. falls in the category of none of my business, unless you're goin' into practice with me."

Nylon whispered as she uncrossed and recrossed her legs. She raised an expectant eyebrow. She didn't say anything, no challenge in her look, just a no-nonsense young woman understanding that Black's last comment didn't call for any response. Plus number three, Black thought.

"First of all ..." He picked up a gilt letter opener by its handle and placed the blade across his palm. "I think we can eliminate a lot of unnecessary talk if I find out what you already know about my operation, okay?"

Sharon thoughtfully bit her lower lip, then smiled. "Every lawyer in Dallas County knows a little bit about you. You pick your clients. Don't try a case but every couple of years or so, and when you do you generally win. You don't advertise. I only know you're looking for someone because I heard it over coffee the other day."

Black shrugged broad shoulders. His waist had expanded some in the past twenty-four years, but he still jogged and did sit-ups to keep from growing a full-sized beer gut. "I got an opening every three or four years," he said. "Youngsters come along and work with me awhile, get to know a few pimps and dope peddlers, get 'em a client base and go out on their own. Hell, I don't blame 'em, I did the same thing myself a long time ago." He scratched his head through thick, graying hair, then held the letter opener once more in both hands. "As for me winnin' cases, there's a reason for that. It's because I don't handle but one case at a time, haven't for years. Allows me to put the blinders on and concentrate on nothin' but the one case. There's advantages to that for a young lawyer throwin' in with me, too. He gets to take on whatever cases he wants—or *she* wants, I'm not used to interviewin' ladies, tell you the truth—and that takes care of my overflow. The fees for the other cases you'd get to keep for yourself, free overhead while buildin' up your own stable of clients. As you know, in this fair county every Criminal Bar member's got to take on court appointments, includin' me. Any indigent case would be your baby. You'd get to keep the court-appointment fee, o' course." Black scratched his chin. "Let's see, Sharon. Six years with the D.A., you made felony prosecutor, you're makin' what, fifty thousand minimum?"

She shrugged padded shoulders in a gray suit to match her shoes. "Close," Sharon said. She wore an off-white summer-weight blouse buttoned to her throat.

"Close enough, anyhow," Black said. "Here, as a base salary you'd be makin' barely more than half of that. With the fees you'll take in on your own cases, you'll wind up with double your D.A.'s income, but it takes time. Be a year or so before you could get back to what you were makin' with the D.A. So how would that sound to you?" He folded his arms, holding the letter opener in his right hand, its blade pointing toward the acoustical ceiling.

She hesitated, likely choosing her words, her smile just a little timid now, not the look of a young woman who'd stood in the courtroom more than once and asked a jury for the death penalty. Finally she said, "The money's about what I expected, Mr. Black."

"Russ. Nobody's called me Mr. Black since my law school profs."

Her lips formed the word Russ, then apparently she couldn't bring herself to say it, and said instead, "I've prepared myself to cinch up my girdle for a while. The deal you're talking beats working for a big firm, where you'd get nothing but a salary and maybe a partnership after ten years or so. I like what you've said so far."

"So far you've only heard the good parts. Now for the bad. I may be easy to get along with, but I'm not exactly runnin' a springboard for young lawyers to get rich off of. On my one or two cases a year, you'd be my co-counsel. Which really translates to bein' my gofer, nothin' more. My cases would take precedent over anything you were workin' on, and that could cost you some

clients. You'd do all my legal research. Hell, I always
hated books, even in law school. You could make suggestions on my cases, but I'd be runnin' the show. My cases
would generally take up about half your time."

She bit her lower lip. "I confess I might have a problem with not making any decisions. I do know the law."

"Hell, yes, you know the law. Five'll get you ten you
know it a damn sight better'n I do. Everybody at the
D.A.'s office knows the law. But face it, you're used to
workin' for the government. When you're a prosecutor,
the court's generally on your side, but where we come
from, the judge is liable to say to hell with the law and
rule against you just 'cause he thinks your client's an
assho—" He expelled breath, then said, "One of the bad
guys.

"What you've got to learn is," Black said, "and this
dudn't have anything to do with the law. You got to
know what prosecutor's lazy, might make your client a
good deal just to make his own job easier, and which
prosecutor's out to hang your boy come hell or high water. Which judge will let you maybe get away with a few
shenanigans in court, and which judge is liable to slap
you with a contempt citation. That kind of stuff you don't
learn in law school, and you sure don't learn it down at
the D.A.'s office. So that's why, in any case I'm handlin',
you can make suggestions, but the final call's up to me.
At least 'til you get some practical experience under your
belt."

She sat up straighter and smoothed her skirt over one
rounded thigh. "Criminal law is all I'm trained for,
Russ." She cocked her head slightly as though she were
thinking: Russ, there, I've said it. "And since I'm suddenly out of a job and can't go to one of the white-collar
firms with my experience, well, criminal law it is. So
whatever you want, I'll have to accept that even though
I might not like it. What I might not like would be worth
it if some of your reputation were to rub off on me. That
and your style. I sneaked away from the office every day
last year to watch you when you defended the Martins."

Black nodded. Ed and Patricia Martin had gone to trial
for poisoning Patricia's father, who'd owned a national
cosmetics firm. Black had won an acquittal, and to this
day he wondered every time he saw a bottle of Random

on the men's cologne counter whether Ed and Pat had been leveling with him. Sure had been a convincing pair.

"Your closing argument was the best I ever heard," Sharon said. "Every lawyer in the D.A.'s office, every defense attorney I know, they all say Russell Black is the best. I never went up against you myself, of course. Only the superchiefs get to try cases against Russell Black." She favored Black with a look of respect.

In spite of himself, Black felt like sticking out his chest. If this young lady was trying to butter him up, she sure knew which buttons to push. He looked at the ceiling. "Superchiefs. Sounds like a railroad, dudn't it? Only in Dallas County do they call 'em that, D.A.'s specializin' in cases that get a lot of ink in the newspapers."

"I always thought it was a little silly myself," Sharon said. "But superchiefs they've been since whenever, before I was born. I've been around enough to know that as a woman practicing criminal law, I'm not going to get many clients other than court appointments until I can prove myself. And working with Russell Black is the best way in this county to do that." Visible beyond her were photos on Black's paneled wall, one of him on horseback, another of him wearing a western shirt, jeans, and a red bandanna around his neck, grinning in front of a steaming pot at the Terlingua Chili Cookoff.

Black dropped the letter opener, put both feet on the floor, and leaned forward with his forearms resting on his desktop. "Now I got to ask you why you're leavin' the D.A. to begin with. The rumors we mentioned a minute ago. I'm not nosy, so nutshell it if you want to."

There was a downward shift to her gaze, an intake of breath as she prepared to talk about something in which she was emotionally involved, and she did her best to compose herself. Sharon Hays watched her own crossed knees as she said, "There's no way to nutshell it."

There was a small twitch at the corner of his eye. His tone gentle, he said, "Take your time, then."

Sharon sighed. "Sexual harassment. A dirty word, huh?" She lifted her eyes, her gaze once again calm and steady, all of the hesitancy gone. "You'll know Milton Breyer."

Black pictured Milt Breyer, tall and lean, a big, ugly bastard but with a pretty-boy way about him, married to big money. To Black's way of thinking, Breyer was the number one offender in the D.A.'s office when it came to spouting half-cocked statements to the newspapers. Black almost said, Yeah, I know the sonofabitch, but then thought better of it. Russell Black hadn't survived nearly a quarter century of practicing law, Dallas County style, for nothing. Better to keep your opinions to yourself, particularly about members of the D.A.'s staff. Never knew when your own words would come back to bite you in the ass. Black merely nodded. "I've tried a few cases against him," he said.

"I already know that," Sharon said. She relaxed her posture, leaning back, scooting her rear end forward a bit. "Well, it was him. It's been going on a year or so. First just a few suggestive jokes. Like I'd say, Boy, do we need to stick it to that guy, some defendant or other, and Milt would go, Well, I'd like to stick it to you, baby. I'm sure not a prude or anything, but that stuff isn't even funny. No matter what I'd say, Milt would turn it around into something sexual, you know? Honest to Pete, I expected him to trot out some Long Dong Silver movies or something. Lately he's been hitting on me to go for drinks, and I'd tell him, Sure, bring your wife along." She sighed. "The other day in court he grabbed my breast."

"The hell you say. Right in front of the judge?"

"Not right in court, in the witness room. Right after the jury brought in the Donello verdict. I quit on the spot after that little scene. Sent my official resignation letter a couple of days later, but I haven't been back to the office since that day in court."

"Rumors are that you did more than just walk out and quit. The story is that you . . ."

"Kicked him in the balls?" Her eyes flashed fire. "You bet your sweet ass I did. I wish I could've done worse than that." Her eyes widened as if to say, What am I saying? Then she lowered her gaze to her lap as she said, "Actually, it was my knee. Kneed him, is the proper description. I couldn't kick. My skirt was too tight, you know?"

"Probably would have been better for you," Black said, "if it hadn't of happened with two defense lawyers lookin' into the witness room from out in the hall. It's all anybody's talked about over at the courthouse the past few days. I saw that Donello business on the news, by the way. Good job, Sharon. Wilfred Donello came by here, and I wouldn't represent him. Greaso child-porno guys I don't need, no way. Howard Saw wound up representin' him, didn't he?" He was watching her, remembering how she'd said, "grabbed my breast," with no embarrassment or nervousness, just someone stating fact.

"Yes, it was Howard," Sharon said. "We expected more of a fight in the Donello case, to tell the truth. Howard Saw didn't seem to have a grasp of what was going on."

It was the first thing she'd said which Black, having a personal rule against knocking another lawyer, didn't particularly like. He decided that Sharon Hays was too fresh from the D.A.'s staff for him to call her hand on that one. Right now at any rate, but later on he'd probably let her know his feelings. "Since Milt Breyer's one of the superchiefs," Black said, "how'd you get to do the TV interview without him shoving you out of the way? He's usually front and center anytime there's a camera rollin'."

"Milt . . ." Sharon's gaze shifted downward for an instant, then she smiled and said, "Milt was indisposed."

Black threw back his head and laughed, a deep, healthy chuckle. "Kind of bent over double." Then, his expression suddenly serious, Black said, "You married?"

She hesitated, clearly surprised by the question and pondering her answer.

"Sharon," Black said, "I'm not pitchin' woo. I was wonderin', one, what your husband thought about the stuff with Milt Breyer, and two, how much problem it'd cause at home if you had to work a lotta long hours. We've got no staff like the D.A., and we have to do the grunt work after the courthouse closes."

She firmed up her chin. "I'm not married, but I have a daughter. Eleven. I like to spend as much time as I can with her, evenings, which was one thing I did like about working for the county. When we weren't in trial, our time was pretty much our own."

"I can't blame you for that," Black said, feeling just a little uneasy, not wanting to ask about the father of her child, not wanting to pry. "You filin' suit against the D.A.? The rumors say you are. That's one thing that would bother most lawyers if they were thinking of takin' you on as an associate. A sexual harassment charge against the D.A., particularly in *this* fair county . . . First thing you know, your client's plea-bargain offers would be zilch. D.A.'s got nearly every judge in his pocket, and you'd find your clients jailed without bond for crossin' the street against the traffic light. I guess you've already thought about that."

"It's the only thing I've *been* thinking about," she said, fiddling with the hem of her skirt. "And I'd love to bring charges. Every time I think about Milt groping me, God. But just for the reasons you're talking about, no, I'm not filing any suit. I need a job a whole lot more than I need revenge. I did make the mistake of talking it over with the federal Equal Rights people. I wish I hadn't, because I hadn't been out of their office five minutes before everybody in town knew I'd been over there, and now that I'm on their list they won't leave me alone. They've already called twice, trying to get me to file charges."

"And they'll keep callin'," Black said. "Which is one reason that anything you say about not filin' suit can't be written in stone. Anybody's got to think, Hey, she might change her mind at any time."

Sharon ran her tongue tip over even upper teeth. "I wouldn't do that. Not if I said I—"

"You're not lettin' me finish. What I'm sayin' is, you're talkin' to one guy don't care what the D.A. thinks. I'm not popular over there to begin with. I don't want your decision about filin' suit to have anything to do with workin' for me. You want to do it, you go ahead. That clear?"

Her mouth softened in surprise. "Working for . . . ?"

"This resumé . . ." He opened the folder and rattled the paper inside. "You were a drama undergrad major and lived in New York?"

Sharon rolled her eyes. "She was gonna be an actress, and all that. I went to acting school after college, voice, dance, the whole works, went in debt up to my tush." She thoughtfully regarded her folded hands in her lap, then raised her gaze. "I worked off-Broadway a year. Melanie was born up there, which was why I decided I had to make a living as something other than a starving artist. Which is also why I was twenty-eight before I got out of law school. Student loans piled on student loans."

"You had to work while you were in law school, then," Black said.

She nodded. "Waitressing mostly. A lot of real trendy

Austin bars and restaurants." She laughed, a pleasant, tinkly sound. "Milt Breyer's not the first man that tried pinching my fanny, believe me. Poor Melanie got to know the day-care ladies very well."

Black pushed the resumé aside, liking it that she was giving the bare-bones sketch, and that she took it all in good humor without going on and on about how tough things had been for her. Black could read between the lines if he cared to. "As far as I'm concerned," he said, "time's a-wastin'. Empty office is over there"—indicating, pointing a finger—"the other side of the library. How long before you can get your gear moved in?"

She smiled an eager smile. "Just like that? I thought you had other people to—"

"Did have. *Did* have, Sharon. Oh, hell, I got to ask you. You can't defend any case you worked on while you were a prosecutor, right?"

Her mouth tightened thoughtfully. "It would be a breach of ethics," she said. "If I made even one appearance in a case like that, the prosecutor would file a motion to have me removed as counsel before you could say, Ready for trial."

Black dusted his hands together. "You ever do any work on the Rathermore case? Heard of it, I guess."

"Who hasn't? But no, I was knee-deep in Donello when they made that arrest." Her interest picked up. "You're representing Midge Rathermore? I thought she had a court-appointed lawyer."

"She did, up until ten days ago. Her mother hired me. We're talkin' a teenage girl charged with hirin' other kids to kill her daddy. You up to somethin' like that? Won't go against your grain or anything."

"No." She smiled. "I'm a criminal lawyer, remember? Nothing's supposed to go against my grain."

"I couldn't have said it better myself," Black said. "Now, one o'clock, she's over in family court for a hearing to certify her as an adult. You ever been in on one of those hearings?"

"Several." Sharon said. "So many kids committing crimes these days, juvie cert got to be old hat at the D.A.'s office."

"Well, I never have," Black said. "Not too many teenagers are lookin' for an old goat like me to represent 'em. Which is really goin' to make me depend on you. Means you got one hour to get moved into your office. Can you do that?"

"You just watch my smoke," Sharon said. She rose, hefted her shoulder bag, adjusted the strap, and took two rapid steps toward the exit. "I've just got a couple of boxes, and they're in my car. Some briefs I've worked on, a couple of paperback law books is all."

"Travel light, huh?" Black grinned. "Good, I like that." She opened the door.

"Sharon?" Black said.

She turned with raised eyebrows. "Yes?"

"Guess you ought to know, Milt Breyer's the prosecutor in the Rathermore case. The D.A. assigned it to him a few days ago, as soon as Donello was over. That going to give you a problem?"

Her soft forehead furrowed, then she said quickly, "The only one it might give a problem is him. Milt's not a very good lawyer, though he is smart enough to have some good lawyers working with him. Having him on the other side, if he's actually going to prosecute the case himself, ought to make our job easier." She took one step into the hallway, then turned back, her features tight. "I hope Milt doesn't bend over and cover his crotch every time I walk near him in the courtroom," Sharon said, then brightened. "On the other hand, maybe I hope that he does. It would give the jury something to wonder about, huh?" She left with a smile on her face.

A lightbulb exploded in Black's head. He got up quickly, followed her over to the door, leaned against the jamb, and thrust his hands into his pockets. She moved in modeling-runway strides, crossed the waiting room to sit on the Naugahyde sofa, crossed her legs, and removed one high-heeled shoe. She dug in her shoulder bag for one spotless white Reebok, dug a sock out of the shoe's insides, and slipped the sock up over her ankle.

"Well, I'll be damned," Black said.

She looked up at him from across the room.

"You knew all along I had the Rathermore case, and that old Milt was goin' to be the prosecutor," Black said. "Didn' you?"

She smiled a tiny smile, then bent her head to pull her sneaker on and snugged up the laces. "I might've heard some rumors," Sharon Hays said.

2

Sharon left Russell Black's first-floor office, hop-skipping in Reebok sneakers down the two steps to the sidewalk, and it was all she could do to keep from breaking into a run. It was the first time that her spirits had been on the upswing since five days ago—*five days?* God, it seemed like ever-loving *weeks*—when she'd put Milt Breyer temporarily out of commission and herself out of a job. Not that she wouldn't do the same thing all over again. She'd gotten the bastard right where he lived, which was exactly what he'd deserved. Just thinking about Milton Breyer made Sharon's flesh crawl.

So it wasn't any regret over what she'd done to dear old Milton which had had her down in the dumps. Her sinking spells of late had been due to the nagging dread—the absolute terror, in fact—that she'd cut off her nose to spite her face. The fear had pursued her day and night, ever since she'd submitted her resignation to the D.A., that as a female with a potential sexual-harassment suit against the county, she'd be too much of a hot potato for anyone to give a job. God knew she couldn't afford her own office. And even if she'd had the money to set up her own practice, she wouldn't have had the slightest idea where her clients would have come from.

But now—zap!—everything had changed for Sharon in the space of twenty minutes or so. Not only was she going to have the chance to go up against Milton Breyer himself in her first trial as a defense lawyer—a prospect which, though she'd never admit it to anyone, had her licking her chops—she was going to be riding shotgun for none other than Russell Black. He didn't know it—and would never know, Sharon thought, would that be embarrassing or what?—but her feeling from afar for the older lawyer went a great deal deeper than she'd let on in the interview.

She hadn't had a crush on him or anything, she told herself with a chuckle, but from a legal standpoint she'd been using Russell Black as a role model ever since she'd been a law student. Even when she'd been a prosecutor, every time that Black had been in trial she'd managed to sneak away for an hour or so just to sit in the back of the spectators' section and watch him work. She'd marveled at his homespun demeanor and razor-sharp questions when he'd been intent on tearing the state's witnesses down—which he did successfully more often than not—and had thought to herself many times, Gee, could I possibly ever do that? Early on in her career, in the secrecy of her bedroom, she'd more than once paraded in front of her mirror—naked as a jaybird half the time—mimicking Black's mannerisms and imagining herself the female Russell Black. In the end she'd settled on a more subdued courtroom manner, which, she felt, was better suited to her personality, but most of her closing arguments had been modified versions of what she'd heard while watching Russell Black stalk in front of a jury. Stalk, that was the proper word for it. There were lawyers who preened in front of the jury and lawyers who strutted, but no one she'd ever seen could mesmerize jurors, make state's witnesses quiver in their boots, and hone in on a case with the intensity of Russell Black. Assisting this guy, Sharon thought, is going to be a constant adrenaline high.

She briskly jaywalked to the remodeled gas station across the street from the back of the George Allen Courts Building, looking both ways for oncoming cars as she did. The old station now served as a covered parking lot, and was the same lot where she'd left her car nearly every day for her first four years as a prosecutor. In those days the criminal courts had been in the Allen Building, and during the same four-year period Sharon had worked her way up through the misdemeanor courts to become chief felony prosecutor in the 368th under Judge Hagood (nasty-dispositioned old bastard, Sharon thought). She'd finally become a first assistant to Milton Breyer (great career move *that* was, Sharon thought), and now had made her gracious exit to civilian life after kneeing her boss in the balls. What sparkling credentials I've got, Sharon thought. She ducked underneath the garage awning and hustled toward her Volvo, at five-nine a tall young woman with the supple walk of a dancer. Her brown leather shoulder bag bumped gently against her hip.

The blue Volvo had seen better days. She'd been driving it for six years. In fact, she'd been planning to trade the car in, but that had been before the Milton Breyer Confrontation, Bout of the Century. So much for a new car—or a new anything else, for that matter—at least for the time being.

She glanced ruefully at the small dent in the Volvo's left front fender, something done in this very parking lot two or three years ago, something she'd chosen to call a little scratch instead of the full-sized dent that it was. It had been a choice between living with the fender or forking over the two hundred and fifty bucks which was her insurance deductible to have it fixed. It was true, as Russell Black had guessed, that she'd made over fifty thousand a year as a prosecutor, but fifty-six, five as a single mother, what with the cost of care for Melanie while mommy busted her fanny in trial, wasn't by any means a bonanza. And now her income was to be skimpier still. She clucked her tongue at the Volvo, murmured, "I hope you've got another hundred thousand miles in you, old girl," then unlocked the car and opened the rear left-hand door.

She'd expected Black to register surprise when she'd told him that she had her things right outside in her car, as if she *lived* in the old heap of a Volvo, but he hadn't even blinked. Actually, hauling around what was left of the belongings accumulated in six years as an A.D.A. had been her idea of thinking positive, like a teenage boy carrying a condom in the hope that opportunity would come knocking, and for once her positive thinking had worked. And—ta—*taa*—there they were, all her lawyerly possessions, packed in twin three-by-three-foot cardboard boxes which sat side by side on her backseat. One box was an Oreo Cookies container and the other had once held El Cid Picante Sauce, and she'd begged both boxes from the manager of the Tom Thumb Supermarket near her home. The six-inch, bright green plastic Teenage Mutant Ninja Turtle figurines scattered about on top of the boxes weren't part of Sharon's legal paraphernalia, of course—God, she thought, my darling little girl, Tomboy Princess—and Sharon quickly dropped the figures, one by one, on the floorboard, halfway expecting Donatello to leap up and shout, "Cowabunga," loudly in her ear. Melanie had outgrown the Turtles, just as she'd outgrown the Care Bears, Big Bird, and everything else passing through her little-girl existence—criminy, Sharon thought, including her clothes—and Sharon planned to drop Donatello and company off the first time she passed a Goodwill station.

The digital clock radio which peeked at her through the crack in the nearest box's lid wasn't legal material, either, not exactly, but as far as Sharon was concerned, the radio was as vital as the paper-bound editions of the Texas Penal Code and the Code of Criminal Procedure. She confessed to being a C&W nut, and had worked out many a final argument and briefed many an issue as she hummed along with Garth Brooks or Jerry Jeff Walker on Country 96.3.

She carefully folded her jacket and laid it on the front seat along with her shoulder bag, rolled up the sleeves of her blouse, and lifted one of the boxes. She balanced her load on her thigh, propping the front edge of the box against the fender while she closed and locked the door. Then, thus weighed down, she stood upright and looked around. Two big, strong male lawyers in suits hustled by on the sidewalk, briefcases held importantly, glanced in her direction, then quickly looked away and continued on into the courts building. No matter, she'd learned to do it on her own a long time ago. She whistled softly the opening bars to "Eighteen Wheels and a Dozen Roses," her spirits still high as she headed across the street with the box resting heavily on her upturned forearms.

A sheen of perspiration had formed on Sharon's upper lip before she'd completed the fifty-yard journey from the parking lot to the steps leading to Black's office. She'd had to stop a couple of times in order to shift her load into a less uncomfortable position. It wasn't particularly hot, the temperature in the upper seventies, but a thick cloud cover blotted out the sun, and it was as if she was wading through the humidity-laden air. It was the first of May. For the next month or so it would rain cats and dogs nearly every night, and sometimes pour all day as well. Then summer would bring a blistering drought which would carry on into early October, at which time the downpours would commence all over. Not to mention the tornado watches and warnings. Dallas my hometown, Texas, Sharon thought, has the worst all-around weather in the Western Hemisphere, and while one could excuse the natives for loving the area, the reason that northerners kept moving to town was a total mystery to her. Must be something in the water, Sharon thought. She had absolutely adored New York City, and if she'd had the good sense to keep from falling in love—and, God, she thought, the good sense to keep my frigging legs crossed—she'd probably still be in the Big Apple, living on Spam, packaged smoked turkey breast, and Kraft American cheese slices while she worked off-Broadway and had the time of her life. But, she thought with a twinge of conscience, if I'd kept my legs crossed, I never would have had Melanie. Tit for tat, Sharon thought.

She took a shallow but determined breath and lifted one foot to mount the steps as, from behind her, a tenor male voice said, "Hey. Hey, I wonder if I could get you to ..." Sharon turned her head toward the sound and blinked.

About twenty steps away and coming in her direction was a man. He wore snow white summer-weight baggy pants and an oversized Hawaiian shirt with green, red, and purple flowers splashed over the fabric. The short sleeves hung below his elbows, and his forearms were skinny and pasty white. His face was pale as death as well, a narrow face with a big, bent honker of a nose. He was clean-shaven except for a pointed brown goatee, and his I-want-to-sell-you-a-condo smile revealed a wide gap between his two front teeth. His hair was thinning, combed straight back, and he wore dark sunglasses in spite of the overcast. A professional-looking camera with a flash attachment hung from a strap around his neck. "Won't take a minute," he said.

Sharon's eyes narrowed warily as she backed away from the steps. "I beg your pardon?"

"Bradford Brie," the man said. "Photographer. Last name spelled just like the soft cheese. I'm shooting a few street scenes for this album I'm putting together, and, hey, you'd be perfect. Beauty at work, you know?"

Sharon felt a slight chill. "I don't pose for pictures, Mr. Brie." If the guy had called and asked for an appointment, she might have felt differently. Instinct told her that there was something not right about this situation.

He raised his camera and squinted through the viewfinder. "Could you maybe turn just a little to the left?"

"I told you, I don't—" There was a sudden flash of light, accompanied by a loud click. *"Hey,"* Sharon said.

"That's the"—click-flash—"way. Natural beauty, but a modern woman not afraid to get her hands a little dirty, hey?" Click-flash. "Perfect, perfect."

A surge of anger went through her. "You stop." She placed the box on the bottom step and faced him with hands on hips. "I've never seen you before in my life." God, he was aiming the camera again. She started to cover her face, but she wasn't quick enough. Click-flash.

He lowered the camera. "Great. Man, would I like to spend an hour with you." His smile disappeared, replaced by a serious pucker at the corners of his mouth.

Sharon's forearms quivered. "You get away from me."

"Man." His shoulders sagged. "Well, if that's the way it is, that's the way it is. But, man, can I ever use these shots. I'm doing an album."

Sharon took a hesitant step toward her box on the steps. "Look, I'm not trying to be rude."

He grinned again. "You could make a living as a model, you know."

In fact, Sharon did know, and had done some commercial photo sessions for Southwest Airlines, in addition to her waitressing jobs, when she'd been in law school. If she'd wanted to get by on her looks alone, however, she could have done some things a whole lot easier than posing for pictures. Had even had a few offers in her time. "What kind of album is it?" she said.

"You work in there, huh?" He jerked a thumb toward the building.

"Yes, I—" Damn, he'd caught her off guard. "What kind of an album?" she said sternly.

"Super." He took a few quick steps away from her, then turned and raised the camera again. Click-flash. "Great. I'll be in touch." He snugged up his sunglasses on his nose, showed wide-gapped teeth in a grin, and hustled away down the block while shouldering his camera.

Sharon yelled after him. "What did you say your name was? You're not using my picture without a release."

He paused and turned. "Brie, just like the cheese. You'll be hearing from me." He went around the corner and disappeared from view behind the building.

Sharon was really frightened. What kind of an album? she thought fearfully.

Sharon had practically forgotten about the strange photographer—or at least had filed the incident into the section of her mind labeled "Scary but Unimportant Happenings"—by the time she'd made her second trip to the parking garage and, huffing and puffing, had carried the rest of her belongings up the steps, through Russell Black's reception area—which held a secretarial desk, chair, and files, but no receptionist that Sharon had seen as yet—past the library and into the cubbyhole of an office which was to be hers. She checked the time. God, only an hour before she and Black were to leave for court. Her struggles with the heavy boxes coupled with the humid outside air had left her quite a bit less than fresh. God, what she wouldn't give to shower and change her clothes. No way could she, however, a quick redoing of her makeup would have to get her by. She opened the first of the boxes, plugged in her radio, set the volume on low ("Small Town Saturday Night" was the jumpy C&W tune in progress), and went to work.

Fifteen minutes later, the boxes were empty, and Sharon's briefs, sample motions, and paperback law books were stacked on top of her desk. The desk was old and pretty banged up, but someone had recently painted it dark brown so that the scratches didn't jump right out and bite you. The swivel chair had a slatted back and wooden seat covered by a portable rubber cushion, and creaked loudly when she sat down. The walls were bare. There was a metal file cabinet in one corner and a dusty imitation rubber plant in the other. The disgusting plant will have to go, she thought, replaced by some real greenery, and she was going to bring a few pictures from home in order to spruce up the place. The ancient chair was soon to be history as well; she was going to have a comfortable place to sit even if it meant digging into her own pocket. She was standing in front of her desk, holding her framed law degree in one hand and a small hammer in the other, and trying to make up her mind as to the best place to hang the sheepskin, when she sensed movement behind her and to her left. She turned.

Russell Black stood in the doorway. He was coatless, wearing a pale blue shirt and navy tie. He jammed his hands into his back pockets, leaned against the door frame and showed a crooked grin. God, Sharon thought, he looks like the sheriff of Last Ditch Gulch. Square, leathery-tanned face with creases around the eyes, a broad, flat, cute-ugly nose, ice blue, stare-'em-down eyes. Interesting face, Sharon thought. Small roll of chub around the middle, barely noticeable beneath the shoulders of a retired football jock. Not unhandsome at all, Sharon thought. She was taller than most men, but her eyes were barely on a level with Black's chin. Even if she wore heels he'd be a half head taller than she. Six three if he's an inch, Sharon thought.

She jumped slightly as she realized that she, as the new person on board, was entertaining her boss with a twangy rendition of "Baby's Got Her Blue Jeans On," which was the song now playing on the radio. Sudden warmth flooded her cheeks as she bent to turn the volume knob. The music faded and died. "I'm sorry. Was it too loud?" Sharon said, and hoped that she didn't look as silly as she felt.

Black didn't seem to hear the question. His gaze swept the room, zeroing in on empty boxes, pausing there, shifting to rest on the stacks of books and motions, taking in all, missing nothing. "Gettin' squared away, huh?" he said. Sharon halfway expected him to add, "pardner," which would have gone right along with his laid-back manner of speech. "Listen," Black said. "I got to apologize for not helpin' you carry in your gear. I don't think real quick some days."

Sharon had had a flare of resentment when the two lawyers had passed her by on the street, pretending not to see her while she'd struggled with her load, but never in a million years would she have expected her boss to pitch in. "Oh, it wasn't much to do," she said. She looked past

him toward the reception area. "Is your secretary out today?" she said.

"Don't have one. I used to have one, but she quit three
years ago. There's a typin' pool up the street that does
whatever letters I need done. The answerin' machine
takes care of the phone, unless I'm in a mood to answer
myself. If the judge calls for a brief, I get my daughter to
type it. She's a business major at S.M.U. and does a
pretty legal paper. Or I guess I used to get my daughter
to do it. That'll be your job now."

For the first time since coming in for the interview,
Sharon felt resentment. He'd told her that she would do
the briefing, she couldn't complain about that, but hadn't
said a word about doing her own typing. When she'd
been at the D.A.'s, she'd merely dictated to the secretarial
pool by telephone, and her correspondence, brief, whatever, had been on her desk the next morning, typed neat
as a pin. Sharon had never even taken a typing course,
and no small part of her resentment was due to the fact
that Black had assumed, merely because she was female,
that she'd be gangbusters on the keyboard. Anyone who
thought that Sharon Jenifer Hays was going to act as a
glorified secretary had another think coming, and that
went for Russell Black or anybody else. She held her
tongue in check and didn't say anything. He had answered one of her unasked questions; his having a daughter meant that he had a wife as well.

"My wife," Black said, as if reading her mind, "used to
do all my typin' years ago. Before she died." He studied
the floor for a moment, and then raised his gaze to say,
"How 'bout givin' me a thumbnail on this juvenile certification business?"

Sharon's flare of resentment had subsided at once, replaced by a sudden sadness when he'd mentioned his
wife's passing, and now the sadness left her for a kind of
heady anticipation. Her ego was no smaller—and, she
liked to think, not any bigger—than anyone else's, and
filling in someone like Russell Black on the law was going to be downright invigorating. Not that she was surprised because he didn't know much about the juvenile
code; a lawyer of Black's stature would never have to.
Years ago, Sharon knew, when Russell Black had first begun to practice law, teenagers seldom if ever had had fel-

ony charges strapped on them. With the current number of murders committed by high school students, however, juvie cert had become a common thing.

Sharon sat in her chair with a protesting squeak of wood. Black continued to stand in the doorway, his salt-and-pepper brows lifted expectantly. Sharon took a couple of seconds to get her thoughts in order, then said, "I suppose I don't have to tell you that they'll certify her. She'll stand trial as an adult. She can't get the death penalty, but they can give her up to life in prison. I believe I read that Midge Rathermore is sixteen."

Black thoughtfully rolled his eyes. "Yeah, I think so."

Sharon would have liked to have given him something brilliant, the new assistant saving the day, but felt sort of down as she said, "Juvenile certification is really a formality. The judge won't even hear the case, he leaves that up to the family court master. That's kind of . . . sort of a junior judge, like the magistrate in federal court. The master can't rule, not officially, he can only make a recommendation to the judge, but the judge just rubber-stamps what the master recommends." She paused to lick her lips, searching Black's face for a hint of a reaction. Approval? Disapproval? Boy, is she ever smart? Black maintained a poker face. Sharon went on:

"There's two issues at stake in the hearing. First, she's got to be at least fourteen, and second, they've got to demonstrate that she understood the nature of her act. That the act was wrong. Legally a juvenile can be certified to stand trial as an adult for any felony, but in practice it's only done where you have a habitual, really a badass kid, or where you've got an unusually heinous crime. Which hiring someone to kill your father is without question. The amount of publicity has a lot to do with it in Dallas County, and really, you can't get more public than the Rathermore case." As Black frowned, Sharon's mouth softened. "Don't guess I'm giving you much encouragement, huh?" Sharon said.

"No problem," he said, waving a big hand as if batting mosquitoes. " 'Bout what I had figured, tell you the truth. The hearin's worth it, though, 'cause they'll have to put some evidence into play. Give us some idea what we're lookin' at, defendin' the little girl."

Sharon hesitated before saying, "I'm afraid not."

His frown deepened. "Huh?"

"It's not like a bond hearing or examining trial, where the state has to put on any probable cause evidence. The charges in a juvie cert hearing speak for themselves. As I said, only two issues, Russ. Is she over fourteen, and did she understand that murdering someone was wrong? They'll probably put a cop on the stand to testify what a dastardly deed's been committed, but he's not going to offer any evidence that hasn't already been in the newspapers. It's like a lot of things that happen in open court. Just a formality, but a hearing has to be held to make it official."

"Damn. Another waste of time."

"Maybe not entirely," Sharon said. "It'll give us a chance to visit with our client in person. Try to see what makes her tick. Have you ever met Midge?"

"Nope, and I'm out of line there. I should've. I've talked to her mother four or five times over the past couple of weeks, and she's damn sure got one relative on her side."

"Well, if nothing else," Sharon said, "the hearing gives you a chance to spend some time with your client other than in the jail visiting room. And by the way. Ten days before a juvie cert hearing seems awfully late in the game to be hiring a lawyer. Looks like she should have had legal representation from day one."

Black said, almost absently, "I told you, she had a court-appointed lawyer. Andy Tubb."

"If you want to call him a lawyer," Sharon said. "He's one I know. He was on the other side of a robbery case I tried."

Black showed sudden irritation. "Somethin' you have to learn, Sharon, like every pup from the D.A.'s office that wants in private practice. You don't go around knockin' other lawyers. Now, I know that's not true when you're workin' for the county, that they spend half their time over there sittin' around drinkin' coffee and sayin', This lawyer dudn't know what he's doin', and, That lawyer got fired off of such-and-such a case. As long as you got that government paycheck comin' every two weeks, you can get away with sayin' just about anything about anybody. But on your own, you're dependin' on other lawyers for your livelihood, referrals and whatnot. Now,

I don't know what went on with Andy Tubb and Midge Rathermore or Midge's mother, and didn't ask. I got to get along with Andy, and stickin' my nose in his business idn't the way to go about it."

Sharon's ego deflated like a ruptured tire, and a slow burn worked its way through her insides. Knifing through her rush of anger, though, was the knowledge that Black was right on the money. It was his manner of putting his point across that really got to her. She tried a meek "I just thought . . ."

"Well, that's somethin' you shouldn't be thinkin'." Black checked his watch. It was a big watch with a big face, the size of a Rolex, though it occurred to Sharon that Russell Black wasn't the Rolex type.

"I wouldn't think that anyone with Rathermore money could have qualified for a state-paid lawyer to begin with," Sharon said, swallowing pride in a big gulp, switching the subject away from other lawyers and their methods.

"The little girl's got nothin' on her own," Black said. "It's all her daddy's money, and since it was him that she's supposed to have had killed, her family's not real crazy about hirin' her legal counsel. Until her mother stepped forward she was goin' to have to take charity." He thoughtfully folded his arms. "What about appeals? If they certify the little girl, can we get it overturned?"

Sharon mentally relaxed. The conflict over her knocking Andy Tubb had vanished as if by magic. "Afraid not," she said. "Juvenile certification isn't even a criminal proceeding. It's civil, so the ruling is based on preponderance of evidence rather than anything beyond reasonable doubt. The judge can rule any way he wants to, and there's nothing we can do about it. She's not under indictment and can't even be charged with the crime until she's certified, and a juvenile doesn't even have Fifth Amendment privileges. There are a few . . . If you could show that she's really childlike, maybe spends all her time playing video games, you've got a chance to beat certification sometimes. The fact is, it's just like about every facet of the law, the D.A.'s office uses juvie cert more as a plea-bargain hammer than anything else. You know, when I was a prosecutor, if we didn't have much of a case against a kid we'd tell him, either plead guilty as a juvenile or we'll certify you as an adult. But on a premeditated crime like this one it's different. I doubt they'll even offer a deal. They'll want to trot her out in public and really let her have it with the cameras grinding. I've only read the newspaper accounts, but this was a pretty brutal killing."

Black winced visibly. "These two youngsters," he said, then cleared his throat and said, "These two youngsters busted into the Rathermores' bedroom in the middle of the night, and beat him to death with a tire tool. Right in front of his wife. She got away by locking herself in the bathroom while they were poundin' on him. Typical of the D.A. in this fair county, they've made deals with the two bloody little bastards to testify against Midge. One of 'em's seventeen and the other fifteen. The seventeen-year-old signed up with 'em to do twenty years, he'll be in about three, and they're not even goin' after the younger kid as an adult." Black snorted. "Bad as the D.A. wants Midge Rathermore, those two kids should have held out. Might have gotten probation, the both of 'em."

Sharon pursed her lips. "With that kind of case, Midge's certification is automatic. We can make some noise in the hearing, but they'll try her as an adult. I'm missing something here, Russ. After what happened, her mother's paying her legal fee?"

"Her natural mother. The woman in the bedroom, the witness—you don't know about Bill Rathermore's second wife?"

Imaginary fingers snapped in Sharon's head. "Of course. Linda Haymon, the TV newswoman. Big headline affair, nasty divorce."

Black stood away from the doorjamb and once more looked at his watch. "Nasty as they come. Listen, we got to get a move on. Hell, I don't even know what questions to ask in this hearin'. If you get any brilliant ideas, let me know." He started to leave, then paused. "Oh, and hey. Turn that volume up some. No reason I can't enjoy some shitkicker music, same as you. I'll get my gear." He headed across the corridor toward his own office.

Sharon went to the door and watched Black go, his gait leisurely and confident, big hands swinging beside narrow hips. Less than an hour on the job, and already her emotions had gone up and down like a berserk yo-yo.

Praise from him one minute, a real dressing-down the next. Well, at least it isn't going to be boring, Sharon thought. She dug into the Oreo cookie box, located her briefcase, and set about stuffing a few papers inside. She didn't have the slightest idea what she needed, but thought she should go to court armed with an overflowing attaché case. Looked more like a real-live attorney that way.

3

Two blocks down the street from Russell Black's office, in a ground-floor converted pawnshop with display windows in front, Howard Saw was having trouble convincing Richard Waite that he should lower his fee for handling Wilfred Donello's appeal. "Fuck, Dicky," Saw said into the phone, "it's a walk in the park. Plain vanilla. Just the usual insufficient-evidence motions and one deal where the judge admitted some things our man said to a detective. Hell, Donello wasn't even under arrest at the time. He wasn't entitled to any Miranda warning out of custody, you know that. You'll never even have to argue the case. The First Court of Appeals will turn us down quicker'n God can get a weather report, and that'll be the end of it. Donello can't afford to appeal it any further." Howard Saw was short, fat, and bald, with puffy rolls hanging down from his throat to overlap his starched collar. He was seated at his desk with the receiver cradled between his neck and shoulder, and he was cleaning his nails with the sharp end of a file. Ten feet above him, twin ceiling fans whirled at medium speed.

There was a brief pause before Waite said, "Ten thousand, Howard. Not a penny less." His words were slightly slurred as if he'd been sleeping.

"Christ," Saw said. "You're wanting to make more off the appeal than I got for representing the guy in a jury trial." Wilfred Donello's file lay open before the pudgy lawyer, weighed down by his forearms as he cleaned his nails. Saw squinted at a row of pen-and-ink figures on the file's inside cover, then shifted his attention briefly to the standard contract, which both Saw and Wilfred Donello had signed. The contract required Saw to handle Donello's appeal at no additional fee. I must have been crazy, signing this sonofabitch, Saw thought.

"Howard," Waite said. "How long have we known each other?"

"Way back a lot of years," Saw said. He pictured Dicky Waite, short and wiry with a pencil mustache. At the moment Waite would be looking at the old law school frat picture which hung in his office, and which featured Saw and Waite with their arms around each other's shoulders in a palsy-walsy posture. Lots of sentimental bullshit, Saw thought. He loosened the knot on his tie by pulling downward with a forefinger. His collar was open, his coat hanging on a hall tree in one corner of his office.

"Right," Waite said. "A lot of years. You didn't touch the Donello case for a penny less than fifty grand, up front. You told the client originally it'd be a hundred, then when he squawked about it you told him that since you believed in him, you'd do it for fifty. Am I right or not?"

"Fifty grand, that's a helluva lot of money," Saw said. "Times are hard." Outside his office in the reception area, a bell dinged as the glass-paneled street door opened, then closed. Saw glanced at his digital clock. Twelve forty-five, the secretary was still at lunch. Saw had no appointments that he knew of, but his sign read, HOWARD SAW, LAWYER, with "abogado" underneath, and the Spanish word attracted a lot of drop-in business. Saw craned his neck, had a glimpse of ice cream white britches and a loud Hawaiian shirt. Saw covered the mouthpiece with the palm of his hand. "Be with you in a minute, huh?"

Dicky Waite was saying over the phone, "Right, Howard, times are hard, and fifty grand is a lot of money for normal people. For Donello, selling all that kid pornography, it's pocket change. So he even bitched about the fifty, and you told him, Hey, if you get convicted I'll handle your appeal at no extra charge. Now he's sitting down at the county and you don't want to fuck with the appeal because it would get in the way of you hustling money from somebody else. Okay, that's your bag. But don't try to jew me down on my fee, Howard. Jesus, I don't even know why we're having this conversation. Ten grand, and that's final. Oh, and, yeah, it'll cost you even more if we got to bond the guy out while he's appealing."

Saw shuddered slightly as he pictured Donello, sneering as they locked him in the holding cell behind the courtroom, Donello threatening his lawyer with a concrete overcoat. "Uh, I don't think there's going to be any bond," Saw said. The chubby lawyer continued to peer into the reception room, squinting for a full view of his visitor. Strange clicking noises emitted from outside Saw's office door. "You drive a hard bargain, Dicky," Saw said. "Listen, I got somebody here."

"Yeah, right. You send the file over with a cashier's check for ten grand. A *cashier's check,* Howard. Let's see, Sharon Hays prosecuted your boy, so the state's case will be up to snuff. Say, you think it's true what they're saying? About how Sharon quit because Milton Breyer was hot to get in her pants?"

"How should I know, Dicky? I'm trying to keep you from getting in *my* pants. I told you already, I got a guy here."

"Ha, ha, Howard. Ten grand." There was a sharp click as Waite disconnected.

Saw hung up and, frowning, entered ten thousand dollars in the minus column on the inside front cover of Donello's file. As he wrote, clutching the ballpoint in a death grip, he said loudly, "Yeah, come on in." And then blinked as a quick, blinding light filled the room. What the fuck was going on here?

Framed in the doorway was a pipestem-thin man in a loud shirt and white pants who peered at Saw through a camera's viewfinder. The newcomer had a pasty complexion and a face like a hatchet blade, and wore dark sunglasses. Saw pointed a thick finger. "If you're from the newspapers, I'll break that fucking camera."

The light flashed again, accompanied by a sharp click. A lingering red haze clouded Saw's vision. The man lowered the camera and grinned, showing wide-gapped front teeth. "No newsman me, no sirree. Get 'em natural, that's my motto. Posed pictures look phony as hell."

"Well, how 'bout posing your ass outside in the street?" Saw said. "I'm busy."

The man took two steps toward Saw's desk. "Bradford Brie, photographer. Freelance. I'm putting an album together on downtown Dallas. Famed attorney hard at work. Great shot."

"I'll give you a shot," Saw said. "Out."

" 'Course, I don't know how famous you are right now," Brie said, inching even closer, raising the camera, adjusting the dial on the lens. "But man, once this album comes out . . ."

Saw had to admit he could use some publicity. Thirty-seven trials lost in succession wasn't exactly dragging in the business. "I really got a lot to do," Saw said.

"Being busy, that's the mark of success," Brie said. "We all got our marks, you know? See, I even got one." He abruptly set his camera on the desk and yanked up his shirtsleeve.

As the red haze faded from his vision, Saw looked closely at the photographer's upper arm. There was a large tattoo on the bicep, a block T with a smaller s looped around the T's base. Saw knew the mark: Texas Syndicate, next to the Aryan Brotherhood the largest, and next to none the most dangerous, organization in the pen. A chill rippled down Saw's backbone. "So you—you done some time," he said.

Brie lowered his sleeve. "It ain't so bad. These days they damn near got more people in the joint than out of it, hey? So, hey"—spreading his palms, his grin broadening—"what's wrong with a man doing a little honest work? Come on, just a couple of shots."

Saw reached inside his middle drawer, found a pack of Winstons, fumbled for a cigarette. "Well, I guess I could spare a few minutes."

"That's the ticket," Brie said, reaching slowly behind him, raising the hem of his shirt, digging now in his back pocket. "And, hey, if you want to—"

Saw's gaze was riveted on Brie's elbow and the bony forearm extended behind the photographer as Brie reached into his pocket. The lawyer's eyes widened. His lips parted.

Brie froze. "Oh. Hey, no problem, I get used to that. Once you been to prison, people think you're always fixing to rob them or something. What I was saying is . . ." He brought his hand out, holding a glossy color photo.

"Maybe you'd like to see some of my work." He dropped the picture in front of Saw.

Saw heaved a sigh of relief. The unlit cigarette dangling from his lips, he picked up the photo and turned it around. His throat constricted.

There was a naked girl in the picture, spread-eagled on a tilted board, her wrists and ankles in shackles, her expression one of terror. She couldn't have been over eleven or twelve, and had no pubic hair. A man in the photo was violating the girl with a frank which was clutched in his fist. Jesus, Saw thought, a weinie, and at the same time he felt a quick tightening in his crotch. The man in the picture wore shorts and a T-shirt, his complexion dark, is face turned toward the camera. Saw's hard-on wilted in a flash. The man was Wilfred Donello.

Saw was able to choke out, "What the fuck . . . ?"

There was a rustling noise as Bradford Brie parted his shirttails in front, a soft, sliding sound as Brie took off his belt and, quick as thought, looped the belt around the lawyer's puffy neck and yanked it tight. Saw tried to scream, but the tightening leather cut off his wind and he could only croak. He clawed at the skinny man's unyielding fingers, kicked out his feet, went over backward with Brie on top. Saw's chair hit the floor with a bang; papers flew and glass tinkled. The photographer's knees pounded the lawyer's chest like pistons. The red haze returned to cloud Saw's vision, grew redder yet, blotted out everything save Brie's wide-gapped teeth. Saw's arms were like rubber and his feet were suddenly numb.

Jesus, Saw thought, I'm just a guy making a living. What did I ever do to anybody? Then, with a final kick of nerveless feet, Howard Saw uttered one last croak and died.

Bradford Brie couldn't understand why Wilfred Donello would hire this dumb, fat fuck for a lawyer to begin with, but that was really none of Brie's business. Doing federal and state time had taught Bradford Brie to keep his nose where it belonged and to let well enough alone. The penitentiary had also taught Bradford Brie what he liked best. Photography. Did Bradford Brie ever love to take pictures.

He rose from behind Howard Saw's desk, raising his

shirt to thread his belt through the loops, and looked quickly toward the outer office. No one coming. Perfect. Just fucking perfect. Brie cinched up his belt, scooped up the photo of Donello and the girl—one of Brie's favorites, he'd taken extra time with the shot, timing his shutter-click in between the girl's screams—and shoved the picture into his back pocket. Then he grabbed up the camera, adjusted the lens, and squinted through the viewfinder.

Click-flash. "Jesus Christ, what a shot," Brie said to the lawyer, Saw's mouth agape, his eyes open and staring at nothing. "Great pose," Brie said. "Great motherfucking pose, you sleazy . . ."

Click-flash.

He used up the rest of the roll of film taking Saw's picture, the puffy, fat face, the fleshy protruding tongue. Brie took photos from both sides, directly overhead, and one absolute beauty of an angle from down on his knees, with the lens aimed at the top of the dead lawyer's head. Perfect, Brie thought, just fucking . . .

His job finished, Brie leisurely unloaded the camera, put the used film away, replaced the film with an unexposed roll. Fourteen shots of Howard Saw, two alive, twelve dead, as well as four (five? Brie wasn't sure) of the absolutely gorgeous lawyer lady. What a day. What a fucking beautiful day. When Donello had told Brie about the lawyer lady, Donello hadn't done her justice. No justice at all.

Brie wished that he could have taken more pictures of her, but he could wait. Bradford Brie was a patient man. He'd get more photos of Sharon Hays. One day soon he'd have all the pictures of the lawyer lady that anyone could want. And then some.

4

During Sharon Hays's time with the district attorney's office, juvenile certification hearings had changed locations. Before completion of the Frank Crowley Courts Building, the facility adjacent to the new county jail, teenager proceedings had taken place in a courtroom beside the county detention home on Harry Hines Boulevard. In those days the trip from cell to court required about five minutes, just long enough to cuff the adolescent prisoner and bring him over. Since the change, however, getting the kids to court on time was quite a rigamarole. Cert hearings now went on in the George Allen Courts Building, just across the street from Russell Black's office, and juvenile detention officers had to rattle cages around five in the morning, herd the teenagers into vans for the ten-mile trip downtown, then chain-gang the kids upstairs into holding cells behind the courtroom by seven, all to be certain that eight o'clock courthouse arrivals didn't trip over any prisoners who were hanging around in the halls.

Sharon understood quite well that the relocation of the hearings didn't have anything to do with convenience. For years the juvenile judges had bitched and moaned about the court facility near the detention home, claiming that the place was hard to find, that the parking was inadequate, etc., all complaints which Sharon knew to be total bullshit. The long and the short of it was that the Allen Building offered nicer judges' chambers, complete with private toilets, and that the downtown location afforded the juvenile judges more opportunity to run into lawyers who would buy lunch and kiss the judges' asses for them.

Russell Black opened the third-floor Allen Building courtroom door for Sharon and stood aside. She entered. The spectators' section was about half full. The waiting group consisted mostly of anxious, hand-wringing parents, and interspersed among the crowd were several lawyers in suits who balanced briefcases on their laps. There were also two reporters from the *Dallas Morning News* present, both of whom Sharon knew: Andy Wade, a slim young man in his middle twenties who wore thick glasses, and who had an absolutely jaw-clenching habit of blowing his nose in the middle of closing arguments, and Rita Paschal, a thick-hipped, thirtyish woman given to oversized blouses and starving-artist jeans who normally covered the federal courts. Andy Wade's usual beat was across town at the Crowley Building, and his and Rita Paschal's presence in juvie court meant that Midge Rathermore's certification hearing was to get plenty of ink in tomorrow's edition. Sharon had already noted a Channel 8 minicam operator, halfway asleep on a corridor bench. TV and all, Sharon thought. She had made her way halfway down the aisle to the bullpen gate, with Russell Black close on her heels, when she made sudden eye contact with Milton Breyer. She paused.

The eye contact wasn't intentional. Sharon locked gazes with Breyer just as he looked up from the newspaper which he had spread out on the railing surrounding the absent court reporter's chair. He wore a solid navy blue suit and a red tie with diagonal navy striping. When he spotted Sharon, Breyer reached out to touch Kathleen Fraterno's arm. Kathleen had been first in line behind Sharon in Breyer's pecking order, and would now be the superchief prosecutor's number one gofer. Fraterno looked over her shoulder to regard Sharon calmly, through mildly curious gray eyes. Kathleen had a narrow, ageless face above a trim and compact figure, and Sharon wondered fleetingly whether Breyer had put the moves on Kathleen as yet. If he hasn't, Sharon thought, it won't be long. She nodded solemnly at Breyer, showed Kathleen a quick smile, and continued on her way through the gate and into the bullpen area. She was surprised at her own coolness; she'd been afraid that the mere sight of Milton Breyer would send her into orbit.

So cool was Sharon, in fact, that she'd carried her briefcase nearly to the prosecution side when, behind her, Russell Black said, "Uh, Sharon."

Sharon stopped and turned.

Black set his briefcase down on the defense table and motioned. "Here," he said. "We set up shop over here."

Sharon's cheeks burned as she crossed over to sit beside her boss. Visible in the periphery of her vision, Fraterno and Breyer exchanged grins. Sharon snapped her attaché case open, withdrew a sheath of papers, and pretended to study them.

Black leaned over and whispered, "Come on. Might as well get it over with."

Sharon said, without looking up, "Get what over with?"

Black nudged her with his elbow and, as she faced him, winked at her. "The introductions."

Sharon's gaze flicked toward Breyer and Kathleen, then back down to the meaningless papers before her. "I already know them," she said.

"If Milt Breyer reacts the same way that you are," Black said, "then we've got him beat goin' in. First things first. First we get all the mumblin's and how-ya-doin's out of the way, then you and I can go about defendin' this teenager." He firmly stood. "Come on, Miss Hays." He held her chair for her while she stood, then followed a step behind her while they approached Breyer and Fraterno. Sharon thought briefly of a long-ago time in grammar school when a teacher had marched her to the principal's office.

Pretending to read the paper at the court reporter's desk while waiting for court to convene, Sharon knew, was one of Milton Breyer's favorite tricks. If Milt remained at the prosecution table, where he really belonged—and which afforded a more comfortable place to read the sports page—the courtroom entry would be to Breyer's back and he would be unable to see everyone who came and went. The makeup of the audience had never mattered to Sharon when she'd been in trial, but Breyer had ulterior motives. It was well known that he planned to run for judge in the next election, and the identity of his listeners was every bit as important to Breyer as the case at hand, if not more so. Breyer folded the newspaper under his arm and waited expectantly. Kathleen Fraterno left the stapled pages she'd been going over where they lay, on the witness box railing, and stepped up to stand beside her boss. Breyer held the paper under his left arm so that his silver wedding ring faced outward. He's slipped the ring on and off so often when entering singles bars, Sharon thought, that he's probably got several duplicates ready in case he loses the original. She stopped before the prosecutors and was conscious of Russell Black's looming presence on her left.

"Y'all know my new sidekick, Miss Hays," Black said.

"I seem to remember her from somewhere," Fraterno said, showing a genuine smile. Kathleen was mid-thirties, a couple of years older than Sharon, and had a decade with the county under her belt. When Sharon had been promoted over her, Kathleen hadn't tried to hide her resentment; Sharon had understood Kathleen's predicament and had been glad that Fraterno hadn't bullshitted around about the way she felt. Later on they'd tried a couple of cases together, one a successful death-penalty prosecution, and Kathleen had showed to be a boobs-out, bang-up trial lawyer. If Milt Breyer had any sense, he'd stay out of the way and let Kathleen prosecute the Rathermore case while he gave all the interviews and took all the credit. Good politician that he was, that was likely exactly what he planned to do. So much for trying the Rathermore case against a fumbling Milton Breyer, Sharon thought. "How you doing, Sharon?" Kathleen Fraterno said.

"So-so," Sharon said. "Better since I got a job. Hello, Milton." She forced her tone to be casual and did a good job of it. Sophomore acting class, Sharon thought, Elementary Method. Remembering the satisfying crunch when she'd brought her thigh up between Breyer's legs even caused Sharon to show a real-live smile. I should have stayed in show biz, Sharon thought.

Breyer patted his hair in a womanlike gesture. Sharon had once seen a tube of Grecian Formula in Breyer's desk drawer, and had delicately kept her mouth shut about it. Now she wished she'd told the world. Breyer's teeth were all capped and resembled a row of piano keys. Sharon recalled a Milton Berle reunion special which she'd watched with Melanie on ABC, and one of Uncle Miltie's stale jokes came suddenly back to haunt her. *Your teeth are like stars. They come out at night.*

"Certainly, Miss Hays," Breyer said. "Delighted you've landed on your feet. We were all worried about you."

Give me a break, Sharon thought. Breyer would have already heard the rumor that his former assistant (and planned piece of ass on the side) had been talking to the federal Equal Opportunity folks, and likely would have lost some sleep over it. At least Sharon hoped he had. She didn't permit herself so much as a blink. "Thanks for your concern," she said, then thought, Hard thigh to the nuts, and smiled at him.

Black now said, "Listen, I guess y'all know I've just recently taken on this case. I haven't even met my client. A continuance on this hearin's probably in order."

Breyer frowned. "It's been scheduled for a while, Russ." Acting as if you were going to give the other side a hard time whenever they asked for something wasn't particular to Milton Breyer. S.O.P. for the Dallas D.A.'s office: make the defense sweat blood over every little detail.

"Lemme finish," Black said. "What I was goin' to say is, I won't bother filin' a continuance motion if you folks could use your good influence with the court to postpone the hearin' about an hour. That'll give us a chance to let the little girl know at least she's got a lawyer."

Breyer placed his tongue against the roof of mouth, poising to form the word no. Kathleen took a quick half step forward. "That shouldn't be any problem," Fraterno said. Breyer closed his mouth. Kathleen smiled and extended her hand. "Kathleen Fraterno, Mr. Black. Your reputation precedes you. It's an honor."

Black's huge, gnarled hand engulfed Kathleen's like a whale swallowing a minnow. "Nice to know ya," Black said. Breyer looked miffed, and Sharon wondered what diplomacy Kathleen would use in explaining to the frigging moron that giving the defense a ration of shit over motions which the judge would grant automatically was nothing but a waste of time. Sharon had wondered more than once during her tenure as an A.D.A. whether Breyer had actually attended law school, or if he'd used some of his wife's money to pay someone to go to class in his place. Having Kathleen Fraterno on the other side would make defending Midge more difficult, Sharon thought, but in ways Kathleen's presence would be a relief as well. Sharon came out of her trance as Black turned to her and said, "Guess we better go meet our employer, huh?"

Sharon nodded, first to Kathleen and then to Breyer, then led the way as she and Black moved toward the exit leading to the holding cell. Black said, barely above a whisper, "Well, at least the little girl won't have to go through these proceedings alone. We're all she's got in this courtroom, Sharon."

She stopped and quickly surveyed the spectator section, the two reporters hunched over steno pads, lawyers and parents seated side by side. "What about her real mother?" Sharon said.

Black said, "Huh?"

"Her mother. You know, the one who's paying your legal fee. She's not attending the hearing?"

Black regarded the floor, then looked up. "No, she's not. Listen, one thing I didn't tell you. Nobody's to know who hired us. If the little girl asks directly who's payin' her legal fee, then we're goin' to have to tell her. Otherwise, as far as Midge knows, we're court-appointed just like her last lawyer was."

Sharon frowned. "I never heard of such a thing. After all, it's her daughter."

Black took her arm and steered her toward the exit. "I'll have to fill you in on that one later. It's sort of a touchy subject. Let's just say she wants to be anonymous unless somebody forces our hand on it."

Sharon had seen quite a few teenagers in lockup in her time, and she'd long ago passed the point of feeling sorry for them. There had been a time in her days as a fledgling prosecutor when she'd gotten flak from her superiors for being too soft on juveniles. Criminals, according to the D.A.'s creed, were criminals, and it was the prosecutor's job to hammer all offenders as hard as the law would allow regardless of the offender's age. If the little bastards were going to go around robbing and shooting people, then no way was the D.A. going to let up on them just because they were kids. Sharon had finally gotten the mes-

sage loud and clear. One of her juvie cert cases had been
a youngster who, two days after his fifteenth birthday,
had blown away two convenience store clerks as they
kneeled begging in front of him. One of the bullets had
passed through a clerk's hand on the way to his brain, the
hand held out in supplication. After that case Sharon had
had no problem at all in prosecuting juveniles.

For the most part, the group of teenagers who milled
about in the holding cell behind the family law courtroom
was typical. There were two tall, skinny boys, their heads
half shaved with the hair on the unshaven portion grown
past shoulder length, each with an identical BORN TO RAISE
HELL tattoo on his forehead. This lovely pair snickered
and giggled as if the prospect of being transferred to the
county jail with the big bad guys—which was the juvies'
next stop once they'd been certified—was the coolest
thing going. The other two kids in the cell, a frail youth
with a nasty scar over his eye and a feminine-looking
youngster with big doe eyes, seemed scared to death.
Midge Rathermore was the only girl, and was separated
from the others. She was outside the barred door, handcuffed to a straight-backed wooden chair, and in spite of
Sharon's ingrained attitude toward prosecuting kids, her
heart went out instantly to Midge. The Rathermore girl, at
the moment the most famous teenager in Dallas County
and easily recognizable from her newspaper pictures, was
definitely hard to miss.

She weighed well over two hundred pounds, and the
greasy diet at the juvenile detention center hadn't done
her complexion any good. There were two pimples on
Midge's chin, one having already come to a head, and
ugly red blotches on both of her cheeks. The beige county
detention smock which she wore was designed for someone half Midge's size. Her big breasts sagged against the
smock's front like balloons in shrunken burlap. The garment buttoned up the side. Two of the buttons had popped
off, and the strained fabric parted to show rolls of fish-
belly white, porky flesh. Midge's posture was pitiful; her
shoulders slumped forward and her big stomach pooched
out. She pressed one of her pimples between dirty finger-
nails. A sorry sight to be sure, but what really got to
Sharon was Midge Rathermore's expression.

Whereas the boys inside the cell were either sneeringly

arrogant or properly terrified, Midge was neither. As Russell Black spoke to the uniformed guard, Midge regarded Sharon with a blank stare. Totally blank. No fear, no resentment. Nothing. Not a hint of a smile or frown. Dull gray eyes, not a spark of life in them, no shift to their gaze. Sharon attempted an encouraging smile. Midge showed no reaction. The fat teenager sat rooted to her chair like a resident of hell, all happiness gone, all emotion drained.

Black was saying to the guard, "We'll need her for about fifteen or twenty minutes."

"Take your time," the guard said. "This one don't give us no trouble." He was a sparrow-shouldered man in his forties whom Sharon remembered from when he'd been a guard down at the main jail. Years ago, working juvenile detention had been a plum of sorts for the guards, a relief from handling the hardened cons in central lockup. No longer. These days teenagers would stick a sharpened spoon between a hack's ribs quicker than the older prisoners would. "Come on," the guard said, "we'll take her next door."

"Next door" was a conference room containing a small table and six chairs, a Mr. Coffee on a rolling server with black dregs in the bottom of the pot, low bookcases filled with the Texas Civil and Criminal Codes and Codes of Procedure. The books were dusty, as if no one had read them in years. The guard seated Midge on one side of the table and cuffed her chubby wrist to a chair arm. He nodded to Black, then to Sharon, said "Take your time" again, then backed out of the room and softly closed the door.

Midge looked in turn at the coffeepot, the bookcases, and then at her lawyers, all with equal lack of interest. Black sat across the table from the teenager, and Sharon positioned herself beside her boss, opened her attaché case, took a legal pad out, and prepared to take notes. Black said in a fatherly baritone, "Midge, I'm Russ Black and this is Miss Hays. We're goin' to be your lawyers."

Midge played with her handcuff bracelet. "What happened to the other dude?" A high-pitched child's voice, no emotion in its tone, distinctive private school accent. On the same wrist which wore the handcuff was a plastic ID band giving her name and prisoner number.

"Mr. Tubb?" Black said.

"Is that his name?" Midge winced as she pressed one of the zits on her chin. The expression of pain was the only emotion she'd shown so far. "Skinny dude with glasses?" she said.

"That sounds like him. I don't know what happened to Andy, I just got your case."

"I didn't like that dude," Midge said.

"I hope you'll like us," Black said.

Midge looked at Sharon. There still was no expression in the teenager's eyes, but there was a slight upturn of her dry, cracked lips. "I might like her," Midge said.

Sharon shrugged and dropped her gaze. A flush crept into her cheeks. What did one say to that? On the legal pad she doodled an oblong.

"Well, I hope you're going to like both of us," Black said. Sharon permitted herself a quick sideways glance. Had there been an edge to Black's tone? Surely not. Surely Russell Black was beyond being miffed because a troubled teenager might prefer his assistant, a female, over Black himself. I don't know, Sharon thought, the male ego is a funny thing. She returned her attention to Midge. Midge continued to favor her new lady lawyer with a mirthless grin.

"Midge, I'm not goin' to ask you . . . First, you tell me somethin'. Do you understand what it is that the police are sayin' you're guilty of?"

Midge's smile suddenly broadened, accompanied by a shrill giggle. "They say I killed Daddy." In spite of herself, Sharon rolled her eyes. A *giggle,* yet.

"Not exactly that you killed him," Black said. "That you had somebody else do it. For now, I'm not goin' to ask—"

"Chris and Troy," Midge said, her expression brightening as if she'd suddenly recalled a couple of chums from her algebra class.

"—if you did it," Black said. "We can get into that later. I just want to make sure you understand what's goin' to be happenin' today. In this court hearin'."

Midge frowned, a little girl denied dessert. "They say they'll take me to the big jail."

"I got to tell you that's a possibility, Midge. In fact, they probably will."

"Can I have chocolate there?" Midge asked hopefully.

Jesus H. Christ, Sharon thought. You poor child.

Black continued as if he hadn't heard. "This hearin's about chargin' you with a crime as an adult. Do you know what that means?"

"I think it means . . . that I'm not like a little girl?"

Sharon searched Midge's face, looking for some sign that the teenager was putting on an act. As a prosecutor Sharon had seen more than one crafty kid put on a performance in an attempt to beat adult certification. The ploy never worked, but some street-wise children would try anything. Not Midge Rathermore, though. She seemed mentally only a baby, and not a particularly bright one at that, a grossly obese little girl whom the system was about to decide was a mature and remorseless killer. There was very little either Midge or her lawyers could do about what the system was going to decide. Sharon swallowed a lump from her throat.

"It sort of means that," Black said. "The punishment they can give a minor is limited. If they try you as an adult and convict you, it means that you can go to the penitentiary."

Midge frowned quickly, then smiled again, the fat baby face going through the range of emotions quick as thought. "I did do what they say. Daddy was bad."

Black coughed into a cupped hand and looked quickly around, as if making certain there was no one else in the room. "Who else . . . did you tell that to anybody else?"

Midge smirked and lowered her gaze, the child caught talking in class. "Tell them what?"

"That you did it."

She kept her head lowered and regarded Black through her upper eyelashes. "I don't know. Did I?"

Black's tone showed irritation. "We can't be playin' games, Midge."

"Midge," Sharon said quickly, and felt Black tense up beside her. Sharon didn't want to make her new boss angry, but being stern with Midge was a waste of time, like reading the riot act to a small baby. Midge now showed a pouty expression, the storm warning of a temper tantrum coming on. "Midge," Sharon said again, "how was your daddy bad?"

Midge's expression softened into a smile as she looked

at Sharon, like an infant relating to an adult whom she liked, wanting to please. "He was bad bad," Midge said.

Sharon decided to let that one alone for the present. "You said a moment ago that you did it, and Mr. Black asked who-all you'd told that. I'm going to ask you the same thing. Did you tell anyone else?"

"That I did it?"

"Yes." Sharon kept her voice calm, using the same tone of voice she'd heard the psychologist use on Melanie; while in the second grade, Melanie had had stress problems over not having a father like the other kids.

Midge seemed deep in thought. "I told that other lawyer dude."

"Mr. Tubb?"

"Yeah."

"Anyone else?" Sharon kept her attitude friendly, with no hint of accusation that Midge had done anything wrong. If the teenager felt rewarded, she would tell all, but if she felt she would be scolded for her actions, she would clam up, and no amount of threatening or pleading would get anything out of her. Sharon pictured herself, struggling to control her temper, coaxing Melanie at eighteen months to eat her applesauce.

Midge pressed on a pimple. "A policeman that came to see me."

Russell Black said under his breath, "Christ."

Midge shot a glance at the older lawyer, and her expression changed instantly from one of wanting to please to one of secrecy. "I was only fooling you," she said. "I didn't tell. It was Susan. Susan told."

Sharon fought the urge to tell Black: Keep the hell out of this and let me handle it. Criminy, with the older lawyer berating this child, they could ask Midge questions until they were blue in the face and never get a straight answer. Sharon repressed her anger and said merely, "Susan?"

"It's her sister," Black said.

Sharon chewed the inside of her cheek. "Older or younger?"

"Fourteen," Midge said. "I *hate* that fucking Susan." She shrilly raised her voice, and the force of her anger jolted like a rush of cold air.

"Now, now." Black tried the fatherly approach again. "She's your only sister, Midge."

Midge screamed at the top of her lungs, "No, goddammit, I hate her." The hallway door flew open and the guard burst in to take a long stride in Midge's direction. Sharon held out her hand to the guard and shook her head. The guard halted in his tracks.

"Midge," Sharon said, "why do you hate Susan?"

"Because she tells *everything*." Tears of rage rolled down the teenager's fat cheeks. "She's always been a tattletale and she's still one." She looked wildly about her. "I think I need to go to the bathroom." The small child's ploy for avoiding unpleasant things.

Black stirred, reached down to pick up his briefcase, and said to the guard, "I guess this is finished."

Sharon touched Black's arm and imperceptibly shook her head. She had to have an answer right now. Later Midge would have had time to make something up. "Midge," Sharon said quietly, "did you feel that your father liked Susan more than you?"

The eyes went instantly deadpan, the fat lips formed a compressed circle. The lone unshackled hand came up; the index finger toyed with a pimple. "He liked fucking her," Midge said.

There was pin-drop silence, a full fifteen seconds of it. The guard's breathing was loud and irregular.

"Christ," Black murmured.

Midge lowered her gaze to her handcuffed wrist. "Can I go to the bathroom now?" she said.

5

"The state has two witnesses, Your Honor." Kathleen Fraterno, professionally cool, arms folded under mildly puffed white sleeves, vest hugging her slim upper body, sitting erect, legs crossed in black knee-length skirt over matching high heels.

"Very well. Call your first, then." Kenneth Tucker, bald as soil in shade, huge bags underneath his eyes, lifelong county employee only recently promoted to family court master, delighting in juvie cert hearings because they gave him the opportunity to don judge's robes and have lawyers call him "Your Honor." Tucker's voice was nasal and a bit raspy.

Fraterno exchanged a glance with Milt Breyer, who was seated beside her at the prosecution table. Peculiar to Texas, lawyers remain seated in court, question witnesses from their respective tables, approach the witness only after requesting the court's permission, and then only to have the witness identify a piece of admitted or prospective evidence. On the defense side, Russell Black sat nearest the prosecutors with Midge Rathermore between him and Sharon Hays. Midge had terrible body odor. Sharon had asked the guard to provide the huge teenager with a smock that fit. The guard had told Sharon with a snicker that the garment Midge wore was the largest available. Sharon had removed her own suit jacket and draped it around Midge's hunched shoulders. The jacket didn't help much, but at least covered the open button holes up the side of the smock. The sleeves to Sharon's

off-white summer-weight blouse were slightly puffed,
like Fraterno's sleeves, and Sharon had shoved the cuffs
up to tightly encircle her forearms.

Fraterno lifted her chin and raised her voice. "State
calls Detective Stanley Green."

Well, fuck a duck, Sharon thought.

Milt Breyer leaned back to peer around Russell Black, and
showed Sharon an obvious smirk. Put sock in it, Milt,
Sharon thought.

There was a rustling in the courtroom, heads turning,
reporters scribbling, as the bailiff ushered the witness in.
Stanley Green was medium height with a square build
and a cowpoke's slightly bowlegged walk. He wore a
dark brown suit and had a golfer's tan, face and neck
bronze, right hand darker than the left. He showed mild
amusement as the court reporter swore him in, then
flowed athletically into the witness chair and folded his
hands.

"Please state your full name for the record." Fraterno's
courtroom voice was clear as a bell and carried perfectly.
In private, Kathleen's speech took on a more husky, even
earthy quality.

"Stanley Randall Green." A heavy Texas drawl, full
brows over a wide nose and thin lips, an honest expression, believable as Will Rogers.

"And what is your occupation, Mr. Green?"

"I'm a detective with the Dallas Police Department.
Crimes Against Persons."

"And in that capacity, is homicide your specialty?"

"Yes, ma'am." Green's response was humble and re-
spectful, which Sharon knew to be some somewhat of an
effort for him. Down deep Stan Green was as sexist as
they came.

Fraterno picked up the pace. "Did you have occasion
on"—she glanced down at her open file, then back up—
"January 8 of this year to go the home of Mr. and Mrs.
William P. Rathermore, Jr.?"

"Yes."

Fraterno performed another brief examination of her
file. "Was the home at 3517 Lakeside Drive, in Highland
Park?"

Another yes. Court Master Tucker's interest picked up.

To Dallasites, a Lakeside Drive address was the be-all and end-all.

"And approximately what time was that?" Fraterno said.

Green seemed to consider his response, and Sharon, along with every other lawyer in the courtroom, knew that the detective was faking it. Fraterno and Green would have rehearsed at length, and the questions and answers would be committed to memory. "I got the call about two in the morning," Green said. "So it would have been close to three when I got there. I didn't get much sleep that night." The detective smiled for Kenneth Tucker's benefit, and the family court master nodded his round head.

"And on your arrival, what did you find?"

"It was a crime scene."

"Do you mean by that that the area was roped off? Officers standing guard? Laboratory technicians gathering possible evidence, things like that?" Fraterno said. Green answered yes to each brief question in turn. "What did you then do?" Fraterno said.

"I went in the house."

"And what did you see inside the house, Detective?"

"I entered through the living room. There was a blond lady on the sofa."

"Did you later learn that the lady was Mrs. William Rathermore?"

Sharon nearly snickered out loud at that one. Linda Rathermore had once been Linda Haymon, the six and ten o'clock anchor on Channel 8, and between the TV exposure prior to, and the social fund-raisers following, her marriage to Bill Rathermore, Jr., possessed one of the better-known faces in the city. It was the first Mrs. William Rathermore, Jr., who had shunned the limelight. Sharon wondered briefly why Midge's mom didn't want it known that she was paying her daughter's lawyers. If it had been Melanie in trouble, Sharon would have been at this hearing with bells on.

"Yes, ma'am," said Green, deadpan.

"Was anyone else present?"

Green nodded. "Detective Burns from Burglary. Patrolmen Tanner and Wimberly, the officers who originally responded to the call. They were talking to the lady."

"And did you have conversation with Mrs. Rathermore at that time?"

"Not then. No, ma'am."

There was a rattling of paper as Fraterno pretended to examine her file, and Green waited patiently for the next question. More Hollywood, Sharon thought. Even the apparently unexpected answer to Fraterno's question would have been rehearsed, the "Not then. No, ma'am" response carefully designed to make the whole thing appear spontaneous. Kathleen Fraterno was pretty good at pretense, Sharon had to admit. Once, when she and Kathleen had tried the death penalty case, Fraterno had had the arresting officer misidentify the victim's sister. The intentional slip-up hadn't mattered in the overall presentation of the case, but had done wonders in convincing the jury that Fraterno and the cop hadn't been in any sort of collusion. It was probably carrying things too far, Sharon thought, to go through the unexpected-answer routine in a hearing such as this, but with Kenneth Tucker on the bench in place of the real-life judge, the strategy should work pretty well.

Fraterno pretended to finish the pretended examination of her file and lifted her chin. "Well, what did you then do, Detective?"

"I went upstairs."

"To the master bedroom?"

"Yes, ma'am."

"And what did you find there?"

"The lab techs were dusting for prints. I, let's see, I don't think the medical examiner's people were there as yet. There was a body on the floor."

"The victim. No one had as yet pronounced the victim officially dead?"

"No, ma'am. I'm pretty sure the M.E. didn't arrive until five or ten minutes after that."

"And are you certain," Fraterno said, "that no one had moved the body, touched it in any way?"

Green thoughtfully scratched his nose. "Procedure would dictate that the lab techs not handle the victim until after the M.E. had finished. I'm pretty sure no one had. I know I didn't touch the body."

"But did you get a good look at the victim?"

"Oh, yes, ma'am. I must have stood there a couple of minutes."

There were more papery rustles as Fraterno dug into her file. She stood holding a large photo, walked around front to the defense side, and handed the picture to Russell Black. Fraterno stood by and brushed imaginary lint from her sleeve while giving the defense a second to look over the photo.

Black held the picture in front of Midge so that he, Sharon, and Midge could see. The corpse in the picture was a mess, a man in a purple robe and pajamas with one side of his head bashed in, face turned unnaturally to one side, eyes partially open in dead-man slits, blood totally obscuring one cheek and dripping gruesomely down to soak the robe and surrounding carpet. Sharon shot a quick sideways glance at Midge. The client sniffled and blew a spit bubble. Wordlessly Black returned the photo to Fraterno. Sharon briefly pictured the jurors' pale expressions when the photo turned up at trial.

Fraterno crossed slim ankles and lifted her face to the bench. "Your Honor, may I approach the witness?"

Tucker leaned back. A spring creaked in his chair. "Yes, proceed."

Fraterno then carried the picture over to the clerk, who applied a gummed evidenced sticker. Then, photo in hand, Fraterno strolled up to the witness box, her gait leisurely and thoughtful, her manner confident. Sharon had done the town with Kathleen a few times, and remembered that Fraterno's walk in good-time clothes was sensuous and even come-on earthy. Kathleen, Sharon thought, wouldn't have made a bad actress. Fraterno handed the picture to Stan Green, who then pretended to study the victim's image. Green, Sharon knew, had a memory like a minicam and knew every detail of the picture like he knew the route to his own apartment.

"I show you," Fraterno said, "what has been marked 'State's Exhibit Number One,' and ask if you can identify it."

"It's a photograph from our files." Green's mild brown-eyed gaze flicked briefly at Sharon, then darted quickly away. Sharon wondered with an inner laugh if she should stand and say hello. How you doing, big fella? Something like that.

"Taken where?" Fraterno said.

"It's the body I saw in the bedroom, upstairs at the Rathermore home." Green's manner was casual, his tone informal. He made one of the best witnesses in the police department. Many cops came across on the stand as if they were reading from a procedures manual.

Fraterno nodded, retrieved the picture from the witness, took a step forward, and handed the photo to Kenneth Tucker on the bench. "The State offers exhibit one, Your Honor," Fraterno said.

Tucker's brows knotted as he looked the exhibit over, his lips curling in obvious revulsion. A real-life judge would have deadpanned it. Tucker cleared his throat. "Objections?"

Sharon and Russ Black leaned forward as one to exchange glances around Midge. Black nodded and mouthed silently, "Go ahead."

Sharon halfway rose from her chair. "No objection." She resumed her seat. Pointless objections were . . . well, pointless. Often the client would be upset because the lawyer wasn't making more noise, which explained a lot of the pointless objections made in court as client pacifiers. Midge Rathermore, however, didn't seem the slightest bit interested in what her lawyers were up to. She merely regarded her filthy nails as though her mind was somewhere far away.

"So admitted." Tucker gave the picture back to Fraterno, then folded his hands.

Fraterno laid the photo on the rail in front of the witness. "Detective, did you later learn the dead man's identity?"

"Yes, ma'am." Green accompanied his answer with a quick nod. "Mrs. Rathermore provided identification."

"And was he William P. Rathermore, Jr.?"

"Yes, he was."

"Thank you." Fraterno gave the picture to the court reporter, who filed it away. The D.A.'s file would contain numerous additional prints: for the defense's use, for admission into evidence at future hearings and, eventually, for the trial itself. Fraterno was through with the photo for now. She had into evidence that there had been a crime as brutal as they come, and that was all she had to prove for purposes of the certification hearing. She had revealed nothing which hadn't already been in the paper, and hadn't tipped any of her hole cards. Kathleen Fraterno, Sharon thought wryly, is one bitchin' lawyer. Milt Breyer watched his assistant from the prosecution's side, and Milt's expression showed open approval. If Milt had been conducting the direct examination himself, Sharon thought, the pompous ass would be chomping at the bit to show this air-tight case he had, and by now Sharon would have two or three pages' worth of juicy notes. But with Fraterno in charge of the hearing, Sharon's legal pad contained nothing so far but doodlings.

Fraterno returned to her seat and faced the witness. "Detective, did you . . .?" She frowned thoughtfully. "First, let me ask you, other than policemen, who was in the house when you arrived?" The pause and frown were more rehearsed theatrics, Sharon thought.

Green shifted comfortably in the witness chair. "Only the lady. Mrs. Rathermore."

Fraterno intertwined her fingers under her chin. "Aren't there children?"

"Two," Green said. "Daughters, both boarding students at Hockaday."

"Hockaday School in far North Dallas?"

"Yes, ma'am."

"So Mrs. Rathermore and her husband had been alone in the house."

"That's what she told us."

Russell Black stirred and shot a questioning glance in Sharon's direction. She slowly shook her head. Fraterno was getting into hearsay now, the detective's recollection of what a witness's statement had been rather than the testimony of the witness herself. In a certification hearing, though, hearsay was admissible, the theory being that the witness would be available for the defense to cross-examine at trial. Black sat back and expelled air through his nose.

"Please tell the court," Fraterno said, "exactly what Mrs. Rathermore told you in her interview."

Black hopped up from his seat. "Objection. Hearsay."

Sharon blinked. Evidently her head shake hadn't gotten the message across.

Kenneth Tucker immediately snapped, "Overruled." He returned his attention to the witness.

Black sat down with a bewildered look, like an NFL coach after a pass-interference call by the referee. Black looked at Sharon. She sympathetically raised her eyebrows and shrugged as if to say, I tried to tell you.

Fraterno repeated her question. Green said, his expression more intense, "Mrs. Rathermore and her husband were getting ready for bed around midnight. Two boys came into their bedroom and beat him to death with a lug wrench."

Fraterno tilted her chin. "Boys?"

"Young men. Teenagers, was Mrs. Rathermore's description."

"But you're certain that the first time Mrs. Rathermore and her husband saw the assailants was when they burst into the bedroom."

"Yes, ma'am."

"No one rang the doorbell," Fraterno said, "and neither Mr. nor Mrs. Rathermore let the assailants into the house."

"Not according to Mrs. Rathermore's statement," Green said.

Fraterno smoothed one of her ruffled sleeves. "Detective, isn't there an alarm system in that house?"

"Yes, ma'am, there is."

"And on the night in question, was the system activated?"

Green nodded. "It was."

"Detective," Fraterno said, "how is the alarm system in the Rathermore home turned on and off?"

Sharon continued to doodle. The Rathermore alarm system had been in the newspapers over and over; cartoon drawings of the huge home and the various panels used to turn the system on and off were as familiar to Dallasites as Jimmy Johnson, Jerry Jones, and the weekly game plan of the Dallas Cowboys.

"There are ten-digit security panels in the upstairs bedrooms, kitchen, and game room, plus a panel inside the front door. There is one code for activating the system and another for disarming it."

"And Mrs. Rathermore was certain that the system was turned on?"

"That's what she said."

On Sharon's left, Midge Rathermore raised her hands

to pat her fat cheeks, then yawned. Sharon's jacket had slipped off one of Midge's shoulders. The teenager's B.O. permeated the air like the stench of dead animals.

"So, then," Fraterno said, "it would be safe to say that no one could have entered the premises undetected without knowing the code to deactivate the alarm, wouldn't it?"

"I'd say so," Green said. "Unless someone had been hiding in the house when the system was turned on."

"And, without warning, these two young men burst in on the couple and killed Mr. Rathermore. Was Mrs. Rathermore harmed?"

"No, ma'am. She locked herself in the bathroom."

"While the two continued to assault and bludgeon—"

"Objection." Sharon was on her feet, acting totally by reflex, and it took an instant for her to realize that the objection had come from her own lips. She softly cleared her throat and let one hand rest on the nape of Midge's neck. "Your Honor," Sharon said, "the photograph is already in evidence. This is a certification hearing, not an argument for capital punishment."

Tucker glanced at Sharon, then at Fraterno, and back again. "Sustained." It seemed that the family court master wanted to spare himself the gruesome details. The regular judge would have likely overruled. Sharon sat down, feeling Russ Black's gaze on her.

Fraterno showed a little smile. She lowered long lashes, then said to the witness, "You were assigned to this case as chief investigating officer, were you not?"

"That I was," Detective Green said.

"You said a moment ago that the weapon used was a lug wrench. Does that mean that you recovered the weapon?"

"The officers found it in some shrubbery."

"A common lug wrench?"

"Yes, ma'am, with a ninety-degree bend and a sharpened point, for removing hubcaps."

"And were there fingerprints on the weapon?"

"No, ma'am. According to Mrs. Rathermore, the attackers wore gloves."

"For the purpose of covering their hands, so they'd leave no prints?"

Now it was Russell Black who stood and offered the

token objection; the killers' reason for wearing the gloves was nothing that anyone had told Green, so the question called for speculation on his part. Before Tucker could sustain, Fraterno said quickly, "I'll withdraw the question," having gotten her point across without having the witness answer. The trick was as old as the law itself, and just as effective. Fraterno pretended to study her notes while making no effort to hide her mischievous grin. Milt Breyer hooked an elbow over his chair back. He was really enjoying himself.

"So, Detective," Fraterno said, "is it safe to say that the night of Mr. Rathermore's death, there were no suspects?"

"Not then. No, ma'am."

"And what about motive? Were there things missing from the house? Valuables?"

"No money," Green said. "There were three hundred-dollar bills in plain sight on the dresser, and no one had touched them."

"Jewelry?"

"No, ma'am. Mrs. Rathermore did a complete inventory at our request, and every piece was present and accounted for. There was a large jewelry box on her vanity, untouched."

Sharon now made her first notes of the hearing. Her husband just beaten to death before her eyes, the lady sits down and coolly inventories her diamonds. Strange. Equally peculiar was the scenario in which, during the beating, the lady had had the presence of mind to hide in the bathroom, and unless the Rathermore john had a steel door and a magnesium bolt, it was also weird that the killers hadn't merely knocked down the door and had a go at her. Sharon wrote LINDA HAYMON RATHERMORE in bold letters on her pad, underlined the name three times, and followed the note with a large question mark.

"Could Mrs. Rathermore identify either or both of the assailants?" Fraterno said.

"No. She said she'd never seen them before."

"So they just came in, killed Mr. Rathermore, and left?"

"Evidently that's what happened," Green said.

"And as of day one in your investigation, Detective, did you have any leads or suspects whatsoever?"

"No, ma'am. Not a one."

Fraterno flipped over a page in her file. "Did that situation later change?"

"Two days later it did. Yes."

"And how was that?"

"Well, we . . ." Green stroked his chin. "We had an informant. A call."

"Was the call anonymous?"

"No, ma'am," Green said. "The call came from a girl named Leslie Schlee."

"And who is Leslie Schlee?"

"She's a student at Hockaday School. In the same class as Miss Rathermore." Green nodded toward Midge, his handsome face now cop impassive. Midge played with a lapel of the jacket around her shoulders, and softly hummed a tuneless tune. Sharon cleared a small lump from her throat. The only knowledge regarding Midge's guilt which Sharon had at the moment had come from Midge herself, the fat, pitiful teenager's own words to the effect that she was guilty, and anything that Midge said could be truth, fantasy, or something in between. Whatever, the certifying of this child as an adult was a grisly joke. The informant's identity had been withheld from the newspapers. Sharon jotted down the name and underlined it.

"And on receiving this call, did you interview Miss Schlee?" Fraterno said.

"Yes. She came to central headquarters. Her father was with her."

"And if you would, Detective, please relate Miss Leslie Schlee's story to the court."

The form of the question was out of line, even in this hearing. Witnesses under direct examination were only supposed to answer questions and not elaborate. One way or the other, though, Tucker would admit Green's hearsay testimony into evidence, so any objection now would only waste time. Sharon glanced sideways at Russ Black. Apparently he had taken sufficient lumps when he'd objected before, and now merely gazed at the witness, the older lawyer's face impassive.

Green folded his arms in the witness chair. "Miss Schlee told us that two boys named Chris Leonard and

Troy Burdette had been the assailants in the Rathermore home."

"And how did Miss Schlee know this?" Fraterno said.

"The boys are St. Mark's students."

"St. Mark's being another North Dallas private school?"

"Yes, ma'am. Mr. Leonard is Miss Schlee's boyfriend. Miss Schlee said that he told her about the killing one night while the two of them were at the movies. She didn't believe that he was really going to do it, and thought he was only bragging. The day after the murder she confronted him, and he said that he and Mr. Burdette had gone to the Rathermore home and done the crime."

"Detective," Fraterno said, her voice now an octave lower, clearly about to drop a bombshell. "Did you discuss a possible motive with Miss Schlee?"

Green now looked toward Midge. His intense expression was rehearsed, of course, just as the surprise answers had been. The theatrics were fooling no one, Sharon thought, except Kenneth Tucker, whose opinion was the only one which mattered. "Yes, ma'am," Green said.

"And what would that be?"

Green's gaze remained riveted on Midge and never wavered. He said, "Miss Schlee told us that Midge Rathermore employed the two boys to kill her father."

"Employed them how? For money?" The question seemed unnecessary, but murder for hire was one of three crimes in Texas which subjected an adult offender to the death penalty. Midge wasn't eligible for capital punishment because of her age, but the prosecutor was getting the point across. Midge was old enough to know the value of a cash offer.

"She paid them nothing at the time. Once the father's estate was probated, she was going to give them twenty-five thousand dollars apiece."

There was a pause as Fraterno riffled through her file, letting the cop's statement sink in. Kenneth Tucker now favored Midge with an openly hostile glare of his own.

"Detective Green," Fraterno finally said, "did you subsequently place Chris Leonard and Troy Burdette under arrest?"

"We did."

"And question them?"

"After we gave them Miranda warnings. Yes, ma'am." Green's eyes were wide with honesty. *Us Dallas Po-lice would never do nothin' to violate anybody's constitutional rights, no sirree.*

"And were the boys cooperative?" Another improper question: the two young killers' attitudes were a matter of the detective's opinion. Sharon thought it over, then decided not to object. Black apparently made the same choice and sat still as a stone. The quicker this hearing was over, the better for the defense lawyers and for Midge Rathermore.

"Not until after they made their deal."

"Deal?" Fraterno feigned surprise. Come on, Sharon thought, that one's not even going to fake Kenneth Tucker out.

"In conjunction with their lawyers and approved by the Dallas County district attorney. They had plea-bargain agreements worked out in exchange for their cooperation."

"I see. And once these arrangements were made, what did they tell you?"

"Basically, they supported what Miss Schlee had already said. That Midge Rathermore arranged for the murder and was to pay them once she'd gotten her inheritance."

Sharon quickly scribbled two sentences on her legal pad. As a minor, Midge wouldn't be entitled to inherit anything immediately. The funds would go in trust until she was eighteen. Of course, neither Midge nor the two hired killers would have to have known that. But any port in a storm, Sharon thought, any tidbit which might shoot tiny holes in Stan Green's testimony.

"And so," Fraterno said, "did you then arrest Midge Rathermore?"

"Yes. A couple of days later, at the school."

"And did you question Midge?"

"No, ma'am. That wouldn't be proper as long as we're dealing with her as a minor."

Sharon nearly laughed out loud. The Dallas cops never arrested anyone without grilling the bejesus out of the suspect, always making sure to have plenty of witnesses ready for denial purposes if the defense raised a stink at trial. She pictured Green, flanked by Fraterno and Milt

Breyer, firing questions at Midge while the obese girl blew spit bubbles and asked for chocolate.

There was silence, punctuated by the flipping of pages while Fraterno examined her file. She let the pages fall from her fingers and closed her jacket folder with a final soft thump. "No further questions," she said.

Green sat calmly on the stand, his chin resting on a clenched fist. Kenneth Tucker nodded to the witness, then looked toward the defense table. "Does the defense wish to cross-examine?"

Cross at this time wouldn't be worth the effort required to ask the questions, Sharon knew. Stan Green was a trained witness and a wonder at dodging issues. As second banana on the defense team, Sharon kept her seat and waited for Russell Black to waive.

Black climbed slowly to his feet. "Just a couple of things, Judge."

Sharon blinked.

"You know me, Detective Green," Black said, smiling at the cop, "so I won't introduce myself. These witnesses you got, the two boys and the girlfriend. You take statements from these people?" The court reporter, a thin Hispanic woman in her forties, stopped with her fingers poised over the keyboard. Sharon decided that the court reporter didn't know whether to put Black's dialogue down verbatim, or perhaps to edit the words into proper King's English. The shorthand machine resumed its muted clatter.

"Yes, we did," Green said.

"Notarized and signed statements?" Black said.

"Yes."

"And will the Dallas Police Department permit the defense, bein' me and Miss Hays there"—pointing at Sharon as Green averted his gaze from her—"to examine and copy them?"

Green frowned and cleared his throat. "I couldn't answer that, not until I talked it over. It wouldn't be my decision."

Fraterno—whose decision the revealing of the statements would be, with a little coaching from Milt Breyer—stood and objected, just seconds late. Green had already let the cat out of the bag.

"I'm withdrawin' the question," Black said, grinning.

"But you did say that the statements exist, and that you have 'em?"

Green hesitated, obviously flustered. Finally he said, "Yes."

"Thanks, Detective," Black said. "Pass the witness."

Sharon's lips curved into a smile of admiration. After they'd certified Midge and indicted her, any witness statements would be automatically available to the defense under discovery. Until their client was actually charged, though, Black and Sharon weren't entitled to see diddly squat. But Black, playing the bull in a china closet role, now had it on record that the statements existed. The state had a big advantage in this hearing in that their witnesses didn't have to appear in person. So, when the witnesses finally testified at trial, they weren't restricted to Green's memory and could say what they damn well pleased. Now, however, if the trial testimony differed in any way from what Green supposedly *recalled* the witnesses to say, since the detective had admitted to having the signed statements, the defense could dig the detective's testimony at this hearing up for attack on appeal. Jolly good show, old boss, Sharon thought.

Kenneth Tucker scratched his round bald head. "Redirect?"

Stan Green hunched forward, hands on knees, ready to stand and leave the witness box.

"Just one more thing," Fraterno said.

Green relaxed, sat back and folded his arms.

"Detective Green, when you went to the Hockaday School to arrest Midge Rathermore, did you have occasion to interview the headmistress at the school?"

Green half smiled. "Why, yes. That would be Miss Etta Taylor. Miss Rathermore was in class, and I had to take the headmistress along while I made the arrest."

"Uh-huh. And during your discussion with Miss Taylor, did she tell you that it had been she who delivered the news of Mr. William Rathermore's death to his daughter Midge?"

"Yes, ma'am, she did."

"And according to the headmistress, what was Midge Rathermore's reaction upon learning that her father had been murdered?" Fraterno folded her hands and waited.

Stan Green looked steadily at Midge. She picked just

that moment to grin at the cop. My God, child, Sharon thought.

"The headmistress told me," Green said, "that Miss Rathermore laughed and clapped her hands."

"Her IQ registered exceptionally high, and her emotional responses were normal." Gregory Mathewson, stomach hanging out over his lap like the girth on Baal. Mathewson was the Grand Poohbah of all psychologists employed by the county on a regular basis, his testimony damaging to the defense in direct proportion to the size of his expert-witness fee.

"And in any of these tests," Fraterno said, sitting back, uncrossing and recrossing her legs, "did Miss Rathermore exhibit less than the maturity one would expect to find in the normal sixteen-year-old?"

"Absolutely not." Mathewson wore dark-framed, I'm-brilliant glasses. He had bulging cheeks and sparse snow white hair, the hair disheveled just so, the studious man too involved in his work to bother with combs and brushes. "In fact, I'd say Miss Rathermore is quite mature for her age." He beamed at Midge, who was now drawing doggies and puppies on a sheet of legal paper which she'd torn from Sharon's pad.

"Doctor," Fraterno said, "in your opinion, would Midge Rathermore understand that it was wrong to murder someone, or to have someone else murder someone?"

"No doubt about it. The subject has a complete understanding of right and wrong."

Fraterno paused, flipping pages in her file for emphasis. Finally she said, "No further questions."

As Tucker offered the defense a chance to cross-examine, Black glanced at Sharon and shrugged. Technically, as the new lawyers in the case, the defense was entitled to suspend the hearing until they could hire their own shrink to examine Midge, but what was the use? Tucker would merely decide that Mathewson's hired testimony was more credible than the defense's hired testimony and recommend certification anyhow. There would be plenty of time to have a different doctor examine Midge between her certification as an adult and the trial itself; not only that, what the defense psychologist was going to say would remain a mystery to the prosecution.

Still, however, Sharon couldn't resist the opportunity to take a few shots. She sat up straighter in her chair. "I have a couple of things, Your Honor." Russ Black drew a breath of surprise.

Mathewson folded his hands over his enormous stomach and waited. The toughest lawyers in the state had fired volleys at the psychologist in the past, and barbs rolled off Mathewson like water off a duck's back.

"Doctor," Sharon said, "in how many cases have you testified for the state?"

Mathewson smiled like Jesus. "I'm not sure."

"Is it more than a hundred?"

"Possibly."

"More than two hundred?"

"It could be."

Sharon stopped at that. In front of a jury she would have built the figure up to five hundred or more, but Court Master Tucker already knew that Mathewson was the state's number one hired gun, and going on and on about the number of cases in which he'd testified would be kicking a dead horse. Sharon now said, "Doctor, during your examination of Midge Rathermore, how did she act?"

Mathewson frowned. "I'm not sure I understand."

"Well, did she blow any spit bubbles?" Sharon couldn't keep the sarcastic bite out of her tone. Lying old bastard, she thought. When she had been a prosecutor, her conscience wouldn't allow her to use Mathewson as a witness, even though she'd received pressure from upstairs to change her mind.

"I don't recall." Mathewson continued to smile.

"Did she ask you for a Hershey bar?"

"Objection," Fraterno said loudly.

"Sustained." Tucker favored Sharon with a stern glare.

Sharon was too worked up to stop. "Let me ask you, Doctor," she said, grabbing the sheet of paper from Midge and holding it up for the psychologist and the family court master to see, "did she draw any cartoons while you were conducting these . . . these *tests*?"

"Objection."

"Sustained. I'm warning you, Counsel." Kenneth Tucker turned red and pointed a finger.

Sharon sighed. She was out of line and knew it. A lawyer wasn't entitled to make vicious attacks on an expert witness, particularly when said lying shit was giving testimony on behalf of the sovereign County of Dallas. Sharon dropped Midge's cartoons on the table and regarded her knees. "I apologize to the court, Your Honor," she said. "I must have gotten carried away."

Kenneth Tucker had no authority to rule on Midge's status and said so. The family court master could only make a recommendation to the judge, and, Tucker said, the judge's ruling would be forthcoming within a week. The judge's ruling, Sharon knew, would consist of the old boy signing an order—prepared by Tucker, of course—without even reading it. On the day the order was ready, the court clerk would make the usual call over to the D.A.'s office, and then Fraterno and Milt Breyer would hot-foot it into the grand jury room to ask for an indictment. The grand jury proceeding would be even more of a farce than the certification hearing, so within a week Midge would find herself in the county jail with the big folks. Tucker terminated the hearing with a wave of his hand. As Sharon turned away from the bench alongside Russ Black, she briefly caught Kathleen Fraterno's eye. The prosecutor locked gazes with Sharon for an instant, then Fraterno lowered her lashes and studied the floor. Personally, Sharon knew, Kathleen didn't have much stomach for this sort of thing. The job as a prosecutor, however, had no conscience. Maybe Milt Breyer did me a favor, Sharon thought, hitting on me until I quit. She took a couple of steps toward the defense table, preparing to retrieve her gear.

Midge's guard had problems. As he led the teenager away toward the holding cell, he reached up to remove Sharon's jacket from around the prisoner's shoulders. Midge grabbed the lapels and pulled the garment tight around her, at the same time sniffling and twisting away. The guard looked helplessly around the courtroom. In private he would have yanked the jacket away from Midge and possibly even roughed her up a bit in the process, but here in the public eye he wouldn't dare. He reached once more for the coat. Midge drew the lapels even tighter around her body.

Sharon walked quickly over. "Let her keep it," she said gently.

The guard said in a hoarse whisper, "It's against the rules, Miss Hays. You know that."

Sharon smiled at Midge and patted her client's thick upper arm. "Well, maybe it is," Sharon said. "But at least let her wear it back to the cell."

Midge's eyes grew big and round as she looked at Sharon with an expression near worship.

"I guess I could stretch a point," the guard said.

"Thanks," Sharon said.

Sharon watched the fat girl leave the courtroom, watched Midge duck her head slightly as the guard followed her through the side exit. Midge lovingly stroked the jacket's sleeve as she disappeared from view.

If there's any way, Sharon thought, I'm going to help that poor baby.

6

Sharon felt nervous anticipation as Russell Black, stone-faced, opened the courtroom door and stood aside for her to go out in the hall before him. Sharon had taken the bull by the horns, both in the pre-hearing conference with Midge Rathermore and in the hearing itself, and she was slightly fearful of Black's reaction. He'd told her in no uncertain terms during her job interview that all courtroom decisions were up to him, yet here she was upstaging Black her first day on the job. She'd already seen her new boss fly off the handle once, over her remark about Midge's former court-appointed lawyer. Likely I'm in for it, she thought with a sort of fearful resignation. As they moved down the corridor with the top of her head on a level with Black's ear, Sharon mentally held her breath.

They'd gone about halfway to the elevators, side-stepping lawyers with briefcases, defendants with worried looks, and clerks who hustled to and fro lugging boxes loaded down with file folders, when Black cleared his throat and said, "Listen, I—"

Here it comes, Sharon thought.

Suddenly Black touched her arm and stopped her in her tracks. Near the elevators Milt Breyer and Kathleen Fraterno were in heated conversation with two men. Sharon had always prided herself on being able to classify strangers she encountered in the courthouse—as lawyer, defendant, or general hanger-on—just by their dress and demeanor, but this pair who were hobnobbing with the prosecutors had her buffaloed. Neither man wore a suit, so they weren't lawyers. Both showed confident, almost cocky grins, so they weren't criminal defendants, either. One guy was mid-forties with long sideburns and a mustache, and was wearing pressed jeans, denim long-sleeved shirt, and gray alligator boots. He was sucking on an unlit pipe. His sidekick was younger, thirty or so, with longish but neat sandy hair which touched his collar. He wore pleated Dockers along with a white knit polo shirt, and as his partner talked a mile a minute to Milt Breyer, the younger of the two strangers looked at Sharon and Black. His lips curved upward in a smile of recognition.

"Don't say a word to 'em," Black whispered. "If they speak to us, let me handle it." He took Sharon's arm and steered her around the foursome toward the elevators, then reached out to press the Down button. Fraterno glanced at Sharon, then looked quickly away. I'm going to have to call her, Sharon thought. Something was bugging the devil out of Kathleen, and Sharon suspected that it didn't have anything to do with the Rathermore case. Sharon clutched her briefcase in both hands as Black stood impatiently by, first on one foot and then the other.

The younger of the strangers excused himself from the group and walked over. "Mr. Black? Hey, Russ, got a minute?"

Black turned toward the newcomer with a sigh of resignation. "Look, we're in kind of a hurry." The elevator doors opened with a swish of air.

The man quickly removed two business cards from his breast pocket, handed one card to Black and the other to Sharon. He smiled at her and stroked one sleeve of his white knit shirt. "You'd be Miss Hays, wouldn't you? Sharon Hays?"

She nodded dumbly. The guy was good-looking, but in a slicko sort of way, the type she might pick for a door-to-door salesman.

Black ushered Sharon firmly onto the elevator. He said brusquely to the stranger, "Nice seeing you."

As the man opened his mouth to speak, the doors closed swiftly in his face. Sharon felt suddenly lighter as the car descended.

She looked at the business card. Apparently the man was Rayford Sly, executive producer of something called

Aviton Productions. The firm's logo was a movie camera mounted on a tripod.

"So you'll know," Black said, "we don't talk to TV movie people. We don't make deals, and we don't have anything to do with 'em."

The car halted, Sharon's feet pressing into the carpet as gravity reversed. She led the way into the building lobby, and Black fell into step beside her. They gave the escalators a wide berth and headed for the rear exit leading onto Jackson Street. Sharon said, "I know some lawyers who've represented people for free just for the exposure. They say that sometimes the TV movie people pay more for the exclusive rights to the story than the fee would've been to begin with."

Black halted and turned to face her. Sharon licked her lips and waited. Two lawyers in expensive suits approached, did a bread-and-butter split to pass on either side, then hustled away toward the elevators.

"What you're sayin's true," Black said. "These people offer big money. Was a time all you saw around these trials was book writers, but that's all changed. Now the movie people bypass the book people, and what they used to pay for the screen rights to the book, they dole out to lawyers and witnesses for exclusives to their stories and take the case direct from the courtroom to television.

"But that dudn't make it right," Black said. "Five'll get you ten Milt Breyer's up there right now negotiatin' his movie deal for the Rathermore case, and once the deal's made, old Milt's gonna be a damn sight more interested in the movie money than what's right for the little girl up there in the holdin' cell. What the movie money does, it means that Milt's got to win the case no matter what. Well, Russell Black don't play that game, and anybody throwin' in with old Russ has got to learn that real quick. Now, let's go." He turned toward the exit.

Sharon swallowed hard, then stood her ground and said, "Russ?"

He stopped and raised shaggy gray brows.

Sharon stepped closer. "Look, as long as you're already wound up, why don't you finish what you started to say upstairs?"

Black frowned. "Huh?"

"I think I already know," Sharon said, "and I'd rather get it over with now so we won't have to talk about it later on. I apologize, I suppose, for stealing your thunder up there in the courtroom. I remember what you said about, you're running your cases and the assistant's supposed to keep her mouth shut. It's just . . . hard for me, you know? I'm used to doing things."

He glanced up at the ceiling, then looked at her. "Oh. Oh, that. Hey, that was good goin', girl. Anybody that goes in the courtroom swingin', old Russ Black wants that somebody on his side. Now come on, we've got to hook 'em." He turned on his heel and led the way toward the rear of the building.

Sharon stood speechless for an instant, then took off after him, her high heels clicking on courthouse tile and her bulging satchel banging softly against her hip. As Black stopped to hold the door for her, she rolled her eyes and shook her head in bewilderment.

Near the bottom of the courthouse steps, Black paused and said, "What the hell . . . ?" He was looking to his left, up Jackson Street.

Sharon halted and followed her boss's gaze. A block away, an ambulance stood at the curb with roof lights flashing. Three black-and-whites were parked near the ambulance with bubble-gum flashers spinning and shooting red beams, and a mob of pedestrians had gathered on the sidewalk. As Sharon watched, four paramedics lugged a gurney from a glass-front office and, with uniformed cops holding back the crowd, loaded the gurney into the rear of the ambulance. On the gurney lay a shrouded body, secured with cloth straps. Two of the medics climbed up to pull on the gurney while the other two pushed from the rear, and the gurney rolled out of sight. One medic slammed the rear gate while another walked around to open the driver's-side door and reached in to throw a switch. The ambulance roof lights stopped flashing.

"Idn't Howard Saw's office down there?" Black said.

Sharon wasn't certain. She'd been to Saw's office only once, during pretrials while she'd been prosecuting the Donello case, and all of the glass fronts along Jackson

Street looked alike to her. "I don't know," Sharon said. "It could be."

"Old Howard," Black muttered. "Be a shame if anything was to happen to him."

7

"Will you be gone a lot?" Melanie said.

"Quite a bit, sweetheart. Now that I don't work for the county anymore, it's going to be different. Someone in private practice has to put in whatever hours it takes to get the job done. And we'll be needing a lot of money pretty soon. Your braces."

"Pew."

"You won't wear them forever. You've already got a pretty smile. You need straight teeth to go with it." Sharon wondered if she'd said the right thing. As Melanie grew older it was harder and harder for Sharon to know what to say. Straight white teeth in Melanie's future were something to look forward to, and projected a good self-image for the eleven-year-old, but Sharon feared her words had implied that at the present Melanie's teeth were crooked and therefore ugly. "Your teeth are already pretty, but then they'll be perfect," Sharon added quickly.

They were sitting on the den sofa, a comfortable but outdated Spanish piece. Spanish had been the rage for about two years during the early seventies, just about the period when Sharon's mother had decided to replace her furniture one piece at a time. Before there had been money for wing chairs and settees, Spanish had been out, and then the cancer had come and Sharon's mother had died. Her dad had lived on in the small East Dallas house until '83, and then cancer had taken him as well. Now that the red brick home was Sharon's—and though she'd been sufficiently flush with cash to replace the Spanish

sofa numerous times—she'd let the couch stay on as a
friendly old memory. There it sat as the den's centerpiece,
in between the modern loveseat and wing chairs, and visitors who thought the combination sort of odd simply
could like it or lump it. The TV was playing on low
volume—*The System* another in the endless string of lawyer shows—but neither Sharon nor Melanie paid the program much heed, both of them grabbing the chance to
spend mother and daughter time.

Melanie brought the sofa pillow up from her lap and
hugged it to her chest, the pillow fringe falling to cover
her forearms. "Mom?" A hesitant tone of voice, a little
girl about to ask questions covering territory where she
wasn't sure she should tread.

"Yes, honey."

A downward cast to Melanie's gaze, a small, timid
smile which reminded Sharon of her mother's look.
"How can you tell when a boy likes you?" Melanie said.

Now, that's a good question, Sharon thought. For her it
had been a long, long time since she'd known the answer.
She assumed that in the fifth-grade set, the boys didn't
cast hungry glances at the girls' asses and legs, and that
no one had to go through the experience of having her
boob grabbed in the county witness room after trial. "Oh,
you can just tell," Sharon said, and added, "I suppose it's
when a boy wants to come around you a lot. Why, does
someone like you?"

"I think so. Jason White sits by me in the cafeteria."

Now, that should set the tongues a'waggin', Sharon
thought. "Is he nice?" she said.

One corner of Melanie's mouth tugged to the side in
thought, her expression a duplicate of Sharon's while re-
searching cases. There was a whole lot of Sharon in her
daughter, as a matter of fact. Melanie was the tallest in
her class, which, Sharon knew, would make her self-
conscious until around the eighth grade, when some of
the guys would grow into gangly beanpoles. If Melanie
ran true to mommy's form, in another year her breasts
would begin to swell; her periods would likely begin at
thirteen and be crampily painful and irregular until the
middle of Melanie's fifteenth year. Adolescence had been
a curse to Sharon, though at the time she'd thought of
herself as cool and all adults as nerds. In the short span

left before she became a nerd to her own daughter, Sharon was going to cherish the feeling of being loved and looked up to.

"I guess Jason's nice," Melanie finally said. "But he's sort of immature." She pronounced the grown-up word carefully, in a grown-up manner. Only a year ago Jason would have been silly. Now he was immature.

"Don't let that bother you," Sharon said. "Males tend to stay that way."

"Immature?"

"You'll learn. Men are just big little boys."

Now Melanie's features tightened, her look a trifle on the crafty side. It was the only expression which Melanie had inherited from her father, which meant that the eleven-year-old's next question was going to be about her dad. "Mom?"

"Yes."

"Was my father immature?"

"Oh, I think we both were." Sharon lived (and sometimes died) by the straightforward answer. She'd made the decision while Melanie was in diapers to be open and honest about Melanie's conception, and then only after lots of study and meetings with discussion groups. Sharon personally thought that Melanie was emotionally better off than the youngsters (fifty percent of all the kids in America, according to published statistics) whose parents were divorced, because Melanie didn't have the problem of being torn between the two. Melanie had understood the situation ever since she'd been old enough to understand anything, and seemed adjusted, but the questions about her father had become more and more frequent of late.

"But didn't you like each other?" Melanie's fifth-grade jargon substituted *like* for *love,* or maybe even more in context, for *get turned on by.*

Sharon lifted, then dropped her shoulders. "We did for a while. Then we didn't anymore."

"Like people divorcing?"

"Well, sort of." Sharon was still uncomfortable talking about the relationship, the really in and with-it aspiring actress and actor as live-in lovers. She'd been four months pregnant when she'd realized that acting was really all she had in common with Rob, and that life was in fact not a stage. Since neither of them had really thought of the arrangement as permanent, there had been none of the bickering and bitching which always accompanied divorce proceedings. In keeping with sensible with-it and ultramodern partings of the ways, Sharon had agreed that since the tiny Brooklyn Heights flat had been Rob's to begin with, it was she who should move, and she had done so. Even when Rob had taken up with Sharon's stand-in from an off-Broadway production within weeks of the split, Sharon and the other young woman had remained on friendly terms, all parties having really in and with-it attitudes. Equally in and with-it had been Sharon's stand with the anti-abortion radicals, so the decision to have Melanie hadn't really been a decision at all. Deciding to return to school back in Texas had taken more deliberation. Though she still missed New York and missed acting even more, it had been a few years since Sharon had felt regrets. Rob, she supposed, was still trooping around Broadway fringes, playing one part after another and taking up with a succession of leads and stand-ins. She'd never asked him for any support, and, given his dream-world sense of values, she supposed that he had never considered offering any.

Melanie snuggled down on the couch and raised her bare feet up on the sofa, pipe-stem legs bent around knobby knees, legs that in a few years would fill out and be supple like Sharon's own dancer's legs. "Will we go to New York someday?" Melanie said. She wore denim shorts which had been Sharon's, and hand-me-down woven belt cinched tight to keep her pants from falling off. Sharon had tried to buy Melanie jean shorts of her own, but Melanie had refused the offer, thinking that wearing grown-up clothes was really big stuff.

"It's likely we will," Sharon said. In the TV program, the swarthy and handsome defense attorney-hero cross-examined the state's stool pigeon witness—berating the witness in a manner which in real life would get the hero's fanny slapped with a contempt citation—and reduced the snitch's testimony to rubble. Sharon glanced at the clock. Ten 'til ten. Still plenty of time for the hero's surprise witness to saunter in and blow the state's case all to hell. In the real world, most defense lawyers looked like Howard Saw, and the only courtroom surprises came from one's own witnesses when they chickened out and changed their rehearsed testimony on the stand. "Bedtime in ten minutes, Melanie," Sharon said.

"Tell me about New York, Mom." Melanie had heard about the Big Apple no less than a thousand times in her life, but loved for Sharon to tell the stories over and over. Melanie's sudden interest, Sharon knew, had a whole lot to do with ducking bedtime talk, and also had a lot to do with changing the subject. Even at eleven years of age, Melanie's understanding that her mother didn't like to talk about her father was quite grown up. Ten minutes of New York, Sharon thought, then to bed with no more screwing around.

"It's big-big," Sharon said. "Tall buildings and sidewalks so crowded with people that at times it's hard to move."

"Did you ride the subways when we lived there?"

You already know the answer, you little fake, Sharon thought. "All the time. Nobody in Manhattan drives a car," she said.

Commander raised his snout from between his paws, regarded Sharon over his shoulder, and yawned magnificently. The German shepherd had heard the New York stories before as well. Tough luck, big guy, Sharon thought, you can bear it with the rest of us. Commander was a police attack school flunk-out, given to Sharon by the trainer on the day after the shepherd had jumped into a simulated bad guy's lap and licked the desperado's face. Oh, Commander did a fairly convincing Rin-Tin-Tin routine, snarling and snapping around the property fence lines, but anyone calling the shepherd's bluff and climbing into the yard was likely to find themselves smothered with love. Which made him the perfect family pet, Sharon thought, mean-as-hell-looking but no danger to Melanie or any of her playmates. Commander was going on six, which meant that Sharon had acquired the dog during her first year as a prosecutor. Time flies, Sharon thought. Commander laid his great head down between his paws and snored.

"Did you stand up on the subways?" Melanie said.

"Most of the time," Sharon said. "We lived close to the river in Brooklyn Heights, at a place on the line where the car was usually full by the time it stopped at our station. If I was doing a play it would be late when I went home. I could get a seat then."

"I want to hear about riding under the river." Melanie snuggled close to her mother, sneaking a quick and guarded glance at the clock as she did. On television, the hero stood up in the courtroom, locked gazes with the sneering D.A., and called—ta-*taa*—the bust-out witness to the stand.

"You never really know you're under the river, sweetheart. The whole subway is in a tunnel, and the tunnel under the river looks the same as any place else on the line." Sharon told the story by rote, like George in *Of Mice and Men,* telling Lenny over and over about the farmhouse with the rabbits.

"You never see the water?" Melanie said coyly, searching for questions now, realizing that the appearance of the surprise witness signified that the program was almost over, digging for anything to put off bedtime.

"It's overhead, but you . . ." Sharon blinked, then narrowed her eyes at the TV screen. In the witness strolled, a street punk, of course, clad in leather jacket, T-shirt, jeans, and motorcycle boots, a greasy-handsome type who winked at the defendant as he passed the rail, who curled his lip at the D.A. as he took the oath, and who spat a wad of gum into a Kleenex just before he climbed up on the stand. Good God, Sharon thought. "You never know the water is . . ." She stood quickly between Melanie and the television. "Time for bed, honey. Now."

Melanie's features squinched themselves into a frown. "*Mah*-um. The program's not over."

Sharon stood firm. "For you it is, honey bunch. Come on, time to hook 'em."

"But why, Mom?" Melanie looked as though the climax to *The System* was the number-one event of the century. "*Why,* Mom?" she said again.

Sharon gently closed her eyes. Because that greasy witness is your father, sweetheart, Sharon wanted to say. Old Rob had finally made it to the small screen.

"Because it's time, Melanie," Sharon said.

"I felt pretty stupid when it was over. Talk about overreaction." Sharon Hays on her bedroom window seat, bare legs curled up beneath her, oversized T-shirt draped over her upper body with the shirt's hem riding her hips. The window was partway open, springtime night sounds filtering in through the screen: two faraway cats in yowling battle with a chorus of crickets in the background. On the far side of the yard, Commander was a dim shape in the moonlight. The shepherd stood in the flower bed and poked his snout through an opening in the stockade fence. Up and down the block, dogs barked and whined in response to the screeching cats. Commander whimpered and his bushy tail moved from side to side. In moments he would howl like a shape-changing werewolf.

"You don't think she'd-a recognized him, huh?" Stan Green, prone on rumpled sheets, his outline blending with the shadows cast by his body, his voice now a slow Texas drawl in contrast with his businesslike demeanor on the witness stand.

Sharon shook her head; strands of perspiration-dampened hair clung to her temples. "No way. She's only seen pictures, two of them, and they're twelve years old."

"Sounds to me like you blew your cool."

Sharon closed her eyes in irritation. Stan Green pictured himself a stud in bed—which he definitely was—a keen personality analyst—which he certainly was not—and had a teeth-jarring habit of stating the obvious. Sharon considered that she'd sunk to the depths, discussing her innermost feelings with a cop who couldn't have cared less, and made up her mind to change the subject to things more on Green's level. Whatever that level might be.

"Maybe you should call the old boy and hit him up for something," Green said.

"That wouldn't make any sense. I've spent the last eleven years *not* asking him for anything." Changing the subject now was going to be difficult; ex-spouses and lovers were Green's favorite topic next to the cases on which he was working. There was a rule against discussing the job outside the department, but neither Stan Green nor any of the other cops whom Sharon knew paid any attention to the rule. Police department heads spent a lot of time trying to find out who had leaked what to the newspapers.

"Hell, he's bound to be making some big bucks," Green said.

Sharon turned her face away from the window, narrowing her eyes in the dimness. Green's body was long and lean, his belly flat and muscular. The filled end of a condom dangled from his spent member like an airport wind sock. Life as a prosecutor, Sharon thought, no commitments, sex life restricted to one law enforcement guy after another who didn't bother to take his rubber off when it was over. "I don't care how many bucks he's making, Stan," Sharon said. "I'd just as soon not even know about his income."

"Well, I'd damn sure be finding out if I was you. Every time I get a raise, my ex old lady sure knows about it." Green propped up on his elbow and lovingly touched his own flexed biceps. Green's former wife was a clerk in city police payroll, who was now sleeping with a divorced FBI agent who used to shack up with one of Sharon's law school classmates, a short, saucy blond who was a prosecutor in the U.S. attorney's office. Sharon's old school chum for a time had slept with Stan Green while he was married to the payroll clerk, so the daisy chain was now complete. Sharon's own experience as one of the law enforcement crowd had consisted of two relationships. The first had been with a fledgling state prosecutor when they'd both been rookies and Sharon had felt she needed someone to lean on. Stan Green was the second, after a series of civilian-issue men who couldn't deal with the fact that their lady friend threw people's asses in jail for a living. The affair with Stan had begun shortly after Sharon had tried a particularly heartrending child-abuse case and had been vulnerable, and Green had provided a much needed outlet for a time. But once the thrill was gone, the problem of communicating with an egomaniac had begun to outweigh the joy of multiple orgasm several times over. She'd been looking for an opening to end things for months, and thought that being on the opposite end of the Rathermore case would make the perfect excuse. Then he'd come over tonight, Sharon had been uptight over seeing Rob on television, and her need for physical contact had taken over. What a screw-up, Sharon now thought.

"Your ex wants to know about your income because of child support," Sharon said. "I don't want any child support because it would mean that I'd have to hear from him. Besides, we were never married." Outside, Commander's whimpers had grown into a steady whine as he pawed the crack between the fence boards. The cat's yowling had ceased, probably just a break in the action, but the chorus of barking dogs had become a din.

Green scratched his hairy chest. "Don't talk to me about child support. My kid's nine. Nine more years of this crap."

Christ, Sharon thought, more tender conversation after lovemaking. She stroked her smooth thigh and bent her head to peer through the window at the far wing of the house. In Melanie's room, gray-green light from the television screen flickered against the closed drapes. Melanie slept like a log; Sharon had checked on her daughter just after she'd let Stan Green in the house. Melanie was getting too old for her mother to have slip-in lovers, another of a thousand reasons for the Stan Green episode in Sharon's life to come to a halt. She pictured the scene if Melanie should wander in some night to find the big cop parked in mommy's bed, and was at a loss as to what she would tell her little girl. You know, darling, mommy gets horny just like everyone else. Fuck a duck, Sharon thought. She said to Green, "You did leave your car parked down the street, didn't you?"

"Next door. What the hell, everybody knows anyhow."

Sharon didn't try to hide the edge in her voice. " 'Everybody' only includes all the cops and D.A.'s, Stan. It doesn't include my neighbors and it doesn't include my daughter." She turned to him, letting her feet dangle from the window seat to touch the floor. "And while we're on the subject, no one knows because of what *I* told them. I thought Milt Breyer was going to give himself whiplash, grinning at me when you took the witness stand today."

Green now proudly touched his pectoral muscle and stretched out his legs, giving the woman a full-length view of his God-given body. "Aw, you know. People talk."

"People only talk when someone gives them something to talk about." She looked over her shoulder out the window. Commander was now on his haunches with his snout raised to the moon. The howl began, low in volume at first and then lifting toward a crescendo. Sharon rapped on the windowsill and said sharply, "Commander. Here." The shepherd cut if off in mid-howl, trotted over to sit beneath the window, and peered up at her with his tongue lolling to one side. One hound dog outside, Sharon thought, another crashed in my bed. She very nearly laughed out loud.

Green now said out of the blue, "I wish y'all could plead that fat girl."

Sharon's hackles rose. She said stiffly, "I beg your pardon?"

"I got a lot to do. If you were going to plead the fat girl, I could quit worrying about her case and concentrate on some other stuff I've got going."

Sharon wanted to scream. A poor dull-witted child, about to be sacrificed to the great god Media Coverage, and as far as Green was concerned—ditto for Milt Breyer, though Kathleen Fraterno would have more compassion—the Rathermore case was just another fat-girl file he'd like to get rid of so that he could go on with his rat killing elsewhere. Through Sharon's anger a warning bell sounded inside her head. Keep your cool, she thought, and you might find out something. She said carefully, "We haven't even talked about a plea bargain. I doubt she'll get an offer to plead, with all the TV and movie interest." She watched Green and cocked her ear to listen.

"You're right, with the money Milt Breyer stands to make on a movie." Green lifted the weighted end of his condom and then dropped it. The jism-filled rubber bounced heavily on the sheets. What a disgusting asshole, Sharon thought. Green said, " 'Course, somebody could make Milt come up with a plea offer."

Green's even mentioning plea bargain meant that the case wasn't as strong as the state was letting on. Sharon had prosecuted two trials with Green as her investigating officer/witness, and both times she'd been tempted to muzzle the detective away from the courtroom to keep him from giving away the farm with his mouth. Now that she was on the other side, Sharon could pump Stan Green and never have a twinge of conscience. "What's the matter, Stan?" Sharon said softly. "Your two schoolboy witnesses have some memory problems?"

"Naw. Those little pricks remember good. It's politics, dealing with these rich kids. The fat girl goes to Hockaday and the boys to St. Marks. The boys' daddies got a lot of stroke with the D.A., political contributions and whatnot, and the papas don't want junior up in front of the cameras for the world to see." As he spoke, he rolled his latex-encased penis between his thumb and forefinger, looking his member over as if infatuated. Which, Sharon thought, he probably is. "You know I'm not s'posed to be telling you this," Green said.

"I know," she said. "It's between us."

"That's the way it has to be. But if you and old Russell Black could work out a plea, those boys' daddies would be tickled to death."

"We'll keep that in mind." Sharon turned her face to the window to hide her grin. "Maybe we'll—"

Beneath and outside the window, Commander moved. He rose from his haunches, growling deep in his throat, and charged across the lawn to the fence. He leaped against the wooden slats, snarling and snapping at something outside the yard.

Sharon lifted her chin. "Commander. Here, boy."

The shepherd ignored her. He backed away from the fence and charged again, hitting the wood with such force that the boards quivered. His growls were murderous.

Sharon stood and leaned toward the open window. "Good God. What's gotten into that dog?"

"Probably nothing," Green said. "Probably just a bitch in heat." He let go of his penis and slid downward on the sheets. "And speaking of that, c'm'ere."

Sharon sat on the window seat and regarded her bare knees. Bitch in heat, she thought. Come to think about it, that's just what I've been acting like. As Commander continued to rage outside, Sharon chewed her lower lip. She touched her thigh. She rubbed her eyes.

"I think you'd better go, Stan," she finally said.

As the big caramel-colored German shepherd snarled and snapped at him through the fence, Bradford Brie thought, One mean-ass fucking mutt that is. I got just the thing for mean-ass mutts, he thought. One jumbo slab of raw beefsteak, laced with a tad of strychnine, comin' up. Not enough poison so that the shepherd dies quickly, no way. Make that fucking dog sick—sick as a dog, Brie thought with an insane laugh—then watch him whimper and whine and beg until he dies. That's just the thing for mean-ass mutts, Brie thought, let 'em know you've outsmarted their stupid fucking ass before they go.

He didn't see the dog as a really big problem. Brie

even got a kick out of the dumb brute, standing just out of reach of the snapping jaws, just far enough from the fence so that the shepherd couldn't bite him. Brie made a game out of it, feinting a charge in the darkness, acting as if he was about to climb over the fence, driving the snarling dog out of its mind. It won't be long for you, you dumb yokel police hound, Brie thought.

Bradford Brie had brought a small Canon camera along with him. He already had shots of the house's front, sides, and rear, using an infrared flash and slowing the camera's shutter speed a fraction, and he now squinted through the viewfinder and pressed the button just as Commander hurled himself against the fence, snapping and growling. Click. Beaut of a picture. This silly dog didn't amount to a popcorn fart, not to a man who'd once outsmarted the bloodhounds down at the Texas Department of Corrections.

Now, them was some mean fucking dogs, Brie thought, those TDC hounds, but they were probably even dumber than this German shepherd. Every prison bloodhound was a member of a pack, and every pack had a leader, and the rest of the mutts would follow the leader straight into hell. If a man wanted to outsmart a herd of TDC bloodhounds, all he had to do was find a maple or elm tree branch and take out the lead dog. Brain that sonofabitch, kill him dead, and the rest of the pack would run for cover. Which was exactly what Bradford Brie had done, killed the lead dog down there in the river bottom, and all the rest of the bloodhounds had scattered like big dumb four-footed quail, baying and howling. Brie sometimes wondered if those stupid fucking guards had ever rounded up their stupid fucking dogs, and frankly hoped the guards were still down in the river bottom hunting for the canine bastards. Killing that dog had brought Bradford Brie four extra days of freedom, hiding out in a farmhouse near Huntsville with a widow woman as his captive slave.

His breath caught as he pictured her, firm ass and big, strong legs, cooking for him and doing just about anything Bradford Brie damn well wanted her to. They'd finally caught up to him when the widow's son had come by looking for his mama, and Brie now understood that not letting her answer the door had been a mistake. He should have let her baby boy into the house and then strangled the fucker; the son had gone away and then had returned a short time later with the county boys. Bradford Brie had been no dummy; he'd understood when the jig was up and had come out grinning with his hands in the air. The four days of good hot food and succulent pussy, Brie thought, had been well worth the beating he'd taken from two county deputies on the way downtown. The court had appointed him a lawyer who'd made Brie a good deal: fifteen years each on the kidnapping and rape charges, a nickel for the escape, all three sentences to run concurrent with the twenty-year beef he'd already been serving for armed robbery. Bradford Brie, in fact, had not received one extra day's time for the escape, not one minute more in the joint for raping and terrorizing a woman over four long nights, and he'd made parole in six years, four months, and thirteen days.

He grinned as he remembered the escape, and squatted down to peer at the raging German shepherd through the fence. Your time's comin', old Shep, Brie thought.

But even if the dog wasn't going to be any problem for Brie, the man he'd seen going in the house might be a different story. Brie scratched his head with fingers like bird claws. He should have figured that a good-looking one like the lawyer lady would have someone coming over at night to put the old pork to her. He hadn't thought that one out carefully, which certainly wasn't typical procedure for Bradford Brie. It had been just past eleven o'clock when the man had come to her door, strutting as though he had a cob rammed up his ass, and Brie hadn't missed the fact that the man had parked his car next door. For some reason the man didn't want people to see him. Was he married? Did the lawyer lady have another guy and this man was just somebody she was banging on the side? Before long Bradford Brie would have the answers, and then he'd know exactly what to do.

After one more feint in the shepherd's direction—and after laughing like a banshee as the dog practically broke his fool neck slamming into the fence—Bradford Brie retreated down the alley and rounded the corner. He was whistling as he climbed into his eight-year-old Chrysler LeBaron. Figure all the angles and don't go in half cocked, he thought. Bradford Brie was one smart guy. He was damn sure smart enough to take his time.

8

The next day was Saturday, but far from a day of rest for Sharon Hays. She was up by six and, clad in knee-length cutoff jeans and oversized Texas Longhorn T-shirt, was on her back porch by seven, beating the stuffing out of two army blankets. They had been wintertime covers for Melanie, and had been folded on the floor of the linen closet since late February. Sharon had sworn every week since then that she was going to knock the dust from the blankets and put them away for the summer, but she hadn't found the time. But now she made time, stretching the roll-up clothesline from Sears across the porch at shoulder level, draping the blankets over the line and, after drawing a deep breath, whaling the tar out of the blankets with a rug beater. She sneezed as the dust flew in sooty clouds, and clenched her jaw to swing even harder. Commander trotted over from his position by the fence, sniffed Sharon's feet, then sat on his haunches and looked as though he thought 7:00 A.M. blanket beaters were nutty as fruitcakes. Sharon paused for long enough to scratch Commander behind the ears, stick her tongue out at him and wrinkled her nose, then continued her assault on the blankets.

She finished in a half hour, folded the blankets away in the top of the linen closet, and said goodbye to the snuggly warm covers until November. Her forehead and upper lip were damp with perspiration, and there was a fine coating of dust grime on her forearms and hands. She went out the front door, padded barefoot down the side-

walk to pick up the folded *Dallas Morning News,* and
paused to wave at Mrs. Breedlove across the street. Mrs.
Breedlove, chubby and gray, returned the wave as she
sprayed her lilies with fine mist from the garden hose.
Mr. Breedlove was retired from Exxon, and the elderly
couple had lived across the street since Sharon had been
seven years old. They had one daughter, Nancy, two years
older than Sharon, who now lived in Boston and worked
for a cruise line. Sharon had intended to write Nancy for
some time now, and as she carried the paper back inside
her house, she made a mental note—for the sixth or sev-
enth time this year—to ask Mrs. Breedlove for her daughter's address. At the very next opportunity, whenever that
might be.

She dumped the paper onto the breakfast table,
whipped orange juice, wheat germ, and one raw egg into
a froth in the blender, and sat down to sip the concoction
while she read the *News.* The other Dallas daily, the
Times-Herald, had folded in late '91. With no local
competition—except for a pesky radical sheet, the *Observer,* which was a free handout in supermarkets and restaurants and survived mostly on income from its
personals section, and which never missed the opportunity to take swipes in print at the *News*—the *News* had
the Dallas media arena pretty much to itself. Sharon
thought the city had really suffered from the *Times-
Herald*'s collapse, and had always considered the *Herald*
the better paper of the two. She skimmed the *News*'s front
page and first-section stories—and wondered briefly
whether Ross Perot was really out to give the Repubs and
Democrats a run for their money, or if the eccentric Dallas zillionaire was merely bored and looking for something to do—then laid the first section of the paper aside,
took a glug of orange juice, wheat germ, and egg, picked
up the Metropolitan page and looked at herself.

It wasn't likely that anyone would recognize Sharon in
the photo. Only her jawline and right arm were visible on
the far left side of the picture as she extended a hand to
comfort Midge Rathermore. Midge's fat face was turned
slightly to one side, her eyes large and frightened, clutching Sharon's jacket as the guard led the teenager from the
courtroom. Sharon thought that Midge was the most pitiful human being she'd ever seen. There was a rule

against cameras in court, and this shot had been taken from out in the corridor, with the lens trained through the window in the hallway door. Sharon scanned the accompanying story, saw that it contained nothing she didn't already know, and was preparing to turn the page when a headline on the lower left caught her eye. She blinked, then frowned.

Someone had murdered Howard Saw in his office. Had strangled the cheap little shyster. There was Saw's picture, his piggish face wreathed in a smile. True, it was an oily smile, which suited Howard to a *T,* but a smile nonetheless. As prosecutor in the Donello case—and given her personal loathing for people like Wilfred Donello, who dealt in kiddie porn—Sharon had been secretly glad that bumbling, porky Saw had been on the other side. The case against Donello hadn't been that strong, and a real-live bang-up attorney might've walked the guy. Now that she was on the defense side of the table, she wondered whether she could ever work up much zeal for representing a sleazebag like Donello. She doubted it, and thanked her lucky stars that she was working for Russell Black, who took on only the cases for which he had the stomach.

So it *had* been Saw's office where Sharon and Black had seen the ambulance as the two of them had left the courthouse. While Sharon had been in the sham of a certification hearing for Midge Rathermore, someone had squeezed the life out of Howard Saw right beside the pudgy lawyer's desk. The killing had taken place only a block from what was now Sharon's office. She couldn't work up a single tear over Saw's death, but the idea of a murder not five minutes' walk from where she was to make her living raised goose bumps on Sharon's neck the size of spider eggs.

She cast the newspaper aside with a shudder. Then she slugged down the rest of her drink and hustled off to waken Melanie.

While Melanie ate breakfast, Sharon showered and changed into baggy white shorts, a man's pale blue button-down shirt with the cuffs rolled up a couple of turns, and white Reebok sneakers along with fuzzy ankle socks. Then she gathered up her purse and briefcase, went downstairs, and sat across from Melanie to jockey the eleven-year-old into finishing off her oatmeal and scrambled eggs. Finally Sharon piled her belongings into the Volvo's front seat while Melanie, carrying what looked to be a half-dozen Sega Genesis video game cartridges, scooted into the back. Sharon hit the switch to raise the electronic garage door, and backed into the street for the two-block journey in brilliant sunshine to Sheila Winston's house.

At first Melanie had been really grumpy over her mother's leaving her for the day—and Sharon, feeling the need to spend the entire weekend with her daughter, had felt slightly guilty and hadn't blamed the child—but the news that she was to spend the time at Sheila's had brightened her considerably. Sheila's daughter Trish was two months younger than Melanie and in the same class at school, and was one of the only kids around who could clean Melanie's plow in the video games. Sharon had recently splurged for two new cartridges, *Nestor's Quest* and *Shadow of the Beast,* and Melanie had practiced on the new games for hours, laying a trap for the next time she face the invincible Trish Winston. As Sharon drove down the tree-lined street with red brick and white frame houses on either side, she kept one eye on the rearview and watched Melanie. The child sat up straight with the video games in her lap, screwing up her features, and Sharon decided that Melanie was putting her game face on.

Sheila's home was in the middle of the second block, a sixty-year-old dark red brick with a wooden front porch and suspended porch swing. The house was in perfect condition, eaves and windowsills freshly painted, and the lawn was clipped and edged as though ready to have its picture taken. Sharon's own yard teemed with springtime weeds, and a twinge of guilt shot through her as she pulled to the curb. To hell with it, her lawn could wait its turn like everything else in her life. Today Sharon had work to do. She and Melanie went up the walk at a fast clip and rang the bell.

Sheila answered in seconds. She wore white baggy shorts and a pale blue shirt turned up at the cuffs. She eyed Sharon's identical outfit and burst out laughing. "Well, at least we're not going to the same party," Sheila said. She wore pale pink lipstick, and her straightened hair was fluffed out around her head like the outline of the Liberty Bell. Sheila's skin was the color of light coffee. That Sheila was black seldom crossed Sharon's mind, and she doubted that Melanie noticed the racial difference at all. Once, when Sheila had come over to help Sharon with yard work, Sharon had noticed Mrs. Breedlove watching from across the street, and her head had been dubiously tilted to one side. It was the generation gap. Sharon's own dad would have had a cow over his daughter buddying around with a black person, and according to Sheila, on hearing that his little darling was palling around with some white-bread bitch, Sheila's father would likely have trotted out his shootin' iron. Generation by resistant generation, Sharon thought, the racial hatred is dying away.

Sharon spun around to model her clothes. "My shirt's a shade darker, I think."

"It's going to look darker on you, anyhow," Sheila said. From inside the house Trish peered around her mom to bat coal black eyes and wrinkle her button nose at Melanie. Melanie wriggled between Sheila and the door frame, and the two little girls made a beeline for the back of the house. As the children disappeared through the sitting room, Sheila said, "Well, come on in. Geez."

"She's already in," Sharon said.

"I noticed." Sheila put her hands on her waist. "Got time for coffee?"

"No way. Miles to go and all that. I owe you one, kid." Sharon had met Sheila in PTA, when Trish and Melanie had been second-graders, and as single mothers they had found they had a whole lot in common. Sheila, in fact, had carried a drama minor while majoring in psychology, and the two women went to a lot of plays together. They also kept each other's children and leaned on one another's shoulders quite a bit, and the racial difference eliminated any feeling of competition between the two. Sheila didn't cross the barrier where dating was concerned, and Sharon's liberation didn't extend to interracial flings, either, so the two of them hit it off better than sisters. "I'll try to be back by five," Sharon said.

"Don't knock yourself out. I'm on the outs with Randall, so don't guess I'll be going anyplace." Sheila rolled her eyes. "End of another beautiful friendship."

"I know the feeling. I'm pretty sure I burned a bridge last night myself."

Sheila leaned against the doorjamb. Her smile faded. "Shar," she said, and then cleared her throat before saying, "I was watching *The System* last night. There was a name in the credits . . ."

"It's him." Sharon folded her arms and regarded the porch beneath her feet. "What can I tell you? It's him."

"Does Melanie . . .?"

"No, she doesn't. Not yet. If he's finally getting a few TV parts, well, this isn't the last time he'll be on. That's the way it works: once you finally get a part, your name goes on the list. We'll be seeing him again." Sharon chewed her lower lip. "You didn't tell Trish who he was, did you?"

Sheila raised a swearing-in hand, palm out. "Not me, no, ma'am. It's your business. But I think you know that, some time, some place, somebody's going to spill the beans. Especially if he's going to be a regular on the tube."

Sharon regarded her toes, then looked slowly up. "I know you're right. It's a bridge I'll have to cross. I've just got to think on the best way of breaking the news to her."

"It's probably going to make her want to see him in person, you know," Sheila said. "Our little girls are growing up."

"I know that, too." Rather sadly Sharon walked to the end of the porch. She turned back. "Thanks for being a friend, Sheila. It'd be tough without you, you know?"

Sharon did her best to shake the blues as she used the McCommas Street overpass to cross Central Expressway into Park Cities, switching the FM dial from Melanie's favorite rock station over to Country 96.3, but the song on the C&W station loomed up to haunt her. "Lookin' for Love in All the Wrong Places." Just perfect, Sharon thought. Then she decided that if she couldn't beat 'em, she'd join 'em, and threw back her head to sing along, belting out the words at the top of her lungs as she tooled her ancient Volvo among the Highland Park mansions. At the corner of Hillcrest and Beverly Drive, a black Mercedes pulled up beside her at the stop sign. There was a fiftyish woman with blued white hair at the Mercedes's wheel, and she directed a curious stare in Sharon's direction. Sharon smiled and waved at the woman, and sang even louder.

Two bad things in one night, Sharon thought. First the shock of seeing Rob on television in all his splendor, followed by the nagging dread that someday soon Melanie was going to demand to see her father. Then the scenario with Stan Green, the hunk of a homicide cop sulking in her bedroom as he yanked up his pants. Actually, since she'd never had any feelings for Stan other than lust, his storming around might have been comical if it hadn't been for the possible consequences. Now, in her very first case as a defense attorney, she had two males on the other side, one she'd kneed in the balls and the other she'd expelled from her bedroom. If hell hath no fury like a *woman* scorned, Sharon thought, then no telling what those two he-man yo-yos might do with their dander up. She didn't know whether or not to tell Russell Black that in addition to the incident with Milt Breyer, she'd now made a jackass out of the investigating detective in the Rathermore case as well. Telling Black was something else she'd have to think on. She didn't want to involve her new boss in her personal problems, but they might spill over into the courtroom at some point. So should she tell Russ? It was hard to know.

She adjusted the radio volume, gave the Volvo the gas, and left the Mercedes in her dust at the intersection. The blue-haired woman angrily beeped her horn.

The law library at Southern Methodist University fronted Hillcrest Avenue like a gothic fortress. The building was three stories high and a half block long. Behind it lay the campus, stretching a mile or two to the northeast, consisting of red brick dorms and classroom buildings, tree-shaded walks and manicured lawns, and with-it students in Docker pants and polo shirts hurrying back and forth among the buildings. Over it all towered the dome on top of Dallas Hall, dead center in the campus quadrangle. Sharon parked across Hillcrest from the college, in front of the University Bookstore in a two-hour zone, and checked her watch. She didn't have any idea how long her research at the library was going to take, but needed to keep up with the time so that every two hours she could hurry back and move the car. Parking anywhere around SMU was a bitch; on campus without a permit sticker was a no-no because the campus cops would write a ticket in a heartbeat and then send a series of nasty duns through the mail if one didn't pay the fine. Sharon dug in her purse and checked her Walkman to be certain that the batteries were ready for action. Then she locked the car, lugged her purse and briefcase to the corner traffic light, and pressed the button on the pole. In a few seconds the light clicked from red to green, north- and south-bound traffic on Hillcrest came to a halt, and Sharon started through the crosswalk. The library building loomed nearer and taller.

Sharon did just about all of her legal research at SMU, and told herself that she came to the college for convenience' sake even though, deep down, she knew better. The county law library downtown was more accessible from the freeway, had gratis underground parking, and contained all the reference material a Texas lawyer would ever need. The truth was that Sharon saw the rich kids' college as an unfulfilled fantasy. While growing up in Dallas, she'd dreamed of going to school out here—and of rush weeks, homecoming dances, Tri-Delts, Phi Beta Kappa, Signa-Fy Nothing—even though in her little-girl heart she'd known that her folks could never afford the tuition. She'd been right, of course. Sharon had spent her college career at U. of Texas-Dallas while holding down a job in Foley's women's wear department, then had gone on to New York to exist on bologna and cheese while attending acting school. Finally there'd been law school in Austin and toting food and drinks back and forth in restaurants with island bars and ferns in hanging baskets, and using most of her tip money to pay for Melanie's baby-sitting. So now that she was a real honest-to-goodness lawyer, if she liked to fantasize a bit while rubbing elbows with the rich folks' children, what was the harm? So, when she wasn't kidding herself, she knew that doing research at SMU had everything to do with a little pretending on her part. That and one other motive.

She reached the eastern side of Hillcrest Avenue and proceeded to stand for a moment in front of the library, craning her neck to gaze up at the mammoth building, feeling like Thumbelina before the giant's castle. Then she squared her shoulders, hitched up her purse and brief-case, and strode purposefully through the entrance.

Sharon's second reason for doing her research at the college leaped at her in the form of an admiring look from a male student after she'd climbed the steps to the second floor of the library. The student sat behind the information desk, was a good-looking kid with fluffy brown hair, and wore a blue knit Tommy Hilfiger shirt. As Sharon came through the turnstile entry, the boy lifted his eyebrows, and as she bent to sign the visitors' register she couldn't resist a smile in his direction. She knew that she looked good, and that she could easily pass for one of the students, and if coming to the campus for research boosted her female ego ... well, Sharon didn't see any harm in that, either. As she laid the pen down beside the register and stepped toward the library shelves, the kid popped up like a jack-in-the-box. "Something ..." he said, then cleared his throat. "Something I can help you find?"

"I don't believe so," Sharon said. "I know pretty much where everything is, but if I need help I'll let you know." She grinned at the boy and continued on her way.

She paused in the aisle for a moment and let her gaze roam up and down a full half block of eight-foot shelves packed with red, green, gray, and black bound volumes of Vernon's Annotated Texas Codes, Civil and Criminal Procedures, Federal Seconds, and American Law Reviews. The northern half of the research room contained codes and research books from the forty-nine states other than Texas. Sharon ignored the out-of-state section and carried her purse and briefcase to a group of study tables. The library was silently crowded; students sat with bowed heads and scowls of concentration as they took notes from open lawbooks. Sharon spotted an empty seat between a red-haired girl in jeans and a slim black youngster wearing thick horn-rimmed glasses, and deposited her belongings on the table between the two. She headed straight for the Texas shelves, then stopped to glance toward the southern end of the building, where the Xerox was. Dime a copy. She retreated, dug in her purse, and found the electronic five-dollar slot card she'd bought on her last research trip. She had enough credit left for thirty-two copies. Might be enough and might not. If she had to, she'd buy another card. She went to the shelves.

In a couple of minutes Sharon returned to the table with four books stacked and balanced on her upturned forearms—the Code of Criminal Procedure in two volumes, the portion of the Criminal Code containing the murder statutes, and the slick paperback giving the 1992 revisions to the code—and dropped her load heavily beside her briefcase. The pile of books toppled and slid; one of the volumes bumped gently against the black student's arm. He showed Sharon an irritated glance. She retrieved the book with a smile of embarrassment. As Sharon pulled out her chair to sit, her briefcase toppled sideways to land atop the thick Federal Second volume which the red-haired girl had open before her. The girl favored Sharon with an agitated smirk. Sharon apologetically shrugged her shoulders, retrieved the briefcase as she had the lawbook, and squeezed in between the two students to sit. I can't help it, kids, if there was another vacant space, I'd take it.

Sometime during the night, in between the time when Stan Green had left in a huff—Christ, Sharon thought, at least the bastard had removed his condom before he put his pants on—and the time when she'd hauled the blankets onto the porch for a good old-fashioned flogging, she had had an idea. Inspiration came to her often in bed, a sudden flash of light cutting through semiconscious sleeplessness which made her sit bolt upright on the mattress. She'd been tossing and turning as she pictured Midge Rathermore, the poor fat teenager with pimples on her face and the psyche of a four-year-old, and the teenager's shocking statement during the interview had come back to haunt Sharon. *He liked fucking her.* Midge's little sister. Midge's father. Likely Midge had made it all up, but what if she hadn't? Bam, bolt of lightening, Sharon sitting up in the darkness, her eyes wide.

Like a lot of her ideas, this one might explode in her face under the brutal scrutiny of the law. But in view of what Sharon knew about the case so far, her sudden inspiration could lead to Midge's only possible defense. Nothing ventured, or whatever, Sharon thought.

She dug her Walkman from her purse, set the dial on

96.3, and clamped the foam-padded earphones on. With Ronnie Millsap's banging out "There Ain't No Gettin' Over Me" in her ears, she opened the murder statutes, jammed her tongue firmly into one corner of her mouth, and went to work. Her foot rocked in time with the music. On her right, the black law student shifted restlessly in his chair. As far as Sharon was concerned, the kid might as well have been a million miles away.

By four o'clock, Sharon had outlasted a libraryful of studiers except for one plump thirtyish woman who sat two tables away. Sharon had made five or six trips to the stacks for more research material, an equal number of forty-yard walks to the Xerox, and three record-time dashes across the street to move the Volvo, once arriving in the nick of time just as a cop was writing her a parking ticket. Her friendly, gee-I'm-sorry attitude had avoided the citation. Other than the book and copy forays and the ticket-saving incident, she hadn't moved from her chair. The four books with which she'd begun had multiplied into twelve, and her uneven jumble of bound volumes spilled over to cover the now empty spaces on both sides of her. A half-inch stack of photocopies sat flush against the front edge of the table; she'd used up all the credits on her card plus a portion of a second card in making the copies from the books. The radio's earphones were canted on her head, the right earpiece lower than the left, and one strand of hair drooped limply onto her forehead. She was beat, but pretty sure she had what she'd come for.

Midge's indictment wouldn't come down for a week, the time required for the clerk to type up the family court master's recommendation and the judge to rubber-stamp his approval, transforming Midge from a troubled adolescent into a scheming adult with a wave of the magic pen. So, allowing for weekends, they were talking a May 12 or 13 indictment. The law required sixty days' intervention between indictment and trial, to give the defense time to prepare. In most cases a series of delaying motions would string the time out a year or more before the trial actually happened. The delays wouldn't come to pass in Midge's case; with the newspaper and TV folks waiting with bated breath—not to mention the movie people who'd been talking to Breyer and Kathleen in the courthouse hallway, the movie guys more than likely having already made a cash offer to Breyer for exclusive rights to his story—the state would push to go ahead. In whatever form Dame Justice might exist these days, Sharon thought, the old gal would never stand in the way of a movie deal.

During summertime trials Sharon always sent Melanie to Sky Ranch, and in the back of her mind she was already making camp plans for the second and third weeks in July. Melanie loved the East Texas camp, just sixty miles from Dallas, and if the Rathermore trial went on longer than expected, the prospect of an extra session of horseback riding, cabin water fights, and campfire sing-songs would make the eleven-year-old jump up and down with joy.

Sharon was convinced that her research was legally right on target, but the distance between being right and winning the case was approximately a million miles. A lot depended on which judge had Midge's case assigned to his or her court. Most judges were hardheads when it came to new wrinkles in the law—especially new wrinkles presented by the defense; all prosecution motions received the court's undivided attention—and Sharon could name only three or four judges in Dallas County who had the legal smarts to listen to her argument. Having Milt Breyer represent the state would have been a definite plus; Milt was as dull-witted as most of the judges. But tack-sharp Kathleen Fraterno would catch Sharon's drift in a minute, and would fight the motion tooth and nail. Nonetheless, Sharon's bolt-of-lightning inspiration was all Midge Rathermore had at the moment. Come to think about it, convincing Russell Black to let Sharon go ahead and use the argument might be as much of a hang-up as winning the point in court.

She mulled these things over as she made four trips to the stacks in returning the books she'd used, then gathered up her purse and now bulging briefcase and left the library. The good-looking kid still sat behind the information desk, and as Sharon went through the turnstile he cleared his throat. She didn't pause, kept resolutely on her way with her sneakers whispering on carpet, but did turn her head far enough to one side so that the boy would catch her responsive smile.

* * *

After she'd dumped her belongings into the Volvo's backseat, she paused with the car door open and looked around. Late Saturday afternoon traffic was sparse. Only a couple of vehicles, a panel truck, and a yellow DART city bus were visible the length of Hillcrest Avenue. The temperature was in the low eighties; sunlight warmed her cheeks, bare calves, and lower thighs. A gentle breeze touched her hair. It was a beautiful day, so what the hell was wrong with her?

Sharon couldn't quite put her finger on the prickly sensation that now paraded from the nape of her neck down her spine. It was . . . fear? Worry? She didn't know. She thought of Melanie and felt a quick surge of panic.

It's nothing but the blues setting back in, she thought, Rob on the television last night and the pitso confrontation with Stan Green. That's all it could be. Those things, coupled with Howard Saw's murder just a block from her office, had combined to give her the creeps. She climbed in behind the wheel, started the engine and, humming along with the country music on the radio, headed for home.

9

As Sharon Hays did research at the university library, Wilfred Donello selected a punk. A really promising punk at that. The object of Donello's attention was a swishy kid of around nineteen, last in a line of new prisoners checking in on the fifth floor of Lew Sterrett Justice Center, an uptown name for the Dallas County main jail. The boy's rear end was like a woman's ass, big and firm, thrusting against the fabric of his tan county-issue jumpsuit like twin bear cubs wrestling under a blanket. This punk even walked like a woman, bim-bam, upholstered butt moving from side to side as a single deputy sheriff escorted the newcomers—two blacks, a pimply white boy, and a couple of Hispanic dudes in addition to the effeminate youngster on whom Donello had his eye—down the corridor toward the twelve-man open bay cell at the northeast end.

Donello slumped against the wall and crossed muscular tattooed forearms on top of his mop handle as the group marched past him. The mop head was immersed in a bucket of gray soapy water. Donello had been pressing the wringer handle to squeeze water from the mop when the new bunch of pisswillies had rounded the corner. *Pisswilly* was a jailhouse term meaning any male under twenty-six—unless they were big enough and mean enough to rid themselves of the moniker—and any homosexual of any age. The northeast corner cell on the fifth floor of the jail was designated housing for prisoners under twenty-six who'd never been down to the Texas

Department of Corrections. Pisswillies all, Donello thought.

As the boy wriggled by him, Donello pulled on his damaged earlobe, pursed thick lips, and blew two smacky kisses. The earlobe had a triangular chunk missing and was for the most part made up of gristly scar tissue. The boy turned his head to look Donello over with full-browed woman's eyes, no fear in their gaze, and continued to watch the older prisoner as the guard unlocked the cell to let the newcomers inside. The boy curved woman's lips into a smile as he entered the cell. The guard closed the door with a metallic bang, cutting the boy off from Donello's view. Christ, that butt, Donello thought. As the burly deputy retreated down the corridor, keys jingling by his hip, Donello bent over the mop bucket to hide his erection.

Tonight Donello would have that boy. Getting inside the cell to visit the punk would be no problem at all, not for Donello, a trusty with pretty much the run of things. Opposed to the general understanding of the squarejohns on the street, who'd never spent a day in lockup and didn't know batshit from beef stew, county jail trusties weren't particularly trustworthy. The guards appointed the trusties, and—with the exception of the D.A's pet snitches, who stayed in an isolated section of the jail, and whose trusty status depended on the importance of the people on whom they'd dropped a dime—generally picked the meanest cons with the longest sentences, people like Donello who were awaiting transfer to TDC. It was then up to the trusties to keep the other prisoners in line, one result being that the guards could spend their workday in the control centers located on each floor, watching television or shooting the bull, and the other result being that the trusties had the run of the jail. The general jail population feared the trusties much more than they feared the guards, and the trusties saw to it that the respect was deserved.

This was Donello's fourth trip to Dallas County lockup, and he was soon to make his fourth trip to the penitentiary. His sentencing wasn't for three more weeks, a month to the day after his conviction. The kiddie-porn beef wasn't his worst offense—though some considered child pornography worse than murder; Donello had done previous time for armed robbery, murder, and sodomy on an eight-year-old boy—but it was likely to net him his longest sentence. The bitch of a prosecutor—Sharon Hays was her name, a tall, pretty thing whom Donello never would have figured to be so freaking mean—had put the Paragraph on him. The Paragraph, a legal requirement for charging one under the Texas Habitual Felon statutes, was a specific addendum to Donello's indictment. As a habitual, Donello was looking at a twenty-five-year minimum sentence.

Donello had it through the jailhouse grapevine—which was a lot more reliable than half-cocked newspaper stories—that the prosecutor had quit her job after the trial because one of the other D.A.'s, a big-shot superchief name of Breyer, had been trying to get in her britches. If the story was true, Donello didn't blame the guy. The way she'd been shaking her ass around the courtroom, any man worth donkey piss would be trying to put his hand in her drawers. Just let old Wilfred Donello on the street for a couple of days, and he'd give her something to whine about for putting the Paragraph on him.

About the only thing Donello had to be thankful for was that his conviction wasn't aggravated. An aggravated charge had to do with use of a deadly weapon, and required that the con do at least a quarter of his time before he was eligible for parole. As it was, even if the judge sentenced him to life, Donello could be back on the streets in seven years or less. Even so, the time he faced on the kiddie-porn beef was more than he'd done for the armed robbery, the murder, and the sodomy conviction combined.

He could forget about getting his case overturned on appeal, that much Donello understood quite well. His appeal chances had gone out the window when someone had murdered his lawyer. The only regrets that Donello had over Howard Saw's death were that, one, Donello had already paid Saw for the appeal, and, two, that Donello hadn't killed Saw himself. Christ, Donello thought, fifty grand to a lawyer who couldn't even win the case over a broad prosecutor. Which attorney the court appointed to stand up with Donello at sentencing didn't matter; all an attorney did at sentencing was stand around and look stupid, and then tell the poor client how sorry he was that the judge had handed down fifty years or some such, and Donello assumed that a court-appointed lawyer could handle those chores every bit as well as Howard Saw.

Donello sensed movement behind him, then the same guard who had escorted the punk to his cell walked up beside Donello and looked down at the mop. Donello hopped to, bending quickly to squeeze filthy water into the pail, slinging the sodden head onto the floor, and scrubbing like a maniac. About the only way to lose one's trusty status was for the guard to catch one goofing off, and a jail-wise con like Wilfred Donello understood the rules. The thick-chested uniformed deputy watched with hands on hips. Donello mopped like crazy.

The guard hooked his thumbs through his front belt loops. " 'Bout time you done some work, old thing." He wore a gray short-sleeve uniform with the county sheriff's shield on the left sleeve in gold thread. Encircling the shield were the words *Integrity, Dependability,* and *Vigilance.* "Old thing" was the name which the guards used for all inmates, young or old.

Donello showed yellowed teeth in a patronizing grin. "Just doin' my time, boss. Keepin' busy makes it pass."

"I seen you lookin' that young'un over, old thing, don't think I didn't."

"What young'un you mean, boss?" Donello turned the mop over and used the scraper to disengage chewing gum from the floor.

The deputy sneered. "What young'un. That young'un you was makin' eyes at, what young'un you think?"

Donello kept his gaze on his work. "I don't fool with no homosectuals, boss."

"Bull *shit.* You don't fool with no homosectual lessen it's nighttime and ain't nobody likely to be comin' around, is what you mean. Listen here, old thing, you got you a vis'tor." The guard used a forefinger to close one nostril, and snuffled up.

Donello stood upright and cocked his head. "Who be visitin' me? I got no people on the street no more." He was a good three inches taller than the guard and had broader shoulders, the forearms of a linebacker, and a scar running from his disfigured ear to the point of his chin. Donello also had thick jet black curly hair and mean eyes set so close together that at times he appeared cross-eyed. The tattoo on his left forearm was a writhing naked woman with long hair. On his right arm was a coiled rattler over the caption NOT TO BE FUCKED WITH.

"I don't keep no appointment book for you gentlemen, old thing," the guard said. "Man calls up from downstairs, says you got a vis'tor, I haul yo' ass down to the visitation room. 'S all I do. You follow me, you hear?" He turned and walked away without another glance in Donello's direction, the deputy's right arm rubbing against his leather John Brown gun holster. Firearms weren't permitted in the jail, but the deputies all wore empty holsters, likely to remind prisoners that, if crossed, the deputies had the firepower to blow one into kingdom come. Donello dropped the mop wetly into the bucket, leaned the handle against the wall, and plodded along behind the deputy.

The route to the visiting room led down two corridors—the first lined with eight-man cells, the second holding solitary prisoners, guys with death-penalty sentences who stared dumbly through the food slots in their cells at passersby—and through a big holding area. The guard stopped before the entry, and Donello assumed the position without being told, spreading his feet, leaning forward against the wall for the guard to pat him down for contraband. The search complete, the deputy clanked open the entry and stood aside. "You rattle when you finished, old thing, you hear?" he said. Donello entered the visiting room.

The room was a bullpen with inch-thick bulletproof plastic windows around its perimeter. The visitors sat in booths which looked into the bullpen. Each visitors' booth contained two chairs, a metal desk, and an intercom phone. It was lunchtime, and only two other prisoners were in the bullpen, a pudgy white man who yelled at a lady over the phone, accusing her of screwing around, and a black teenage boy who stared numbly out while a gray-haired man with tears streaming down his face looked in. In a couple of hours the room would be packed. Donello squinted, searching the booths one by one until . . .

Christ, Donello thought. He sat down in front of a window and picked up a phone. "I thought we made a deal," Donello said.

Bradford Brie's sunglasses lay before him on the visitors' booth table. "How you doing, pal?" Brie said. His eyes were pale blue. Crusts of sleep were stuck between his lashes. The hand which held the phone had filthy nails.

"The deal was," Donello said, "that we ain't having no contact."

"I miss talking to you." Brie inclined his head to peer around Donello into the bullpen. "We got any friends in there?" Brie said. "Guys we know?"

"Bobby Jett," Donello said. "Guy used to shell the peas on Coffield Unit. You remember Bobby, huh?"

"Yeah, sure, I know his sister," Brie said. "What they got Bobby on?"

"He's doing a misdemeanor trespass he pled down from a burglary," Donello said. "Couldn't nobody put him inside this building he done, you know? Bobby says he could have beaten the case flat, but they offered him sixty days on the trespass so he took it. He'd have done six months waiting for a trial on the felony anyway, you know how that works."

"Yeah." Brie giggled through his nose. "You can beat the rap, but you can't beat the ride." His Hawaiian shirt was yellow with big blue flowers. He yanked on his goatee. "Anybody else?"

Donello transferred the phone from his scarred ear to the normal ear. "Couple of guys, but that's got nothing to do with what I'm talking about. We're not supposed to be having contact."

"I heard you before. Hey, it's lonesome out here."

"Jesus Christ, Bradford. I told you I wouldn't say nothing about you, and I didn't. They asked me a lot of things, too, about who was taking them pictures and all. You coming down to the jail, you might as well say, Hey, I'm this guy's partner."

"I signed in as somebody else. I got this driver's license."

"Don't matter," Donello said. "A lot of people down here know you by sight. What if somebody sees you and drops a dime?"

"I'm not worried."

"Good that you ain't. I am." Donello narrowed his eyes. "You got rid of them other pictures, huh?"

"I'm keeping them for a while. Some of those girls got parents, you know? People might pay for the negatives."

"That ain't the deal," Donello shouted, then looked guardedly around and lowered his voice. "I'm s'posed to say nothing about you, you're s'posed to get rid of the pictures. How come we're not communicating?"

Brie picked up his sunglasses and stuck an earpiece into one corner of his mouth. He peered around Donello again, then dropped his gaze. "Look, Wilfred. You're not fooling around in there, huh?"

Donello swallowed. "What kind of a question is that, asking a man? It's different in here, you know? We got women on the street."

"We kind of had an arrangement."

"We didn't have no arrangement on the streets," Donello said. "Any arrangement you got in here don't go once there's women. We already talked about it, three or four times. I ain't no fucking queer."

Brie gestured with the sunglasses. "I just don't like the idea, you with somebody. You know what I done to them guys that cut you up down on Coffield Unit. That scar on your face, you know? That's kind of what I'm talking about, sometimes somebody means something to a guy."

"You quit it. You keep that queer talk up, I'm ending this visit." Donello made a move to hang up.

Brie lifted a bony hand. "No. Wait. I won't say anything else." His expression was earnest.

Donello replaced the phone to his ear. "No more talking like queers. That's disgusting. You get rid of them pictures like we said."

Brie hesitated, then said, "I showed one to a guy."

Donello arched an eyebrow, not saying anything.

"Your lawyer," Brie said.

"He's dead."

"Well, he looked at the picture first." Brie put his shades on and grinned.

It took a second for it to sink in, what this crazy Bradford Brie was saying. Donello finally said, "Man, that was you?"

"You said the guy was dogshit. Didn't do anything for you but take your money. That D.A. lady, too, she done bad things to you," Brie said. The gaps between Brie's teeth appeared larger than normal. Must be the bullet-proof plastic, Donello thought, distorting the image.

Donello stabbed the air with a forefinger. "You listen to me. I got nothing to do with no murder."

Brie shrugged. "Who said you did? I'm just trying to show you, I can't stand anybody doing bad to you. Man or woman."

Donello cocked his head. "You done something to that D.A. lady?"

"So far I just took her picture." Brie sniffed. Tears welled up in his eyes. "Tell me you ain't fooling with no-body, man. I can't stand that."

"I done told you . . ." Donello trailed off. All he needed was a big queer scene right here in front of everybody. He forced his tone to be gentle. "No, man, I wouldn't do that to you. Some things are permanent, you know?"

When his visit was over, Donello rattled the door for the guard, waited five minutes, then rattled again. Finally the deputy came, ambling along, taking his time, and admitted Donello back into the innards of the jail. Donello returned to his workstation, picked up his mop, and began to scrub the floor. His mind was working furiously. For now his thoughts centered on Bradford Brie; Donello had even forgotten the punk.

Wilfred Donello now had information about a murder which had come down, and his sentencing was still three weeks away. He'd never been a snitch in his life, but he'd never been looking at a twenty-five-year minimum, either. He still could cut a deal, he was sure of that, but he was considering the proper timing.

The wad of gum was still stuck to the painted concrete. Donello bent to dig at the tacky mass with his thumbnail. Be nice, Donello thought, if I could wait until Brie gets through with what he has in mind for the lawyer lady. Everything would be damn near perfect if I could hold off until then.

10

Sharon had a guilt trip over deserting Melanie for the law library on Saturday, so on Sunday she took her daughter and Trish Winston to Six Flags Over Texas. Sharon did a lot of things outside the budget for Melanie—the cost of a trip to Six Flags for three never fell short of a hundred-dollar bill—and often wondered if she was spoiling the child. She was enough of a self-analyst to realize that her generosity had a lot to do with hustling to make up for Melanie's lack of a father, and she watched her daughter's relationship with other children very closely for signs that Melanie might be turning into a brat. So far Sharon hadn't seen any telltale evidence that she was ruining her daughter, and until she did notice such signs, she wasn't going to worry about it. Raising children, Sharon thought, was one continuous knock on wood.

Sunday marked the first time in the year in which the temperature reached ninety degrees, and the amusement park teemed with girls in shorts and halter tops—most of them showing pale wintertime skin ripe for a bitch of a sunburn—and husky teenage boys in tank tops and loud Bermudas. Sharon wore thin white cotton slacks, Nikes, and a pale green summer blouse, and finally relented to let Melanie drag out the hand-me-down jean cutoffs. To escape the heat as much as possible, Sharon kept Melanie and Trish on the log and canoe rides. The long slides and final drenching plunges into water did provide cooling relief, but by mid-afternoon Sharon's hair had twisted into damp, tangly clumps. Melanie and Trish ate three funnel cakes apiece, covered with strawberry compote and powdered sugar, and for once Sharon said to hell with her waistline and had two of the delicious cakes herself.

Later in the day, Sharon let the girls ride the Texas Chute Out and Shockwave roller coaster on their own while she sat them out on a bench in the shade. For one thing, mommy was pooped, and though she'd never admit it to the kids, rides which sent one high in the air to do loop-de-loops and teeth-rattling dips scared mommy to death. Furthermore, sitting all alone while Trish and Melanie whooped it up on the rides gave Sharon time to think about the Rathermore case and what she'd found out the day before at the library. Dammit, she just knew she was right. The first thing tomorrow morning she was going to make an all-out assault on Russell Black, doing her damnedest to convince the older lawyer to give her the go-ahead sign.

It was while the kids were on the roller coaster when the first strange chill hit her. Sharon was seated on the green wooden bench along with a plump lady in pink britches and what looked to be half of a grammar school class, little boys and girls who twisted and turned and just wouldn't be still. Two hundred yards away, the Shockwave whipped through one of its double upside-downers. Sharon squinted to pick out Melanie and Trish, but saw only a jumble of waving arms, as though the roller coaster car was a hundred-legged insect.

Sharon was suddenly cold. Ice cold. Goose bumps raised instantly on her forearms and she shivered.

The feeling passed in seconds. Sharon looked all around, at a man selling red, green, and blue helium-filled balloons which tugged upward against restraining strings; at a woman in a yellow straw sun hat; at a child whose ice cream had melted all over his hand. Just the normal Six Flags crowd, parents worn to a frizzle and kids yelling for more. It's only a sinking spell, Sharon thought.

The second blast of icy coldness struck around eight o'clock, as Sharon walked between Melanie and Trish through the amusement park's self-serve parking lot. It was almost dark; the overhead fluorescent lights shone brightly from silver poles. After the tumult of Six Flags, the parking lot was strangely silent. Sharon's Volvo was between a station wagon and a pickup truck, just fifty yards away.

The coldness shot through Sharon's being like a giant icicle. She stopped in her tracks and looked fearfully around, seeing no one. Melanie looked curiously at her mother. Sharon grabbed both little girls by the hand, and the threesome sprinted for the Volvo. When they reached the car, both Melanie and Trish nearly collapsed with giggles.

As Sharon poked the key into the door lock, she continued to scan the dimness warily. It had to be her imagination. But just for a second there, Sharon had been certain that someone unseen was watching her.

11

A spring cool front blew into Dallas early Monday morning, and with it brought fearsomely boiling clouds, thunder blasts, and buckets of rain. In nearby Rockwall, Texas, a cyclone touched down, knocked over a trailer park and drive-in grocery, then twisted merrily on its way. Sharon awoke around four as lightning illuminated the sky like daytime, followed in a half second by thunder which rattled the windows. She buried her head beneath her pillow and snuggled down among the covers, and the steady drumbeat of rain lulled her back to sleep in minutes.

With sheets of water cascading from the rooftops, wild lovemaking filled Sharon's wee-hour dreams. She often had such dreams when it rained, and always her lover was faceless. A muscular male dream body appeared, its features hidden in shadow, to stroke her endlessly; first with gentle, then, as she writhed under his touch, frenzied hands. Finally the dream man mounted her with tender-violent thrusts which left her giddy with ecstasy. Rolling thunder accompanied her final jaw-clenching orgasm.

The radio alarm woke her for good at six-thirty to David Allan Coe's tenor with twangy guitars in the background. She dressed in semi-light as she listened to the morning traffic reports on Country 96.3. It was pouring outside, and driving downtown was going to be a nightmare.

She woke Melanie twenty minutes earlier than normal, and pressured the eleven-year-old through breakfast.

Commander didn't help matters much, the buff-colored shepherd sitting beside the table with his head cocked in a begging attitude. The second time that Sharon caught Melanie slipping the dog a chunk of buttered toast under the table, she brought the activity to a screeching halt. She grasped Commander's collar firmly and ushered the shepherd onto the back porch, there to cower and whimper under the overhanging roof. I suppose this makes me the original Hard-Hearted Hannah, Sharon thought. She then contributed to Commander's delinquency by tossing him a chunk of toast herself, and finally hustled Melanie into clean Guess' jeans and a gray Harvard University sweatshirt. Convincing the child that she'd catch pneumonia if she didn't wear her bright red rain slicker and overshoes required more pressure from mommy.

By quarter to eight she had Melanie deposited into the Volvo's backseat and, squinting to peer past the thunking windshield wiper, drove down to stop in front of Sheila's and beep the horn. Trish came charging through the rain, pink rubber splashing sidewalk water, and dived in alongside Melanie. The two girls then twisted and giggled all the way to school, and once Sharon came within inches of rear-ending a blue Dodge pickup after turning her head to threaten the little darlings with mayhem. Finally she sat at the curb and sighed with relief as the kids dashed madly for the cover of St. Thomas Episcopal. The private school was a drain on Sharon, just as it was on Sheila, but the two young mothers had agreed in countless bull sessions that private school beat the alternative, Dallas Independent School District, hands down. Just the previous week at a public middle school, a seventh-grader had shot the playground coach. Her carpool duties over for the day, Sharon pointed the Volvo's nose to the southwest and made her determined way downtown. Sheila would pick up and keep the kids at her place until Sharon got home; Sharon felt deep guilt that Sheila bore the heaviest childcare load. But Sheila didn't seem to mind a bit, which, Sharon thought, was what real friends were all about.

She wanted to park in the covered converted gas station across from the office, but decided that six-fifty a day was too steep even in a frigging blizzard. She left the Volvo in a two-buck lot across the freeway south of downtown, then sloshed through a nine-block trek in heavy drizzle with her head bent beneath her umbrella and her loaded briefcase bouncing off her raincoat. During the walk she decided that the six-fifty might well have been worth it.

Once at the office, Sharon paused just inside the entry, held the umbrella out the door, and shook off what water she could. She hung her slicker on her hall tree, dropped the umbrella's curved handle over a hook, and found the Mr. Coffee in the utility room. The pot was filthy, Russell Black apparently being a dump-the-dregs-and-fill-it-back-up man, so Sharon attacked with soap and water. Finally, with hot brown liquid dribbling and making steam rise, she lugged her briefcase in to the Xerox and copied her research work. For the next half hour Sharon watched sheets of water jelly the windowpanes as the green fluorescent moved back and forth, back and forth, with a series of dull clunks. After she'd made a duplicate set of research notes for Black, she went into her office to sit, silently rehearse her argument to go ahead with her Midge Rathermore defense project, and, for the most part, twiddle her thumbs.

Around ten-thirty, the door leading from the street swung open. Sharon craned her neck to peer out into the reception area, and caught a glimpse of Russell Black's craggy features as the older lawyer ducked into his office. She counted to sixty, giving him time to ditch his raincoat, then carried both sets of research papers past the reception desk, paused outside Black's door to catch her breath, and walked in without knocking. "Russ, I've got some . . . oh."

Black wasn't alone. Seated across from him was an attractive brunette woman, around forty, wearing a light brown cotton sweater and pleated skirt. One corner of the woman's mouth tilted in curiosity.

"Excuse me," Sharon said, backing up. "I'll come back when—"

"We were just talkin' about you." Black motioned Sharon inside, and she gently closed the door and took a forward step. "I want you to meet Deborah North," Black said. "Midge Rathermore's mother. This here's Sharon Hays, my new sidekick."

Deborah North's wealth of brown hair had a few strands of gray mixed in, nothing that a little touch-up

wouldn't have gotten rid of. Sharon thought that dye jobs
were the height of vanity, and Deborah North's lack of effort to cover up her gray said a lot about the woman's
ego. Ms. North's smile was pleasant, if a trifle strained.
"Miss Hays? Glad to know you."

Sharon stepped forward to shake hands. "The plea-
sure's mine." Formal and businesslike, the second-banana
lawyer meeting her boss's important client for the first
time.

Black told Sharon to sit, and as Sharon placed both sets
of notes on the edge of her boss's desk and sank down in
a visitor's chair, Black said, "I was just fillin' her in on
the certification hearin'."

Sharon nodded, not seeing that what she'd heard required any response on her part. What she really wanted
to know was something she'd never ask: why this woman
had come to her daughter's aid by hiring a first-class lawyer, and then after doing so wanted to remain anonymous.

Deborah North's purse was on the floor; she reached
inside and brought out a tall pack of Virginia Slims.
You've come a long way, baby. "Do you mind?" A strong
woman's voice, slightly husky in tone. Her question was
directed at the room in general, but her gaze was on
Sharon.

Though she didn't smoke and never had, she wasn't a
non-smoking nut. She watched her own diet and got
plenty of fresh air, but thought that people who went
around condemning anyone with a tobacco habit had real
problems, like those who openly sneered at gays in order
to cover their insecurity over their own sexuality. "Go
right ahead," Sharon said.

Black produced a small glass ashtray which he slid to
the front edge of his desk. Deborah North popped a cigarette into her mouth, then paused with her thumb on the
flint wheel of a red plastic disposable lighter. She raised
an eyebrow. "May I call you Sharon?" She flicked. Flame
appeared. She puffed, inhaled, and blew out smoke as she
bent to put the lighter away.

"I'd prefer you did," Sharon said.

"Good. I'm Deb." Deborah North balanced her cigarette on the ashtray. Rose-colored lipstick smeared the filter like a wound.

Black stood. "Listen, I need a coffee jolt and I've got

a couple of calls to make. I'd wanted you ladies to get acquainted anyhow, so I'll make myself scarce. No, keep your seats. I'll use your place, Sharon." He circled his desk and left the room. Just like that. This is Sharon, this is Deb, and now you two can talk things over. Sharon wondered briefly whether Black really had things to do. His motives were hard to figure.

When they were alone, Deb North said, "Russ tells me you have a daughter."

Sharon nodded and smiled. "That's right." The first whiff of smoke entered her nostrils. Initially it was a shock to her senses, but she'd quickly get used to the fumes. Rob had smoked when she lived with him in Brooklyn Heights, and she'd finally reached a point that she didn't even notice the odor.

"Then you're going to be wondering about my relationship with Midge," Deb said.

Sharon chewed thoughtfully on her lower lip. "Only to the extent that it might affect Midge's defense."

"Thanks for being businesslike, but you really don't have to. I'm not proud of myself where my children are concerned."

Sharon lifted a hand. "Look, Deb, I don't condemn."

Deb picked up her cigarette. "Well, you should. So you'll know, Russ leaving us alone wasn't his idea. I asked him to. You already know that Midge had a court-appointed lawyer, don't you?"

"Andy Tubb," Sharon said.

"Right. I had a long interview with Mr. Tubb, and aside from listening to him quote his fee and lay out his glowing plans for defending my daughter, I just couldn't get through to him. I think it's important for Midge's lawyer to understand a few things about her. That's why when Russell Black told me his new assistant was female and a mother to boot, I decided to hire him and let Mr. Tubb go his separate way."

Well, I'll be damned, Sharon thought. She'd spent an extra two hours polishing up the old resumé the night before her appointment with Russell Black, when the guy already had checked up and had known all about her. Which explained why he'd fallen all over himself to hire her. If Midge Rathermore's mother had told him that Midge needed a two-headed lawyer, Black probably would have conducted interviews at a freak show. Sharon wasn't sure whether or not she should feel resentful. She'd have to think on it.

"A man," Deb said, "would never even think about my relationship with my daughter, but a mother's going to pick up in a second that there's a problem. And I've got to tell you, I'm mostly to blame for where Midge is right now. And now that I've said that, ask what you want to know."

Sharon watched smoke rise from the cigarette's end. She wondered what Rob's reaction would be if Melanie were to find herself in the same boat as Midge Rathermore. He wouldn't understand, if he cared at all. "When did you and Midge's father divorce?" Sharon said.

"It was final five years ago. Exactly two days before he married Linda Haymon. We were separated three years before that, and while we were separated he and Linda lived together. I haven't really spent any time with my daughters in eight years." Deb's gaze lowered in guilt.

"And your last name, North. That's your maiden name?" Sharon reverted to her training as a prosecutor, just asking the questions, not being emotional. Keeping her feelings in check in the Rathermore case was going to be tough.

Deb continued to watch her lap. "No. It's another married name. You'll already know that the Rathermore name means money. Do you know where Midge's father's money came from?"

"Not really. Oil, I suppose, that's where most of the wealthy got it in this town."

"You're half right. Midge's grandfather—William Rathermore, too, by the way, Bill was a junior—did get his money in oil, but what he really was was a thief. Do you know what slant-well drilling is?"

Sharon smoothed her navy skirt along her thigh. "No, I don't. What I know about the oil business you could put in a thimble."

"Well, it's stealing, even though it's pretty slick. What Rathermore Senior would do, back in the thirties, he would buy leases on land located near producing wells. The people selling the leases knew there was no oil underneath the land, and had the old man pegged as a nut. They sold him the leases dirt cheap and sat back to watch him go broke. He was crazy like a fox, though." Deb glanced at the ashtray. Her Virginia Slim was burnt nearly to the filter. She flicked gray ash from the end, took a final drag, and stubbed out the butt.

"The old darling would drill," Deb went on, "at a forty-five-degree angle, right into the wall of a neighboring well, and hijack the oil. Millions on millions of barrels he stole, and then when he had a nest egg of, say, fifty million dollars or so, he simply retired. Even today there are a lot of people in East Texas who wonder how he struck oil where everyone else drilled dry holes. They chalk it off to dumb luck."

Sharon's mind wandered, her gaze absently on the window beyond Deb North. The rain showed no signs of slacking, water pouring in sheets down the windowpane. She sighed. "That's fascinating, Deb, but really I—"

"Don't see what that has to do with Midge's defense," Deb said. "Please humor me, Sharon. It's all I can do to keep from running screaming into the streets over what I've done to my little girl." Deb had worry lines at the corners of her nose and mouth which her makeup didn't quite hide. "Listen, Bill Rathermore, Senior, was only thirty-eight when he moved to Dallas and bought that big house on Lakeside Drive, and he was incredibly rich with nothing to do. He ran through eight wives in ten years, the fifth of which was Bill's—my husband, Bill's— mother. She was nineteen when Bill was born, and six months later the old man paid her off and moved her out just like he did the rest of his wives. Females to him were nothing but places in which to deposit his semen.

"I met Bill in college," Deb said, "at the University of Oklahoma. I'm from Midwest City, an Oke City suburb. My dad worked for the water department, and the only way he could afford to send me to college was for me to live at home and drive back and forth to Norman every day. O.U. was Bill's fourth school. He'd managed to flunk out of three, and nearly flunked out at O.U. as well, but he was my first exposure to real money. The first time I saw that house, but wow. I don't know that there's anything I wouldn't have done to get in that family." A tear formed suddenly and ran down her cheek. She bent to dig in her purse, found a Kleenex, and blew her nose.

Sharon leaned forward. "If you'd like to continue this some other time . . ."

Deb waved her off, looked for a wastebasket, disposed of the Kleenex. "I'm started now, and if I don't finish what I have to tell you, I may never have the nerve again." She took a deep breath and expelled air from her lungs. "So anyway. The first time I went home with Bill, just for a weekend between classes, was the only time I met the old man. He was in his late sixties then, and I was twenty, but that didn't stop him from putting the moves on me. I'm not joking, Sharon. You've had a few moves put on you, right? You can tell."

Sharon nodded. "You can't explain how you know. But you do."

"Sure. And as long as I'm confessing, I can't swear that if Bill Senior had lived long enough, had been around after Bill and I got married, that I wouldn't have wound up in bed with my own father-in-law. Not that the old man turned me on. It's just that, that's how much the money got in my eye."

"Anyway," Deb said, "I didn't ever have to be confronted with that lovely choice, because barely a week after that first visit Bill Senior was dead. Shot in a dive near Fair Park, the old bastard, sitting in a booth between two hookers. So, barely twenty-two, Bill inherited the whole enchilada, quit school, and married me. What a date with destiny that was. Just before I walked down the aisle, my own dad hugged the daylights out of me and said, 'Honey, I've got a bad feeling about all this.' I'll never forget the look on his face."

There was the muffled noise of a door opening and closing as someone entered the reception area from the street. Sharon tensed to rise, then relaxed. Russell Black had set up this conference, and Russ could damn well wait on the customers himself until the meeting was over. Sharon returned her attention to Deb.

"Bill," Deb said, "when we were married . . . Well, he inherited his father's attitude about women. Oh, he'd hump me most every night, but unless he wanted sex I might as well have been another stick of furniture. It's not a real self-image booster, you know? Less than six months after the wedding I found out that, in addition to me, he was humping the maids, the neighbors, and anybody else who was willing. And you know what? I was so eaten up with being the wealthy Mrs. Rathermore, going to the Crystal Charity Ball functions and Cattle Barons' ball and whatnot, that I looked the other way. I got to know a lot of rich women during that time, and I'll tell you, I wasn't the only one who knew her husband was screwing around. Most of those men look on their wives as just another possession."

Sharon lifted her rump to scoot forward in her chair and crossed her legs. She was, she thought, getting too wrapped up in the story, and reminded herself to take it all in from a lawyer's neutral viewpoint, realizing she was hearing only one side. "Deb," Sharon said, "I've got to ask you something."

Deb reached nervously for another cigarette and thumbed her lighter. "Yes?"

Sharon pictured Midge, the chubby teenage face impassive as she'd said that her father had had sex with Midge's sister. Sharon said, "Did you ever have any indication that there might have been ... any sort of incest within that family?" Sharon had had many discussions with Sheila Winston on the subject, and knew that incest is usually inherited, the children learning it from the parents.

Deb froze with the lighter a half inch from the cigarette's end. "Why do you ask?"

"Something Midge said yesterday."

"Did that bastard do something to her?"

Sharon blinked. "I'm not sure."

Deb lit and inhaled through trembling lips. "It wouldn't surprise me. I never saw any incest, but that's about the only aberrant behavior I didn't see while I was married to him. It kills me to confess this, but I lost so much self-esteem, I went along with whatever he wanted. I ... God, how to say this." She bent forward from the waist and regarded the floor. Sharon was speechless, wanting to comfort but not knowing how. Raindrops pelted the windows like a thousand tom-toms.

"All sorts of ..." Deb was struggling to get a grip, but didn't seem to be making it. She spoke as if choking on her words. "Once down in New Orleans, I solicited a hooker because Bill wanted a threesome. I was ... the third, you know? I think even the hooker looked down on me. Another time, this was in Galveston at a convention, I picked up a young man in a bar and brought him back to our hotel so Bill could watch us." Her gaze steadied somewhat. "The list goes on and on, Sharon, if you want to hear more."

"I don't want to hear anything," Sharon said, "that we can't use somehow in Midge's defense. No reason for you to run yourself through the wringer unnecessarily."

"Oh, but there is," Deb said. "But you're right, I should be doing it in a shrink's office instead of a lawyer's. I think we'd probably make better progress if you asked questions. That way you wouldn't have to hear me go on and on."

"Why don't we talk about," Sharon said, "the things that led up to your eventual divorce?"

Deb managed a bitter laugh. "That's easy enough. It was just before Easter, the year Midge was five and Susan was three. I'd been out shopping for virginal-looking Easter outfits for me and the girls. We always attended services at First Methodist, mainly, I guess, because that's where we were most likely to get our pictures on television. Family of the month, you know? I'm sure of this now, this was the Thursday before Good Friday. I came home in the early afternoon, a couple of hours early, and walked in on Bill. He had a woman in bed right in our own room. I wasn't particularly shocked, frankly, given my husband's habits, but this woman looked quite young, and seemed . . . prettier, more sophisticated perhaps, than his normal fare. Both of them had been drinking, I remember a quart of Chivas on the nightstand. There I stood in the bedroom doorway watching them thrash around, and all I could think of was, When will they be finished so I can go in and change? I'm not kidding, I just didn't give a damn at that point.

"After they'd finished," Deb said, "Bill gave me this big grin like he loved for people to watch him doing it, and then he said, 'Deb, I want you to meet your replacement.' "

Sharon's jaw dropped practically into her lap. "Son of . . ." She swallowed. "Linda Haymon?"

Deb nodded. "At first I thought he was putting me on," she said. "But Linda didn't think it was a joke. She said, formal as could be, 'So pleased to meet you.' That's when I realized that the nightgown she'd been wearing—it was ripped and thrown on the floor—the nightgown was one of mine. Both of them started giggling like crazy.

"I ran to the downstairs bathroom," Deb said, "and threw up for about an hour, I think." She pulled at the hem of her skirt with shaky fingers, dragged on her cigarette, laid it in the ashtray, then quickly picked the cigarette up and puffed again. Her brown eyes were slightly bloodshot.

"I've seen a lot as a prosecutor," Sharon said. "But that's the strangest . . ."

"It gets even worse. I'll tell you something else, I don't think it was an accident that I walked in on them. I think my dear twisted husband planned the whole scene, and I think that if I hadn't been a couple of hours early, he'd have had her hang around until I got home. He simply wanted to hurt me as much as he possibly could. God, I think he invented sick."

Sharon's flesh crawled, but she shook out of her trance to say, "Deb, we will probably want you to testify to what you've just told me. It shows the deceased's character, and Linda's as well. She'll be the state's star witness against Midge. Criminy, with testimony like this . . ." She reached across Russell Black's desk for pen and pad.

"I don't say it would be the funnest thing I've ever done," Deb said. "But for my daughter, sure. I'd do it. It would be the very least, to make things up to her."

"While we're on the subject of Linda," Sharon said, "anything you know, anything you can think of about her background? Skeletons in the closet are dirty tricks, but there's no really clean fighting in the courtroom."

Deb shook her head. "I never really tried to find out about her. I never really wanted to believe she existed. Just what the public was aware of, that she was a newscaster, of course. What the public doesn't know is that I knew what was going on a long time before the final breakup. Oh, I had her phone number."

Sharon thought, then shrugged. "I'm afraid to ask how you got it," she said.

"Oh, Bill gave it to me. Whenever he left home to go God-knows-where, usually I didn't have a clue where he was and didn't give a damn. But every time he was headed for her place, he'd say, 'You can call me at Linda's if you need me.' God, but he thought that was funny."

"It's hard for me," Sharon said, "to hear all this just as a lawyer, because I'm also a mother. You'd think he'd have more concern for his kids."

"I think," Deb said, "that it's inherent in the Rathermore bloodline that the men don't have concern for anyone with the exception of themselves. What they want in the heat of the moment. The way Rathermore Senior, the old man, worked it, once the children were born the mother was to have no more influence over them. Rathermore children reported to the nannies and to their father. Never to their mother. I believe that one reason Linda's marriage to Bill lasted as long as it did is that they've had no kids. She could devote all of her time to keeping him . . . occupied. If you know what I mean."

"I suppose you've done some study," Sharon said, "on what drove him to be like he was."

"I've had four million miles of counseling over the past eight years," Deb said. "I can only tell you what the psychologists tell me. Bill wasn't good-looking and wasn't even particularly intelligent. He had this really weak chin, almost no chin at all, shoulders like a sparrow, and a big stomach. He flunked out of three colleges and would have flunked out of a fourth if his father hadn't died and given Bill the opportunity to quit before he busted out. He had a lot of women, but none of them, including me, ever wanted him because of him. Money's the only thing Bill Rathermore had going for him. Period.

"The money gave him power," Deb said. "He had enough to buy anything he wanted, people included. It's taken me a long time to face up to what I became during those years, but I finally have. Degrading women, making them grovel before him, would just be another part of the whole."

"Of his wanting power?" Sharon said.

"Control is a better word. He could control me, he could control Linda, he could control his children. He was likely in shock in the moments before he died, that he couldn't just reach out and control those boys who were beating him to death."

"I suppose," Sharon said, "that when you'd finally had

enough of the affair with Linda, that's when you separated from him?"

Deb widened her eyes. "Are you kidding? God, no, not Deborah Rathermore the socialite. I just involved myself in fund-raisers and whatnot, and let him do whatever he wanted. We finally split three years later, when Midge was eight, and it was Bill who kicked me out, not the other way around. He thought all along that Linda was better suited to the image he wanted to maintain, and when he finally got around to it he got rid of me."

"With a big settlement, I suppose." Sharon said.

"Yep. And if you can believe it, I fought the divorce for three years. That's how hung up I was on being Mrs. William Rathermore, I just couldn't bear the thought of being just plain old Deb again. His lawyers finally made an offer I couldn't turn down, so I took the money and ran. I get thirty thousand a month for life, and for that mess of pottage I gave up my own children. I'm really the one who should be in jail. Not Midge." Deb sniffled and dabbed at her eyes.

"And in all this time you've never seen the girls?" Sharon said.

"Not once. I live in Oklahoma now, right around the corner from my mother and dad. I married once, to a man named North, and it lasted eight months. It seems my second husband was only interested in my money. Is that a turnaround or what?"

Sharon thought that Deborah North was the most miserable woman she'd ever seen. "You know," Sharon said, "if we use you as a witness, the prosecution will throw every dart at you that they can. Did Russ tell you that?"

Deb nodded as she fumbled for yet another Virginia Slim. "I'm ready for whatever. What my daughter thinks is the only thing that matters. I don't think I can face Midge after I've deserted her all this time."

Sharon wondered how any mother could get in this situation. She had fought for Melanie since the child's conception, and knew she would as long as there was breath in her body. "What do you think Linda stood to gain from the affair? The marriage, sure, but . . ." Sharon said.

"Taking up with Bill would be just a way of furthering her own public image, I suppose, but I'm only guessing at that."

"I don't see that a highly publicized affair would help her image any," Sharon said.

"Come on," Deb said. "Affairs don't hurt anybody's image anymore. It's the thing to do among the social set."

The lady's got a point, Sharon thought. Affairs were in and with-it, sort of like off-Broadway actors and actresses living together and then amicably splitting the blankets. "So there's nothing at all you can tell me about Linda's past?" Sharon said.

Deb pursed her lips. "Not before she and Bill. There is something that Bill told me once."

"Anything about her could help." Sharon steadied the writing pad on her thigh.

"Well," Deb said, "while we were separated, I had a few meetings with Bill. His lawyer, my lawyer, you know? Every time I saw Bill, he'd try to get to me with some kinko sex story. He loved telling me that sort of thing."

How could it be more sicko than doing it with his own daughter? Sharon thought.

"He told me once," Deb said, "that Linda was heavy into exhibitions. Doing it with other people while Bill watched them."

"I've heard that sort of thing isn't that rare," Sharon said.

"Tell me about it," Deb said. "According to Bill, the chauffeur would solicit the men."

Sharon sat up straighter. "Do you know the chauffeur's name?"

"He's dead," Deb said vacantly. "Charles, the chauffeur, he was past seventy when we divorced. No, Bill would want it so no one knew firsthand except him." She zeroed in on something across the room, near the ceiling. "It would give him control over Linda," Deb said. "And that's what Bill Rathermore was all about, you know?"

12

After she'd accompanied Deborah North to the exit and said her goodbyes, Sharon had to sit down. Right there in the reception room, she sank into a typist's chair and hugged herself. She thought that if she ever had to go through what Deborah North had, she'd be a permanent rubber room candidate, and thanked her lucky stars that her own life seemed pretty much in order. Slightly more composed, she crossed over to her office and went in to talk to Russell Black.

He had his feet up on the corner of her desk, his ankles crossed, and was reading a Publishers' Clearing House mailer which had been lying on Sharon's desk for two days. The radio was on very low volume, David Allan Coe's "Please Come to Boston" like faraway background music. Sharon sat in her visitor's chair. "Is that some of the important work you had to do when you left us alone?"

Black slid the come-on letter back inside the bulky envelope and laid the whole mess aside. Ed McMahon beamed at Sharon from near Black's elbow. "The odds against winnin' anything from Publishers' Clearing House," he said, "are about the same as the odds of beatin' the state in a criminal trial. Or so a lot of lawyers tell me. You've got a fan." He tossed a thick brown envelope over in front of her. "Fella brought this by. He seemed upset that you weren't here."

Sharon picked up the package. The cover was blank, no address, nothing. She undid the clasp and pulled out a set of eighty-by-ten glossies: Sharon on the sidewalk in front of the building, Sharon carrying boxes of files up the steps. Sure, Sharon thought. Bradford Brie, Photographer. The strange-acting guy.

"He stopped me when I was moving in Friday and took my picture," Sharon said. "I asked him not to, but he did anyway. He said he was doing an album."

"Be careful," Black said. "There's a lot of nuts runnin' around."

"I didn't exactly just get off a load of hay, Russ. I'm always careful. To get down to brass, boss, what would you have done if I hadn't taken this job? Hunted up another female? Any female?"

One shaggy eyebrow lifted. His eyes twinkled. "Deb told you about our talk, huh?"

"I think you should have told me that before you hired me. I thought it was because of my record; now I find it was just because I'm a woman."

Black picked up the Publishers' Clearing House ad and rubbed the edge under his chin. "Let's just say you fit into the plans real well. But before you get your britches in a knot, young lady, listen to me. It's true that Mrs. North wanted a female on Midge's case, but that had nothin' to do with me hirin' you. I already had my mind made up on you, sight unseen."

"Come on, Russ. I heard about the job over lunch."

"And I knew you were lookin'," he said. "Which is why I put the word out, knowin' sooner or later you'd hear."

"Now you're being flattering," she said. "Why would you put me through the interview at all if you were already set on hiring me?"

"So you could make up *your* mind. I never go into anything without checkin' up on it first."

Sharon folded her arms. "Checking up how?"

"By checkin' up. That's all you need to know."

"It'll do for now," Sharon said. If Black thought he'd never hear of the subject again, she had news for him.

"Good," Black said. "Now let's talk about somethin' important. What did you think of Mrs. North?"

"That's one troubled lady. Has she told you all those stories about Midge's father?"

"About his crazy sexual outlook?" Black said.

"Yes."

"She told me. Tell you the truth, Sharon, I don't feel real comfortable discussin' such with a woman. I'm glad you two ladies could chat."

Sharon looked at her lacquered nails. "What she says could fit right in with this plan I've got for Midge's defense." She cut her eyes upward to check his reaction.

Black grinned. "Why am I not surprised you've got a plan?"

"I spent some time at the library over the weekend."

His smile broadened. "Why am I not surprised at that, either? I hope it didn't mess up any dates or anything you might have had goin'."

"I've managed to mess up those sort of plans on my own," Sharon said. "Have you ever handled a battered-wife case under the new law?"

"Nope. I've read a few things about it."

"A lot of convicted women are getting out of prison," Sharon said.

"So I've heard. Has somethin' to do with premeditation."

"That's an oversimplification, but yes," Sharon said. "Hot blood has always been a defense to murder charges. If someone's killed in a fight, the hot-blood theory makes it an accident. Manslaughter. The law has always been that if the prosecution can show a cool-down period, say you walked around the block after someone threatened you and then sneaked up and blew them away, then the hot-blood defense goes out the window. That's all changed now where battered wives are concerned."

Black interlocked his fingers behind his head and leaned back. "I've looked into it. The battered wives, now they can slip up on the old man when he's asleep, shoot him, and still call on hot blood as a defense, the theory bein' that they can't defend themselves while their husband's beatin' them up."

Sharon nodded. "It's called the burning-bed law, after the movie with Farrah Fawcett. A few hundred women have already had their convictions reversed and gotten out of prison because of the new wrinkle." Her tone was excited. When she knew she was onto something, it was all she could do to keep from bursting into song.

"Okay, I'll buy that," Black said. "An old boy that

beats up his wife deserves to get shot. What's all this got to do with Midge Rathermore, though? She dudn't happen to be married to anybody."

"No, but if what she told us about her father and her sister is true, plus if what Deb North says about the father's sex habits checks out, Midge and her sister are surely going to qualify as abused kids."

Black's eyebrows moved closer together in a confused frown. "That's really stretchin' it. Particularly in this fair county, where the defense has got two strikes goin' in. I've never seen where anybody's tried to apply the battered-wife defense to an adolescent killin' a parent. I doubt we'd even get a judge to listen to the argument, especially where the little girl's supposed to have hired somebody to do it."

Sharon sat eagerly forward. "There's precedent for it, Russ. Right in the law books."

"Precedent how? This new stuff's been law less than a year, not even long enough for there to be appellate decisions."

Sharon couldn't resist a mischievous grin. "The precedent's in a place where Milt Breyer would never think to look, and I doubt that even Kathleen Fraterno would find it. It's under family law. The same section they used to certify Midge as an adult, by the way."

Black continued to scowl, but his features softened some in interest. "This is a criminal case, girl. Family law has nothin' to do with it."

"Family law may not," Sharon said, "but the Supreme Court of the United States has everything to do with it. What the high court has to say applies to every facet of the law, civil or criminal. Look, you know about the Florida case that's been on the news, where the kid actually got himself removed from his parents' home because of neglect?"

"I saw it on television, along with everybody else," Black said.

"This is the same theory," Sharon said. "*Akin* v. *Akin*, it's an '87 Massachusetts case. The kid is abused and runs away from home. The court says when the child is the victim of gross abuse, he can have his minor disabilities removed and, for all practical purposes, divorce his parents. They let the kid stay in this foster home where he was living."

"Yeah, but he didn't kill his mother and daddy."

"That's not the way the good old S.C. worded their decision. They say—and I'm quoting from memory, but the case is on your desk—they say the child can take *any* measure to protect itself from abuse. It goes back to the constitutional right to life, liberty, and the pursuit of whatever, which is the very same right on which a self-defense exculpation of murder charges is based. And constitutional law, boss, applies in any arena. Civil or criminal."

Black was running out of arguments. He said rather weakly, "As a minor, though, our little girl didn't have any constitutional rights."

"That's right," Sharon said, "but now they've certified her as an adult. If they'd charged her as a minor under the delinquency laws, this wouldn't work, but now she's entitled to the same rights as anybody else." Filling Russ Black in on her research made Sharon excited all over again. Her theory sounded even better under the scrutiny of daylight than it had in the shadows of the law library.

Black uttered a low whistle. "Jesus H. Christ."

"And the twelve apostles," Sharon said. She pointed toward the door. "Your copy's over there, boss. Look it over and try to shoot some holes in it."

Black thoughtfully checked his watch. "I'm goin' to look up your cases in the books to make sure you're not missin' something."

Sharon grinned. "Feel free."

As Black headed for the exit, Sharon went around, sat behind her desk, and picked up the envelope containing Bradford Brie's photos. Just picturing the strange photographer gave her the creeps, but Sharon had enough of an ego not to be able to resist looking them over. Who knew? The pictures might be flattering after all.

The more that Sharon looked the pictures over, the better she liked them. Creepy as the man with the pipe-stem arms, huge Adam's apple, and crooked, wide-gapped teeth had been, he wasn't bad with the camera at all. He was very good, in fact, and Sharon should know; in law school she'd posed for some real pros, people whose photos had appeared in *Redbook* and *Cosmo*. Bradford Brie, Photographer, Sharon thought. No address, no phone number. Strange as all get-out, Sharon thought. She wondered where she could get a copy of the album Brie was putting together.

She took one picture from the stack, set it aside, and slid the rest of the photos back into the envelope. The picture she'd retained was her favorite, the one of herself half bent over from the waist, files on her upturned forearms, showing a wealth of well-formed thigh as she climbed the steps to the office. She particularly liked her expression of concentration in the picture, and admired the way that Brie had caught her at just the right instant. Action photos taken of a moving subject were no easy trick.

Sharon wondered what it would cost to have the pictured framed in chrome. One corner of her mouth tugging in thought, she picked up the Yellow Pages. It might be vain to hang her own picture on her office wall, she thought, but it wouldn't hurt anything to get a few price quotes. It would give Sharon something to do while Black went over her research notes.

It took the better portion of two hours, but when Russ Black returned to Sharon's office he was excited. "I think you're right," he said.

Sharon put her list of framing prices aside and closed the Yellow Pages. "I know I'm right."

"We can't be goin' off half cocked," Black said, sitting down across from her.

"That's why I spent most of the day in the library. Believe me, if there was a hole in it, I'd have found it."

Black propped his knee against the edge of her desk. "Don't be talkin' this around over drinks with anybody. I damn sure don't want Milt Breyer gettin' wind of what we're up to, at least not 'til after she's indicted."

Sharon placed her thumb on her lower lip, her forefinger on her upper lips, and pressed the two lips together.

"Good as it is," Black said, "it all depends on which judge hears the case. Luck of the draw."

"I know," Sharon said. "But even if we draw a dunderhead that won't listen, we'll have ammunition on appeal.

Somewhere up the line, some court will get the picture. Appellate judges aren't all morons."

"We need to be gettin' evidence together," Black said. "If we can't prove abuse, we're whistlin' in the wind."

"I know that, too. The day after the indictment, just watch my smoke. I'll be digging up witnesses from all over. Just call me Nancy Drew."

"Are you planning on bein' a witness?" Black said.

Sharon leaned back. An attorney cannot investigate one's own case; to do so risks disqualification as lawyer and a stint on the stand. A first-year law student understands this, and Sharon felt foolish. Chalk it up to zeal, she thought.

"Deborah North has approved some money to hire an investigator," Black said. "I've got a guy in mind."

"If he's a good one, he'll be worth whatever he costs." Sharon was grateful that Russ Black hadn't blistered her ears; for once, any dressing-down she'd received would have been deserved.

Black rose, walked over to the open doorway, leaned against the jamb, and thrust his hands into his back pockets. "You looked outside?"

Sharon got up and walked around her desk. "Not lately."

"Well, look, then," Black said.

Sharon moved up beside her boss and gazed through the front office window. Sunlight had broken through the clouds. On the sidewalks and in the streets, puddles shrank, and clean, dry concrete showed between patches of standing water. Sharon stepped into the reception area, nearer the window. In the sky directly over the courthouse, strung between remnants of thunderheads against a bright blue background, was a perfect half-circle rainbow.

13

Sharon couldn't understand what Sheila Winston was saying over the phone, and said so. "There's some kind of static."

"It's not on my end," Sheila said.

Sharon switched the receiver from one ear to the other, shifting her position on the Spanish-style sofa as she did, and frowned at Commander as the shepherd scratched on the door leading outside. Ordinarily Sharon needed a cannon to drive the dog into the yard for the night—along with a heart of stone, Commander rolling on his back with his tongue off to one side in a begging attitude—but this evening he'd been asking to go out ever since supper. Even when Melanie had gone protestingly off to bed, Commander had forsaken his usual stunt of diving underneath the eleven-year-old's covers and had continued to hang out near the den exit. Sharon had nearly opened the door for the dog several times, but something had stopped her. Sharon glanced at the clock: 10:20. If she didn't let Commander out soon, she was liable to have a damp spot on the carpet. Commander whined softly. Sharon said into the phone, "That's better. The line seems clear now. The way Melanie yanks the cord around, trying to talk to her friends while she rummages through the kitchen cabinets, I'm surprised I've got any connection at all. Now, what were you saying?"

"I asked if you wanted a vahs," Sheila said.

"A what?"

"A vahs. Don't ask me, I'm just the dumb shopper. I

kept saying, 'That thar vayse is shore 'nuff purty,' and this saleswoman would go"—Sheila deepened her voice and talked through her nose—" 'It's one of our more popular vahses.' She was some kind of Yankee, New England or someplace, and I guess she thought I was Ghetto Gertie. A desert scene with cactus flowers. It's pretty, okay, but it just doesn't fit with my green carpet."

"Oh, Sheila." Sharon was cracking up. Sheila Winston had an interior designer's taste and would have known damn well what would and wouldn't go at her place, but also would have pictured Sharon's pale gold carpet and light tan cowhide chairs and would have realized that the vase would blend perfectly at Sharon's place. Sheila was like that. Spending hours shopping for a back-to-work gift for a friend, then pretending she'd bought the vase by mistake, fit right in with Sheila's modus operandi. "How much was it?" Sharon said. "I'd insist on paying you."

"Nah. I told you, I'm stuck with it."

"If the plant leaves are the right shade of green," Sharon said, "it might fit in at my office. God knows, something needs to."

"Wherever," Sheila said. "How's work going, by the way?"

"It's been kind of a drag, to tell the truth. Monday we had some action. I got to meet Midge Rathermore's mother, and my boss agreed to let me use some stuff I've been working on to defend the little girl. Since then we haven't hit a lick. Here it's Thursday, only three days later, and I feel like it's been a month since I've done anything."

"While you're sitting around," Sheila said, "there's an article you might like to read. It's by a Yale psychiatrist, on the problems of filling both parental roles. A little on the commercial side, but it isn't bad."

And it would advise single parents, Sharon thought, to let the absent parent play as much of a part as possible in child-rearing. Sheila was as dear to Sharon's heart as any person on the face of the earth, but when Sheila felt she had a point to make, shaking her off was like trying to disengage alligator jaws. Sharon said, with little conviction, "Well, maybe I'll read it."

"God grant me nothing to do for a while," Sheila said, obviously sensing opposition and deciding to wait for a

better time. Sharon was certain that the subject of Rob
and Melanie would come up over and over.

"It's different with you," Sharon said. "Your practice is
at home, and when you don't have somebody's head to
shrink, you can work on your yard or something. Downtown I just sit around and stare at the street." Sharon
wore her standard stay-at-home grodies, pale blue running shorts she'd had since high school and an oversize
Moot Court T-shirt. She was barefoot.

"So dig up more clients," Sheila said.

"I'd love to if I knew where. I really shouldn't complain, and I know it, but working for a lawyer who handles one case at a time isn't as neat as it sounds. At the
D.A.'s I always had a stack of files hanging fire, so if one
case had nothing going I could work on another. Sitting
around waiting for them to indict our client, gee, it's like
waiting for a time bomb to go off."

"If it's tough on you, how do you think the client
feels?"

Sharon's jaw tightened in sadness. "I'm not even sure
she knows what's going on. You should see this poor
child. The damn newspapers are portraying her as some
kind of teenage Lizzie Borden, but I'd like for one of
those frigging reporters to spend an hour with her. *Commander.* Hush that." The dog cut himself off in mid-
whine, and sat on his haunches to regard Sharon with an
accusing cant to his snout. *Come on, lady. Lemme out of
here.*

"I guess the state used old Gruntin' Greg Mathewson
as their expert witness to certify her, huh?" Sheila said.

"None other. I don't know why you don't start collect-
ing a few expert witness fees yourself." Sharon straightened her leg, pointed and wiggled her toes. A slight
cramp began in her calf. Back to the old treadmill, she
thought.

"I would if I didn't like to sleep at night," Sheila said.
"Make that, I like to live with myself. I've been having
problems sleeping as it is. I've got this woman that,
someone's stalking her."

"That sounds like a fun analysis visit," Sharon said.

"Tell me about it." Sheila's voice softened, her tone
now just a bit frightened. "This lady's a bundle of rags,

Sharon. She can barely keep any food down. It's always something that's going to happen to someone else, right?"

Sharon curled up her legs on the sofa and sat on her ankles. "Let's hope it stays that way."

"It's worse when you don't have the slightest idea who it is. This creep, the other night he left a bag of shit on her doorstep. Human feces, can you believe it? He was hiding in the bushes, I'll give you odds, and giggling like a moron while this poor woman screamed her head off."

There were long seconds of silence, a faint crackling noise over the line as both women imagined what it would be like to have the worst female nightmare of all come true.

"What have you done about camp?" Sheila finally said. Her tone was more upbeat as she changed gears, though the lightheartedness in her voice was obviously forced.

Sharon leaped at the opportunity to change the subject. "I made reservations at Sky Ranch for the second week in July, because it's likely that's when the Rathermore case will be in trial. It's Melanie's fourth year up there, so if I have to change at the last minute, the camp people will probably cut me some slack. Trish is still going, isn't she?" Sharon wasn't as worried as she had been during Melanie's first summer at camp, but still liked the idea of Melanie having her best friend along.

"You betcha," Sheila said. "If she didn't have her reservations at the same time as Melanie, Trish might assassinate me in my bed." There was a pause, punctuated by paper rustling, then Sheila said, "I've written it down on my things-to-do list for tomorrow. Call Sky Ranch, second week in July. Wow, a week without the kids. Good time to fall in love for a few days, huh?"

"Or a few hours," Sharon said. Commander had resumed his insistent pawing at the door. "I've got to go before this dog drives me up a tree," Sharon said.

"Me, too. Be careful, Sharon, huh?" Sheila disconnected.

"Yeah," Sharon said softly. She replaced the receiver on the hook, her mouth tugging in worry. Good God, a bag of feces on the woman's doorstep. Which is probably what Stan Green would like to leave at my place, Sharon thought wryly. She got up and went to the door, then scratched Commander between the ears as she said reproachfully, "Hold your horses, will you?" Then she turned the dead bolt and opened the door.

Commander raced into the night as if his fur were on fire. His claws scraped wood as he charged across the deck and bounded into the yard. Commander never volunteered to leave the house at bedtime. Never. Frowning in apprehension, Sharon reached around the jamb and flicked on the outside lights.

The sudden illumination revealed spires of Johnson grass waving over unmown Bermuda and a swing set which towered like a gallows. Sharon went out onto the deck. The redwood warmed her bare soles.

Commander had pell-melled out to the fence separating the yard from the alley, and now picked something up in his mouth and lugged his prize in among the shadows cast by the swing set. The thing in his mouth was heavy and pliant, hanging loosely down from both sides of the shepherd's jaws. Sharon narrowed her eyes. It could be a dead animal: a rat or a baby rabbit. There was a vacant lot a half block away, a perfect springtime breeding ground, and the previous year Sharon had chained Commander after the fourth or fifth time he'd assassinated an infant bunny and brought it proudly up on the doorstep. The babies liked to roam. Sharon thought she'd successfully closed the small hole at the bottom of the fence, but now wondered if the bunnies had found a new hatch. She stepped to the edge of the deck. "Commander. Here."

The dog was a shadow among deeper shades of darkness behind the swing set's slide. He dropped his burden between his forepaws and stood stock still, but made no move to approach her.

Sharon stepped down into cool, tickling grass and circled the swing set, thinking for the thousandth time that Melanie had outgrown the damned slide and swings and that she should get rid of them. Commander whimpered as Sharon approached. Just enough police school training remained for him to hesitate at her command, but whatever lay between his feet had enough of his attention that he wasn't about to go off and leave it. Sharon stroked the dog's head. "Dumb old flunk-out," she murmured, then bent to pick up the thing from the ground. It was slickly wet and dangled weightily from her hand. She moved back into the light and had a look.

She was holding a raw steak, with a thick rind of fat encircling its perimeter and one jagged piece of bone clinging to its edge. The red meat was marbled with fingers of gristle.

Sharon lifted the steak to her nose and sniffed; there was a faint sour odor like rotten eggs. She peered into the darkness beyond the fence. Was someone out there?

He was hiding in the bushes, I'll give you odds, giggling like a moron while this poor woman screamed her head off.

A sob climbed up from Sharon's throat. She grabbed Commander by his collar and, carrying the meat in her free hand, hauled the dog through the yard, across the deck, and back into the house. She locked the door from the inside and sagged against the den wall. Commander whined and sniffed at the beefsteak. Sharon patted his head. Her hand was trembling.

It was obvious that the cop didn't consider attempted dog poisonings a high-priority item. "You keep the dog in?" he said. He glanced at Sharon's bare legs, then looked quickly away. A report form on a clipboard rested on his thigh. So far he'd filled in Sharon's name and address.

"He stays in the yard unless he's on a leash," she said. "Every once in a while he'll scoot out through the front door when my daughter leaves it open, but we run him down as soon as we can." Sharon was uncomfortable, sitting on the sofa in gym shorts as the policeman looked her over as if she were naked, and she wished she'd pulled on a pair of jeans before this guy and his partner had arrived. The steak, sealed inside a Ziplock bag, rested on the sofa between Sharon and the cop.

"I know you probably watch him as much as you can," the cop said, "but these animals are tough to keep up with. What I'm saying is, he could be roaming when you don't know it. A lot of people, you know, get het up over dogs messing around in their yards." He was around twenty-five with a pudgy face and brush mustache. His billed uniform cap lay on the coffee table, and he was doing his best to talk this schizo woman out of filing a complaint.

"I know all that, Officer," Sharon said. "That's why I watch my dog and don't let him wander around."

A heavy footfall sounded on the deck, then the second policeman entered the house. Commander dutifully brought up the rear, sniffing in curiosity at the cop's pants leg. The newcomer was a tall, skinny drink of water with pimples on his neck, a bit older than his partner but still a couple of years short of thirty. In a few years, Sharon thought, Melanie and her friends will be ripe for this pair. She didn't like the idea.

"There was somebody out there, all right," the second policeman said. "There's footprints in the mud outside the fence, and more pieces of mud in a trail down the alley." He glanced at Sharon's legs and didn't look away nearly as quickly as his partner had. The plastic bill of his uniform hat practically touched his nose. He put one hand under Commander's snout to raise the dog's head and look him over. "He doesn't look any the worse for wear," the cop said.

"If he'd eaten any of it," Sharon said, "you wouldn't be saying that." In an offbeat sort of way, she was glad these two were leering at her. She'd been on the verge of hysteria when she'd dialed 911, and had cried some while waiting for the squad car to arrive. Now, with these two ogling her and not particularly trying to hide the fact, her shock had subsided and she was merely good and mad. She curled her shins underneath and sat on her ankles. The two cops watched the leg show. "Of course someone was out there," Sharon said. "That piece of meat didn't just walk into the yard."

The younger cop tapped his clipboard with the eraser end of his pencil. "I think you need to know, ma'am. Once we turn this meat in at the lab, they're liable to have you come down and fill out a bunch of forms. Probably will, in fact. There's a lot of red tape. I smelled the meat myself. It's poisoned. I don't see where the type of poison makes any difference." He glanced at his partner.

"Not unless you're interested in catching whoever did it." Sharon put on her sweetest smile. "I don't mind filling out the lab forms. I work downtown, anyway."

The second cop sat in a wing chair and crossed long legs. Commander sat nearby on his haunches, panting.

The dog eyed the meat. Sharon scooted the bag and its contents away from the edge of the sofa cushion.

"I know it makes you mad for this to happen," the skinny cop said. "But I got to tell you, miss. If we do catch this old boy, his punishment won't amount to much." He had thick lips and a pointed nose. He took off his hat, revealing mouse brown hair receding from his forehead.

"It's a class-B misdemeanor," Sharon said. "Thirty days plus a two-hundred-dollar fine. Normally it's pled down to a class C, and the perpetrator pays about fifty bucks court costs. I still want to know who did this."

Commander's panting punctuated ten seconds of silence, after which the younger cop said, "You a lawyer or something?"

"I was a prosecutor with the D.A.'s office, and sometimes I go to lunch with Jill Thomas. She's over the misdemeanor section." Sharon folded her arms. "I'd like this to be a formal complaint, please."

The younger cop took his gaze quickly away from Sharon's legs and poised his pencil over the complaint form. He cleared his throat. "What time was this?" He was suddenly all business, his neck flushed slightly and his tone more subdued.

"Ten twenty-five on the dot when I let him out. Forty-five minutes ago, taking into account the half hour it took for you to respond to my call." Sharon watched the skinny policeman. He sat up straighter, his expression now formal, and zeroed in on the far wall. When Sharon had answered the door, the older cop had been drinking a Coke from Kentucky Fried Chicken, and had later tossed the empty, ice and all, into the kitchen garbage. Sharon put both feet on the floor, crossed her legs, and let one bare foot rock up and down. Neither cop so much as glanced at her.

"I think the steak was out there long before that," Sharon said. "The dog had been scratching to get out all evening."

The young cop wrote something on the form. He looked up and opened his mouth to speak just as the telephone rang.

Sharon got up, crossed the room, and picked up the receiver. Her back to the policemen, she said, "Hello?"

"You asleep?" The rumbling voice on the line belonged to Russell Black.

Sharon bent her head forward. "Not exactly."

"Bad news," Black said. "They've already indicted our little girl."

Sharon watched the carpet. "Damn."

"I made a deal with Milt Breyer," Black said, "that he'd let me know before they went into the grand jury. He told me he'd call me the minute the judge signed the adult certification order. Lyin' bastard."

Sharon permitted herself a small grin, and couldn't resist saying, "I thought we didn't talk about other lawyers, boss."

"It's different when it's just between us."

"That's not what you told me."

"Well, that's what I'm sayin' now," Black said. "Don't worry, I didn't trust old Milt to begin with. I got a spy down at the jail, on the warrants desk. They're movin' Midge from juvenile down to the county tonight. If it wadn't for the spy, the first we'd know about it was when the clerk called to tell us they were arraignin' her on the adult charges."

Sharon softly closed her eyes, picturing the grossly overweight teenager and what was likely to happen once they had her booked in with the big folks. "What time are they moving her?" Sharon said.

"About a half hour from now. I guess there's not much for us to do 'til in the mornin', but at least we can run over and visit her as soon as they open up."

"No," Sharon said hesitantly, then said more firmly, "No, Russ. I'm going down there."

"Tonight?"

"That's what I said."

"I'm not stoppin' you," Black said. "But I don't know what you think you can accomplish."

"I just think someone should be with her. I know I'd want somebody there if it was my daughter. See you in the morning, boss." Sharon hung up, then faced the two policemen. "I'm afraid I have to leave, gentlemen."

The two cops appeared relieved. The younger one stood, holding his clipboard. "Well, if we can be of further help, let us know."

"Oh, I will," Sharon said. "Not only that, I'll be at

main police headquarters tomorrow to formalize my complaint. You fellas want to give me your badge numbers? Or maybe you can meet me and I won't have to get the duty officer to call you in." She smiled at them. "Say around two in the afternoon, okay?" Sharon said.

"Baby-sitting's one thing," Sheila said. "Dog-sitting is another. Jeez, how much is in here?" She rattled the huge sack of Alpo which she had clutched to her chest, and bent her head to peer inside the bag.

"For Commander it's a week's supply," Sharon said. They were in Sheila's kitchen just inside the screen door. Trish and Melanie were bedded down in Trish's room, though Sharon doubted that the giggly little girls would get much sleep. Visible through the screen, Commander sat on the bottom step with his head cocked in a puzzled attitude.

"I'm not keeping this monster for a week, Sharon. Friends are friends, but, you know." Sheila wore a white shortie gown. Slim coffee-colored legs bent at the knees as she stooped to place the dog food on the floor.

"It's just for tonight," Sharon said. "I'll guarantee you, I'll pick him up by nine in the morning. And in return for you taking the girls to school tomorrow, I'll pick up two days in a row. Scout's honor."

Sheila threw a dubious look in Commander's direction. "I can see you bringing Melanie, but I thought the dog guarded the house while you were gone. How come I'm guarding him?"

"I can't go into it now. Just trust me," Sharon said. On the drive over, Melanie had grumped sleepily in the back while Commander nearly caused a wreck by sloppily licking Sharon's face. If she took the time to fill Sheila in on the whole mess, she'd never make the jail in time. "I'll tell all tomorrow," Sharon said. "Promise."

"Well, okay. Just this once. Can you feed him out of a bowl, or does it take a barrel?"

Sharon moved a step in the direction of the front door. She'd changed into jeans and scuffed white leather sneakers, and had given her hair a lick and a promise. "A big bowl," she said. "A mixing bowl is what I use. I've got to go." She hesitated, then said, "Sheila, have you got a gun?"

"Jesus, no, I'd shoot myself. Listen, if the old Mace

doesn't do the trick, I'm afraid I'm all theirs." She dubiously raised an eyebrow. "What would you need a gun for?"

"No reason," Sharon said quite softly, then strengthened her voice and said, "No reason, Sheila. Just thinking out loud, all right?"

Sharon arrived in the Lew Sterrett Justice Center basement just as they brought Midge through the tunnel into the glare of spotlights held aloft by gaffers as TV people pointed minicams. Midge wore ankle irons and handcuffs fastened to a chain around her waist. The mountain of a girl shuffled along in shackle-resisted baby steps, a burly deputy on either side as she moved slowly through the lobby toward the booking desk. Her unwashed hair hung in greasy strings; her eyes were wide in a dull stupor.

Sharon quickened her pace, her rubber soles whispering on painted concrete. A knot of reporters blocked her path. In the center of the group stood Milton Breyer, clad in a navy blue suit and tie, with Stan Green alongside wearing slacks and a sports shirt. Breyer smilingly answered the newspeople's question while Green responded to inquiries with lantern-jawed silence; the Dallas County district attorney had brought another one back alive. Sharon grimly lowered her head and tried to walk around the group. Stan Green saw her and peevishly dropped his gaze.

A youngish male voice on Sharon's right said, "Miss Hays. Miss Hays, any comment?"

Sharon turned. Andy Wade of the *News* approached, thick lenses shining in the glare like spacemen's goggles. A Channel 8 minicam pointed its lens in her direction.

Sharon peered around the reporter to fix Milt Breyer with a look that might wilt roses. Breyer looked down at his shoes. Sharon faced the reporter. "This isn't my show, Andy," Sharon said. "It's Mr. Breyer's. Talk to him."

"But it's your client," Wade said, steadying a steno pad, pencil ready. "At least tell me how she's going to plead."

Sharon expelled a breath. "What is it with you people? I guess the whole crew of you just happened to be in the jail basement at midnight in case a story breaks."

Wade lifted, then dropped his shoulders. "I'm not sure.

Somebody called the newsroom, I guess. Come on, any comment?" His voice took on a pleading tone.

Sharon had a comment, all right. A comment about D.A.'s who sneaked into grand jury rooms for indictments, then called press conferences in order to put helpless overweight teenage girls on display for the world to see. She opened, then closed her mouth. Finally she composed herself and said, "I haven't seen the indictments. We'll save our response for the courtroom, if it's all right. Let me through, please."

She shouldered her way in between Wade and a female reporter with the *Observer* whose name Sharon couldn't recall, and made her way past the mob. Midge was now halfway from the tunnel to the booking desk. One of the cameramen yelled something to the nearest deputy. The potbellied county man stood back in order to give the camera a better angle. Midge blinked dully at the lens.

Sharon quickly positioned herself between Midge and the camera. "For Christ's sake, leave her alone," she said. She quickly approached Midge. The deputy took a step forward to block her off. Sharon hissed, "I'm her lawyer. Stand back." The deputy hesitated, unsure of himself, then moved aside. Sharon draped a protective arm around Midge and helped her toward the booking desk. Automatic Plexiglas doors hissed open. Three more uniformed deputies, two Hispanic men and a young black woman, waited at the desk.

Sharon put her lips close to Midge's ear. "I'm sorry, Midge, they sneaked up on us. If we'd had any warning, we could've bypassed all these newsmen."

Midge looked up. Blinding light painted a shadow of her nose on her right cheek. On her chin a ruptured pimple drained. "Where am I?" she said.

"It's the main county jail. This is where they're going to keep you now." Sharon lowered her lashes in pity.

A female guard, a not-unpleasant woman in her thirties, approached to remove Sharon's arm from Midge's shoulders. "I'll have to take her now," the deputy said.

Sharon stepped helplessly away. Midge's eyes were wet black jelly. Sharon tried to smile, but her mouth seemed frozen.

"I want to go home," Midge said. "Please. When can I?"

The guard tugged her between the double doors toward the booking desk. The doors hissed closed. Sharon stood alone in the jail lobby as all around her cameras aimed.

Andy Wade said loudly, "Come on, Miss Hays, we go way back. Just one statement, huh?"

Sharon turned mutely to face the reporter. Her nose was suddenly stuffy, her vision blurry with unfallen tears.

14

Dallas County assistant D.A. Edward Teeter, chief felony prosecutor in the 357th District Court, already knew two of the three lawyers who now sat across from him. On Teeter's left was Richard Waite, whose habit of filing appeal notices barely under the time-limit wire had earned him the nickname "Deadline Dicky." Dicky Waite was rat thin with a pencil mustache, and wore designer jeans along with a tan Ultrasuede sports coat. Waite was strictly an appellate lawyer, seldom appeared in court, and dressed in whatever manner he pleased. I'm lucky, Teeter thought, that the guy's not down here in his bathing suit.

Directly across from the prosecutor, on Dicky Waite's left, sat Vernon Riggs. Impeccably dressed in a black three-piece, Counselor Riggs was bald as an egg and sported a full mad scientist's beard. Riggs had recently won an acquittal in a robbery case with Ed Teeter representing the state. Teeter hated Riggs's guts for whipping his ass in the courtroom, but being on Edward Teeter's permanent shit list didn't place Vernon Riggs in the minority. Teeter, in fact, hated every attorney who didn't work for the D.A.'s office, and even despised some of those who did.

The third visiting lawyer was a man whom Teeter had never seen before. Teeter half rose and extended his hand across his desk. "Ed Teeter. I don't think we've met."

The stranger was medium height, medium build, with medium-length brown hair, and wore a charcoal gray suit with a starched white shirt. A bright red tie was his only distinguishing feature; the man was as ordinary-looking as Ross Perot. Teeter thought that if he didn't get a good make on this guy, he'd never recognize him if he saw him again. The stranger took Teeter's hand and exerted a medium grip. "Samuel Jones," the stranger said. "Jones and Jones."

I'll bet even the guy's shirt's a medium, Teeter thought. He resumed his seat and smiled. "Three lawyers come to see a man on Monday morning, the man must be in trouble. What can I do for you guys?" Teeter's smile appeared painted on and showed no warmth. All three visiting lawyers knew that the smile was a phony, Teeter *knew* that they knew it, and the four of them had an understanding.

Dicky Waite crossed his legs and folded his hands around his knee. "Eddie, we got a small disagreement we think you can solve for us."

Teeter's office was up on the Crowley Building's eleventh floor, but he now held forth at the judge's assistant's desk behind the 357th courtroom, adjacent to the jurist's chambers. Teeter bent forward to peer through the partly open doorway into Judge Ralph Briscoe's pad. Rascally Ralph was in there, all right, iron gray locks inclined as he studied a magazine. Teeter hurriedly got up and closed the door, then resumed his seat. "Man, I can't even referee the clerks' arguments around here. How am I going to help three lawyers?" Teeter had a round face and pointed nose to go with an overhanging belly and pipe-stem legs. He wore his office suit, dark brown in contrast to the dress-for-power black he donned for trials.

Vernon Riggs stroked his smooth scalp, then pulled on his beard. "The problem has to do with a case in this court. State versus Wilfred Donello. You need to get the file?" He opened his briefcase to remove a thick manila envelope.

It was all that Teeter could do to keep from curling his lip; a man who beat Ed Teeter in court owed him one for life. In Riggs's case, Teeter wouldn't settle for less than a quart of blood. "I might," Teeter said, "and I might not. Depends on what you want. I'm pretty familiar with the Donello case without the file."

Samuel Jones, the stranger, sat forward and touched his fingertips together. "It's your case? I thought—"

"It's an inherited case," Teeter said. "Sharon Hays actually tried it. She quit, as I'm sure y'all know. Milt Breyer was the main prosecutor on Donello, but now he's on the Rathermore case. They indicted the Rathermore girl last week, so that will be Milt's full-time occupation for a while. There's nothing left on Donello but the sentencing, so for the duration the case is mine. Not much to that bastard's sentencing, to be honest with you."

"He'll get some time, huh?" Waite said.

"You betchum, Red Ryder," Teeter said.

"Ed," Riggs said, drawing a stapled sheath of papers from his envelope, "I know you're a busy man, so we'll be brief. Wilfred Donello called my office the other day, and I visited him in the jail. In a manner of speaking, he's retained me."

"So he's got a lawyer," Teeter said. "Good. He needs one."

"The problem is," Riggs said, "that according to Mr. Waite here, *he's* Donello's lawyer." He looked at Dicky Waite, who nodded emphatically.

Teeter rocked back in the judge's assistant's chair. "So he's got two lawyers. That's twice as good." He grinned. It wasn't that unusual for a jailbird to wind up hiring two lawyers; the dirtball would hire one attorney and then, if the first lawyer didn't get any results, would retain another guy without dismissing the first attorney. The confusion among attorneys tickled the D.A.'s office to death; having two lawyers duke it out made it easier to put the screws to the defendant.

Samuel Jones pinched his chin. "There's very little humor in this situation, Mr. Teeter."

"There's not? Let me guess." Teeter pointed a finger. "You represent Donello, too. Now he's got three lawyers. What, the fucking guy's going for a record?"

Jones raised a hand, palm out. "No need to be profane."

Teeter glanced back and forth between Waite and Riggs. "Where you come up with this fucking guy?" Teeter said. Riggs shrugged. Waite regarded the far wall.

"The fact is," Jones said, "that I represent Howard Saw."

Teeter blinked. "Now, that's real nice, Mr. Jones. Howard Saw's dead. But if you want to represent him, feel free."

"His estate, that is," Jones said. "I'm strictly a probate attorney."

So that's why I've never seen this guy, Teeter thought. "How much did old Howard leave?" he said.

"That isn't the issue." Medium conservative attorney Samuel Jones obviously was having a hard time controlling himself. Which was exactly the position in which Ed Teeter loved to put people. Jones adjusted the knot on his tie. "I'm just expressing my position in this matter. Now that I have done that, I'll fall silent and let these fellows carry on."

"Good," Teeter said. "You do that."

Vernon Riggs heaved a sigh and rolled his eyes. "There's a full docket this morning, Ed. In thirty minutes I'm pleading a guy in the 277th, at ten o'clock I got to be down in the 356th for a bond hearing. I'd like a few minutes to talk to my guy in the 277th before he cops to murder if it's okay."

Teeter motioned toward the door. "Be my guest. I'm not stopping you. You guys came to me last time I checked."

"That's right, we did." Riggs pulled on his beard. "I'll tell you what, though. If you keep on making with the jokes instead of listening to the problem, I'll bypass you and talk to the judge."

Teeter opened his mouth to tell Riggs where to get off, then hesitated. Riggs was just the kind of prick who would go to the judge, and the number one duty of the chief felony prosecutor in a district court, on days when a trial wasn't in progress, was to see that the judge didn't have anything to do. As long as he kept the judge happy, he could do pretty much as he pleased, but if Riggs was to interrupt Judge Briscoe's magazine reading, there'd be hell to pay. Teeter relaxed his posture. "Well, what is it," he said, "that you guys are having a problem with?"

"As I already told you," Riggs said, "Wilfred Donello wants me to represent him in connection with certain things. I quoted him a fee."

"Sounds reasonable," Teeter said. "But what's he want to *hire* a lawyer for? A court-appointed guy can stand up

at his sentencing just as well. Either way the guy's going
to get the maximum."

"That's what I thought," Riggs said. "But it turns out,
Mr. Donello's got other things in mind than his sentencing. The fee I quoted, well, he doesn't have any money.
He gave all his money to Howard Saw before his trial,
and the fee he paid Saw included the cost of the appeal
in case Donello was convicted. Now Mr. Donello says he
doesn't want to appeal, but wants a refund from Mr. Saw
so that he can retain me."

"Sounds pretty simple to me," Teeter said.

"It would be if Howard was alive. But now the only
way I can be paid is to file a claim against Howard's estate, with Mr. Jones the probate attorney over here.
Which I did, legal and proper, a form executed by Wilfred
Donello and notarized. Which brings us to this problem
we've got."

Riggs paused to shoot a less than friendly glance at
Dicky Waite. Waite expelled air through his nose and impatiently tapped his foot. Riggs went on:

"It seems that there's already a claim, in the same
amount as my claim for fees, filed by Mr. Waite here. According to Mr. Waite's claim, he's representing Mr.
Donello in his appeal. An appeal with which Mr. Donello
no longer wishes to proceed."

Waite folded his arms. The sleeves of his Ultrasuede
coat showed deep creases. "Ten grand," he said. "Howard
owed me ten grand."

"All I could do to help with that," Teeter said, "is to
check the file to see if there's an appeal notice." He gazed
beyond the seated lawyers at the trophy displayed above
the sofa. The trophy was the prize in the annual judges'
and prosecutors' slow-pitch softball game, and was held
for a year by the winning team's most valuable player.
Engraved on the statuette's base was last year's score:
Felonies 22, Misdemeanors 18. Teeter had slugged two
homers and held the Misdemeanors to thirty-seven hits,
and he thought that the awarding of the trophy to Judge
Briscoe was nothing but politics.

"We've already checked," Riggs said, "and there is no
appeal notice on file."

"I got until tomorrow to file notice under the time
limit," Deadline Dicky said. "Look, everybody knows me

and Howard were fraternity brothers. He calls me up and makes me a deal over the phone, not fifteen minutes before he died. If Howard was alive, we wouldn't be having this conversation. His word was his bond."

"If that's true," Riggs said, "then how come the notation, made in Howard's handwriting on the inside cover of the file, says you demanded a cashier's check before you were lifting a finger? Everybody that's been to law school knows that unless you received a consideration you didn't have any deal. No consideration, no contract, it looks like to me."

"I'm not sure what I've got to do with this," Teeter said, "but what's wrong with filing two claims against Howard's estate? That way Donello could get whatever he wants from Riggs, and Waite could go on with the appeal. Donello could have his cake and eat it, too."

"That would suit me and Vernon just fine," Waite said. "Only *he* won't go for it." He pointed at Jones, who placed his elbows on his armrests and rested his chin on his intertwined fingers.

"Mr. Saw lived high," Jones said. "It's true there was quite a bit of cash in the estate, but I've got a claim from the IRS for over half of it. That takes precedence. Then there's a sworn note to Caesar's Palace—"

"In Vegas?" Teeter said.

Jones nodded. "In addition to that there are credit card bills and whatnot. After everything's settled, Mr. Saw's estate comes to twenty-one thousand and change."

"I guess there was enough to bury Howard," Teeter said.

Jones smiled a conservative smile. "Oh, Howard had a burial policy. I recommended that when he first came to me to draw up the papers."

Teeter scratched his nose. "So what's the problem? Twenty-one thousand, ten for Dicky, ten for Vernon, still leaves a grand or so."

Jones sat back and fiddled with his ear, not saying anything.

"The problem is," Riggs said, "that if I get my ten thousand and Dicky gets his ten thousand, there's not enough left over for his fee." He pointed at Jones.

Teeter looked from one visiting lawyer to another. Finally the prosecutor spread his hands, palms up, in a shrugging gesture. "Well, hey. It looks like you've got some compromising to do. I still don't see what the D.A.'s office has to do with—"

"We've already hashed it out," Riggs said, "and nobody wants to compromise. I've proposed a solution to Dicky that we do what's best for the client."

Waite snorted. "Sure. As long as you get yours."

Riggs ignored the skinny lawyer. "Here's the proposition," he said. "What Donello wants from me, he wants me to talk to the district attorney, which is you in this case, Ed. He wants me to talk to the district attorney about making a deal for him. So I made a suggestion to these two guys. I'm going to tell you, just supposing, what the offer my client has in mind will be. My *proposed* client. If you as the D.A.'s rep tell me that we can make an arrangement for Donello, he's going to waive his appeal in writing. That way Dicky Waite here won't be entitled to a fee. But if we *don't* have a makeable deal, then I'm going to withdraw."

"I still don't like this," Waite said glumly. "Either way he gets his." He pointed at Jones. Jones folded conservative manicured hands in his lap.

Teeter blinked. "Let me get this straight. Wilfred Donello's coming to us, wanting to make a deal."

"That's what he says," Riggs said.

"Jesus Christ," Teeter said. "Seeing as how he's already convicted, I don't see that he's in much of a bargaining position."

"The judge will go along with whatever sentence the D.A. recommends," Riggs said. "You guys can give him probation if you're a mind to."

"Sure we can," Teeter said. "We can do anything we want. But Jesus Christ. Donello?"

Riggs scratched his chin through his beard. "Mr. Donello wishes to offer certain information in exchange for leniency."

Teeter studied his nails. Now the conversation was drifting into his ball yard. "He wants to be a snitch, in other words." He still didn't like Vernon Riggs, but for now was prepared to put his animosity on hold. Snitches were the system's lifeblood, and coming up with a gold-plated informant would be a feather in Teeter's cap.

Riggs's mouth tugged to one side. "Well, if you want to call it that."

"Sure, we make deals all the time," Teeter said. "I'll listen to anything. But if he wants to tell us about some guy running a red light ... hey, you know, fuck you, Donello."

Probate lawyer Jones threw Teeter an irritated glance, then resumed his conservative posture.

"In my opinion," Riggs said, "Mr. Donello's information is entirely worthy of consideration. Of course, it's for your ears only, Ed. Even though I don't officially represent him, what Donello told me falls in the attorney-client category. Also, if we can't make a deal, you can't use the information."

Dicky Waite suddenly pounded the arm of his chair. "This is horseshit. I mean, they got me in the middle, you know? Either way this guy gets his." He pointed at Jones. "Now Riggs has got this secret information that I don't even know what the fuck it is. I could make Donello the same deal if I'd of gotten to him first."

"But you didn't," Riggs said. "He called me, remember?"

"Fuck," Waite said. He leaned his cheek against his clenched fist.

"That's between you guys," Teeter said. "You and you"—he pointed at Waite, then at Jones—"go out in the hall. Me and Mr. Riggs have got some serious talking to do."

Dicky Waite and Samuel Jones sat on a bench in the narrow corridor outside the judge's assistant's office. The office door was closed; shadows moved over the frosted glass insert. The judge's hallway entry was open; as the waiting attorneys watched, Rascally Ralph Briscoe tossed a *Time* magazine aside and picked up *Entertainment Weekly*. Dicky Waite nervously studied the floor. Samuel Jones returned his attention to the Bar Association bulletin he'd been reading. The hallway clock showed five until ten.

There was a sudden click and rattle. The assistant's door opened and Vernon Riggs came out with Ed Teeter close on his heels. The prosecutor seemed excited. Dicky Waite sagged on the bench.

Teeter gestured with his hands. "This is strictly hypothetical, right? I mean, we've got nothing solid as yet."

"Right," Riggs said. "Nothing's finalized until you get the bargain reduced to writing. Then you and I will take a trip over to the jail for Mr. Donello's signature and talk to him in person. My guy tells you nothing until the judge agrees to the sentence." Riggs glanced at the clock and folded his arms. "Shit, I missed my guy's plea in the 277th." He shrugged. "Win a few, lose a few. What the hell, it's a court appointment."

Waite bounced up from his seat on the bench. "I've been thinking this over, Vernon. Tell you what. I'll take five, you take five. Mr. Jones can have all of his probate fee."

Riggs exchanged looks with Teeter. Riggs smiled. "Fuck you, Dicky," he said.

Waite studied the floor. "I should have been a probate guy, you know?"

15

Sharon didn't think that the salad at Joe Willie's Restaurant, in the tunnel underneath Bank One Center, was as fresh as in the past. The lettuce was the proper shade of green, the tomato wedges firm, the croutons crunchy, but there was something about the salad's overall appearance. She poured ranch dressing in a circular pattern, mixed the dressing in with her fork, took a bite of romaine lettuce, tomato, and bell pepper, and chewed thoughtfully. "Tastes a little wilted," she said.

Kathleen lifted her forkful of green-speckled pasta. "That's why I always get the fettuccine. One day the salad's good, the next day I wouldn't eat it on a bet." She poked the noodles into her mouth and had a sip of iced tea.

Sharon thought that if she had Kathleen's metabolism, she'd be chowing down on the pasta with carbonara sauce as well. Kathleen could consume a gallon of ice cream every frigging day and still look like a gymnast, for God's sake. Sharon's bathroom scales had told her last night that she'd gained four pounds, and she'd been up this morning before dawn to go an agonizing mile and a half before taking Melanie and Trish to school. Once in New York she'd starved herself practically to death for two weeks before auditioning as Blanche Dubois in *Streetcar*, then had lost the part because she'd been a head taller than the guy playing Kowalski. "Maybe next time I'll have the fettuccine," Sharon said.

"Next time we should try the West End," Fraterno said. "There's a new Good Eats Restaurant."

Sharon made a face. "It's too crowded. I'd like a little privacy when I'm talking business."

Fraterno's expression clouded. It was the first time the two had seen each other outside the courtroom since Sharon had quit the D.A., and she suspected that being an adversary made Kathleen somewhat uncomfortable. "How's your dog?" Fraterno said.

Sharon's lips parted. "Oh," she said. "Word gets around."

Fraterno spun more fettuccine onto her fork. "Cops talk, you know that."

"Commander's okay. The poison was strychnine. I'm keeping him in day and night for a while. I want to talk about Midge Rathermore."

"There's no one meaner than someone who wants to hurt an animal," Fraterno said.

"Kathleen," Sharon said. "I've got to know about discovery."

"You know I can't make any commitments without talking things over with Milt." Fraterno's hair was jet black and flowed halfway to her waist in back. In court she tied the hair up. Today she wore a dress that was half black and half yellow, with the colors divided vertically, and pale yellow medium heels. Sharon thought that Kathleen's trial attire was always perfect; her tastes outside the courtroom, though, left a bit to be desired. When they'd both been prosecutors and had done some running around together, Sharon had taken Kathleen shopping and had made some subtle suggestions. The result had been that Kathleen's stunning figure, displayed properly, had given men whiplash when the two women did the town together. Left to her own devices, Sharon thought, Kathleen has reverted to form in her dress. The yellow-and-black outfit wasn't flattering at all. "Milt's calling the shots," Fraterno said.

"I work for Russell Black, too. That doesn't mean I don't know what's going on in the case."

Fraterno stiffened noticeably. "I'm just one of the grunts."

Which Sharon knew to be an out-and-out lie. Milt Breyer's style was to glad-hand the press, make appearances anytime the television folks were around, and depend on his assistant to try the case and keep Milt advised of what was going on. Sharon's tone took on a slight edge. "And I'm just trying to defend this child," she said.

"She's a murderess." Fraterno's face turned to prosecutorial stone.

"Now you sound like Milt Breyer," Sharon said.

"What's wrong with that? We should have more people who approach their work the same way."

Sharon couldn't believe her ears. It hadn't been a month earlier that Kathleen had kept Sharon in stitches with her Milton Breyer impression, complete with goosestep walk and phony educated manner of speech. Sharon searched Fraterno's face. Kathleen was as serious as malaria. What could have changed? Oh, Sharon thought. You're screwing him, Kathleen. Aren't you? The thought of Kathleen in bed with Milt—or anyone in bed with Milt, for that matter—made Sharon's stomach churn. But there was no other answer, and it would account for the Halloween costume of a dress, which a clod like Milton Breyer would think the living end. Sharon lowered her lashes and concentrated on her plate.

"About the discovery," Sharon finally said.

"Yes?" Icy, reserved.

"It's been two weeks since the arraignment, Kathleen. The trial is set for six weeks from now, and we're smart enough to know that with all the media coverage there aren't likely to be any continuances."

"A motion for continuance," Fraterno said, "would be up to Judge Griffin. The state doesn't plan to ask for one, I'll tell you that much."

Sandy Griffin had been the luck of the draw, and Sharon and Black had celebrated when the Rathermore case had landed in her courtroom. Though a former prosecutor herself, Griffin was under forty, a Texas Tech law school grad, and one of the only Dallas County judges with the imagination to listen to Sharon's argument comparing abused children with battered wives. Like all Texas jurists, however, Griffin was elected. As a politician, she'd sooner break a leg than cause the press or movie people a moment's inconvenience.

"So we're in agreement that we're looking to go to trial July 6 or thereabouts," Sharon said. "That's not much time. Ten days ago I sent a letter over to your office asking to see the evidence against our client, and I haven't heard a word from it."

"Our mail room's been in a turmoil," Fraterno said, blank-faced.

Sharon blinked. Kathleen Fraterno had gone from friend to foe with one wave of Milton Breyer's magic wand. Or magic penis, whatever, though Sharon would have been shocked if there was anything supernatural hidden in Milton Breyer's underwear. Sharon said, "Okay, Kathleen, up front. Is it going to take a formal hearing for us to get discovery?"

Fraterno pursed her lips. "Well, it might."

"So finally we're being honest," Sharon said, wondering how honest it had been for the state to pigeonhole a letter as important as a request for discovery. "If you don't want to cooperate, Kathleen, I suppose we'll have to go for a full-blown examining trial."

Fraterno's reaction was a defiant half smirk. Examining trials were a pain in the ass, a procedure whereby the defense could force the prosecution to lay its case out, witnesses and all. Normally, examining trials took place prior to indictment, with the end result being a judge's recommendation as to whether or not the case could proceed to the grand jury. Midge hadn't been entitled to an examining trial as a minor, however, and Sharon had already confirmed that she could now ask for one, her conviction bolstered by a short chat with Judge Griffin. Fraterno wouldn't know about the talk with the judge, of course, and her smirk was based on her belief that the state could defeat a motion for an examining trial. "You'll have to do what you have to do," Fraterno said.

Sharon tightly gripped her fork and, mashing down, murdered a crouton in half. "I suppose we will. Making us go through all this is a little silly, Kathleen."

Fraterno moved her half-eaten plate of fettuccine to one side and placed her tea directly in front of her. "I can't control problems in the mail room."

"An intentional problem. We're entitled to your evidence."

Fraterno used a thumbnail to draw a line in the frost on her glass. "No one said that you weren't."

"One reason I was glad to see you on the case was that

we wouldn't expect to go through the same bullshit with you as we would with Milt. I guess I was wrong."

"I suppose you were."

Sharon had felt a wave of pity when she'd realized that Kathleen had something going with Breyer, of all people, but anger now blotted out any other emotion which Sharon might have room for. "So we're forced into an examining trial. God, Kathleen, I thought you had more class than this. What the hell has changed?"

"I don't see that anything has changed except for the uniform you're wearing," Fraterno said.

If she had any inkling of how close she was to wearing Sharon's wilted salad like an Easter bonnet, she might bolt from the restaurant. Sharon moved her salad bowl out of temptation's reach. "I'm a lawyer, you're a lawyer, and the law hasn't changed. One thing we always agreed on, it's pointless to give the other side a hard time just for the sake of giving one."

"It's also rather pointless," Fraterno said, "to put a black mark on a man's reputation just for the sake of doing it." Her hand was wrapped around her glass, and for just an instant Sharon expected claws to sprout catlike from the prosecutor's fingertips.

Sharon narrowed her eyes. "What did you say?" Two women at a nearby table interrupted their conversation to turn and stare. Sharon knew she was speaking too loudly, but at the moment didn't give a damn. "Say that again," she said.

Fraterno lowered her eyes. "Nothing."

Sharon drummed her fingers, then folded her hands in her lap and lowered her voice. "I'm only going to say this one time, Kathleen, and I don't really know why I'm telling you this much. I've never said one word to anyone about Milton Breyer. Period."

Fraterno look up slowly. "*You* say."

"That's right, Kathleen. I say. I talked about what happened between Milt and me to Russ Black, during my job interview, and then only because I was worried about how it might affect my job. And you can bet your sweet ass that Russ hasn't told anybody else. The only reason anyone knows what went on is that two lawyers happened to be looking into the witness room when Milt reached out and tweaked my breast. I confess I may have overreacted a bit, but the next guy who grabs my boob when I don't invite him to is liable to be walking doubled over just like Milton. And for you two to try to railroad this poor teenage girl into prison just because Mr. Breyer has his feelings hurt . . . Well, the two of you should be in jail instead of Midge Rathermore."

Fraterno sat up indignantly. "Now, don't be accusing me. This murder case was in the mill long before you became one of the defense team."

"I'll grant you that," Sharon said. "But as far as I know, your office wasn't withholding evidence until Milt became the prosecutor and I went to work for Russ. Oh, to hell with it. I'm glad we had this conversation. At least we know to go ahead with our motion for examining trial." Sharon stood and scooped up the check from the table. "My treat, Madame Prosecutor. See you in court." She stalked to the cash register, nearly running over two busboys on the way, and was so testy in handing over her American Express card that the woman behind the register asked if something was wrong with the food. Sharon had even forgotten that the salad wasn't up to par; she shook her head at the woman, signed the ticket, and left with her eyes front and her spike heels clicking angrily on corridor tile. She'd climbed out of the tunnel and proceeded a half block down Main Street before the blood pounding in her temples had slowed to where the traffic noises penetrated her ears.

Sharon was so angry that she nearly walked past the portrait shop on her way back to the office. Landers Photography was a narrow storefront on Elm Street and difficult to notice, and it was only when the aerial shot of downtown Dallas caught her eye from the display window that Sharon realized she'd passed the entrance. She doubled back, said breathlessly, "Pardon me," to the man with whom she almost collided in her about-face, and entered the store. She dug in her purse, presented her claim check to a fiftyish woman in a print dress, and stood first on one foot and then the other while she waited for her order. As she hefted her purse up onto the counter, lunchtime pedestrian traffic paraded back and forth outside the display window.

You've blown your cool, dopey, Sharon thought.

Throwing a fit in front of Kathleen Fraterno would only
add fuel to the fire. Sharon pictured Fraterno and Milt—
the revolting bastard—laying up in the old sack together
as Kathleen said, "And then she grabbed the check, tee-
hee, and then twitched her butt on out of there, tee-hee,
and then, oh, Milton, *don't ever stop doing that*." Sharon's mouth tugged to one side as she tried to figure a
way to turn the restaurant scene to her—and Midge
Rathermore's—advantage. She didn't see any way. The
saleslady showed Sharon a curious look as she returned
from the back and laid a wrapped package up on the
counter. "Everything all right?" the lady said.

"Fine. Just fine." Sharon turned on a smile, which required more than a little effort. The woman smiled in return. Sharon picked up the package and turned it around.
"Mind if I have a look?"

"Be my guest." The woman was a grandmotherly early
sixties with gray hair and rosy cheeks, and wore wire-
framed Mrs. Santa glasses. "You must be proud of that.
Who took it?"

Sharon ripped thin white paper and looked at the natural pose of herself, Oreo cookie box held in front as she
ascended the steps to Russ Black's office. The photo shop
had done a corker of a framing job, plain chrome siding
with a dull plastic, nonreflecting insert to protect the picture. "Just a guy I met," Sharon said. "Strangest thing.
Do you really like it?"

"I wouldn't say if I didn't," the lady said. "If you know
how to get in touch with the photographer, I'd like to talk
to him about doing some things for us on a contract basis."

"If I ever see him again, I'll tell him," Sharon said. "I
wonder if he could take a portrait of my daughter. She's
eleven. I think this guy could do a good job on her."

16

Bradford Brie had every intention of making contact with Sharon Hays, and very soon. Anybody who had it in for Wilfred Donello could expect to reckon with Bradford Brie, and could expect that they would not enjoy the reckoning. It was the way things were with guys who'd been close in prison. There was a bond for life. To his way of thinking, the fact that Bradford Brie bent over and grabbed his ankles for only one man in this world said all about the relationship that needed saying.

Antsy as he was to get his hands on Sharon Hays, no way was he going to be stupid about it. A dumb guy, maybe one of those Aryan Brotherhood types who talked a good game but were the stupidest cons in the joint, one of those guys would have gone in after the woman just a day or so after poisoning her dog. Doing that would be dumber than shit, Brie thought. The woman was no moron, and right after she'd lost her dog her guard would be up nine miles high. Likely right now she had the black-and-whites cruising by her place two or three times a day. It would take a couple of weeks for the police to lose interest and go to goofing off, which was what squad-car cops did best of all, so Brie decided to leave Sharon Hays alone for a while. Let her cool down for a time, that was the smart way to go about it. Then, once she'd gotten to thinking that things were back to normal, *boom*. Hit her before she knew what the hell was going on.

Brie regretted that he hadn't been able to hang around and watch the German shepherd die. Brie had intended

to watch every delicious second—old Fido galloping
dumbass out into the yard, wolfing down the meat, then
dying nice and slow while kicking and clawing at the
dirt—and had even loaded down his pockets with film
and brought his camera along. Just as dusk fell, he'd
tossed the four-pound hunk of meat and bone over the
fence, gristle and sinew peppered with strychnine, spinning lazily through the air to land, rebound, then settle on
the grass. Brie had at first wanted to use arsenic, but had
read up and learned that strychnine would put more
wrenching pain in the shepherd's gut. With the hook
baited, Brie had sat down in the alley, camera ready, and
waited for the shepherd to come outside and die.

But an elderly woman had scared Brie away. The photographer still couldn't understand it, a wrinkled old
broad, seventy-five if she was a day, screwing around in
her flower bed across the alley from the lawyer lady's
house. What in hell had the old crone been doing outside
at that time of day? Brie wondered. The woman had worn
baggy pants and a huge sunbonnet, and had been putt-
ering around her rosebushes, shears in hand, a snip here
and a snip there. She'd paused in her work and, hands on
hips, had gaped at Brie across her low picket fence. The
woman's eyes had narrowed under her hat brim, and
she'd set her wrinkled lips in a line of disapproval. Brie
had pretended not to notice the old broad, had just sat
there fiddling with the adjustment on his camera lens, all
the time measuring the height of the picket fence, certain
that he could vault over into the old woman's yard in half
a second. He'd nearly gone after her, too, tensing his
muscles for the charge, but just as he had risen into a
starting crouch, she had turned from her rosebushes and
headed for her back porch at top-speed waddle. Brie had
plenty of experience in casing burglary prospects, and if
there was anyone who knew when one of the neighbors
was headed inside to use the phone and report something
suspicious, that person was Bradford Brie. He had actually risen, put his camera aside, and had taken a couple of
steps toward the old lady's fence when the man had appeared.

Brie had about crapped in his drawers when the wrinkled old fart had come out through the woman's back
door. The old man, stooped in the standard aching-back

posture, had waited on the porch as the woman approached. She'd set down her basket of roses and gestured with her shears in Brie's direction, talking to the old man a mile a minute. Christ, even as old and helpless as the couple had been, there was no way that Brie could have taken care of both of them. He didn't have a gun—no way was a smart ex-con like Bradford Brie going to be caught with a piece on him—and while he was using his bare hands on one of the old people, the other would be inside calling the law.

So Brie had decided to split. He'd left at a fast walk, scooping up his camera and adjusting his sunglasses on his nose, and had actually smiled at the old couple as he'd whistled his way down the alley in the direction of his car. See, old folks, nothing to worry about, just a man out here taking a few pictures.

Once inside his beat-up old Chrysler, Brie had taken a white-knuckled grip on the steering wheel and had a talk with himself. Christ, but he'd wanted to feel the old woman's neck in his hands, hear the soft pop of bone as her windpipe collapsed, watch her eyes bulge from their sockets, her tongue poke out of her mouth as she gasped for air. But killing the old woman would have ended all chance for Brie to make contact with the lawyer lady, so he had bided his time. As he'd driven away, he'd been careful not to exceed the speed limit.

Aside from giving Sharon Hays a cooling-down period after the loss of her dog, Bradford Brie had other things to worry about. He was almost broke. Money had been good before Wilfred Donello had gone to jail, but since his conviction, Brie had yet to earn a dime. He needed money. It would require some travel, but Brie knew exactly where a man handy with a camera was always in demand.

So, on the morning after Brie tossed the poisoned meat into Sharon Hays's backyard, he tooled his LeBaron over to Pep Boys'. There he hovered over the mechanic while the worker changed the oil, changed the filter, and replaced all of the hoses under the Chrysler's hood. Brie didn't like the size of the bill, and let the assholes at Pep Boys' cashier's desk know about it. Christ, but those mechanics were a bunch of crooks. With the LeBaron in road-worthy condition, Brie traveled south on I-35. As the Dallas skyline grew smaller in the rearview, he sang over and over the only Spanish-language ditty to which he knew the words. The song was *"La Cucaracha."* Brie's voice cracked occasionally as he sang, and he couldn't carry a tune in a bushel basket. What he lacked in style, he made up for in enthusiasm.

Two weeks later—at the precise instant, in fact, when Sharon Hays entered Landers Photography to pick up her picture—Bradford Brie stepped on a cockroach. *Crunch,* take that, you hideous fucker. Bug bone snapped. Brown juice squirted on the sole of Brie's shoe and sprayed the nasty linoleum floor. Never in Brie's life, not even in the Texas Department of Corrections, had he seen so many roaches. Christ, he'd been living with the bastards.

Brie wiped his shoe on the pink throw rug as he stepped closer to the bed to aim the camera. The bed posts were rusted iron; cotton stuffing poked out here and there from the mattress. One filthy sheet lay on top of the mattress in a crumpled pile. On the bed were two naked people, a bearded olive-skinned boy in his twenties and a girl of fifteen or sixteen. The girl's skin was midway between black and brown. Her belly was taut, and there were pale stretch marks on her abdomen. Her long hair was black and greasy, and showed dandruff like oily flakes of snow. Springs creaked as she bent to take the boy's erect penis in her mouth. Her breasts hung; her big brown nipples touched the mattress.

"Not too fast," Brie said. "We don't want him shootin' off, not yet." The button on the camera clicked, the room filled with instant blinding light. Brie reached out to adjust the portable screen, moving it closer to the bed. " 'At's it, honey," Brie said. "Take it on *down.* Deepthroat that fucker, atta babe. Jose. Hey, Jose, you gotcha a real *seen*-yor eater here. *Seen*-yor eater, get it?" Clickflash. Brie cackled, lowered the camera, raised the camera again, and squinted through the viewfinder with one pale-skinned eye. His sunglasses lay on a scarred table with the eyepieces folded over.

The girl continued to take the boy's penis in and out, in and out. She raised one lid and regarded Brie with a bored brown-eyed stare.

The Hispanic man who was seated beside the table

yawned. He had a Fu Manchu mustache and goatee, and wore faded, ripped jeans along with a skin-tight Dallas Cowboys T-shirt. The shirt rode up to reveal a round, taut belly. A whirring video camera was beside the man, mounted unattended on a tripod. One bright light was on a stand by his shoulder, its beam directed on the bed. "Them pipple don't understand what you're saying," he told Brie.

"Maybe not, Jose." Click-flash. "Maybe not, but they know what I'm telling 'em. Come on, darlin', you're supposed to be enjoying yourself. Me and old Jose ain't paying for no deadass pussy. You want to get paid, you put something in it."

The girl redoubled her efforts, rising up on her haunches, the movement of her head accompanied by a slurping noise. A drop of perspiration rolled around her waist, leaving a rivulet in its wake, and dripped onto her thigh. The boy on the bed put his head back and closed his eyes.

"See there?" Brie said. "They understand good, Jose. It's the universal language, you know?"

"My name is Guillermo," the man beside the table said. "Le's don' be forgetting that chit."

"Yeah, okay, I got a bad memory. All the way, Dallas to Nuevo Laredo, I tell myself, fucker's named Guillermo. I'm bad on that, ain't I, Jose?" Click-flash. "Yeah, darlin', yeah. Oh, yeah, work it on out."

"Twelve years I been telling you, my name Guillermo. All the time on Wynne Farm, we picking that cotton and chit, you keep calling me Jose. You keep forgetting my name, we liable to have big problems, bro."

Brie paused and regarded Guillermo over his shoulder. "We can't have no disagreements, Jose, we got too much of a good thing going. We get crosswise, we both wind up in the same cell with Wilfred Donello."

Guillermo reached up under his shirt to scratch his stomach. "You don't want to go to no Mexican jail, bro. These joints down here make TDC look like a fuckin' Hyatt House."

"So I hear." Brie's nose wrinkled as he aimed the camera. "Yeah, so I hear. But you and me don't have to worry about that. This here makes a hundred and sixteen rolls of film, Jose. Fifty-eight for me, fifty-eight for you. Tomor-

row I'm going back to God's country. You're going to
owe me thirty-eight hundred Uncle Sam U.S. dollars, any
problem with that?"

"No problem at all," Guillermo said. "You keep doing
good work, you keep getting paid." He patted the video
camera. "I still get the tapes, huh?"

"All yours, babe. I wouldn't give two cents for no
moving pictures, man. You show them smokers to a
crowd, you got too many people talking. These wallet-
sizes, you can sell them one on one and never get no heat
from it. I told you before, showing them fuck movies is
going to get your ass busted."

"You leaving tomorrow? I thought you staying another
week." Guillermo scratched his beard and dubiously eyed
the video camera, as if he was picturing himself caught in
a motel raid.

"Naw." Click-flash. "Naw, I got business. Jesus, honey,
hold on a minute." He reached out over the bed and
touched the girl's shoulder. She looked up, blinking in the
spotlight's glare. "Just one little second, hon," Brie said.
"You finish him with your hand. *Su mano, comprende?*"

The girl nodded. She wrapped her fist around the boy's
penis and flogged away, her tiny hand looking as if it
were encircling a baseball bat. The boy moaned and
writhed on the bed.

"That's right, darlin'," Brie said, moving around for a
better angle, clicking the button. "Go on, go on. Get it,
you hear me?"

Semen spurted onto the girl's chin and breasts. The boy
bucked up and down.

"Good one. Good *wan.*"

Finished with their performance, the couple rose. The
girl tore paper towels from a roll, handed a wad to the
boy, then used a fistful to wipe herself.

Brie turned to Guillermo. "Meet you outside here, say,
ten o'clock in the morning. I get the money, you get the
film."

"Right on, bro." Guillermo's head tilted in a listening
attitude as the girl spoke to him in rapid Spanish. He answered her. The naked boy said something, also in Spanish, and Guillermo answered him as well. Finally
Guillermo turned to Brie. "They wonder if you want them
tonight. A freebie. These pipple, they busting to please."

Brie snapped the camera open to remove the exposed film. He grinned. "Yeah? Sure, why not. The more the merrier, hey?"

Brie rose early the next morning, scooting carefully down the center of the bed and standing from the end to keep from disturbing the boy and the girl. He'd slept in between the two. The boy lay on his stomach with one hairy leg bent and his knee resting close to his chest. The girl slept on her side with her cheek on the palm of her hand. Brie paused to watch the couple. Jesus, what a scene, huh? He pictured himself, sometime during the night, humping the girl from behind while the boy crawled up between his legs to lick the gringo's balls. One for the books. Brie crept around the room to retrieve his clothes.

One of his pants pockets was turned inside out. He considered waking the boy and girl to whip the daylights out of them, then changed his mind. What, fifty bucks? Wasn't worth the effort, and anybody dumb enough to go to sleep with his bankroll unprotected deserved to lose the money. He went into the bathroom to retrieve the rest of his money, which was encased in Cling-wrap and suspended inside the filthy toilet tank. Back in the bedroom, he stepped into his dirty white pants and zipped them up. His loud Hawaiian shirt smelled of perspiration. He put it on. When he picked up his shoes, roaches scattered in all directions.

Brie loaded the lights, camera, and battered suitcase into the LeBaron, then drove over to meet Guillermo. The Mexican was on time as agreed, and handed Brie a wad of American money in exchange for fifty-eight rolls of prime-quality pussy film. Brie had thought of something during the night, and now slung his arm around Guillermo's shoulders to make a request in hushed tones. Guillermo nodded, then led the way on foot two blocks down dusty streets with water-filled gutters to knock on the door of an adobe shack. An old man answered. Brie then paid the old man two hundred dollars for four sets of steel handcuffs, fifty feet of quarter-inch rope, and an eighteen-inch dildo. Two sets of cuffs were for the lawyer lady and her daughter; the spare cuffs were just in case the lady's nigger friends happened to be along. Bradford Brie thought of everything. He didn't expect to have to deal with the jungle bunny and her picaninny, but a smart and stand-up con like Bradford Brie came prepared. Besides, a little salt-and-pepper action would make good film.

Barely an hour later, Brie stopped at the border checkpoint on the U.S. side of the Rio Grande bridge. He told the Customs people that he had nothing in his car except for his clothing and picture-taking equipment, then snugged up his sunglasses and watched the tourists—women in slacks or shorts, men showing white legs in Bermudas with cheapass cameras dangling from their necks—stream back and forth between the States and Mexico while the federal assholes searched the LeBaron's trunk. Finally the Customs agent made a notation on a clipboard and waved the old Chrysler through. Brie had known that the feds wouldn't search his pocket; the stupid assholes never did.

With Mexico now behind him, one smart con named Bradford Brie pointed the LeBaron's nose north on the San Antonio highway. It was a six-hundred-mile drive to Dallas, and Brie would take his time. By now the lawyer lady would have gotten over the poisoning of her dog, and would just now be letting down her guard. And that's just the way a smart con like Bradford Brie wanted the broad. He briefly pictured Sharon Hays's little girl, her scrawny legs as she'd dashed through the rain into the schoolhouse. Brie wasn't certain, but thought the child was old enough to sprout some pubic hair.

17

As Kathleen Fraterno called state's witness Christopher Leonard to the stand, Sharon Hays leaned back and whispered to Anthony Gear, "The redhead, third row. He's the other one."

Anthony Gear was seated just behind and in between Sharon and Midge Rathermore at the defense table. Gear was a private detective who had retired from the FBI three years ago. He was in his fifties, dark-complexioned, with sagging jowls. His face was lined with sun wrinkles. Gear wore dark slacks, a plaid sports coat, a yellow shirt, and a dark green tie. Russ Black had employed the detective two other times, and had told Sharon that Gear wasn't any more of a goof-off than any other private cop. Given Black's opinion of retired law enforcement people in general, the older lawyer's assessment was high praise. Sharon had called Deborah North in Oklahoma City, and Midge's mom had borne the additional expense without batting an eye.

Gear directed his attention three rows deep in the spectator section. State's witness Troy Burdette was seated in between his parents. Burdette's mother wore a pale red suit and a fifty-dollar Neiman-Marcus upswept hairdo. The witness's father was in a blue pinstripe suit that was five hundred dollars off the rack if it was a dime. Troy Burdette had bright red hair and wore an oversized gray polo shirt. If Sharon hadn't known that this kid had helped bludgeon a man to death, he would have had her vote for Most Likely to Succeed. True to form, the state had permitted its witnesses to remain free on bond for the duration of the Rathermore trial. Though the cushy deal cut for the two young murderers was reduced to writing, it wasn't engraved in stone. The boys' sentencing wasn't to occur until after Midge's trial, and the degree to which the state lived up to its bargain was dependent on the witnesses' testimony. So goes justice, Sharon thought.

Defense counsel had waived The Rule for purposes of the examining trial. The Rule, if invoked, would have required that all witnesses stay outside the courtroom during testimony, and the waiving of The Rule had caused glances of triumph between Fraterno and Milt Breyer. The prosecution's joy, Sharon knew, was just fine with Russell Black. The Rule was a sham to begin with; Breyer and Fraterno would have filled their witnesses in on testimony during breaks in the action anyway. With the witnesses in the courtroom, Anthony Gear could have a good look at Leonard, Burdette, and, hopefully, Midge's stepmother, Linda Rathermore. Gear turned to Sharon and whispered, "I've already got Burdette on my list." Sharon nodded and returned her gaze to the front.

Christopher Leonard raised his right hand. The clerk asked Leonard if he swore to tell the truth, the whole truth, and nothing but the truth, so help Leonard God. Leonard responded with a subdued "I do," just as the D.A.'s would have tutored him. This boy was tall, dark-haired, and rangy as a rookie golf pro. As he listened to Fraterno's initial question, he broke into a what-me-worry grin. The jury's going to love this pair, Sharon thought.

"Please state your full name for the record."

"Christopher Thomas Leonard." Voice straight from *Dobie Gillis*.

Sharon tuned out the testimony and madly searched her notes. Prior to the court's convening there had been a meeting in Judge Griffin's chambers, during which Fraterno had raised the roof over the defense's shotgun approach at Midge's certification hearing. The judge had instructed that whichever defense attorney began questioning of a witness, the same lawyer had to ask all questions until another witness took the stand. Black had pow-wowed with Sharon, and the two had agreed that he was to ask the questions today while she attended to other knitting. She located a name on her legal pad, wrote

"Leslie Schlee," on a phone slip, underlined the name twice, tore off the page, and nudged Anthony Gear. Gear leaned forward.

Sharon whispered, "This chick. She's the one that originally snitched on these boys. We need to know all about her and why she's not on the state's witness list. Chris Leonard's her boyfriend. Or was." She handed the slip to Gear. Gear nodded, folded the slip, and put it away.

Sharon turned to the front to find Judge Griffin staring daggers at her. Sandy Griffin had wavy blond hair, a smooth forehead, and a pointed chin. She had left the D.A.'s office to run for judge during Sharon's third year as a prosecutor. As a lawyer, Judge Griffin had been every bit as thorough as Kathleen Fraterno, which was saying a mouthful. The judge shunned all social activity—which had caused speculation among some as to whether Sandy Griffin was a lesbian, which Sharon considered a crock—her only apparent passion the law. She would listen open-mindedly to arguments from both sides, and she didn't stand for any bullshit in her courtroom. Sharon showed the judge an apologetic smile and pretended to concentrate on what the witness was saying.

Fraterno's question was: "And it was just this year that you transferred from public to private school?"

Sharon already knew the answer. The fine young man now testifying on behalf of the state had been a student at W.T. White, a public high school, and had stolen the principal's car. The court had granted juvenile probation, and daddy had opened his wallet to send the kid to St. Mark's. Had really straightened the boy out, Sharon thought. Now he's only a murderer. Leonard answered yes to Fraterno's question.

"Would you please tell the court how you first became acquainted with Midge Rathermore?"

On Sharon's right, Midge yanked on a wad of greasy hair that was plastered together. On Sharon's special request the court had ordered Midge provided with clothes that fit, the result being that she now wore a male prisoner's jumpsuit the size of a circus tent. Her body odor permeated the surrounding area; when Anthony Gear had first spotted the client, the detective had visibly winced.

"Midge?" Leonard said.

"Yes." Fraterno was alone on the prosecution side, her

company being two empty chairs that normally would have held the respective fannies of Milton Breyer and Stan Green. After the preliminary jousting in the judge's office, Breyer had made excuses and left. Milt had announced over the weekend as a candidate for the currently vacant congressional seat for the North Dallas/ Highland Park district, and likely was off to meddle in politics. Stan Green, Sharon knew, was seated at the rear of the courtroom with Linda Rathermore. The homicide cop would be giving the state's star witness some last-minute prompting, and likely would be trying to figure the closest route into Linda's pants. Fat chance of that, Sharon thought. Fraterno folded her hands and waited for Leonard to answer.

"First time I ever saw Midge was at a dance," Leonard said.

"A school function?"

"Yes, ma'am."

"St. Mark's and Hockaday are socially coordinated, aren't they?"

Leonard showed the Alfred E. Neuman grin. "Beg pardon?"

"I mean, Hockaday invites St. Mark's boys to their dances, and vice versa."

"Yes, ma'am, that's true. This was a Christmas dance last year."

"And who introduced you to Miss Rathermore?" Fraterno said.

"Nobody, exactly. There were all these guys around her."

"Was one of them Miss Rathermore's date?"

Leonard looked at Midge. His grin widened. "Oh, no, ma'am. Nobody'd ask old Midge for a date." He snickered, and an answering giggle came from the spectator pews. Sharon turned. Troy Burdette had a hand cupped over his mouth. After a stern nudge from his father, young Troy straightened up.

Coldness clutched Sharon's insides as she glanced at Midge. Since her transfer to the main jail, her complexion had cleared and she'd even lost some weight. Sharon was familiar with the Lew Sterrett menu from her days as a prosecutor, and understood why Midge was thinner. "Thinner" didn't mean "more attractive" in Midge's case because the weight loss had created folds of loose, blotchy skin. The pitiful teenager regarded her own intertwined fingers. Nothing in life, Sharon thought, could be more heartbreaking than being the girl whom no one wanted to date, and even Midge was bright enough to feel the pain. Sharon blinked a tear back and concentrated on the testimony.

Fraterno spoke in a flat monotone. "So she had no date, but there were boys around her. What happened next?"

Christopher Leonard continued to smile. "This guy, I think it was a guy named Randy, told me they were fixing to get her outside."

Sharon gently closed her eyes as, on her left, Russ Black drew a breath. Since the purpose of the examining trial was to get the state's case out in the open, objections at this point would be foolish. But criminy, Sharon thought, do they have to get into this?

"Get her outside?"

"Yes, ma'am. For . . . you know."

Sharon looked at Judge Griffin, whose gaze was riveted on the table before her. Even the judge was having a hard time with this.

"For sex?" Fraterno said.

"Yes, ma'am."

Fraterno paused for effect, then said, "And did they?"

"Sure did."

"Chris, weren't there chaperones at these school functions?"

"They had some, some teachers and parents. Nobody paid much attention to us."

Now even Fraterno sounded put off. "So you and the other boys took Miss Rathermore outside?"

"To a car. Yes, ma'am."

"And you'd never seen Miss Rathermore before that night."

"Seen her, yeah." Leonard's grin was so maddening that Sharon wanted to stalk to the witness stand and slap the boy's face, contempt citation or no. "Old Midge is hard to miss." Leonard's smile broadened.

"Young man." Sandy Griffin sat stiffly forward, her voice like that of a drill sergeant. "I'm going to instruct you to answer the questions without the added humor. If you think these proceedings are funny, maybe they'll look more serious to you from jail." The judge looked at Black like, That's all the help I can give you.

The smirk disappeared from Leonard's face, and he looked down at his knees.

"Chris," Fraterno said, "how many boys had sex with Midge Rathermore that evening? As best you remember."

On Sharon's right, Midge sniffled. A tear rolled down, streaking blotchy skin.

"It's hard to say," Leonard said. "Must have been twelve or thirteen. I was way back in line."

Anthony Gear touched Sharon's elbow from behind. She turned as he jerked a thumb toward the rear of the courtroom. "This note," he whispered, offering a folded slip of paper. "Lady back there wants you."

Sharon gazed past rows of reporters, who were madly scribbling on steno pads, and zeroed in on the courtroom exit. Good God, Sharon thought.

Deborah North stood behind the last row of spectator pews. Deb was watching the witness stand, an expression on her face as if she were viewing a horror movie. Her mouth was open in shock.

Sharon made tracks. Ignoring the questioning look from Judge Griffin, she went through the gate and hurried up the aisle. Stan Green and Linda Haymon Rathermore were in the two seats nearest the aisle on Sharon's left, two rows from the back. Linda was blond and showcase beautiful, with the confident posture of someone used to being in the public eye. The homicide cop seemed out of his element, clodhopper Romeo beside Royal Princess. He glanced up at Sharon. She ignored him, reached the rear of the courtroom, and hustled Deborah North out into the corridor.

"I'm sorry you had to hear that," Sharon said.

Deborah North sank onto a bench like a deflating tire. "My sweet Jesus," she said.

Sharon sat down as well. "I want you to know that's the first time we've heard that garbage."

"Even if it's true," Deb said, "what's the point?" She wrung her hands.

"It goes to the character of the defendant," Sharon said, "which the state is entitled to present. I'll have to think on it, but that crap might backfire in front of a jury. It shows that Midge might not be, well, all there."

"That she'd do that . . ."

"I know," Sharon said. "I wish you hadn't come. My message was just for you to call me."

"I couldn't stand sitting up there in Oklahoma doing nothing, so I drove down this morning." Deb wore matching green slacks and blouse, with a light green scarf at her throat. She touched the scarf. "I'd meant to go shopping and come by your office later, but I couldn't stay away."

"Has anyone from the prosecution tried to contact you?" Sharon said.

Deb shook her head no.

"Well, they might. They know you're her mother. Listen, I called you because if we're going to help Midge, we're going to have to change some ground rules."

Deb raised one plucked brown eyebrow.

"None of us can communicate with Midge," Sharon said. "She'll brighten if you want to talk about what's on at the movies, but anytime we try to discuss the case, she clams up. Her contribution thus far is less than zero. Defending a client who won't help you is next to impossible."

"I suppose it hurts her," Deb said. "It hurts me, too."

"That makes three of us. Believe me. Here's what we're facing, Deb. Midge is emotionally disturbed, but an insanity defense is out of the question because the crime is premeditated. The defense we're about to hang our hats on has to do with sexual abuse, father against daughter. Her sister . . . Susan, is that right?"

Deb looked at Sharon like, yes, it is.

"According to the only information we've been able to get out of Midge, he abused Susan. I suspect he may have tried to put the girls in competition for his attention in some way. If we have a chance in this world, we're going to have to prove the abuse against Susan, and Susan's own words are the only things that can help us. We need for Susan to testify."

Deb seemed far away, an exceptionally attractive woman approaching middle age, not wanting to face up to the fact that she'd given up her children, taken the money, and run. Sharon's own choice to raise Melanie the best way possible come hell or high water gave her trouble working up sympathy for Deb. Sharon had a boat load of compassion for Midge, however, and needed Deb's help in the worst of ways.

"I'm listening," Deb finally said.

"Susan's vanished," Sharon said. "Oh, the prosecution knows where she is, you can bet on that, and so does Linda Rathermore. Susan withdrew from Hockaday School three days after the murders, and the people at the school don't know beans about her whereabouts. Anthony Gear—that's the investigator we've hired—I suspect Mr. Gear can locate Susan pretty quickly, but finding her is only part of the problem. The only chance we're going to have in getting Susan to talk about what happened is for you to intercede, Deb. It'll strip you of your anonymity, but I think it's the only way. Susan won't respond to me or Russ Black any more than Midge is doing. We have to have your help, and I mean with something besides your checkbook."

Deb fumbled with her purse. "Can I smoke here?"

Sharon glanced up and down the hall. "All these county buildings are designated smoke-free, but wait a minute." She got up and went down the hall to a utility closet. Two custodians were inside, smoking like fiends, their feet up, shooting the bull. The smoke in the closet was thick as acrid fog. Sharon excused herself, found an ashtray on a shelf, and returned to Deb. "Puff away," Sharon said. "If anyone says anything, I'll cover for you."

Deb lit up with trembling hands, puffed, inhaled. "I haven't told you this. But I did talk to Midge once, four years ago."

Sharon sat on the bench, crossed her legs, and folded her arms.

"It took some doing," Deb said. "Friend of a friend, a lady who taught Midge in grammar school. I arranged for this woman to take Midge to the school office and call me in Oklahoma. I remember my one and only line. 'Hello, darling. This is your mother.' "

Deb watched smoke drift toward the ceiling. "She didn't say anything for . . . about thirty seconds, I guess." Her face twisted in anguish. "Then she screamed something like, 'My *mother*? I *hate you*.' She said a few other things as well. Called me a wrinkled old bitch, if my memory serves me correctly. Do you wonder why I haven't tried to contact the kids anymore?"

"I know that was tough," Sharon said. "And I can't

promise there won't be another scene. But something's got to shock both Susan and Midge into talking to us, and I don't know anything other than a confrontation with their real mother that might help."

Deb's mouth bunched at the corners. "What do you want me to do?"

"As far as Susan goes," Sharon said, "we can cross that bridge when and if Mr. Gear locates her. But I want you to go with me to visit Midge tonight, in the special lawyers' visiting area at the jail. I'll arrange for us to be alone with her. For what it's worth, you can count on me for a shoulder to lean on."

Deb stubbed out her cigarette. Smoke rose from the ashtray in a thin bluish line. "I'll go," she said. "I'll do anything that might help. But get ready to hang onto me. If my daughter rejects me again, I might run screaming out of the room."

Kathleen Fraterno's tone now hinted of horror afoot. "Chris, are you certain that's what she told you?"

"Positive. Yes, ma'am." Christopher Leonard, mop of black hair swept low on his forehead, straight from *Beverly Hills 90210*.

"In the food court at Valley View Mall, where you kids gathered from time to time?"

"In front of the taco stand," Leonard said. "Midge ate a lotta tacos." The corners of his mouth turned up, then immediately straightened.

"And this was right after she gave you the slip of paper with the security code written on it. The code for disarming the Rathermores' burglar alarm."

"Sure was."

Fraterno bent forward in her chair to peer around Russell Black and Sharon, and to fix an accusing gaze directly on Midge. "This is very important, Chris," Fraterno said. "So there will be no question. Repeat for the court what Midge Rathermore said to you at that time." She leaned back and calmly watched the witness.

"She sa—" Leonard's voice broke. He cleared his throat. "She said that she wanted him dead."

"Her father?"

"Yes, ma'am."

"Dead."

"Yes, ma'am."

Fraterno rustled her file while, all through the courtroom, pens and pencils scratched as the reporters wrote madly away. Finally Fraterno looked at Russell Black. "Pass the witness," she said.

Sharon reached over to pat Midge's hand. Midge was watching Christopher Leonard with a look near hero worship. Thank God the jury's not here, Sharon thought. Defense attorneys normally waived cross in examining trials, not wishing to expose any hole cards, but Sharon and Black had agreed to ask a few questions in Midge's behalf. The defense was desperate for witnesses of their own.

"I'm Russell Black, Mr. Leonard," the older lawyer said, "representin' Miss Rathermore. Now, you said earlier that you and Mr. Burdette spent quite a bit of time over at the Rathermores', is that right?"

"Yeah," Leonard said, then caught Fraterno staring daggers in his direction and said more softly, "Yes, sir."

"So the Rathermores' house was a gathering place for you kids?"

"We went there a lot."

"To eat, watch a little television . . ."

"Kind of fool around, yes, sir."

". . . kind of rally around in a cozy atmosphere."

"Objection." Fraterno testily folded her arms.

"Sustained," Judge Griffin said. "Stick to the issues, please, Mr. Black."

"Sure thing, Judge. Were there any other kids makin' a habit of hanging around the Rathermore house, Mr. Leonard?"

"A few, sometimes."

"Mr. Leonard, do you know a young lady named Leslie Schlee?"

"Sure. Yes, sir."

"Was she at the Rathermores' sometimes?" Black said.

"I guess she was."

"Okay. Did Leslie Schlee, or anybody else, did anyone besides you and Mr. Burdette back there"—pointing at the spectator section, where the redhead sat between his parents—"hear Midge Rathermore make an offer to you two in exchange for killing her father?"

"No. It was just us three."

"Just you three," Black said. "What kids came over besides Leslie?"

Leonard flashed Fraterno a glance of alarm. "I'm not . . ."

"I'm askin' you," Black said, "what other teenagers, friends of yours, frequented the house at the same time you and Mr. Burdette were over there watchin' television and playin' Scrabble and whatnot. And plottin' to murder this man in his bedroom."

"Objection," from Fraterno.

"Sustained," from Judge Griffin, accompanied by an exasperated lifting of her eyebrows.

"I'll withdraw the last part," Black said. "Who else hung out over there, Mr. Leonard?"

Leonard seemed helpless; clearly the prosecution hadn't schooled their witness for this line of questioning. Unexpected queries in cross-examination generally brought the most truthful answers given in the courtroom. Sharon favored her boss with a look of respect.

"There might have been one or two others," Leonard finally said.

"One or two others. Can you remember any of their names?"

"Not except for Troy. The other kids, we didn't know them."

"How many other kids were there, Mr. Leonard?"

"Sometimes . . . fifteen or twenty, I guess."

Black stiffened in shock, and Sharon pressed so hard on her pencil, taking notes, that she nearly broke the point. As many as twenty high school kids, sitting around waiting their turns for sex with Midge, or perhaps even good old congenial Mr. and Mrs. Rathermore. Sharon quickly wrote a note on a yellow stick-up and passed it over her shoulder to Anthony Gear. "We need to find some of these kids," she whispered to the detective.

"And you can't give us one single name?" Black said.

Sharon noted that Fraterno was scribbling as well. The prosecutor laid down her pen and gave the witness a quizzical look.

"I never heard any," Leonard said.

"You sure of that?" Black's shaggy brows moved closer together.

"Yes, sir, I'm sure."

Black swiveled his head and looked at Sharon like, Anything else? She shrugged her shoulders. "No further questions," he said.

It was nearly five, so Judge Griffin recessed for the day. Midge docilely followed the bailiff back to the holding cell while Black held an off-to-one-side conference with Kathleen Fraterno. Sharon hadn't spoken to Kathleen since lunch at Joe Willie's, and purposefully remained at the defense table, polishing up her notes. Anthony Gear hustled to the back and out into the hall; Sharon had arranged for the detective to meet with Deborah North to pick her brain. Sharon felt a hand on her shoulder. She turned her head around.

Stan Green bent close and said rather sheepishly, "Didn't you get my messages?"

Christ, Sharon thought, his horn is honking. "All five of them, Stan. You used up nearly the whole tape on my machine." She lowered her head and continued to write.

Green lowered himself into a chair beside her. "Goddammit, Sharon, I need to see you."

Sharon pursed her mouth and expelled air. "It's over, Stan."

"No, it's not." His jaw thrust forward. "It's not over 'til I say it's over."

Sharon blinked in sudden anger. "God, what are you, Yogi Berra? It's finished. Kaput. You're wasting your time. And while we're at it, quit calling me and hanging up. Please be adult enough to say something when I answer the phone."

Green narrowed his eyes. "I don't know what you're talking about."

"I'm talking about grown men who act like children, calling women at three in the morning and then hanging up. One of these times a man may answer."

"I've never done anything like that in my life," he said.

Sharon studied his expression. He didn't look as if he was lying. Stan Green had an infantile streak a mile long, but . . .

"I don't believe you, Stan," Sharon finally said. "Who else would be calling me at that time of night?"

18

Assistant D.A. Edward Teeter entered the conference room and quickly assessed the situation: Vernon Riggs, dressed in a high-dollar blue suit, lounging in a chair with his shin propped against the long, polished table's edge; Wilfred Donello alongside his lawyer, Donello's close-set eyes glaring hatred, tattooed forearms showing muscle like twisted rope. Riggs's beard was freshly barbered, the top of his head smooth as sanded wood. Donello wore white jail-issue shirt and pants. Teeter halted just inside the door and pointed at Donello. Teeter said to the guard, "This guy's not handcuffed."

The uniformed sheriff's deputy, a thin-faced, clean-shaven man in his thirties, stood alone in the corner of the room. "You just said bring him over from the jail, you didn't say nothing about cuffing the guy. He's not going to pull anything with me standing here." The guard adjusted the revolver inside his Sam Browne holster for emphasis.

"Well, I'd just as soon," Teeter said, "that we don't have you shooting a gun off in the courthouse. The judges might get nervous, you know? So handcuff the asshole."

The guard frowned, but stepped quickly forward to cuff Donello to one arm of the chair. Attorney Riggs watched with an expression of mild amusement. Once Donello was cuffed, Teeter sat down across from prisoner and lawyer and grinned. "Mr. Donello," Teeter said. "How you doing?"

Donello rubbed his shackled wrist and gave a look like, How you think I'm doing?

"Things aren't going so well for you," Teeter said. "Well, maybe this will make you feel better." He set his briefcase on his lap, braced the edge of the case against his belly, and unsnapped the catches. He handed Donello's lawyer a letter in duplicate. "Here go, Vern," Teeter said. "One snitch contract, sealed, delivered, and ready for signing."

Riggs held the letter by one corner and fished in his pocket for bifocals. He read silently. Donello cracked his knuckles.

"I never been a snitch in my fuckin' life," Donello said.

Teeter squinted to make certain Donello's handcuff was secure, then breezily crossed his legs. "Let's just say," he said, "that you've never had the right opportunity. All you hardasses come over sooner or later. Being on the right side makes time easier to do. Trust me." Christ, Teeter thought, look at the arms on the guy.

Donello's expression said that he didn't trust the D.A. as far as he could spit. Donello started to say something, but Riggs stopped his client with a wave of his hand. Riggs took off his glasses and laid them on the table, lenses down, with the earpieces sticking up in the air.

"This isn't exactly the way we discussed." Riggs waved the letter.

Teeter stayed deadpan, but inside he was laughing. Jerking defense attorneys around was the way he got his jollies. "What's the problem?" he said. He winked at the guard.

"I think you already know the problem," Riggs said, dropping the letter alongside his glasses. "We talked about time. Ten years, you said, and my guy could be on the street in eighteen months. My client's agreeing to inform, but you're not specifying how much time he's going to do. Under this deal the judge could go ahead and give him the maximum."

"We're dropping the habitual clause in the guy's indictment," Teeter said.

"He can still get ninety-nine years," Riggs said. "Big deal."

Donello struggled, trying to rise. The handcuff chain

tautened and clinked. The guard stepped forward in a movie gunslinger pose. Donello sat down. "I knew not to trust these fuckers."

That's the ticket, Teeter thought, get 'em by the balls and then stick it to the guy. "Hold on," he said. "You got my word, the ten goes. Trust me." He smiled.

Riggs flattened his hand and made a sawing motion. "With nothing in writing, no way."

"Okay," Teeter said. "Let me tell you how it is. I'm not making any promises to this guy until I know his information's legitimate. He says he can give us the guy did Howard Saw. There's a lot of people around town think whoever offed Howard should get a medal. But I'm a prosecutor. I got to prosecute, right? So if Donello gives up the guy, a deal's a deal. But no way am I going to specify short time in writing until I got the fucking guy downtown here. What if we give Mr. Donello the ten and then he don't know shit, huh? I'm going to look pretty stupid."

Now it was Riggs's turn to put on an Honest Abe expression. "His information's good, Ed. We've got to meet one another halfway."

Teeter stabbed the air with a finger. "Let me tell you what's halfway. Your man is halfway to doing so much time he'll be eating baby food by the time he hits the streets. I'm halfway to walking the fuck out of here and forgetting the whole thing. It's just another case to me. Now. He gives us information about Howard Saw, sits up and testifies like a little man, the ten years is solid. One fuckup between indictment and conviction on your boy's part, and there's no deal. *Nada.* Take it or leave it."

Riggs put on his bifocals and pointed at the letter. "Well, what's wrong with reducing *that* to writing? What you just said. If Donello renegs, the deal's off. What's wrong with that?"

Teeter had known before he entered this meeting that he was going to pull the carpet routine, and decided that the time was right. "What's wrong with it," he said, "is that I'm not putting shit in writing. You got that. Now. You see that line?" The prosecutor pointed at the open corridor door. The conference room carpet was beige. The hallway carpet was green. The two carpets were joined in the doorway by a line of stitches. "I'm headed out of here," Teeter said. "You want the deal, you make up your mind, right now. Once my foot lands on green carpet, the deal's off. I got no more time to fuck with your client."

Teeter stood and straightened his coat. He picked up the letter and put it away in his briefcase. Riggs sat still, not saying anything. Teeter hefted his briefcase and took measured steps, one, two, three, four, and prepared to walk through the doorway. The carpet routine never failed. Determination was the key, no hesitation, convincing the defense lawyer that you were walking the fuck out and there was no turning back. Teeter lifted his foot.

Donello said, "Wait a minute."

Teeter relaxed, withdrew his foot from the hallway, and stepped down on beige carpet. He turned, smiling. "Yeah?"

Riggs pointed at a chair. "Sit down, Ed."

Teeter returned to sit. Ah, the carpet routine. He crossed his legs. "Okay, I'm listening."

Donello wiped his mouth with the back of his hand. "I got more than I told you."

"Oh?" Teeter said. "Imagine that."

"More information," Donello said.

Sure, he does, Teeter thought. Nothing like the old carpet routine to get 'em to singing the high notes. "If you got more, you might make a better deal," Teeter said.

"This guy I'm talking," Donello said. "He done Howard Saw, okay. But there's somebody else he's planning to off. A woman."

Teeter lifted his eyebrows. A snitch telling about a murder was one thing. But *preventing* a killing? Edward Teeter, veteran county prosecutor, saving a victim's life? He could see the headlines now. "Interesting," he said, leaning forward. "Tell me, Mr. Donello. Who is this woman?"

19

Sharon chewed her lower lip, crossed her fingers, and would have crossed her toes if there'd been more room in the pointed ends of her shoes. For a lawyer to become emotionally involved in one of her cases was unprofessional at best—and destructive at worst—but Sharon couldn't help her feelings. Every time Midge Rathermore showed one of her pitifully vacant looks, every time the mountain of a girl slouched into court or the jail visiting room wearing clothes which fit her like flappy tent material ... well, at just the sight of Midge, Sharon's heart dropped into the pit of her stomach. There simply had to be a way to get through to the child.

And if Sharon was nervous, Deborah North was a basket case over her first meeting with her daughter in eight years. Sharon wondered if she should have brought a tranquilizer along. As the women waited in the attorney visiting booth at the jail for Midge's entrance, Deb wrung her hands until her knuckles were white. Her nails dug into her palms, leaving bloodless lines.

There was no bulletproof plastic shield in the attorney section; all that separated the prisoner and visitor was a row of thin steel bars. A six-inch slot was under the bars, a hole for passing papers back and forth, and in the attorney visiting section prisoners and visitors could touch one another. Opposed to the closely monitored bullpens, in the attorney section guards stayed outside the booths and minded their own business because the Constitution guaranteed prisoners privacy in meetings with their lawyers.

More than half of the drugs in the jail came in through this room, Sharon knew; there were attorneys in Dallas County who made as much money smuggling dope into the jail as they did from the practice of law. A year earlier the sheriff had petitioned the court to allow searches of the lawyers' briefcases, both on entering and leaving the booths. The Constitution had prevailed, the petition of the sheriff summarily denied.

There was a sudden clank and rattle, a meshing of gears, and the door leading from the jail innards slid sideways on oiled rollers. Deborah North uttered a sob. Sharon stiffened her posture as Midge entered the room, blinking, her round shoulders slumped. The teenager moved forward to sink into a chair, and gaped dully at her mother. Sharon searched Midge's face for a sign of recognition, but found none.

Deb said, "Darling?" Her voice had lost all quality, her tone tinny and nasal.

Midge's eyes widened. "Mama?"

Sharon held her breath.

Deb nodded slowly. "Yes, honey. It's me."

Don't reject her, Midge, Sharon thought, she's all you've got left.

Midge reached out to clutch the bars. "Where have you been, Mama? They're trying to hurt me in here."

Wilfred Donello dictated his statement to a county stenographer, implicating Bradford Brie in Howard Saw's murder and further outlining Brie's plan to harm Sharon Hays. Donello executed the statement in front of a notary a few minutes after noon. Assistant D.A. Edward Teeter then prepared a probable cause warrant for Brie's arrest, and cooled his heels outside Judge Ralph Briscoe's office for the better part of an hour while the jurist met with his campaign secretary before getting Briscoe's signature on the warrant shortly after one-thirty. Mission accomplished, Teeter dispatched a courier three miles east to Main Dallas Police Headquarters. The courier, an efficient young female deputy with a no-nonsense attitude, delivered the papers to the city warrants desk in short order, and duly noted the time of her arrival at 2:07 P.M. She returned to the Crowley Courts Building and reported to

A.D.A. Teeter that the process for expediting Bradford Brie's capture was now in motion.

The police warrants secretary, who was involved in reporting three earlier arrests to the Burglary Division, mistakenly attached Bradford Brie's warrant to her reports and routed the entire mess upstairs. Once in Burglary, the warrant went to an evening shift detective's in basket, where it remained for several hours because the detective's wife was ill and he was late reporting for duty. Brie's warrant, of course, wound up on the bottom of the detective's stack, so that it was nearly seven in the evening before the officer discovered the warrant's presence on his desk, and was quarter after seven before he figured out that the warrant wasn't intended for him. The discovery prompted a thirty-foot stroll into the shift lieutenant's office, where the detective said to the loo, "How's come we're supposed to be doin' work for the fuckin' Warrants Division?"

A telephone conversation ensued between the Burglary lieutenant and the Warrants shift boss, the culmination of which was that Burglary advised Warrants that if they weren't upstairs after their piece of paper in fifteen minutes, the Burglary lieutenant would see to it that the warrant became a toilet tissue substitute. The lieutenant from Warrants did indeed make an appearance in Burglary shortly thereafter, bringing with him the evening shift captain, who held an hour-long meeting with both irate lieutenants in an attempt to determine exactly who was responsible for the fuckup. The meeting adjourned without a resolution to the problem, and the warrant finally made its way to the proper police division at quarter past nine. The Warrants Division then jumped into action.

At ten minutes until ten, two unmarked vehicles barreled out of the police basement garage, wound their way through downtown to the Cadiz Street viaduct, and sped across the bridge toward Oak Cliff. One car was a Chevy, the other a Plymouth, both four-doors with dark paint jobs, overhead street lamps reflecting globes of light from roofs and hoods as the Chevy led the way. Far below, the Trinity River's surface was black as midnight. Flame danced in occasional shoreline fires as downtown street people retired for the night, heating canned beans or melting heroin in rusty spoons.

The Chevrolet carried four plainclothes detectives; in the Plymouth sat three tactical forces officers, two male and one female, all wearing dark blue uniforms and flak jackets and all armed with riot guns. The car's noses slanted downward as they left the bridge, then moved along Zangs Boulevard to turn west on Jefferson.

Detective Martin Ray sat in the front passenger seat of the Chevy. He was worried about the validity of the warrant, and said so. Paper rattled as he held the official document in the dim glow from the dash light and squinted at the signature. "The judge must have been drunk when he signed this sonofabitch." Ray was a fireplug of a man with a thick neck and square chin. He had twenty-one years on the force under his belt, fifteen of those years in Homicide, and he'd seen enough warrants thrown out in court to be suspicious.

Detective Gregory Gomez was even stockier than Detective Ray, and wore sideburns which extended below his earlobes. The sergeant raised hell every night at shift muster about Gomez's hair, which bothered Gregory Gomez not one iota. He was driving the Chevy, had made detective only six months earlier after two years as a patrolman, and subscribed to the kickin' ass and takin' names theory of law enforcement. "Not our problem," Gomez said. "We got a warrant, so we pick the guy up. So what?"

Detective Ray scooted down in the seat, propped his leg against the dash, and relaxed his neck against the headrest. "I'll tell you so what, sonny, not that you're going to listen. It doesn't make any difference who screwed the warrant up; if we have to shoot the guy or something, they'll throw us to the dogs. They'll claim we didn't follow instructions. Our fine politician bastard of a chief will suspend us and call the investigators in. I've seen it before. I tell you something else, too. We got some worry, because this guy we're going after is somebody we might have to shoot."

Gomez slowed, reading passing street signs. There were one-story rundown shops on both sides of the street; a half block ahead on the left was the marquee at Texas Theater, the place where, nearly thirty years earlier, Dallas's finest had taken Lee Harvey Oswald into custody. "You mean the suspect? He's a badass, huh?"

"Yeah," Ray said. "Bradford Brie. Ten years ago when we handled this guy, he'd killed two liquor store clerks in a holdup. Poor bastards were begging for their lives, down on their knees. The warrant was a piece of shit like this one, and I'll never forget this guy. Skinny guy looks like he couldn't bust an egg, but don't let it fool you.

"We had this half-assed warrant based on what some snitch told the D.A., and go busting in on old Brie like gangbusters. There's this whore in there with him, and Brie tries to use her as a shield. None of you guys"—Ray turned his head to include the two young detectives in the backseat in the conversation—"remember Ricky Mills, this patrolman, he's long retired. But this Brie shot Ricky in the shoulder, and was damn sure ready to blow the hooker away when we tackle the guy from all sides. Beat the shit out of him, okay?"

"Sounds like he had it coming," Gomez said.

"Yeah, sounds like," Ray said. "Him and Ricky both wound up at Parkland Hospital, Ricky with a gunshot wound and this Brie asshole with a broken jaw and two busted ribs. Tough fucker, I'll give that to him. Busted jaw and ribs, it still took four of us to handcuff the guy.

"And guess what," Ray said. "Right, we wound up getting sued over this lousy warrant we had. The court threw out any evidence we found at Brie's place, which happened to include the murder weapon from the liquor store job. Adios to the murder conviction, and it was a combination between the plea bargain on the robbery and the lawsuit settlement that Brie gets any time at all on the deal. Two of the four officers that jumped the guy wound up with thirty-day suspensions, and I was lucky I didn't get suspended myself. Sorry fucking system."

The veteran detective swept the car's interior with his gaze, looking over the fresh-faced youngsters in back, Gomez holding the steering wheel and yanking nervously on his right sideburn. Overhead street lamps sent parallelograms of brightness moving through the car's interior. "So I'm telling you guys," Ray said, "if we do find this man, be on your toes. This guy ain't some dildo. Mr. Bradford Brie knows the ropes, and he'll be looking to get something on us. Plus he'll blow you away without batting an eye. One mean bastard we're talking. Guys like this, they should reinstate the lynch mob."

* * *

Detective Ray paused near the curb to wave the tactical people on, directing two SWATs around the north side of the ramshackle house and one to skirt the south side, lithe officers running in crouches with riot guns extended in the moonlight. Once they were all behind the shack, a couple of the tacticals would take the windows and the other would train gun sights directly on the back door; then they'd await the signal to charge in and go to Bullet City. After the SWATs had disappeared from view, Ray checked right and left. Everything seemed all systems go, one young plainclothes cop hanging loose near the front porch; another crouched, pistol drawn, behind the un-marked Chevy at the curb. Ray now concentrated on the house itself, sagging roof and worm-eaten wooden porch, black tarpaper showing on the walls in places where ter-mites had eaten the wood away. Finally the veteran detec-tive glanced at Gomez on his right, the round Hispanic face screwed into a scowl of readiness. Ray breathed a si-lent prayer, a good Presbyterian man hoping the fuck that his own jiveass partner didn't blow him away in the con-fusion. A single faint light glowed within the house.

Ray touched Gomez's shoulder, and the two policemen walked side by side across the barren yard, twin fireplugs with bull necks, each clad in a brown suit, picking their way among broken bottles, mashed Budweiser and Lone Star cans, and an occasional mound of dog manure. Half-way to the house, Gomez stepped in a depression, stum-bled, then righted himself. He murmured, "Shit."

Once up on the porch, the detectives flattened against the wall on either side of the door frame, pistols drawn. Ray knocked on the wall with big round knuckles, three loud thumps. They waited, their breath hissing faintly, their gazes meeting across three feet of door frame. In the distance crickets *chirruped*. In a house a half block up the street, a light went out. Ray knocked again. Rotting wood vibrated dully.

Ray paused. He still wasn't certain that the warrant in his pocket gave him probable cause to enter. He chewed his lower lip.

Detective Gregory Gomez, who didn't give a rat's ass about probable cause and never would, backed away, lifted a size ten double-soled shoe, and kicked the door right beside the handle. The wood crumpled like cellophane, sagging inward and twisting, and the door swung open on broken hinges. Gomez grinned at Ray, winked, and went inside.

Either they get me away from this pissant, Ray thought, or I'm asking for a transfer. Five seconds passed before Ray crossed the threshold and stood in stifling darkness. His nose wrinkled with the odor of burner-singed grease.

As Ray's eyes became accustomed to the darkness, shapes appeared and clarified. Gomez hulked stock still, ten feet ahead and to the right. Directly in front of Ray was a hall extending to the back of the house, and directly beyond the hallway was a screen door leading outside. As Ray watched, the female SWAT officer came in through the screen, riot gun ready. Ray said loudly, "It's just us up here." The girl nodded, stepped sideways and out of his line of sight.

Ray stepped back to the entry, felt for a switch, and flicked on the overhead. Sudden unshaded light filled the room. Ray stood on wrinkled blue linoleum in a sitting area occupied by one sagging vinyl-topped table and one grease-stained brown sofa. On the table was a Kentucky Fried Chicken box, and inside the box was a pinkish leg bone, stripped of meat, and a half-eaten thigh. Beside the chicken box was a Coke can, which Ray gingerly lifted using his handkerchief. The can was half full and lukewarm. The detective shook the can with his ear close to the ring-tab hole. The drink was flat as maple syrup. Ray stepped to the door and yelled for the other two plainclothes men to come inside.

"Guy don't seem to be here," Detective Gomez said.

"You go busting in like that without waiting for a signal again," Detective Ray said, "and you won't have to worry about the guy. What you'll have to worry about is me."

In the hallway, beside the bathroom, they found a closet converted into a darkroom. Throughout the rest of the house, clothes lay in jumbled piles on the floor and furniture and filthy plates and dirty silverware were scattered about, but the darkroom was immaculate. Bottles of processing fluid were clean and neatly labeled, and pre-

cisely typed development procedures were thumbtacked
to a bulletin board. Hundreds of pictures were stuck on
the wall, all of naked kids, some alone, some in two-
somes or threesomes. The children appeared terrified. A
row of brand-new photos hung by clothespins from a
drying line. In the fresh pictures a teenage Hispanic couple performed sex on a ragged mattress, in every position
known to man.

"What a sicko, huh?" Detective Gomez said.

"Likely we can't use any of this," Ray said, "thanks to
you busting in."

One of the SWAT officers said, "Hey. I've seen her before." He indicated a picture on the table, beside the developing pan.

Ray stepped nearer the table. In the picture was a pretty
young woman carrying a box up the steps of a downtown
office building. "Me, too," Ray said. "She's a prosecutor.
Or was. Let's see, what the hell is her name?"

20

Sharon stopped in the justice center parking lot to tell Deborah North, "I think you've come a million miles today."

Deb's features literally glowed in the overhead floodlights. "I took up so much time just getting to know her," Deb said, "that you didn't get a chance to ask her a thing about the case." The two women stood to one side of the attendants' shed, where a thin black youngster sat on a stool and collected parking fees. Out on near-deserted West Commerce Street, an old car with one flickering headlamp rattled by. Jail visiting hours ended at ten, and the trip down the elevator and into the asphalt lot had taken twenty minutes.

"That's exactly how we wanted it," Sharon said. "I think now that we've cracked her armor, the rest will come. We'll take our time with her. Tomorrow night we'll see her again, okay?"

"I can't wait," Deb said. "Listen, I'm checked into the Adolphus Hotel. Care to join me for a drink?"

Sharon wanted a drink, and wanted to visit with Deborah North even more. She was dying to see what made this woman tick, that she'd give up her children and live with the loss for all this time. But it had been a long day, and Melanie had been with Sheila ever since school had let out. "Definite rain check, Deb," Sharon said. "I've got my little girl."

"Sure you do." Deb's gaze cast downward, then back up. She smiled. "Sure you do. See you tomorrow." Then she was gone, walking briskly away, head down. Three parking rows from the shed, she stopped beside a Lincoln Town Car, jingled keys, lit a cigarette, climbed in, and started the engine. She backed up, reversed directions, and cruised slowly past the shed and out onto Commerce.

Open mouth, insert foot, Sharon thought. "I've got my little girl," she'd said, while Deb had left her own child in jail and was headed for a dreary hotel room. Tonight before Melanie went to bed, Sharon would give her daughter an extra hug.

She had left her Volvo near the back of the lot, and now threaded her way in between the parked cars, her heels clicking mutedly on asphalt as she left the artificial light and moved in moonlit darkness. The sounds of her footsteps rebounded from the nearby jail wall and hung for seconds before dying slowly away like mountain echoes. She'd reached the side of the Volvo and had inserted her key in the doorlock when the coldness hit her.

It was the same icy sensation she'd felt in the Six Flags parking lot on Sunday evening, the same creepy-crawly eeriness she'd experienced on Saturday across the street from the law library, and she now backed up a step and looked around, seeing no one. It's the creeps, she thought, nothing more. Silly. Silly as hell. Then she dived in behind the wheel like a rabbit into its hole, and hit the electric switch to thunk the locks into place. It was a full minute before her pulse slowed to near normal.

The crawling creeps imbedded their fangs into Sharon's consciousness so deeply that by the time she'd made the trek to her own East Dallas neighborhood, she was practically a basket case. When halted at traffic lights, she gripped the wheel until her fingers stung. It seemed to her that the bogeyman drove every other car on the road, and that behind each glowing set of headlights sat a hunchback with wrinkled skin and a wart on his nose, cackling, *Heh, heh, heh, my pretty,* biding his time until he could get his talons on her soft . . .

She scooted into Sheila's driveway with her nerves in ragged threads, and practically sprinted from the car up on the porch and rang the bell. She thought she heard scuttling noises on the lawn behind her, and squinched her eyes tightly shut and pounded the door with her fist.

Sheila answered with her features wreathed in alarm. "Is something wrong?" she said, peering past Sharon into the night.

Sharon looked fearfully across the lawn. There was no one there, or course, only the rustling warm wind. She breathed a sigh that was part exasperation and part fear. "Look, Sheila," she finally said. "You wouldn't have any brandy, would you?"

Two ounces of apricot liqueur sat in Sharon's belly like a warm lead golf ball as she learned that Melanie had reached the third level of *Nestor's Quest* on the Nintendo game while Trish's guy had died while still in level two. "That's nice, honey," Sharon said. "How much homework did you get done?" They were a block from home. The headlamps shined on reflector buttons as they bounced through the intersection where Sharon caught the bus when the Volvo was in the shop. Been a couple of months, she thought, it's about time for something in the old heap to go haywire. As if reading her thoughts, the Volvo's engine skipped a beat, then chugged dutifully on.

Melanie wriggled in the passenger seat and turned her face to the window. "I didn't have any homework." Her seat belt strap was twisted just above the catch.

"That's also nice," Sharon said. "You never have any homework. The note from your teacher last week said differently."

"I've made those lessons up," Melanie said.

Sharon pursed her lips. This single-mother bit was a nightmare at times. Melanie was bright—was exceptionally gifted, in fact, scoring in the ninety-nine percentile on the TASS and Stanford Achievement Tests—a condition which, Sharon thought, the child had inherited from Rob. Learning had never come easily for Sharon, but Melanie could make A's at the fifth-grade level while standing on her head. By eighth grade she would be in accelerated honors classes, but for the time being school bored her to death, and she often fudged on her homework. When she did, the notes would come home from the teachers, Sharon would ride herd on studies for a while, and Melanie would escape the hangman's noose with a string of 100's. While Sharon broke her neck practicing law, however, she simply didn't have time to monitor Melanie's lessons often enough. She pressed on the brake pedal harder than necessary and halted abruptly in her driveway.

"If you've made up the lessons, you've made them up," Sharon said. "I'm going to ask your teacher. I'm telling you, Melanie, one more note from school and the Nintendo competition is history."

"*Mah*-um." Melanie unsnapped her seat belt and opened the door.

Sharon cut the engine and dropped the keys into her purse. "Don't *mah*-um me, young lady. I mean it." She climbed out of the car feeling guilty, wondering if she was taking the crawling creeps—bolstered now with a half ounce more than Sharon's limit of alcohol—out on her daughter. She said in a more friendly tone, "Only what, two more weeks of school?"

"Week and a half." Melanie half jogged alongside her mother, obviously relieved to steer the conversation away from school work. "When do I go to camp?"

Sharon slapped a mosquito away from her neck; the vicious little critter had taken a nip, and the flesh on her throat swelled and itched. "Second week in July," she said. She fumbled for keys and inserted one in the front door dead bolt lock. Inside the house Commander whined and scratched. "Mommy's going to be in trial that . . ." Sharon paused with the door partway open, her gaze across the street. "Week," she said softly. The crawling creeps paraded up and down her spine like a spider herd.

Parked in front of the Breedloves' house was a beat-up old convertible, a Chrysler LeBaron. Sharon had never seen the car before, of that she was certain, and the presence of a stranger in the neighborhood made the antennae shoot up automatically. The car was dented like a WWII combat tank, and there was a chunk of chrome missing from the rear bumper. Mr. Breedlove was a nut about his autos—a '73 Buick and an '84 Pontiac—and kept them in mint condition, and he'd never permit the disgusting old Chrysler to sit in front of his home if he was aware of it. Christ, Sharon thought, it's the bogeyman for sure.

She decided that the spookiness of the evening coupled with the apricot brandy had made her delusionary, and mentally kicked her own behind as she depressed the thumb latch and swung the door open wide. Melanie dashed inside and hugged Commander while the shepherd quivered all over and licked the child's face. Sharon paused for a final glance at the old Chrysler. You've gone bonkers, you dummy, she thought. Completely out of your mind. Chuckling at her scaredy-catness, Sharon then went inside. Once in the entry hall, she quickly locked the door.

Chasing Melanie in to bed took Sharon's mind completely off the old car parked across the street, Midge Rathermore's examining trial, and anything else other than the exhausting process of getting the child down for the night. No little girl in America, Sharon thought, could possibly be as exasperating as Melanie Hays when the child set her mind to being stubborn. Something else she had inherited from old daddyo, Sharon thought.

First Melanie demanded three separate drinks of water, and wailed when questioned as if she were on the Gobi Desert and the nearest oasis were fifty miles away. Then she wanted the New York stories for the five zillionth time. Much as it burned Sharon's conscience, she flatly denied the story request, knowing that once she started Melanie would ask to hear each big-city tale over and over until mommy was ready to pull her hair.

Then there was the sudden concern over Commander. Melanie would *just die* if she couldn't wait until the dog's nightly constitution was finished before she hit the hay. Ever since the attempted poisoning, Sharon had monitored Commander very carefully, letting the shepherd into the yard only in the early morning and just before bedtime. She wasn't sure how Commander's bladder was holding up to the change in routine, but thus far she hadn't seen any soiled spots on the carpet. Sharon told Melanie that she would bring Commander to Melanie's room as soon as the shepherd was through with his business—which Melanie already knew very well to be the rule—then marched the child firmly back to her bedroom. Finally Sharon stood, arms folded and doing a toe-tap, over Melanie until the child was in pajamas and tucked beneath the covers. Mommy then breathed an exasperated sigh of relief, turned off the lights, and retreated to the den with Commander shuffling along beside her.

She flicked on the yard lights and led Commander out onto the deck, stooping to pick up the flashlight as she did. It had taken a week or two, and Sharon had employed the German training collar for the first time since Commander had been a pup, but she'd finally convinced the shepherd that under no circumstances was he to bound into the yard until she'd given him the go-ahead. Sharon didn't know if she'd ever get over finding the strychnine-laced steak. Overly cautious? Well, maybe, she thought, but acting a bit silly was better than winding up with a dead dog on her hands. The night was unusually cool for late May; in another couple of weeks the after-sundown weather would be muggy and stifling, and would remain so until mid-September. Sharon stepped down onto the grass and looked around.

Nothing was on the ground out in the open save for a broom and rake which Melanie and her playmates used as stick horses. Sharon propped the broom and rake against the side of the house, then cast the flashlight's beam into the shadows surrounding the swing set. She probed that area, checked beneath the fence all around the yard, and looked closely around the edges of the redwood deck. Nothing.

At the far corner of the house she was crouched down to inspect the rosebushes, when there was sudden movement on her left. She leaped erect as if touched by live current; the flashlight flew from her hand and bounced on the grass, shooting its beam in wild and crazy arcs. A half-grown bunny then emerged from the bushes and regarded Sharon with dark, frightened eyes. The bunny then hopped to the fence, scuttled and wriggled out through a small hole, and disappeared. Sharon held one hand over her pummeling heart as she retrieved the flashlight. God, she could see the headlines. Fearless Lawyer Frightened to Death by Wild Rabbit. From his vantage point on the deck, Commander regarded Sharon as if she were a madwoman. Sharon stuck out her lower lip to blow her bangs away from her forehead as she shot Commander the bird. Insane Lawyer Gives Finger to Dog, Sharon thought.

Finally satisfied, she told Commander, "Go to it, boy. I'll let you back in the house as soon as I scrub the old bod." Commander hopped down into the yard, and trotted over to piss contentedly against the swing set. At least he's still got a use for the slide and swing, Sharon thought, even if Melanie doesn't. Christ, she'd gotten a German shepherd for protection and now she was guarding the dog. Ruefully shaking her head, Sharon went inside.

In her bedroom she considered getting down on all fours and peering under the bed, then changed her mind. To hell with it, Sharon thought, if the bogeyman's hiding in here, he's just got me. Muttering, rolling her eyes at her own silliness, Sharon stood before her closet and wiggled her feet out of her shoes one at a time. Then she lifted her skirt up to her waist and bent to strip out of her panty hose.

So jumpy was Sharon Hays that the simple act of taking a shower was a fearsome ordeal. She stood side-straddle to the nozzle jets, soaping her belly and thighs, her eyes narrowed into slits as she peered through the opaque shower curtain. She thought that any second the bathroom door would swing open, and a blurred moving shape would approach the shower stall. Then a gnarled hand would yank the curtain aside and . . . Christ, Sharon thought, there he'll be, Anthony Perkins in the flesh, his eyes black holes in his face, his lips pulled back in an insane grin. Perkins would be wearing a granny dress and stringy black wig, and he'd hold a foot-long butcher knife aloft as light flashed from the blade. Then he'd slash her; she'd back up against the tiled wall and futilely grab at the knife, and the blade would cut her to ribbons while the wild background music reached a crescendo. Finally she'd flop onto the floor like a dead fish, one eye wide and staring as her lifeblood swirled down the drain. My *God,* Sharon, she thought. She gritted her teeth and jammed her head beneath the nozzle. Plummeting hot water soaked her hair and cascaded down her body. She reached blindly for the squeeze bottle, forced a mound of shampoo into her palm, then lathered and rinsed her hair. Normally she wouldn't have washed her hair until tomorrow night, but she'd decided that with the extra perspiration brought on by the crawling creeps she would likely look a fright in court in the morning if she didn't shampoo.

Midge Rathermore's examining trial would go on for

two more days, three at the most. Sharon and Russ Black had pow-wowed after that day's session, and had decided not to question the two teenage killers any further. Information about the other persons who'd frequented the Rathermore home was about all they could expect to get from Troy Burdette and Christopher Leonard until the trial itself, and the defense was better off letting well enough—and Judge Griffin's attitude—alone until then. Anthony Gear, the new private eye, was trying to find out something about Leslie Schlee, so the defense was through with Leonard and Burdette for the time being. Linda Haymon Rathermore was also scheduled for a stint on the stand, however, and that would be a horse of a different color.

Deb North's information about Linda's penchant for sexual exhibitions wasn't admissible in court because it was hearsay; Bill Rathermore, the originator of the statement, was no longer among the living and therefore not available to testify. Russ Black had done some snooping around—he had connections which made Sharon's jaw drop in astonishment—but, surprisingly, hadn't turned up a thing about Linda's background. Her past seemed a total blank; it was as if she'd suddenly appeared out of the mist, walked into the television studio, and auditioned for a spot on the news program. Linda, of course, was the only eyewitness to the murder, and if the defense was going to make an attack on her, they needed something for Anthony Gear to sink his teeth into. Black had tossed the hot potato into Sharon's lap; cross-examination of Linda during the examining trial was up to her.

Sharon silently rehearsed her questions to Linda as she finished rinsing her hair, then reached for the knobs and shut the water off. The bathroom was suddenly quiet, the drips from the nozzle like tomtoms. Her hair soaking wet, half blind from water in her eyes, Sharon gripped the edge of the shower curtain to yank it aside. She froze.

My God, she thought, is someone *out there*? A dim shape was outlined against the curtain, something big and menacing near the sink. She firmly shook her head. Anthony Perkins, right? Sharon thought. Well if you're out there, Anthony, screw you. She managed a throaty laugh as she pulled the curtain open with a rasp of hangers and reached for her towel.

And recoiled in terror as a flash of light filled the room, followed immediately by a second blinding flash. Sharon backed up to the wall and hugged her breasts. As the red haze cleared from her vision, she gasped.

Bradford Brie sat on the counter beside the sink; he lowered his camera and let it dangle from the strap around his neck. He wore a yellow panama hat with a bright red band, dark sunglasses, and a loose-fitting Hawaiian shirt with a blue and green flower pattern. He picked up a pistol from the counter and pointed it at her. The bore looked to Sharon to be about two feet in diameter.

Brie showed crooked yellow teeth in a grin. "Those shots will come out perfect," he said. "The mist." He reached behind him to trace a line in the mirror frost. "Better than air brushing. Trust me."

Though she stood in a cloud of warm mist, she was suddenly freezing cold. "How did you get in here?" She tried her best to make her tone forceful, but her voice sounded like a child's.

"Getting in was easy, pretty lady." Brie's tone was matter-of-fact. He was in full control, obviously enjoying her fear, savoring every moment. "Front window. I'd have been inside waiting when you got home, only that beast of yours don't like people coming in the house. Jesus, mutt's got a constitution."

Sudden anger welled in her. "Did you poison my dog?" She forgot her nakedness and took a menacing step forward.

He laughed, laid the gun aside, and took her picture. Sharon covered her breasts with one hand and her pubic area with the other. She'd never felt as helpless—as out-and-out humiliated—in her life. She reached for the towel rack.

He picked up the gun and gestured. "No, uh-uh. No towels. Jesus, those water drops on your skin make for good poses." Sharon backed away from the towel rack, her gaze riveted on the pistol. His grin broadened. "That's it. That's much better. So I got to tell you, I 'preciate you putting the dog outside. I was afraid I'd have to shoot him, tell you the truth. Wake the fucking dead."

The inside of her mouth was dry cotton. "What do you want?"

He chuckled nasally, then coughed into his cupped hand.

Sharon had prosecuted many rape cases, and the victims all told one common tale. The attack itself, they said, wasn't nearly as bad as the shock of encountering the attacker. Not even the beatings they'd taken could match the mental torture. "You won't hurt me, will you?" Sharon said weakly. Sweet God, she thought, please let this be over with.

He stood and opened the door leading into the bedroom. "Come on. That's right, pretty lady, come on, now." He waved the gun.

Slowly, her legs like rubber, Sharon stepped out of the tub and moved woodenly to the doorway. Don't upset him, she thought. Whatever you do, don't set him off. Her sopping hair clung to her forehead and ears, and water dripped on her bare shoulders. The refrigerated air in the bedroom was shockingly cold.

There was a rump-sized depression on her quilted bedspread, and Sharon pictured him sitting there, grinning and waiting while he listened to the noise of the shower. She supposed he would take her on the bed. Would he tie her? Hold a knife to her throat? There was a coiled rope on the bed, alongside several sets of handcuffs. Sharon gently closed her eyes. She was certain that she was going to throw up.

He came in behind her and crossed over to the dresser. She'd laid the framed pictures, the ones he'd taken outside her office, on top of the dresser, and had planned to take them tomorrow to the office. He lovingly touched the chrome frames. "You like these, huh? They're not bad, but you ain't seen nothing yet."

Her mouth quivered. "Look, I've got a little money."

"No talking." His features twisted; he stepped up close and touched the pistol to her left breast. Cold steel hardened her nipple. He was an inch or so shorter than she was, and there was onion on his breath. His hat brim was a hair-length from her forehead. "Jesus, all you broads. You got to talk, you know? I don't want no talking unless I ask you something."

Without warning, he backhanded her across the face

with the pistol. She cried out in shock and sat down hard on the bed. She wondered dully whether the blow had cut her face, then touched her jaw and stared numbly at two red drops on her fingertips. Strangely, Sharon felt no pain.

"Now, I don't like doing that," he said. "Messes up my subject. You want to keep making pretty pictures, you listen to me."

Sharon had taken classes on what to do in these situations. The instructor had been a police tactical squad officer who'd played the rapist while the students—all female assistant D.A.'s except for the woman who supervised the district attorney's file department—took turns practicing judo moves or playing mind games with the guy. The reality, Sharon thought, is quite different from the classes. In class, the throat-constricting terror had been missing. She tried to call on what she'd learned, folding her hands over her bare thighs and forcing her expression to be calm. "May I ask something?" Always ask permission. Crazies want to be in control.

He tilted his hat back with the barrel of the pistol. "What?"

Sharon licked her lips. "Why me? I've never seen you before the other day." Keep his mind occupied, she thought. They all like to brag to their victims before they . . . A shudder ran through her.

"No, but I seen you. You hurt a friend of mine."

"Oh? What friend is that?"

He snugged up his sunglasses with his middle finger. "I'll tell you something. Save you some breath. All that psychological bullshit, I've heard it before. All you people think you can fuck with a guy's head, you know?" He bunched his fingers together in a come-here motion. "Stand up, pretty lawyer lady. And don't try no mind games with me. I know stuff you ain't even heard of."

Sharon stood as resignation came to her. It was going to happen. That he knew she was a lawyer told her he'd likely been through the system, and what he was saying made a crazy kind of sense. There were men, she knew, who resisted all psych analysis, who were too far gone for help. She'd have to go along and pray he didn't kill her.

He handcuffed her wrists, his face impassive as the

bracelets closed with a rachety sound. He turned and removed the key. At least my hands are in front, Sharon thought. She made up her mind that if he gave her any opening at all, she was going to make the most of it. Don't resist, she thought, but if he lets his guard down for the barest instant . . .

"Where do you want me?" she asked softly.

He picked up the rope and spare handcuffs, then went to the door leading to the living room. "I don't want you no place yet," he said. He beckoned. "Come on. We're going to get cutie-pie."

Her brain was foggy from the blow to her jaw. Cutie-pie? Who is . . .? She got it. Haltingly she said, "Please. You don't mean my little girl."

"She ain't so little, Mother. I like them skinny legs of hers. Mother and daughter, make a good portrait, you know?" He sneered and beckoned again.

"Oh, no. Listen, oh, no. I'll do anything. Please. Oh, please." Sharon's speech was rapid and uncontrolled, flowing without her conscious thought.

"*Goddammit,*" he screamed, and Sharon recoiled in terror. "Goddammit," he said more softly, "I told you not to fuck with me." He grabbed the chain between her wrists and yanked. Sharon felt herself propelled forward like a rag doll as he flung her through the doorway. "You move your goddam ass when I tell you, you hear?" he hissed.

She fell heavily on the living room carpet and rolled over. There were thumps and guttural snarls as Commander hurled himself against the back door from outside. Easy, boy, Sharon thought, and uttered a silent prayer that this crazy didn't kill the dog.

Brie came out of the bedroom carrying the rope and handcuffs along with a paper sack. He reached into the sack and produced a huge erect penis made from hard rubber, then bent and held the dildo inches from her face. "Big 'un, ain't it?" he said. "You ever seen one like this?" The maker had spared no detail, even to the blue veins on top of the hardened shaft. Sharon gagged.

Carpet fibers tickled her shoulders. The fall to the floor had cleared her head, and through her terror she now felt a burning resolve. Until he'd mentioned Melanie, Sharon's only thought had been self-preservation, but now all such self-serving emotion flowed out of her system. She wasn't letting him anywhere near Melanie, and all she thought of now was the best chance to make her move. As she lay on the carpet with the fearsome dildo inches from her face, Sharon made up her mind that she was willing to die.

He shoved the dildo under his arm and swept the pistol barrel in an upward motion. "Don't worry if you ain't seen one before. They're easy to strap on, pretty lady. You'll see, nothing to it. *Ssst. Ssst.*" He made the hissing sound with his tongue against the roof of his mouth. "Up, now. Come on."

She climbed slowly to her feet and led the way through the living room toward the front of the house. Toward Melanie's room. Sharon had forgotten her nakedness, and her fear was completely gone. She just wanted one chance, one opening, before she reached the child's bedroom, and if the opportunity didn't come she was going to rush the lunatic anyway. To hell with this bastard who was invading her home. Sharon lightly gritted her teeth.

"It just came to me, you know?" Brie said, waving the gun, chuckling as he moved along behind her. "One night down there in Mexico I was shooting this album and I thought to myself, hey, what about a mother-daughter spread? Then this old guy showed me this hummer of a dick I got here. Jesus, Roy's horse, Trigger, would be proud of this sonofabitch, don't you think? Twenty bucks was all it cost me, too. You got any idea—"

Sharon stepped down into the sunken living room. The lights were out, the only illumination filtering through her still open bedroom door. Brie's singsong voice penetrated her consciousness, but she wasn't listening to the words.

"—what a dong this size would cost up here in the States? I seen one like it, only not near as good with the veins and hole in the head, I seen one like it at this X-rated bookstore on Industrial Boulevard, and guess what. Hundred and fifty bucks for the fucking thing, can you believe it? I tell you something, I'm going to have to shoot your picture while you're putting it on. Otherwise people will think you're some kind of hermaphrodite, that's how real the bastard looks."

Sharon reached the step up into the hall. Only a few more feet, ten or fifteen steps separating her from the entrance to Melanie's room. Her body tensed. She kept her gaze straight ahead.

"Only thing is," Brie said with a honking nasal laugh, "I can't figure out whether you should give it to her in the snatch or up her ass. I like the front fuck, you know? But a lot of people get their jollies the other way. Disgusting, yeah, but there's no accounting for people's taste. Guess we'll have to try 'em both, huh? What you think, Mother? How you think cutie-pie would like it best? Hold it, Mother. Hold it right there."

Sharon halted in her tracks, unsure, and swiveled her head to look at him. His face was hidden in the shadow of his hat brim. Oh, she thought. Sure. The light. He stepped to the side to flick the switch which would illuminate the hallway. He'll have to reach for the switch, Sharon thought, and he'll have to turn his head to the wall if only for an instant. She mentally braced herself, took a half step backward, and tensed her knee to spring.

"Can't see where the fuck we're going, huh?" He groped at the wall with the hand which held the rope and handcuffs. The metal bracelets clinked together. His head moved to his right as he looked for the switch. Sharon drew a deep breath.

And the doorbell *bong-bonged.*

So unexpected was the sound, so totally impossible that anyone would be coming to call now, of all times, that Sharon froze with one foot suspended in midair. God, who could it . . . ? Brie was motionless as well, his hand on the wall, his head cocked inquisitively, captor and captive in frozen stop action.

The chimes sounded a second time.

Now Brie turned full-profile to her as he squinted through the entry hall at the front door.

Sharon charged. She brought her handcuffed wrists up over her head, took a long running stride, and launched herself. Brie yelped in surprise and turned toward her, the gun swiveling to point at her, the set of his mouth showing that he knew all along that he wasn't going to make it.

She swung her weighted wrists like a woodman axing a tree, first contacting his hat and crushing the crown, then feeling the satisfying crunch of metal on bone as the cuffs smashed into the top of his head. Then her arms

IN SELF-DEFENSE   211

were around his neck; she squeezed for all she was worth, her bare breasts flattened against him, her legs coming up to wrap themselves around his waist. Sharon sank her teeth into the side of Bradford Brie's throat like a frenzied vampire, all forgotten except that this foul-smelling creature had come into her home and threatened her little girl. A growl like a tigress's fought its way out of Sharon's throat and split the silence.

Bradford Brie screamed and fell on his side with Sharon on top, her teeth grinding, ripping flesh. She tasted salt. The gun clattered on entry hall tile, and at the same time the spare cuffs and rope flew in the opposite direction. Sharon was faintly aware of something rubbery bouncing on the floor beside her ear. A penis, she thought, it's the *goddamn revolting rubber dick that this scum has been waving in my face*. She clamped her jaws even tighter. Brie yelled like a banshee, clawing at the fury which ripped at his throat. Flesh ripped as he squirmed away from her. Sharon spat out a ribbon of skin. She rolled sideways on the floor, got both hands around the handle of the gun, and fought her way up on her knees.

Clutching his wounded throat, blood seeping from between his fingers, his hat a mass of crumpled straw, Bradford Brie sprinted for the door. Sharon had never fired a gun in her life—was deathly afraid of firearms, in fact, and for two years had ignored the D.A.'s memo directing his staff to take turns on the police firing range—but she did know which end was which and where the firing mechanism was located. She pointed the barrel of the gun squarely between the fleeing man's shoulder blades and yanked hard on the trigger. The trigger wouldn't move. Dammit, she thought, the *frigging trigger is frozen*. Something raced through her subconscious, some long-ago something she'd heard about safety catches, as Brie flung the door open and thundered out into the night.

Dammit to hell, Sharon thought. More than anything she'd ever wanted to do in her life, she'd been dying to kill the bastard.

Homicide detective Stan Green was too godawful drunk to know what time it was or, for that matter, to give a damn. He'd begun his evening at five o'clock in the af-

ternoon with a few toots at the bar in Pappadeaux Seafood Restaurant in the West End, and by seven had had
more than a snootful. He hadn't gone to the upscale Ca-
jun fish joint with the idea of getting drunk, but to mull
over strategy in the Rathermore case with Kathleen
Fraterno and Milton Breyer. After three Hurricanes
(hundred-proof Bacardi mixed with orange, lemon, and
cranberry juices, sweet-tasting with the kick of four
Clydesdales) while watching the happy hour crowd—
young singles mostly, girls in skin-tight jeans and bare-
midriff blouses showing golden springtime tans as they
batted eyes and gave come-ons to young men with razored hairstyles—move and shake, and two solid hours of
observing Breyer and Fraterno play with each other's legs
under the table while pretending to talk about the case,
Stan Green had no longer given a shit whether Midge
Rathermore had offed her daddy or not.

Actually, Midge's guilt or innocence had never mattered to Green to begin with. Putting evidence together
against the overweight teenager had only been part of the
job. The Rathermore case was the eighty-seventh homicide on which Green had worked in the past year and,
aside from the publicity, wasn't any different from the
other eighty-six. The procedure was always the same:
first Green zeroed in on the suspect and then set about
making a case. No one could say that he hadn't worked
like hell on the Rathermore investigation, either, and for
busting his ass what was he getting? Peanuts, he thought
as he drained his second Hurricane. Those goddamn
movie people weren't willing to pay Stan Green a third of
what they'd offered Milton Breyer.

And Breyer, the ungrateful horse's ass of a politician—
who hadn't known goatshit about the Rathermore case
until Green had filled him in on the details—what had
Breyer done? Well, for starters, the married s.o.b. was
fucking Kathleen Fraterno—which was the only thing
preventing Green from taking a shot at the assistant prosecutor himself—and for finishers, Breyer hadn't offered
to share a nickel of his movie money. Breyer's cheating
on his wife didn't bother Stan Green one iota, having
done more than his share of extramarital screwing around
in his time, but the fact that the prosecutor was married
might come in handy should Green have to resort to

blackmail in order to get his cut of Breyer's television deal. Hell, Breyer's wife was already rich, what did old Milt need the money for? With the proper amount of Hollywood cash, Stan Green could pay off his boat and trailer, shut his ex old lady up about the past-due child-support payments, and do some living of his own. Maybe take a little vacation, huh?

The more liquor Green had consumed at Pappadeaux, the more resentful he had become, the result being that by seven o'clock the detective was in an alcohol stupor, staring sullenly into space while Breyer and Fraterno continued to feel each other up underneath the table. The last straw for Green had come when the movie people themselves—David Whit, the producer, a guy in his forties with a Gable mustache and sideburns, wearing pimpy-looking high-dollar boots and designer jeans, and Whit's assistant, Rayford Sly, who Green suspected was a fag—had stopped by the table to buy a round of drinks and check up on how the case was going, and had completely ignored Stan Green. Had *ignored* the detective as if he wasn't even there, as if it had been Milton Breyer instead of Stan Green who had put together the evidence against Midge Rathermore to begin with. Green had taken the snub for as long as he could—which in his condition was a total of about thirty seconds—then had told the lot of them, Fuck you very much, and had raged and cursed his way out of the restaurant into the parking lot. He'd located his car after stumbling up and down four parking rows, had yanked open the door to flop disgustedly behind the wheel, and finally had careened off into the night.

Since he'd already worked up a snootful, he hadn't been about to go home. He'd headed straight for Bryan Street, the section in between Peak and Haskell avenues lined with sawdust-floored beer joints, and had proceeded to make a night of it. The handsome, rawboned cop liked the Hispanic joints along Bryan Street because he could speak the lingo after a fashion, and because in the Spanish honky-tonks people treated an officer of the law with the respect he deserved. There were plenty of joints on the strip where a cop didn't even have to lean on anybody for a freebie. On Bryan Street the bartender was likely to pop open a Bud or a Lone Star for an officer of the law and waive the buck-fifty charge without being asked, and without the cop having to roust a customer or two in order to get the bartender's attention.

It was on a bar stool at the Rocket Lounge, with olive-skinned couples boot-scooting on the dance floor to Johnny Paycheck on the jukebox, that Green thought hungrily of Sharon Hays. The nerve of the woman, sending a sure-enough stud like Stan Green packing. No female in his life had ever treated him that way; if there was any by-God busting up to do, he had always been the one with the say-so. Right then and there Green decided to give Sharon one more chance, decided that he'd head on over to her house so she could tell him what a mistake she'd made. Likely she'll get down on her knees and beg for it, Green thought. Damn straight she will. He wasn't sure just how much of a ration of shit he'd give her. Jesus, was she ever going to grovel at his feet. Finally he'd give in, of course, taking her into the bedroom and giving her the solid country fucking she was dying for, but not before he made her worry that she wasn't going to get it. There wasn't a woman in the world that Stan Green couldn't make holler for more. His mind made up, the slight stiffening in his crotch growing into a full-sized boner, he had downed the last of his beer in a single gulp. Then off he'd staggered, hell-bent for leather.

All of which preceded the scene at God-knows-what-time-of-night, with Stan Green listing in place on Sharon's front porch as he thumbed the doorbell. Out in back of the house, Sharon's big tan German shepherd was raising a ruckus, snarling and snapping. Must be a bitch in heat in the neighborhood, Green thought, then giggled drunkenly and thought, Well, actually there's two of 'em, one someplace nearby to drive Commander into a frenzy, another inside the house waiting for old Stan Green to come callin'. He laughed out loud and pressed the button again.

As someone yanked the door open from inside, Green backed away a step and spread his arms. Come to daddy, darlin', he thought, you act real nice and ol' Stan might not even make you beg for it. She sure was in a hurry to open that door. Green decided that she'd seen him through the peephole, and just the sight of him had made her pants so hot that she'd ... Jesus Christ, Green thought, here my darlin' *comes*.

The detective grunted a startled "oof" as a wiry man, head down and wearing a crumpled straw hat, charged onto the porch and collided with Green, nose to breast-bone. The man struck out blindly at the cop, twisting and squirming, opening a gash alongside Green's nose with a fingernail. Green didn't know what the fuck was going on. He acted on pure instinct, grabbing the man in a bear hug, the two scratching, biting, and cursing as they tumbled sideways from the porch into the flower bed. They rolled over and over on damp earth, first the skinny man on top, then the detective.

Still drunk but growing more sober by the second, Green managed to stay on top and pin the wiry arms with his knees. The two men glared at each other. Blood ran from a gash on the skinny man's neck. His hat toppled from his head and lay canted against a row of lilies. He had thinning hair and a big, bent honker of a nose.

"Who in hell are you?" Green said breathlessly.

The man squirmed and wiggled to free himself. Green increased the pressure with his knees.

Suddenly two pale bare arms extended themselves between the men. The delicate wrists were handcuffed. The slender hands clutched a .45 automatic, which they placed solidly against the skinny man's forehead. He stopped moving, his eyes darting wildly back and forth. Now Stan Green was really confused. He looked to his right. Sharon Hays stood stark naked in the light of the moon, her hair wet and clinging. She smelled of lilac soap.

The detective's mouth opened like a fly trap. "Who in hell is this guy?" His words were slurred.

Sharon never took her gaze away from the prisoner. "Take the gun, Stan," she said.

Green scratched his head. This was the weirdest fucking thing he'd ever seen.

"Stan," Sharon said. "Take the frigging gun."

Woodenly Green reached for the pistol and closed one hand around the grip. Sharon released her hold on the grip and stood erect. Green swiveled his head to look at her. His nose was inches from her bare inner thigh.

"Quit looking at my crotch, Stan." Sharon gestured

cuffed hands at the prisoner. "Him," she said. "Hold the gun on him. I'll be right back."

She skirted the two men to go up on the porch and inside the house. Somewhere in the detective's head there was a buzzing noise, but he held the gun steady. The man beneath him panted through crooked teeth. Green shrugged and grinned at the guy. If he ever figured out what the fuck was going on, he might even get mad. The scratch alongside his nose burned like fire.

In seconds Sharon returned carrying a coil of rope and several sets of handcuffs. She dropped everything into the flower bed save one set of bracelets, closed one around Green's wrist and the other around the prisoner's. Then, after hissing, "Don't move a muscle," she searched the skinny man's pockets and located the handcuff key. Finally she stood back.

Green focused boozily on the pale-skinned naked woman, then peered at the pile of handcuffs in the flower bed. "You gotten into something kinky?" he said.

She sighed. "No, Stan, I haven't." She pointed at Green and said, "You cop," then pointed at the skinny man. "Him criminal," she said. "See if you can hang on to him while I put something on, okay?"

Sharon dressed quickly, then went down the hall to waken Melanie. During the scuffle Sharon's adrenaline had pumped like crazy and she'd had no sensation of fear, but now she trembled like a leaf. She swallowed, turned the handle, and entered the silent bedroom.

Sharon's daughter slept like an angel, her head turned to one side with her cheek resting on the back of her hand, her back rising and falling in little-girl sleep breaths. Sharon said a silent prayer of thanks, and also asked the Lord to make Melanie's life cheerful and free of worry. It was certainly someone in the Hays clan's turn. Boy, Sharon thought, Sheila's going to think her best friend's turned into a lunatic. She gently closed her eyes, then bent to kiss Melanie's cheek and shake her daughter into grumpy wakefulness. As Melanie tried in vain to bury her head under the pillow, Sharon wondered how a drunken Stan Green would fare in transporting the prisoner downtown. As she shook Melanie harder, Sharon decided that she'd better call for a squad car.

21

Bradford Brie grinned through the one-way mirror and stuck out his tongue. He poked his thumbs into his ears and waggled his fingers. Then he walked up to the glass and licked it. Finally he pointed at the mirror and silently formed the word "You," then made a big *O* with his lips and squeezed his crotch.

"Lovely," Sharon said. She was on the other side of the glass, watching Brie move about inside the police interview room. He now sat down at a bare wood table and crossed his eyes. "You'd almost think he knows we're out here," Sharon said.

"There's always a funny man," assistant D.A. Ed Teeter said. "Monkey see, monkey do. You're really pretty lucky, Miss Hays. You're positive this is the same guy that took your picture?"

Sharon hooked her elbow over the back of her chair and crossed her legs. "Sure it's him." She wore stretch blue denims and an orange cotton oversized knit shirt.

"Bradford Herman Brie," the prosecutor said. "Four years ago he broke out of Coffield Farm and held a woman hostage in her house for nearly a week. She was in therapy for a few months after that. Finally she killed herself."

Sharon looked at her lap as she smoothed her hair and bit her lower lip. "He wanted my daughter. You can handle all these cases as a lawyer, but it never seems real until it happens to you."

Teeter was seated on the conference table with his feet

dangling and his hands gripping the table's edge. He wore a button-down sports shirt and pleated brown slacks. It was almost four in the morning, and Sharon had been at the station for over three hours.

"You've given a statement," Teeter said. "I suppose that's all we need for now."

Sharon watched through the glass as Brie picked his nose. "How can that be all?" she said. "The only statement I've given has to do with seeing him downtown and him taking my picture."

Teeter regarded his knees. "We can get the rest later."

"I'm in the middle of an examining trial," Sharon said. "After which we're going to break our necks getting ready for the real thing. I'd as soon give my entire statement now, while it's all fresh."

"You seeing him around the corner from Howard Saw's office," Teeter said, "that's corroboration for what our other witness has to say. We can use you."

"Your other witness being Wilfred Donello?"

"Yes, ma'am," Teeter said.

"That's fine for Howard Saw's murder," Sharon said. "But what about the little matter of his breaking into my home?"

Teeter nervously cleared his throat. "It's sure something to hold on to."

Sharon arched an eyebrow. "I'm not sure I follow."

Teeter brushed lint from his pants leg and looked up at the ceiling. "We're talking a real bad actor here, and before we do anything else we've got to prosecute the more serious charge. That's the murder. I'm not sure if we can get the death penalty, but we'll try for it. You know the law, Miss Hays. Howard Saw wasn't a cop or a fireman. I think we'll go at it from the angle that Mr. Brie in there was trying to rob old Howard. At the very least we can get him an aggravated life sentence. That'll keep him off the street for fifteen years minimum."

Sharon rubbed her forehead. Texas death-penalty statutes applied to murder for hire, killing of a police officer or fireman in the line of duty, and murder during the commission of another felony, such as a rape or robbery. For any other murder the maximum sentence was life in TDC. The offense was aggravated if committed with a deadly weapon, which in Howard Saw's case meant the belt which Brie had used to strangle the guy. "What I'm hearing is that you're not going to prosecute this scumball for what he's done to me, right?" Sharon said in a monotone. "That's nice for you people. I'm sure the district attorney can take a shower without worrying a bit."

"Not exactly, Miss Hays. We're not saying we *won't* prosecute."

"Well what are you saying? Exactly."

Teeter scratched his chin. "Look. Monday I go to the grand jury on the Saw murder. If we get him for that, it's plenty. There's no reason for you to have to testify to what this guy did at your place if we're going to hammer him for the Saw killing. We've got your best interests in mind."

Sharon curled up her legs and sat on her ankles. She wore Top-siders without socks. "Do you think I'm addle-brained, Mr. Teeter?"

He lowered his head, rubbed the back of his neck, and didn't say anything.

"The Dallas County district attorney's office doesn't give a hoot in hell what I go through," Sharon said, "as long as they can get a conviction. You get another notch in your belt if you convict this guy for breaking into my house and trying to assault me and my daughter, regardless of what happens on the Saw murder."

Teeter covered his mouth and coughed into his hand. "Well, maybe we should hold the other case in abeyance until the Saw murder is history. After that, maybe a second indictment. I'll be honest with you. I don't think another case against this guy is going to be necessary, not with the ammunition we've got on the Saw murder. He told the whole thing to Donello. The two of them used to be boyfriend-girlfriend in the joint." The prosecutor grinned as if he'd just revealed one for the tabloids.

Sharon was beginning to get it. Her jaw clenched. "Where's Detective Green?" she said.

Teeter looked at his watch. "Detective Green?"

"Yes. You know, the witness who'll supply corroboration for my story about the break-in. Is he sleeping it off?"

Teeter looked around the room like a second-story man in search of a quick getaway. "I think Stan's . . . he might have gone on home."

"As soon as y'all called Milton Breyer to report what happened," Sharon said. She stood, folded her arms, and looked down at her feet. "I think I see, Mr. Teeter. For you to prosecute, your booze hound of a detective would have to tell what he was doing on my doorstep at that time of night. Well, you want to know?"

Teeter dropped his gaze. "It's none of my business."

Sharon's eyes flashed fire. "Oh, yes, it is. Everything is your business if you're prosecuting a case." She put on her sweetest smile. "Your good detective was hoping for a piece of ass, Mr. Teeter, not that he was going to get to first base. So what you've got here is, one, your complaining witness is a female with a potential sexual-harassment suit against the district attorney, which makes you not exactly chomp at the bit to handle the case to begin with, and two, your other witness doesn't want to testify because it might be embarrassing to him."

Sharon spun on her heel and peered inside the interview room. Two investigators had joined Brie, two guys in white shirts with rolled-up sleeves sitting across from the suspect. One of the cops offered Brie a cigarette. He turned down the smoke with a crooked-toothed grin.

Sharon whirled back to face the prosecutor. "I'll tell you what, Mr. Teeter. I don't know just how far I want to push this, but that vermin in there had in mind to harm me and my little girl. If the district attorney screws up and lets that guy back on the street, then Mr. Brie is the one that's going to need protection. From me. And if that's not clear enough, I'll be glad to say it into your tape recorder."

22

Sharon Hays would be the first to admit that her ambition to be an actress had had more than a little to do with ego. Being on stage in the spotlight had been one monster of a high, and even today she fantasized occasionally by taking a few bows in the privacy of her bedroom. It had been a long time since she'd had curtain-up butterflies, but as she entered the courtroom on Wednesday morning, the wings beat in her stomach like riverboat paddles. The third day of Midge's examining trial had them hanging from the rafters.

As Sharon paused just inside the doorway to look the situation over, all thoughts of the near disaster at her house involving Bradford Brie temporarily disappeared. Andy Wade and Rita Paschal from the *News* were in the courtroom, of course, just as they'd been the first two days of the hearing, but now both of them seemed uncomfortable. Whereas during the previous testimony they'd had the media section—which in Sandy Griffin's courtroom were the first two spectator rows on the judge's right—to themselves with plenty of spread-out room, today the *News* reporters were wedged in like a couple of sardines. On both sides of them sat men in shirtsleeves and women in slacks and business dresses, all with heads cocked attentively and pads and pens held ready. Sharon had heard the rumor yesterday (from the courtroom bailiff, who knew better than anyone what was going on) that there'd be a couple of reps from *People* magazine on hand today. That would account for some of the congestion among the media. Papers from San Antonio, Houston, and possibly even the *New York Times* would have heard that *People* was interested in the Rathermore case, and would have decided that something hot was brewing in Dallas. At least a couple of the writers present would be book authors, present on a freelance basis while their agents shopped proposals on the New York markets. Sharon could always spot the book writers; they were the ones huddled the most jealously over their notes, glancing suspiciously fore and aft, hoping against hope that they'd caught something in the hearing that their competition wasn't aware of.

Sharon excuse-me'd her way around two men who were craning their necks in search of a vacant seat, then hurried halfway down the aisle and paused again. Angry warmth coursed up the side of her neck as she zeroed in on the area near the gate leading to the bullpen.

So Milton Breyer had heard the media rumors and picked today to finally put in an appearance. Old Milt looked as if he'd just returned from the beauty parlor, where the stylist had poured on an extra quart or so of Grecian Formula. The prosecutor had worn his Judgment Day suit, coal black with creases like stiff paper. As Sharon watched, Breyer leaned over the rail to shake hands with the head movie guy, the older man with sideburns and a mustache. Today the producer had on a pale blue western-cut suit and Sharon wondered briefly whether the movie guy wore those godawful outfits back in Hollywood. The production company's second banana—Rayford Sly, Sharon thought, that was the name on the card the guy had handed her as she'd stepped onto the elevator—stood off to one side with his head bowed and his hands folded in front. The main movie man held Breyer by the elbow as he introduced the prosecutor to a newcomer. She was a striking brunette with every hair and grain of makeup exactly in place, and as she reached over the rail to shake Breyer's hand, she turned partway so that Sharon had a profile view. Sharon blinked in surprise. She'd never seen the woman in person, but this slick-looking chick was a co-anchor on *Hard Copy*. Christ, the national TV tabloid. Ready whenever you are, C.B., Sharon thought. She stood in the aisle for a few seconds to survey the rest of the courtroom.

Deborah North must have arrived at the crack of dawn in order to nail down her front-row aisle seat, and now she determinedly sat her ground while those at the opposite end of her pew scootched sideways, their expressions irritated as they made room for a woman who must have weighed three hundred pounds. Deb wore a gray dress with a white collar. Sharon went down the aisle, leaned over, and whispered in Midge's mother's ear, "How'd it go last night?"

Deb's face lit up like a moonbeam. "She remembered things I never thought she would. A couple of them when she was only two."

Sharon squeezed Deb's shoulder. "Good goin'," she said. "Now, I want you to take your time. Don't push Midge, but as soon as you think she's ready, I want to bring our investigator over to talk to her. That's Anthony Gear, he's the guy who'll sit between Midge and me at the defense table. The sooner Midge can talk to him, the sooner he can dig up witnesses and evidence to refute the crap they're going to throw at us."

Deb nodded. "Soon."

"Great. Just remember, you're the best therapy Midge can have right now." Sharon winked and smiled, and continued on her way.

She shouldered in between Milt Breyer, the movie guy, and the *Hard Copy* woman without speaking, and went through the gate. As she neared the prosecution table, headed for the defense side, Kathleen Fraterno said hesitantly, "Sharon?"

She turned. She'd say this much for Kathleen, the workhorse of the prosecution team wasn't putting on the dog for the media the way Milton Breyer was. Kathleen was her usual courtroom self, wearing a slim navy blue dress and matching medium-heeled pumps. Other than the usual courtroom banter, Sharon hadn't spoken to Kathleen since lunch at Joe Willie's, the day when she had lit out from the restaurant as if her pants were on fire. Since then her anger toward Kathleen had been replaced by a strange sort of pity. Fraterno had worked her tail off on the Rathermore case—that was apparent from her courtroom showing—and her reward for grinding her nose down to the bone was an occasional hump from Milton Breyer. What a booby prize, Sharon thought. She went over to where Kathleen sat and said impersonally, "Hi."

Kathleen closed her case file and turned in her chair. "I just wanted to tell you I heard about your trouble. I hope everything's all right. Is your daughter . . .?"

"Melanie?" Sharon said breezily. "Nah, she's fine. She didn't even wake up while it was going on." She felt pretty good herself, considering that less than thirty-six hours earlier she'd been parading naked through her house while a madman waved a gun at her. Yesterday in court she'd nearly fallen asleep during the second teenage killer's testimony. Last night she'd hit the sack at eight and slept clear through to seven-thirty in the morning, with Sheila Winston subbing on the carpool duties. "Thanks for asking, Kathleen," she said.

Fraterno threw a guilty look in Milt Breyer's direction, then stiffened her posture. More formally she said, "Well, if there's anything I can do . . ."

Sharon glanced at Breyer as well. He was watching the exchange between his assistant and the enemy with a disapproving scowl. Sharon considered thumbing her nose at the egotistical prick, but ended the conversation with a quick nod in Fraterno's direction. "Thanks again, Kathleen," she said, then hurried over to the defense side.

Russell Black wasn't putting on a show for the media or anybody else. His charcoal pinstriped suit needed pressing, and his lizard boots were dusty. He was turned around in his chair, glumly regarding the spectator section. As Sharon approached, he said, "What we need here is a good trapeze act."

Sharon set down her briefcase, smiled, and reached out to straighten the knot on Black's tie. "There, that's better," she said. "Quit scowling so much, boss. Gee whiz, you're going to smear your greasepaint."

Sharon thought that the pains Judge Sandy Griffin had taken prior to her entrance into the spotlight were sort of pitiful. Judge Griffin was a plain woman to begin with, and given her alleged sexual preference, any attempt on her part to gussy up would be greeted with raised eyebrows. But nonetheless, here she came into the arena wearing fourteen tons of makeup, her cheeks a bright pink, her lipstick thick and cardinal red, and enough purple eyeshadow to cover a clown convention. God, but it's garish, Sharon thought. No one, but no one—with the exception of Russell Black, of course—seemed immune to the public eye. Judge Griffin assumed her seat in a royal posture. Sharon was afraid that if she made eye contact with Griffin, she'd burst out laughing, so she averted her gaze. Somewhere in the spectator section a woman snickered.

If the judge heard the snickering, she didn't let on. She quickly called the court to order and told the bailiff to fetch Midge. The bailiff exited right as the audience swiveled heads like tennis fans. When he returned with Midge in tow, Sharon gasped out loud.

Midge's hair was beautifully washed and combed, soft as down with a wave across her forehead. Her jailhouse smock was clean as a pin, starched and pressed, and for once the garment fit. Sharon knew from her days as a prosecutor that pressed jail uniforms didn't come easy, and required a bribe to the inmates who worked in the laundry. There were also inmates who would do hair in exchange for cigarettes or ice cream. Sharon turned to look at Deborah North. She beamed at Midge as if she were wearing her first prom dress. So much for the source of the inmate bribes, Sharon thought. Deb had learned the ropes in a hurry.

Midge's face was scrubbed clean, and her complexion seemed clearer. As she took her place beside Sharon at the table there wasn't a whiff of body odor. Overnight, Midge had been transformed from a disgustingly filthy fat girl to a pleasant, plump, and almost attractive young lady.

Once Sharon was able to pick her lower jaw up from the floor, she patted Midge's arm and whispered, "Your hair looks very pretty."

Midge blushed and grinned. "A lady washed and combed it. She's a hooker."

Sharon's smile froze in place. Well, what had she expected for a couple of packs of Pall Malls? Ralph from Neiman's? "That's nice, Midge," Sharon said.

Judge Griffin banged her gavel. "To continue the hearing. Call your first witness, Madame Prosecutor." Sharon suspected that Griffin, political animal that she was, would get some serious coaching on application of her makeup before the trial itself began.

Milton Breyer stood up and cleared his throat. "If the court please. I'll be conducting the state's case today."

If Breyer's action miffed Fraterno, she wasn't showing it. Her head was down as she intently studied her notes. That Breyer wanted to become lawyer for a day was hardly a shock. With all the national press and movie guys in attendance, Sharon wouldn't have been surprised if a girl in spangled tights had appeared and set up a platform for Milt to stand on.

Judge Griffin showed no emotion. "Very well. Call your first witness, sir." Griffin, along with all the other judges in the county, had seen the media transform prosecutors into showboats thousands of times, and Sharon suspected that the judge was secretly suppressing a yawn.

"The state calls," Breyer said importantly, "Linda Haymon Rathermore."

Oh God, Sharon thought, to be a star. Midge sucked in air through her nose.

There was a loud rustling accompanied by a turning of heads as Stan Green escorted Linda down the aisle as if he were giving her away in matrimony. Linda walked in snow white spike heels as though she'd been born in them, a confident showcase walk, back straight, head tilted regally. She wore a pale lavender suit with padded shoulders. Her blond hair was fluffed out just so, her nails done in matching lavender, diamonds on her fingers and earlobes like twinkling stars. Stan Green was dressed in a navy blue suit. As he opened the gate for Linda and stood aside, he glanced at Sharon, then looked quickly away. Sharon resisted the urge to sneer.

Okay, folks, she thought, this is the act you've all come to see. She dug in her briefcase for pen and notepad as Linda Rathermore stepped up to the court reporter and raised her right hand.

"So to repeat," Milton Breyer said, "you were reclining on the bed reading a book. Near eleven, is that right?"

"That's about right," Linda said, her perfect newscaster's voice amplified by a microphone. Her legs were crossed, one shapely nylon-encased knee showing, her hands folded in her lap in attentive respect. "I know it was past ten-thirty because the newscast was over."

"The same newscast you yourself narrated prior to your marriage?"

"Yes, sir." A modest lowering of sky blue eyes.

Christ, Sharon thought, if they bring up her TV career one more time, I'm going to barf right here on the table.

"And your husband," Breyer said, looking toward the newspeople, "where was he?"

"Bill liked to exercise. I think he was doing sit-ups."

Sharon frowned. The photos she'd seen of William Rathermore didn't depict a physical-fitness nut. The guy had had a pretty good-sized gut, in fact. Sharon made a note to check out Rathermore's conditioning habits. Likely there was nothing there, but one never knew.

"And that's when the boys came charging in?" Breyer said.

"Yes." Linda's shoulders moved in a shudder.

"And you had no warning? No sound outside your bedroom?"

"Well ... the security panel."

Breyer rested his elbows on the prosecution table, made a pyramid with his hands, and placed his chin on his fingertips. Ah, yes, the security panel. "Will you please explain that?" he said.

The question was nebulous and enough out of order to be absolutely ditzy. Sharon nearly objected on general principles, just to show Breyer what a jackass he was being, but held her tongue. Sandy Griffin would sustain an objection, but then Kathleen Fraterno would set her boss straight, and Breyer would merely reword the question.

Linda said, "We heard a series of beeps. Someone using the panel to disarm the security system."

"Which requires a code?"

"Yes, sir."

"A code known to who, Mrs. Rathermore?"

Linda appeared deep in thought. "Me. Bill, of course. And Bill's two daughters, for when they were home from school."

"From Hockaday? The boarding school?"

"Yes."

"No one else knew the code."

"No, sir. We'd thought about giving it to the butler and

maid, but for security reasons we changed our minds. When the people were on duty during the day we simply left the system off."

Breyer's voice lowered an octave. "Was the defendant, Midge Rathermore, is she one of the daughters you mentioned?"

Linda's gaze flicked distastefully at Midge, then settled back on the prosecutor. "Yes, sir. Midge knew the code."

"I see. Mrs. Rathermore, how much time elapsed between your hearing the alarm turned off and these boys' entrance into your bedroom?"

Linda wrung her hands. "Only seconds. Not over half a minute."

Midge Rathermore shifted in her chair. Not only was the teenager well groomed for a change, there was a noticeable defiance in her posture which Sharon had never seen. If Linda's morals were as down in the gutter as Deborah North had said, Midge must despise her stepmother. Sharon hoped against hope. If Midge was now ready to fight, her defense might not turn out to be hopeless after all.

Breyer now assumed a tone of utmost sympathy. "Mrs. Rathermore, I'm now going to ask you to describe what happened next. Take your time, please. The court will understand if it's difficult for you."

Linda's hands twisted violently in her lap. "All right. Of course." There was a tearful catch in her voice.

Sharon couldn't take her eyes off the witness's hands. Over and over the twisting and squeezing, the white-knuckled gripping of the thumb. There was something familiar about the way Linda Rathermore's hands remained at rest as she listened to the question, then writhed in her lap as she answered. Sharon would have to think on it. The answer would come to her.

"Well, the door opened. Slammed open, there's still a mark on the wall," Linda said. Now a tear ran down her cheek, as if on cue.

It *is* on cue, Sharon thought. Sure, body language, elementary method acting. The twisting together of the hands, the programmed catches in Linda's voice. Sharon's New York stage coach had taught her to slightly tighten the larynx muscles just before speaking, and the tears were even easier than the voice. Just close the nasal passages and breathe rapidly, and the old ducts would flow like open faucets. If properly controlled, the rapid breathing would come across as a series of tune-up sobs. You're hamming it up in front of the wrong chick, old Linda, Sharon thought. During her off-Broadway days, the size of Sharon's paychecks had made bawling on cue as easy as falling off a log.

As Linda Rathermore haltingly and tearfully told how the boys had bludgeoned her husband to death before her very eyes, Sharon began to write like crazy. She had an idea.

Sharon whispered to Anthony Gear, "You ready?"

He winked and nodded. Today the detective wore a pale blue sports coat with navy slacks, not quite the Mike Hammer effect, but better than the garish plaid he'd had on the previous two days. Gear thumbed the clicker on his ballpoint and bent over his legal pad. Sharon rustled through her notes as she prepared to cross-examine Linda Rathermore.

Sharon was suddenly overcome with stage fright. Christ, she couldn't believe it. All those years on stage, all that time as a prosecutor, and here she was shaking like a leaf as she began her first cross-examination in private practice. She decided that her bout of nerves had something to do with the way Russell Black was looking at her, his thick brows furrowed like Zeus. She averted her gaze from Black, and the butterflies' wings slowed a fraction.

Sharon drew a shallow breath. "Linda Haymon Rathermore. I assume Haymon is your maiden name?"

"Yes." Linda showed no emotion, her face impassive like a candidate for Honest Woman of the Year.

Sharon intensified her tone of voice. "Was Haymon always your name? From birth?" She cut her eyes at the bench. A grain of mascara fell from Judge Griffin's lash and lodged in thick eyeshadow.

Linda looked at the prosecution table as if searching for help. "No, it wasn't."

Sharon glanced inside her file. Pretending to study notes while gathering one's thoughts wasn't an exclusive trick to Kathleen Fraterno. "Wasn't your name originally

Harmon?" Sharon said. The butterflies barely rustled their wings now as Sharon got into the thrill of the hunt.

Linda brushed imaginary lint from her skirt. "That's right."

"Very similar names. Could you tell us the reason for the change, Mrs. Rathermore?"

Linda's self-confidence was faltering. Both Breyer and Fraterno now exhibited concerned frowns, and Kathleen wrote something down. The prosecution wasn't ready for this, Sharon knew, and no wonder. Anthony Gear had found the name change only yesterday during a routine check of courthouse records, and the expression on Linda's face told Sharon that she might be hitting a small jackpot. "Could you, Mrs. Rathermore?" Sharon repeated.

"I had—" Linda said rapidly, then cleared her throat and said, "An agent suggested it."

"Possibly because another newscaster was already named Linda Harmon?" Sharon knew an objection was coming, but asked the question anyway. Her nervousness had subsided; she was now cool as a cucumber. Was having a pretty good time, in fact.

"Objection," Fraterno said, half rising. "Your Honor, we don't see the relevance of this."

Oh, yes, you do, cutes, Sharon thought. She considered reminding Judge Griffin that, in view of her ruling that the defense was confined to one lawyer at a time, then Fraterno shouldn't be objecting to cross questions asked of Milt Breyer's witness. Sharon didn't bring up the issue, however. She didn't want anything diverting Sandy Griffin's attention away from Linda's name change, and besides, if everyone had to wait for Milton Breyer to get the point, this frigging examining trial might never end. Sharon spoke slowly and carefully: "Your Honor, this is a preliminary procedure to trial. We're entitled to broad discovery here."

The judge's call was a toss-up, but Sharon was counting on Sandy Griffin's curiosity. All of the reporters and spectators were dying for Linda to answer, all sitting expectantly forward, and Sharon figured Judge Griffin to be every bit as nosy as the next gal. The judge said, without hesitation, "Objection overruled. Repeat your question, Counsel."

"My question was," Sharon said. "Did you change

your name because someone in your chosen field was already using your maiden name?"

Linda fidgeted. "I might have. I don't recall."

"Well, then, was news broadcasting your chosen field?"

Silence. Fraterno half rose from her seat, then sat back down.

"Or possibly," Sharon continued, "did you originally aspire to be an actress? That would better account for the change in names, and the fact that you'd be using an agent." Talk about shooting from the hip, Sharon thought. If this blew up in her face, she wasn't going to be able to face Russell Black, who was now just as much in the dark as were Fraterno and Breyer.

"It seems . . . I think I may have wanted to act once."

Aha, Sharon thought. She practically sagged with relief. "Mrs. Rathermore, where are you from originally?" It had seemed strange that no one, including Deborah North, had been able to dig up any background on this woman, and now Sharon knew why. They'd all been checking under Linda's assumed name.

"Baltimore," Linda said. "The . . . Baltimore area." Her hands remained at rest.

Sharon cocked an ear. Pen scratched on paper behind her as Gear took his notes. Get all of this, Mr. Private Eye, Sharon thought. "And where did you attend college?" Sharon said.

"U.M. Maryland."

"Was journalism your major?"

Linda brushed a golden lock with her fingertips. "No, it wasn't."

"Well, did you graduate?"

"No." Practically a whisper.

"Speak up, please." Sharon looked at the court reporter, a jolly black woman who was now straining to hear.

More forcefully Linda said, "No, I didn't."

"In what year did you graduate from high school, Mrs. Rathermore?" Christ, no one even seemed to know this woman's age.

Linda gave the prosecution side a look which said, Get me the hell down from this witness stand. Fraterno seemed absorbed in her notes. Milt Breyer beamed at his witness, but made no move to object. Linda ran the tip of her tongue over even upper teeth before saying, "Nineteen sixty-nine."

Sharon rummaged through her file to hide her surprise. This chick had more miles on her than one would have imagined; Linda Rathermore could easily pass for early thirties. Compared to her, Sharon thought, I'm a mere infant.

"Thank you," she said. She glanced at Anthony Gear. The private detective showed a quick nod. Having given Gear plenty of food for investigative thought, Sharon now looked for a way to end it without exposing anything she had in store for Linda at trial. She thought of one more skeleton which might be rattling around in Linda's closet. "Mrs. Rathermore, how did you first meet Mr. Rathermore?"

"At a party. A friend introduced us." Linda's voice practically dripped relief. She'd be well prepared for the defense to grill her about her affair with William Rathermore. Sharon pictured Breyer and Fraterno telling Linda, "If they ask you this, you say such and such."

"Who was this friend?" Sharon said.

"Arnold Millen, I think."

"Who is?"

"He was the news director at the station. *Is* the news director."

"Did you know that Mr. Rathermore was married at the time?"

"Since it was a mere introduction," Linda said testily, "I had no reason to inquire." As a scriptwriter, Sharon thought, Milt Breyer would make a pretty good shortstop. Since I'd just met him I didn't see any reason to ask, would have been a much more natural-sounding answer.

"When was it," Sharon said, "that the relationship developed into something more?"

"After more meetings," Linda said, "when we were thrown together."

Sharon paused to think. Any answers Linda would give to this line of questions would be prosecution programmed. Judge Griffin was looking just a bit bored, and Sharon felt that if she dragged the cross-examination out much longer, the judge would begin to get mad. Besides,

Anthony Gear should have little trouble digging up the details of Linda screwing around with a married man; the whole affair had been blown up big in the papers. Sharon decided to let well enough alone. "I have no further questions at this time," she said with finality.

Linda's eyes widened, clearly in surprise, and Breyer and Fraterno exchanged exasperated glances. All that rehearsal for nothing, Sharon thought. The judge appeared surprised as well, and began drumming her fingers. As Linda rose to leave the witness box, Sharon said, "Oh. Just one more thing."

Linda sat down and waited expectantly.

"Mrs. Rathermore," Sharon said, "do you like the Soles method? Or do you find Reasor's school of thought more effective?"

As she spoke, she twisted her hands, wringing them in an exact duplicate of Linda's earlier movements during direct examination. Both the judge and Russell Black looked at Sharon as though she'd just stripped stark naked, but Linda Rathermore wasn't puzzled at all. Her gaze dropped nervously to her lap. Sharon considered a few crocodile tears, but it had been a long time. Once in New York she'd giggled onstage while trying to work up a tragic cry, and the director had never let her live it down. Kathleen Fraterno's jaw dropped as realization dawned.

Sharon relaxed her hands and favored Linda Rathermore with a quick, saucy wink. "Your Honor, I'll withdraw the question," she said.

As Sharon headed down the corridor toward the elevators, Russell Black said, "Who in God's name is Soles?" He was moving alongside her in testy strides; they'd just sidestepped the movie producer's second banana, Rayford Sly, as he stood impatiently outside the courtroom.

"Who?" Sharon said.

"Soles. And the other guy, Reasor. I thought you were onto something." Black pressed the elevator's Down button. From down the hall Andy Wade of the *News* shouted, "Mr. Black. Got a minute?" Black shook his head at the reporter.

Sharon held her briefcase handle in both hands with the case itself touching her thighs. "They're drama coaches.

Both of them wrote books on body language. That was between me and Linda, Russ, she's a trained actress. Five'll get you ten that she somehow stumbled into a newsroom when she was between parts. It happens all the time since the TV folks quit using professional journalists and switched to the beautiful people."

The elevator doors parted, and Sharon and Black crowded onto the car with eight or ten spectators who'd been at the hearing. The spectators all watched the ceilings and walls and pretended not to eavesdrop. Sharon felt suddenly lighter as the car started down.

"How'd you know that about her?" Black said.

"I didn't. Not 'til she started the hand-wringing act during direct examination. I don't know how she felt about her husband's death when it happened, but all that tear-jerking on the witness stand was strictly ham and eggs. She was using textbook body language."

Black rose on the balls of his feet, then sank down on his heels. "I guess we'll be shooting our boy Gear up to Baltimore to find out more on that woman."

"I think the first order of business," Sharon said, "is those teenagers who hung out at the Rathermores'. I'm making his Baltimore reservations for next week."

The elevator halted on the ground floor. Black exited after Sharon, and as they walked amid the crowd toward the exit he said, "Takin' a lot on yourself, ain'tcha?"

Oh, God, the male ego, Sharon thought. She gulped. "I just thought—"

"Not that there's anything wrong with it," Black said. "But let's don't be forgettin' who's runnin' this show." He picked up his long-legged pace, head down.

Sharon did a double-take. Was he dressing her down or wasn't he? In ten years or so, she thought, I might figure him out. "Whatever you say, boss," she said.

23

Bradford Brie, who'd done enough jailin' to last the average man a lifetime, sat on his haunches to peer out the food slot in his cell door while he ate his dinner. The food was typical Sheriff's Hilton: one fried chicken thigh, blood red in the center, a mess of runny beans and a glob of canned chocolate pudding, all served in a Styrofoam tray with the only utensil a plastic spoon. The beans were mixed in with the pudding and the chicken was dipped in both. There was a cup of red Kool-Aid sitting on the floor. Brie's napkin was a wad of toilet paper torn from the roll beside his stool. He smacked as he chewed and slurped Kool-Aid to wash down a mouthful of beans.

The chicken was cold, the beans foul-smelling, and the pudding tasted like chalk, but Brie didn't mind. He was an adjuster. No experienced con expected a jailhouse meal to have any taste; food in the county was just something to keep a man's belly from growling. Prison chow was much better; Brie rated Dallas County Jail food, on a scale of one to ten, around a four. He was glad that as a murder suspect he was entitled to a private cell. In the open-bay tanks, the niggers would gang up on a man and take his food.

To Brie's way of thinking, the noise level would require more adjusting than the food. This jailhouse was loud, baby, was it ever. There was a TV set in every day room up and down the corridor, every set was on a different channel with the volume up as loud as it would go, and the din would give the average man a headache. The niggers all liked *Soul Train*, Brie knew, while the bikers all were queer for rasslin', and which program played on what TV depended on which group could whip the most ass, the bikers or the niggers. There were no acoustics in the Lew Sterrett Justice Center, only bare concrete ceilings and floors, so the TV sounds blended into one never-ending blast of noise. Bradford Brie set his mind to tune the racket out.

Last night they'd handcuffed him to a chain gang of twenty men, crammed the lot of them into the back of a van, and moved them from city jail down to the county. It was a part of the process which Brie had committed to memory. First the city, then, after the detectives had figured out that Bradford Brie was one stand-up con who wasn't saying shit to anybody, on to the county. Here they'd hold him for a while and then turn him loose. He understood that the entire bust was one big bluff on the part of the Dallas police.

All of the detectives' questions had been shots in the dark, Brie thought. Absolutely no way could they make a case on him for killing the fat punk of a lawyer, Howard Saw. There'd been no witnesses, and Brie was certain he'd left no prints. No one other than Wilfred Donello knew who'd offed the lawyer, and no way would Wilfred Donello ever snitch on a man. No fucking way. Brie and Donello had been too close for too many years for that to happen. All he had to do was keep his mouth shut, and in a few days he'd be free as the air. He finished his meal and set the tray and cup in his pan slot. In a few minutes one of the trusties would come to haul the garbage away.

The thing that itched at the back of Brie's mind had to do with the break-in at the lawyer lady's house. Not a word about that from the detective, and he couldn't believe it. That would be an easy case for them to make against him; he'd been caught leaving her house, hadn't he? If he hadn't been unlucky enough to run into the big drunk ox on her porch, he would still be running. With the woman and the drunken ox as witnesses, why weren't the police charging him with assault? Or burglary at the least. Twenty years, and with the pistol he'd carried to aggravate the charges, he would be looking at a full man's nickel before parole.

He thoughtfully brushed chicken crumbs from his

jumpsuit pants as he went over to sit on his bunk. Though a confirmed slob on the outside, Brie was a cleanliness nut in lockup. Keeping one's house and clothing spic and span was one of the only bits of pride left to a convict. His jail uniform was pressed and fit him perfectly, one of the perks of being a stand-up con who knew the ropes. Last night during in-processing, while the other new men had received ragged hand-me-downs tossed at them by cursing trusties, Brie had had a talk with the trusty in charge of the laundry. The talk had netted him a pressed set of clothing twice a week in exchange for a carton of cigarettes. The price had nearly doubled since Brie's last trip to county jail, but since he didn't smoke himself he thought that fresh clothing was worth the cost.

He gingerly touched the Band-Aid on his neck. The laceration which the lawyer woman had bitten into his flesh burned like fire. She had one coming for that, and Brie aimed to see that she collected. Picturing Sharon Hays, long-legged with fine, bouncy breasts as she'd stepped dripping from her shower, brought a crooked-toothed grin to his face.

And suddenly he understood why the police hadn't questioned him about Sharon Hays. Sure, the bitch didn't want to testify against him. Bradford Brie had raped four-teen women in his life, including a twelve-year-old whom he tied down and beaten to a pulp with a wire coat hanger, and not a single one of the females had ever faced him on the witness stand. Brie didn't understand why the bitches preferred not to talk about the attacks—he certainly liked to talk about them, spending a lot of time in the joint swapping pussy stories with other cons—and didn't care. The point was that women didn't like to talk about anyone wanting to rape them, and the lawyer lady was no different. Her silence would clear the way for Brie's release, which was fine with him.

Brie had started a letter before lunch, and he now picked up a legal pad and Bic disposable pen from his bunk and continued with his writing. The mattress on which he sat was made of green plastic, stuffed with rags, the product of one of the TDC work farms. The frame of his bunk was solid steel, bolted to the wall and floor. Brie had been working on his letter for several hours with his tongue jammed firmly into his cheek, and had had to yell to the guy in the adjacent cubicle for help in spelling a word or two. He didn't read and write very well, but what he did write was emotional. Making certain that Wilfred Donello understood exactly where he was coming from was important to Brie in the overall scheme of things.

There were shuffling footsteps in the corridor, accompanied by the *whush* of a trash bag dragged along the floor. Brie tore the three finished pages from his legal pad, got down on his haunches, and duck-walked over to his door. He thrust his letter through the food slot and waved it around. "Trusty," he said loudly. "Yo, trusty."

In seconds a face appeared in the opening. It was a black man, forty or so (though Brie had a harder time estimating niggers' ages than he did with white men), who had one drooping eyelid and a gold tooth in the front of his mouth. The trusty scraped Brie's finished meal into the garbage bag, then said, "What you want, bro?"

"Hey, yeah." Brie grinned. "Listen, I got to have this delivered to a man." He held the letter against his chest and folded it neatly in half.

The black man narrowed his one good eye. "Cost you a deck. Free-world smokes, none of the Bugler roll-your-own shit."

"No problem, man. I got money in my account."

"If you don't pay, you be hurting," the trusty said.

"You're talking to a man's done some time," Brie said. "I say I'll pay, I pay you."

The trusty reached through the slot and took the letter. "What man you want to get this?"

"Wilfred Donello. Big man with a scarred ear. White dude, everybody knows this guy. He's a trusty, same as you."

The trusty wadded the letter and tossed it back inside the cell. "Fuck you. I don't deliver no mail to no Donello. Not for no price."

Brie's face twisted violently. "I give you two decks, whatever kind of free-world smokes you want. Money don't matter to me."

"You don't get it. They done moved Wilfred Donello this morning, into the snitch wing. Hope he get fucked in the ass up there, dropping a dime on somebody. Best you don't be talking no Wilfred Donello around here, something might happen to you." The trusty stood up and continued on his way, dragging the garbage bag behind.

Brie put his face to the slot. "Hey. Hey, no," he yelled. "You're thinking of the wrong man. Wouldn't no Wilfred Donello snitch on anybody. Hey, I know this guy a long time."

24

Three floors downstairs from the cell where Bradford Brie had dinner, Midge Rathermore was getting a jail-house perm. She loved having her hair done while listening to Sonya sing the blues. Sonya believed she could have been a professional vocalist—the slim black hooker pronounced it "pro*fesh*nul"—if only her mama had provided her with lessons. In fact, she might yet sing for a living once she'd saved enough from turning tricks, which was just something she did to get by until the right somebody discovered her talent. Sonya had told Midge all of this right after she'd become the heavy teenager's only friend in the cell block, which she had done on the day the commissary cart had brought Sonya four pints of ice cream and a carton of free-world Marlboros. Regardless of her motive, Sonya's rendition of "Summertime" wasn't bad at all. She told Midge that a boyfriend, her legitimate man, had taken her to State Fair Music Hall to watch the road show of *Porgy and Bess,* and as well as Sonya knew the words, Midge was certain the story was true. Midge believed everything Sonya told her because Sonya was her friend.

The women's wing at Lew Sterrett was exactly like the men's section of the jail—bare cement floors with steel bunks, tables and chairs anchored in place—but the girls had better learned to improvise. Keeping their hair clean and attractive was a major problem; heated rollers were out, of course, as well as anything else electric which could be modified into a weapon. Pasteboard toilet paper centers became rollers, secured in place with plastic paper clips. Once rolled, the hair was allowed to air dry, then the soggy toilet paper cylinders came out and the hair was fluffed with a brush as best as possible. Before a not un-friendly guard had set up the windfall from Midge's mother, Sonya had done hair for cigarettes and candy. Now that her monetary problems were solved, Sonya concentrated on keeping Midge happy and being her friend.

A metal bench and table in the dayroom served as a vanity, with Midge drowsily listening to Sonya's crooning and *General Hospital* on the television as background noise. Sonya moved around behind Midge, firmly turning the teenager's hair around a toilet paper roll, clipping, reaching for another roll and paper clip, combing, fitting the ends of Midge's hair onto another pasteboard cylinder. White, black, and Hispanic women lounged on benches all around, staring vacantly at the television, some chewing gum, all patiently doing time in loose-fitting cotton smocks.

This part of the women's section was for nonviolents: hookers, druggies, shoplifters, and the like, women with no history of violence whom the jail classification system declared weren't into any type of sexual abuse. There was a separate wing for females who were into lesbianism, both consensual and forced, and Midge's age had dictated to jail personnel that she be kept away from the butches. It wouldn't have mattered to Midge if they had housed her with the violents; sexual abuse was nothing new to her, and she would have gone along with anything the other inmates wanted if only someone would be her friend. If Sonya had wished, Midge would have gladly spread her legs.

So it had been as far back as the dull-witted girl could remember. She had only a faint recollection of the time before her mother had gone away, and even back then Midge had spent little time with either of her parents. Nearly all of her days and most of her nights had been under the nanny's supervision, and while the nanny had been efficient enough, she hadn't been really caring.

During those early years it had been Midge and Susan, and Midge had showered every ounce of love she could muster on her baby sister. She had played with Susan like a doll, hugging and pampering the smaller child endlessly. Then, when Midge was around six and Susan about four, the younger sister had surpassed Midge intellectually. It was when Midge realized Susan was smarter than she that her love for her baby sister had begun to dissipate. She'd felt that Susan had delighted in showing her up.

Mother had gone away for good when Midge was eight and had the mental capacity of a three-year-old. She had been heartbroken at first, but as time had passed, her feeling for her mother had become hatred as well. Food had been Midge's method for filling the void inside her; indulgent nannies had catered to her every whim in that regard, and by the age of ten she had weighed a hundred and fifty pounds.

In recent weeks her feeling for her mother had become again one of devotion; puppylike, Midge Rathermore responded to any outreaching that resembled love in any form. When she had been thirteen and her father had begun to take Susan into his bed, Midge had longed for the same privilege. Her father had rebuffed her, and Midge had hated him for it. She had hated her stepmother, Linda, as well, feeling that she kept her father away from her.

Her relationship with the boys had been another attempt on Midge's part to get someone to like her. She had been detached from the sex, saying nursery rhymes and singing songs as the boys had their way with her. She had wanted them for friends, and had felt she must satisfy them sexually to earn their friendship. She had thought Chris Leonard and Troy Burdette to be witty, and when they had first spoken of killing her father, Midge had gone along with them, feeling that she'd do anything if only they would be her friends. The arrangement to give them part of her inheritance had meant nothing to Midge; the dull-witted child had no real understanding of money.

Sonya interrupted her singing to say softly, "Turn your head toward me, honey." Midge obliged, smiling at her newest friend and gently patting the hooker's hand. Sonya parted Midge's wet hair with a comb and resumed her song.

Midge liked Sharon Hays so much that at times she felt her heart would burst, and it terrified the teenager to think that sometime Sharon might go away. The older lawyer,

Mr. Black, meant nothing to Midge, but the teenager would do anything to keep Sharon's friendship. Sharon wanted details of what had happened between Midge and Troy and Chris, and Midge wouldn't have minded at all telling Sharon the truth about William Rathermore's death. But she was afraid that Sharon, on learning what she wanted to know, would go away just as Midge's mother had once done. Midge felt that the only way to keep Sharon's interest was to hold back the truth as a secret. As long as Sharon didn't have the answer, she would continue to be Midge Rathermore's friend.

25

Ever since the attack at her house, Sharon's nerves had been unraveled yarn. She was sleeping alternate nights, first lying awake until dawn as each tiny noise in the house brought her into a panicked sitting position, then so bleary-eyed the following evening that she was completely zonked by nine o'clock. today was Saturday, and Friday night had been dusk-to-dawn wakefulness. Sharon feared that the drone in Russell Black's voice might put her out like a light.

"I think runnin' down Linda Rathermore's past is top priority," Black said. "You got any problem with that?"

"None, boss," Sharon said with a yawn. "Only that you've said this before. We're doing it." Having been on board for a while, Sharon had lost her awe for Black's office setup. The veteran lawyer's quarters still were impressive—handball court-size mahogany desk, rich red carpet with three-quarter-inch padding, visitors' chairs with red velvet cushions, celebrity-like photos of Black adorning the walls—but there were a few ragged edges. The carpet beneath the window was sun-faded, and a dime-sized chunk of wood was missing from the edge of Black's desk. There was nothing *wrong* with the office decor, but Sharon thought the place needed a woman's touch.

"I keep askin'," Black said. "But I'm not gettin' any results."

Sharon felt like stretching out on the floor, and hoped that Midge would forgive her for the thought. "Monday morning Mr. Gear's headed for Baltimore. And no matter what we find out about Linda, we've still got to tie her in with William Rathermore's abuse of his daughters. If Linda was the person on the grassy knoll at the Kennedy assassination, and it has nothing to do with Midge and her sister, it won't help us." She wore white jeans and blue running shoes along with a navy blue knit shirt, and her ankle rested on her knee. A legal pad lay across her inner thigh. Melanie was spending the day at Sheila's. Visible through the office window, a cleanup crew swept the steps at the old county courthouse. It had rained three days the previous week, but now, moving into late June, Dallas was in for a three-month scorching.

Black nervously pinched his chin. "Speaking of Midge's sister—Susan?"

"That's right."

"We got anything on her whereabouts?"

"None, only that she's withdrawn from school. Mr. Gear's working on it, that's all he'll tell me."

"For what he's chargin', he ought to be workin' on somethin'." Black wore a wash-faded golf shirt and tan cotton pants. There was a stain on the shirt. Egg yolk, Sharon thought. "You got your pretrial motion in order?" Black said.

Sharon rubbed her eyes. "It's not a motion I've got in mind."

Black's eyebrows moved closer together. He should trim them, Sharon thought. Black watched her with ice blue eyes that mirrowed a mind as quick as lightning bolts.

"What I thought I'd do," Sharon said, "I thought I'd get into the abuse question when we cross-examine Linda."

"That's dangerous. You need to put the abuse question in front of the judge in pretrial."

Sharon firmly shook her head. "Not with Sandy Griffin. I don't want Fraterno sensing what we're up to until the very last second. I'm sure of my research, but I don't want to give her time to dig up any cases that might muddy the issue."

"How've you got the cross-examination pictured?" Black said.

"Linda's?"

"Yeah."

"The way I see it," Sharon said, "no matter what she says on direct, I'll hit her right off by asking if she ever saw William Rathermore sexually abusing his daughters."

"To which she'll automatically say no."

Sharon put both feet on the floor. "To which she won't have a chance to say anything, because Fraterno will object before I finish the question. Which is how we'll introduce the abuse issue."

"In front of the bench?" Black said.

"In chambers, more than likely. Oh, there'll be a bench conference and then a recess. Kathleen will say we're just trying to incense the jury against the victim, and that's when I plan to trot out my theory on battered wives, extended to battered children. Judge Griffin will likely call for briefs."

"Which we've already got, thanks to your trip to the law library."

"And which Fraterno will have to hump to come up with," Sharon said. She almost added that Milt Breyer might have to go horny while Fraterno researched the law, but decided that such a catty remark would be unprofessional. It would be sort of to the point, though, Sharon thought.

"We're bankin' a lot," Black said, "on the judge allowin' us to get into the abuse question. If she sustains Fraterno's objection, we're dead in the water."

"We'd be dead without it anyway, boss. We'd be stuck with beating Linda Rathermore up on the stand, and we're probably going to have to do that anyway."

"Is our client openin' up any?" Black said.

Sharon inhaled and exhaled. "Some. Her mother's done wonders with her. Midge even talked to Mr. Gear for about an hour, night before last. The problem is that what she says doesn't help."

"That child's got real hang-ups."

"It's much worse than that, Russ. She hired those boys, or thinks she did. We can make all the noise we want to. Midge is such a mixed-up kid, gang-bangs and the works, we could probably make a case that those two studs egged her into it. But she promised them part of her inheritance for killing her dad, and there's not any way around it."

"Don't guess we could put her on the stand," Black said.

"We'd be cutting our throats. Aside from the fact that she'd give this ditzy grin and tell the jury she did it, Midge isn't mature enough that I'd trust her. She might tell us one thing, then get on the witness stand and say something else."

"What in hell's wrong with these kids today?" Black rocked back and looked at the ceiling.

Sharon let her legal pad dangle from her fingertips. "I've got a different theory than most people. The basic problem is no different than it's ever been. Every high school class in history has got at least one Midge Rathermore. The unattractive girl so mixed up that the boys have an easy time with her. It's nothing more than a desire to be popular. To feel wanted and loved." Like me sleeping with Stan Green? Sharon thought. The corners of her mouth tugged involuntarily downward.

Black's cheeks relaxed in pity. "Ours was Estelle Bigby. They used to take turns with her in the balcony at the picture show. Every one of those guys should have had their butts thrown in jail."

Including you? Sharon thought. She tried to picture Black as he'd looked in high school. Conjuring up such an image was near impossible. "Back then," she said, "they didn't know what they do now about sex abuse. Chances are, every one of those girls had an older brother, stepfather, whatever."

"This is Midge's real daddy we're talkin' about," Black said.

"To the child it makes no difference, from what I understand. Any older male, sort of an authority figure. He slept with Susan and rejected Midge. Like lighting a stick of dynamite."

"Back in my day," Black said, "I don't recall anybody tryin' to kill the parent."

"That much has changed," Sharon said. "A lot of people want to blame drugs, but I don't see any evidence of that with Midge. I think it's the power of suggestion. Too much in the newspapers and on TV. Did you get our psychologist's report on Midge?"

Black scratched his head. "Didn't tell me much."

"Look again. Her IQ's a shade below dull normal. In

public school I doubt she could pass. Abused or not," Sharon said, "Midge Rathermore didn't think up any murder plot on her own. Somebody planted the suggestion."

Black frowned. "Who?"

"Maybe those boys themselves. Who's responsible for suggesting it to them. God only knows."

Black opened his drawer, took out Sharon's research file, and dropped it on his desk. "The whole case, right here," he said. "Jesus H., a lot depends on this."

"I know," Sharon said.

When she went across the hall to her office, she sat down and stared at the three books on her desk. Her trusty ever-ready penal code and the family law section of the statutes were stacked, with the *Standard Synopsis on Victim's Rights* off to one side. In addition to working on the Rathermore case, she'd bought the victims' rights paperback with the idea of finding out if she could force the D.A. to prosecute Bradford Brie for breaking into her house. She wasn't having much luck in that regard. She pushed the paperback aside and opened the penal code to the book-marked section on criminal responsibility. It was in the back of Sharon's mind that, failing in the effort to have Midge's case fall under the abuse category, she could try to defend Midge based on the teenager's understanding of right and wrong. That effort, Sharon knew, would likely be in vain.

As much as she tried to concentrate on the code, her mind wandered and her gaze drifted to the transom above her door. Likely her problem was lack of sleep. One didn't see transoms in offices anymore; this building was more than fifty years old. She regripped the edges of the book and forced herself to look at the page. And let her gaze roam to the transom again. Finally she turned the book facedown and reached for a small pile of unopened mail. The first envelope she looked at brought her into shocked wakefulness.

The letter, addressed to her in care of the Dallas County district attorney's office, bore a thirty-day-old postmark. Once the letter had circulated through the office for several weeks, someone in the D.A.'s mail room had finally bothered to forward the envelope to her. The envelope had been slit open and stapled closed, and Sharon wondered which nosy assistant prosecutor had read her mail. The letter inside showed a New York City return address, but the postmark on the envelope was from L.A. It was a message from Rob, the first Sharon had received from him in the twelve years since they'd split the blankets. She wanted to drop the folded piece of correspondence into her wastebasket, but could no more do that than she could fly. Curiosity compelled her. She read.

Dear Muffin:

I was recently shocked to learn from Betsy that you and I may have a child. Is this true? If so, it is devastating to learn that I am a father after all these years.

I have a starring role coming up in the pilot of *Sixty-First Precinct,* a police drama in which I play a homicide detective. The pilot airs in August. In connection with this I'm making a promotional tour through Dallas on the 17th and 18th, and think we should get together. If what I have heard is true, then I of course wish to discuss my assumption of parental responsibility to the child. Please contact me, and if you have indeed borne my child, include photos of our offspring.

Affectionately as always,

Rob

Sharon tossed the letter aside in disgust, then hugged herself as depression set in. The message was typical of him. His sudden interest in Melanie was likely prompted by his agent, who'd figured out that if Rob was likely to be elevated to stardom, he'd better cover his ass before his illegitimate child came up to haunt him in the tabloids. "Betsy" would of course be Betsy Willis, who had become Rob's shack job within days of Sharon's vacating the Brooklyn Heights apartment, and his "recent" enlightenment had likely come about within hours of Melanie's birth. "Muffin" had been his cutesy nickname for her—the moniker had no basis whatsoever other than the fact that Rob thought having endearing names for his lovers was something Cary Grant would likely do—and the inclusion of the name in a letter such as this made Sharon absolutely want to puke. "Affectionately as always," Sharon thought, was likely a close added by some adlebrained typist in Rob's agent's office. Fuck you, but Merry Christmas anyway.

He had been on television once more this week, a bit part as a wiseass repair man on *Murphy Brown*. This time Sharon had sat stiff as a stone beside Melanie on the sofa, and had managed not to fly off the handle. Rob had a sensitive mouth, a nice trim physique, and the ego of a three-year-old. Sharon wondered if he had matured any. She felt that she had grown up, so why couldn't Rob grow up as well? Artistically, living with him had been just the thing for that period in Sharon's life, but that had been then and this was now. Sexually Rob had been adequate, though nothing to set the bells a-ringing.

Sharon had a fat picture of Rob's "assumption of parental responsibility." There would be regular—and generous, depending on his future Neilsen ratings—support checks, and just enough visits so that photographers could catch him romping with his daughter. Not *my* child, Sharon thought. Absolutely, positively, no frigging way. She and Melanie had done just fine, thank you, for eleven years, and a father figure was something that Melanie simply didn't . . .

Sure, there are thousands of successful products of one-parent homes, Sharon thought. Midge Rathermore, for example.

But that's different.

Or is it?

Well, Midge's father was a pervert, Sharon told the voice inside her. That makes it different.

And Melanie's mother, the voice inside Sharon said, is a lawyer who sometimes stays in trial for weeks at a time. So what?

She felt like screaming. She stuffed the letter into her purse. She'd have to talk this development over with Sheila. Who would tell her, just as she always had, that Melanie needed contact with a father figure. Trish's father, bastard that Sheila felt he was, nonetheless had Trish on alternate weekends and two weeks during the summer.

Sharon expelled an agitated breath and picked up the law book, concentrating on the print so hard that she saw double. She read the same sentence over three times, comprehending nothing, then set the book aside once more.

Christ, what she needed was to take a couple of days off and get violently laid.

Oh, yeah? the voice inside her said. Laid by whom?

Sharon sighed. Stan Green had the body of a wide receiver and a me-hungry-me-eat, me-horny-me-fuck mentality. Pillow-biting ecstasy followed by conversations with a moron.

Sharon glared at the poinsettia in the corner, the one she'd bought to replace the disgusting imitation rubber plant which had been there on her first day. The rubber plant, Russell Black's idea of a decoration.

He owned a razor-sharp mind and used a gruff exterior to hide a kind heart. And had egg on the front of his shirt.

Jesus Christ, the voice said, you're not thinking about sleeping with Russell Black, are you? Girl, you're really on the edge.

No, Sharon answered, but I'd like to put Russ's mind in Stan Green's body. Would that be a combo or what?

Suddenly the intercom buzzed. Sharon picked up the receiver. "Hi," she said dreamily, then assumed a more businesslike tone and said, "Hello?"

"Hot-foot it on over here, Sharon," Russ Black said.

"I just left from over there," Sharon said, then realized she was talking into a dead phone, Black having disconnected. She trudged across the hall and entered.

Black stood by the window, looking out. He turned and grinned. "My detective just called," he said.

Sharon sat down. "Mr. Gear must have done something good. For the past week he's been *my* detective."

Black's smile broadened. "You ain't wolfin'. Remember Leslie Schlee?"

"Sure. The girl that snitched Chris Leonard and Troy Burdette off to Stan Green."

"That's her. Grab your gear, Sharon. In a half hour we're goin' to interview the young lady.

26

On the ride out to interview Leslie Schlee, Sharon concentrated on the scenery in an effort to keep Rob's letter out of her mind. She sat beside Russell Black in the front seat of the older lawyer's Buick, her arms folded and her gaze shifting alternately to either side of the wide, tree-lined Highland Park boulevards.

She could probably count the number of times she'd visited homes in wealthy Park Cities on the fingers of both hands. When she was a little girl, it was an annual event for her parents to drive her through Highland Park at Christmastime to view the decorations. Sharon would never forget gaping in awe at the lit-up Santas and reindeer, and at the thousands and thousands of red, blue, and green lights which covered the trees and the fronts of the mansions. Her dad used to remark that the people on Lakeside Drive spent more on Christmas glitz than the Hayses had paid for their modest East Dallas home, and Sharon supposed that he hadn't been far from right. In her little-girl daydreams she had often lived in one of the Lakeside Drive palaces and had had a staff of servants to boss around. Always in her daydreams she'd been a movie star.

The castle-sized houses were built on a hillside which sloped steeply upward from the banks of Turtle Creek, and had no lawns to speak of. The angle of the slope rendered mowing virtually impossible, and Lakeside Drive residents opted mostly for English ivy as a breathtaking ground cover. The stately elms and sycamores which dotted the creekside properties provided ample shade so that the ivy would thrive, but anyone, Sharon knew, who thought that the creeping vines with their broad dark green leaves were easier to maintain than grass simply had no experience with the expensive ground cover.

Early on in her gardening career, shortly after her father had died and she'd inherited the East Dallas house, she had decided to try English ivy in her own front yard. Her reasoning had been that since her job with the D.A. left scant time for mowing and pruning, the ground cover would take over the yard on its own and make her small East Dallas property virtually maintenance free. Well, she'd been partly right. The English ivy had taken over her yard. It had crawled up the trunks of two pecan trees and strangled them to death, and had covered up the front of the house and twisted around the eaves like a herd of boa constrictors. Weeds had thrived among the ivy and waved their ugly heads tauntingly above the vines, and had very nearly driven Sharon insane. The last straw had come when Mrs. Breedlove had remarked that she was considering sending in the National Guard to make sure the ivy wasn't attacking Sharon in her bed. It had cost two months' county prosecutor's salary to have the English ivy dug out, but the cost had been well worth it. Now, as Russell Black steered the Buick along Lakeside Drive, Sharon wondered how much of an army was required to maintain the vicious but gorgeous stuff which covered the hillsides. Must cost a fortune, she thought.

Midway down the block, Black put on the brakes and moved over to the side of the street. With the motor idling, he bent his head to look up the slope. "There's our crime scene, girl," he said.

She leaned toward him for a better view, and a chill went through her. She'd forgotten for the moment that the Rathermores had been Lakeside Drive residents. Hearing about the murder from a lawyer's perspective made the whole thing seem like fiction, as if she'd been watching a play or reading a novel, but finally looking on the place where the tragedy had unfolded gave her a sobering sense of reality. The towering gothic home sat high above street level. There were round, tall spires at the two visible corners like gun turrets, and the roof was peaked and covered with brown wooden shingles. Right there, Sharon thought. According to Christopher Leonard's testimony, the boys had crept straight up the hillside under cover of darkness, their breaths shallow, murder on their minds. Sharon relaxed in the seat and hugged herself.

"World's gone crazy," Russell Black finally said. He gave the Buick some gas and moved on.

About two hundred yards farther down Lakeside Drive, he left the street to pull into an exposed aggregate circular drive. The drive slanted upward at a forty-five degree angel, then leveled off in front of a porch of ornate red stone. The entrance was an oak door with a huge brass knocker. So thick was the forest of trees in front that the house had been invisible from the street. Anthony Gear's white Land Rover was parked directly in front of the door. Black stopped behind the Jeep, got out, and went around the Buick toward the passenger side. Sharon reached for her door handle, then relaxed. It was another of Russell Black's eccentricities that he opened all the doors for women who were in his company, and anytime she forgot and opened a door for herself, she felt the older lawyer's resentment; he wouldn't come right out and say that he was miffed, but his posture would stiffen slightly and he would become morosely silent. Black's politeness had taken some getting used to on Sharon's part. When she'd been a prosecutor and had tried cases alongside male assistant D.A.'s, she had felt fortunate when she hadn't had to lug the man's paraphernalia around in addition to her own, as if she were a packhorse. She thought that being treated with respect because of her gender was something which could spoil her in a hurry. Black opened the passenger door. Sharon climbed out and led the way up the drive toward the house.

The Land Rover had mud on its tires. Sharon thought that a private detective who drove around in a vehicle which looked as if it were headed off on a jungle safari was sort of weird. It wasn't the only strange thing she'd noticed about Gear, but also she thought that he wasn't any more of an oddball than other current and former FBI agents whom she'd met. They all had their own way of doing things. And so far, she had to admit, Gear had shown to be one corker of an investigator. Sharon led the way up on the porch. Black raised the knocker and slammed it down; the banging echo rumbled through the interior of the house like The Haunting. Sharon and her boss waited in beams of sunlight slanting down through thick overhead branches.

She gazed down the slope. "Some layout."

Black folded his hands in front of him. "Waste of people's money. Guys living in these houses along here, they're just asking to get robbed." Sharon had never been to Russell Black's house, but was certain that it was no bigger than he needed for it to be. Nothing pretentious about old Russ. Sharon knew a lot of men who made a big to-do of having money—a lot of them making more of a show than they could really afford—and she'd found most of those guys pretty shallow. With Russell Black one got exactly what one saw. The door swung open on oiled hinges. Sharon peered into the house.

A tall man, skinny as a war captive and wearing a tie and tails, said, "Yes?" What, Sharon thought, are you kidding me? Next a ghost in armor would appear. Or Anne Boleyn, her head tucked underneath her arm.

Black cleared his throat. "Russell Black. And this is Miss Hays. Here to see Mr. Schlee. I think Mr. Anthony Gear's hiding in there someplace, too. We work with him."

The butler stood aside to usher them into a stone-tiled entry hall featuring a two-story domed ceiling of stained glass. Just inside the door was a six-foot grandfather clock whose pendulum swung monotonously back and forth, back and forth, ticking and tocking. Twenty feet ahead was a staircase. The polished wood banister gleamed like new auto paint. The beige-carpeted steps led up to the second floor, leveled off into a foyer, then took off upward again for parts unknown. The butler led them around the banister toward the back of the house. "Mr. Schlee is in the den," he said. His tails waved below his bottom like flags. In her white jeans and sneakers, Sharon felt like Little Match Girl. If Russ Black was embarrassed by his own cotton pants and egg-stained shirt, he didn't let on.

They entered a den that was forty feet long if it was an inch. The room's main attraction was a fireplace of uneven stone which cast shadows on its own surface. There was a stuffed elk's head mounted dead center over the mantel, its antlers spread like twin firs. Mr. Schlee obviously didn't worry about utility bills; the refrigerated air raised bumps on Sharon's forearms.

At the far end of the room was a long sofa, and on it sat Anthony Gear in his trademark plaid sports coat, yellow shirt, and tie. A healthy-looking guy in his forties was seated on the other end of the divan, wearing a tennis outfit and spotless white shoes. He had graying temples and a dark sunlamp tan. The butler led the newcomers over to stand in front of the sofa, said stiffly, "Mr. Black to see you, sir," bowed, and withdrew.

The detective handled the introductions, his weather-worn face impassive as a poker player's. "Mr. Schlee, that's Russ Black, and the lady's Sharon Hays. This is Leslie's dad. We've been talking."

Schlee stood, shook Black's hand, and threw a wink in Sharon's direction. "Curt Schlee," he said in a business-like tone. He had slim, hairy legs. Sharon resented the patronizing wink, and immediately labeled Schlee as a dyed-in-the-wool sexist.

Schlee resumed his seat, crossed his legs, and rocked one white sneaker up and down. "There are some ground rules for seeing my daughter."

Gear sat down as well and didn't say anything. He'd made the contact; the rest was up to the lawyers. Black sank into an easy chair adjacent to the sofa. Sharon glanced about, then pulled an armchair away from a table containing an ivory chess set and seated herself beside her boss. As far as Curt Schlee was concerned, his guests apparently could fend for themselves. Sharon's resentment of him was growing by leaps and bounds.

Black favored Schlee with an impersonal blink. "Thanks for having us over, Curt. And your rules suit us as long as they don't interfere with us lookin' out for our client."

"Who is Midge Rathermore?" Schlee's mellow tenor voice carried the tone of a man used to having his orders followed.

"Who is Midge Rathermore." Black's tone said that he didn't follow orders from anyone. This should be interesting, Sharon thought.

"You know I'm a lawyer," Schlee said.

"No, I didn't," Black said. "There are a lot of lawyers I don't know."

A sudden light blinked on in Sharon's head. Sure, Collins & Schlee. One partner was the former national director of the IRS, had resigned when Carter had brought the Democrats swooping into office, then had set up private practice in Dallas to help local Repubs hide their assets from the Carter regime. The other half of the firm was the personal lawyer for both U.S. senators from Texas and a score of congressmen. Sharon wasn't certain which partner was the politician and which was the income tax man, but when one mentioned the firm of Collins & Schlee, one was talking mucho stroke and then some. To say that Russ Black and Curt Schlee were both lawyers was like saying that Van Cliburn and Jerry Lee Lewis were both piano players.

Sharon cut in. "I know the firm, Russ. He's—"

"I didn't catch your name." Schlee grinned, his gaze roaming up and down Sharon's body in the standard tits-and-legs once-over. She was getting about all of this guy that she could stomach.

"Sharon Hays," Black said. "She's my cocounsel." He had caught Schlee's attitude as well, and his tone said, She's not my flunky and she's not a candidate for any moves on your part, bud. Sharon nodded slightly and favored Schlee with a steady gaze.

"Glad to meet you," she said. "His firm does corporate work, Russ."

One corner of Black's mouth tugged toward his ear. He didn't say anything.

"As I was saying," Schlee said, bending at the waist to scratch his lower leg, "if you want to talk to Leslie, there are restrictions. That's the way I put it to the D.A.'s office, and that's the way I'm putting it to you. Sending your detective"—he jerked a thumb at Gear, who defiantly folded his arms—"around yelling subpoena doesn't scare me one iota. Leslie tells you nothing unless you agree not to call her to testify."

Now Black frowned. "I can't make that guarantee. It depends on what she has to say."

"Well, if you can't, we're wasting time," Schlee said. "I can't afford to have my child mixed up in this. I've kept her name out of the newspapers so far, and I intend to go on doing that."

Good God, Sharon thought. On Curt Schlee's list, his daughter's well-being was way down below the publicity which Schlee himself couldn't afford. Sharon changed her opinion. She didn't merely dislike Schlee, her feelings went much deeper."

"All I can give you is this," Black said. "If what she tells us can be gotten into evidence any other way, we won't put her on. But if we need her, we'll subpoena her. We got a client."

"And I've got a daughter." Schlee pointed a finger. "You try playing hardball with me, and you'll be putting on a witness when you don't have the slightest idea what she's going to say. That I promise you."

Black leaned forward and rested his forearms on his thighs, sizing up Curt Schlee, obviously wondering how far he could push it. His tone softened. "I'll say this much for you, Curt. I've been practicing law around here a bunch of years, and I've never seen anybody tell the D.A. how the cow ate the cabbage the way you have. You must be a campaign donator." Black's speech was suddenly crisp and precise, all of the backwoods preacher's dialect gone. He could turn the good-ole-country-boy act on and off at will.

"I give some," Schlee said.

"Well, you listen to me," Black said, "We're representin' a mixed-up teenage girl here. I don't say she's lily white, but it's way off base to try to railroad her into the penitentiary in her condition."

Schlee looked with satisfaction at the elk's head over the mantel. "I'm glad that's not my problem, sir. I was only doing my duty as a citizen, having Leslie talk to that detective to begin with. I don't see I've got any duty to have her talk to you at all."

Sharon sat up straighter. "You mean, talking to the police wasn't Leslie's idea?"

"Of course not. She's a teenager. Nobody would have known anything if we hadn't overheard her."

"Overheard?" Black said.

"On the phone. Kids stay on the phone constantly. The best way to know what's going on is to record them."

Hoo, boy, Sharon thought. "You record her phone calls?" she said.

"Every one. It's one way to keep her on the straight and narrow."

And the best way to make her hate her parents, Sharon thought. Sheila Winston counseled a steady stream of troubled teenagers, and she had told Sharon that many of them had problems no greater than that their parents acted like parole officers rather than loving moms and dads. If Leslie didn't feel trusted, she'd perform on the level expected of her.

From the den entrance a clear female voice said, "Curt?"

Sharon swiveled her head. The source of the voice was a slim, compact woman with honey blond hair, wearing a pink cotton jogging suit. Her face was flushed from exertion, her skin unwrinkled.

"I'm handling this," Curt Schlee said.

"That's what I'm afraid of, dear." The woman crossed over to stand near the sofa. She nodded in turn to Black, Sharon, and Anthony Gear, then said, "I'm Virginia Schlee. What's going on? I heard someone mention Leslie's name." The lady of the house could easily pass for mid-thirties, but Sharon thought she was probably closer to fifty. For many Highland Park wives, a good cosmetic surgeon was the key to living the good life and keeping hubby at home.

"These people"—Schlee made a contemptuous gesture directed at the room in general—"are the defense lawyers for Midge Rathermore. I've told them the ground rules."

Virginia Schlee stiffened her posture. "No, you haven't, Curt. You've told them your rules, which are whatever you think will offer the most protection for you."

Schlee rubbed the top of his tennis shoe. "We've been over this, Virginia."

"No, we haven't. You've been over it. We never should have covered for that slime while he was alive, and now we're not about to continue the charade."

Sharon and Black exchanged glances. Anthony Gear sat forward in interest.

"You keep quiet. We're asking for trouble if we tell these people the time of day," Schlee said.

Virginia rested her fanny on the arm of the couch, flattened a hand behind her, and crossed her ankles. "Y'all will excuse my husband. He's thinking about running. He doesn't know for what office as yet, but he's already begun his campaign." She had high cheekbones and the complexion of a face-cream model.

Schlee's mouth curved downward in a petulant frown.

Virginia alternated her gaze between the three visitors as she said, "Y'all want to question Leslie, I suppose."

Russ Black rested his chin on his lightly clenched fist. "There's been testimony about Leslie in pretrial hearin's, Mrs. Schlee. For reasons which your husband's now explained to us, the prosecution's decided not to use her as a witness. If she can help our case, we plan to."

The lines around Virginia's mouth softened. "We should have made a clean breast of it from the beginning. Now that we want to, the district attorney's office doesn't seem to be interested in the details."

Sharon assumed a woman-to-woman tone. "I've got a daughter myself, Mrs. Schlee. Please believe that we don't want to put Leslie through any more than absolutely necessary."

Virginia glanced at Curt Schlee, who regarded the carpet. She stood. "I'll go get Leslie now."

Schlee lifted his head. "Virginia, wait."

She glared. "And if you don't want to hear this, Curt, you might go on to your tennis game. Frankly, I'm not sure I care what you do."

Leslie Schlee's toes pointed slightly in when she walked, and she sat like a sorority rushee. She wore spotless white baggy shorts which ended just the correct distance above her knees, along with a red Bugle Girl shirt with the collar turned up. She had her mother's complexion and her father's perfectly formed legs. Her makeup looked like a Neiman-Marcus professional job, and probably was.

"Pleased to meet you," Leslie said. Perfect diction, the greeting as if programmed on Curt Schlee's office computer. She sat between her parents on the sofa. Anthony Gear had moved over to make room, and now seemed more of a spectator than part of the group in the den. To Curt Schlee's credit, he hadn't gone off to play tennis. The game probably hadn't been important businesswise or politically, Sharon thought. Otherwise Schlee likely wouldn't be sitting here.

"Leslie, these questions we've got," Russ Black said, relaxing in his easy chair. "We'll make this as quick as we can."

"Don't hurry," said Leslie politely. "I've talked this over with my mom. Anything you want to know." Virginia Schlee patted her daughter's hand. Curt Schlee sagged like a deflated raft.

"A lot of it we already know," Black said. "You were datin' Chris Leonard, is that right?"

Leslie blinked. "No, sir, it isn't."

"I'm sorry? Miss Schlee, the state's witness ... you know Detective Stan Green?"

The teenager blinked again. "Yes, sir."

"Well," Black said hesitantly, "Detective Green said at Midge's adult certification hearin' that ..."

Leslie looked at her father. Once during Sharon's freshman year in college, she'd been afraid that she was pregnant. It had turned out to be a false alarm, but she'd had to sit down with her mother and dad and tell them about it. At the moment Sharon felt very sorry for Leslie. Curt Schlee ignored his daughter and seemed quite interested in something located above the stuffed elk's head.

Virginia squeezed Leslie's hand, then said, "Mr. Black, so you won't have any more surprises, I'll get something out of the way. My husband has only told you part of what happened. It's true that he found out what was going on by tapping Leslie's phone. But Leslie never met with that detective in person but once, after Curt had already gone to the police station and given Detective Green the boys' names. The story about Leslie having dated one of those boys is pure fiction, made up between my husband and the police in order to explain Leslie's role. She won't be allowed to date until she's sixteen, which is two months from now." She smiled at Leslie. "Go ahead, darling," Virginia said. Curt Schlee regarded the floor.

"I never met those two dudes," Leslie said, "until one day over at Midge's house."

"It's just two doors down," Virginia said. "Leslie and Midge have been friends since, oh, they were nine or ten."

"So Midge was your friend and not Chris Leonard?"

Black said. Gear had taken out a small spiral pad and pen, and now wrote something down.

"Well ... Midge didn't have many friends," Leslie said. "I liked to go over to her house, but I can't exactly say she was my friend. I didn't want anyone at school to know I was going over there."

Sharon and Black looked at each other.

"Midge could get good dope," Leslie said. "That's the only reason anybody had anything to do with her. And most of the kids thought Midge's parents were pretty cool."

"Cool how, Leslie?" Sharon said.

Leslie looked at her father. Schlee bent his head and gazed down between his knees.

"How were Midge's folks cool?" Sharon said.

Leslie folded her hands demurely in her lap and smiled. "They gave us dope. Uppers. Some blow."

Black's voice came out in a soft rumble. "Did they use it themselves?"

"No, sir, not that I ever saw. They kept it for kids that came around." Leslie's gray eyes wavered with uncertainty. "Mr. Rathermore ... liked to mess around with the girls."

"I suppose," Black said, "that's why he gave them the dope."

Leslie shrugged. "Sure, that was the deal when you went over to Midge's. None of the girls let him mess around because they wanted to. That guy was awful old."

Sharon's stomach churned. Virginia Schlee averted her gaze while her husband buried his face in his hands. This child is only four years older than Melanie, Sharon thought.

"I have to ask you, Leslie," Black said. "Did Mr. Rathermore ... mess with you?"

Curt Schlee's head popped up. "I don't see what that has to do with—"

"I don't like askin' the question any more than you like hearin' the answer," Black said, raising a hand. "But it looks like we'll have to use her as a witness."

Schlee said with warning in his tone, "Leslie."

She ignored her father and said evenly to Black, "Yes, sir. He did."

"You know that Mrs. Rathermore isn't Midge's real mother, don't you?" Black said.

"Oh, sure. Linda talked about that all the time, when she wanted to put Midge down. She'd go, You don't think that's *my* kid, do you? Something like that. Midge would cry, but that's what Linda was wanting. Midge hated Linda, like, awesomely."

Sharon firmed up her chin. "Leslie, did you know Midge's sister, Susan?"

Leslie raised one foot from the floor, squirmed on the couch, and sat on her ankle. "Yes, we all went to Hockaday together. Susan's younger, a couple of years."

"Was Susan there when y'all were taking drugs?" Sharon said.

"Yes." No expression in Leslie's voice, eyes vacant and matter-of-fact.

"Did Susan take them, too?"

"All the kids did. Susan probably more than any of us."

"Did Mr. Rathermore ever mess around with Susan that you remember?"

"Yes, ma'am. Never alone, but a few times she'd be with some other girls and they'd all . . . you know."

"Get into bed with Mr. Rathermore?"

"Yes, ma'am."

Sharon swallowed hard. "Leslie, have you talked to Susan lately?"

"Sure. Just last night," Leslie said. Curt Schlee lifted his head in shock. Likely he hasn't reviewed today's tapes, Sharon thought.

"Where is Susan, Leslie?" Sharon said. "She's not in school."

Leslie raised her eyebrows. "Didn't you know?"

Sharon and Black exchanged confused looks. "I'm afraid we don't," Sharon said.

Virginia Schlee broke in. "Susan Rathermore is in the hospital. Do you know Havenrest?"

Sharon nodded. Havenrest was Dallas' most uppity-up psychiatric hospital. Lovely grounds, lawns like carpets, tall, beautiful trees. Bars on many of the windows. Many padded cells.

"Two days after her father died," Virginia said, "Susan

cut herself with a razor. Slashed her wrists and arms. She's been at Havenrest ever since."

Black gave Sharon a questioning look. She nodded as she said, "It's typical. Classic sex-abuse victim, self-mutilation. They get violent with guilt." She mentally included Sheila Winston as an expert witness for the defense. Sheila despised expert witnesses because most of them would say anything they were paid to, but she'd jump at the chance to get into the Rathermore case once Sharon filled her in on the details. *Sheila will testify without charging a fee,* Sharon thought.

"Mrs. Schlee, I've got to ask you," Black said. "You seem to know a lot about what went on over at the Rathermores'."

Virginia laughed mirthlessly. She bent forward to glare around Leslie at Curt Schlee, then faced Black. "We didn't know what was going on over there," Virginia said, "or Leslie never would have been involved. But our daughter got friendly with Midge to begin with because Curt thought it politically correct to have Bill Rathermore for a buddy. Curt pushed Leslie into the relationship with Midge. Thought it would be nice for our kid to be one of the Rathermore children's playmates. What he didn't know was that it wasn't exactly Midge who wanted to play with Leslie. It was Midge's father."

"Leslie, these things you're telling," Black said. "Have the police and district attorney known about them all along?"

Leslie looked at her mother. The teenager's upper lip quivered, and for the first time Sharon thought that the girl might break down.

Virginia placed a hand on her daughter's arm. "I'll answer that one, Mr. Black," Virginia said. "With a question. Since the homicide detective, in cahoots with my husband, concocted the story about Leslie's having only dated one of the boys, what do you think?"

Black lowered his head, muttering. Sharon wrote on her notepad, "Stan Green is a lying horse's ass," then scratched through that and wrote instead, "Prosecution's knowledge of kids having sex w/Bill Rathermore—*investigate.*"

"Leslie," Sharon said, "what about Mrs. Rathermore?

Did she know that Mr. Rathermore was messing around with those girls?"

Leslie touched the front of her honey blond hair. "She was right there in the house. While some of the kids were in back with Mr. Rathermore, the rest of us would be in the living room talking to Mrs. Rathermore and doing some dope. Or drinking, some of the kids. I never drank any." She glanced at her mother as though abstaining from alcohol was a point in her favor.

The thought that there were people in the world like Linda Rathermore made Sharon absolutely ill. "Did Mrs. Rathermore ever participate in the sex?" Sharon asked.

"Not with any of the girls," Leslie said.

Sharon turned a page on her notepad. "With the boys who came over?"

"I never saw her," Leslie said. "But I've heard."

"But you can't remember any specific time when Mrs. Rathermore might have had sex with any of the boys?"

Leslie seemed deep in thought. "No, ma'am."

"So you couldn't testify to that."

"I don't suppose," Leslie said.

Sharon explained to Virginia Schlee, "Leslie couldn't testify to anything someone told her. It would be hearsay."

Virginia permitted herself a little smile. "My husband's a lawyer, Miss Hays."

Curt Schlee seemed to shrink. At the moment it was easy to forget that he was a lawyer, or anything else other than a jerk who'd sacrificed his own child's well-being for political reasons. Finally Sharon said, "Who told you about Mrs. Rathermore and the boys, Leslie?"

"Midge. Susan, too, I think."

The answer didn't help. The defense team had already made up its mind that putting Midge on the stand would be suicide, and with Susan currently in Havenrest's rubber room, it didn't appear that she would be much good as a witness, either. "No one else told you about it?" Sharon said.

"No, ma'am."

The corners of Sharon's mouth tugged in disappointment. She expelled a breath.

"Let's talk about," Black said, "when you met those boys at the Rathermores'."

"Troy and Chris," Sharon added.

Black cleared his throat and crossed his legs. "The first time you ever saw them in your life was at the Rathermores'?"

Leslie shook her head. "No, I'd seen those dudes. Around at some dances."

"But you'd never talked to them?"

"No, sir. I was over one day and Midge and those two guys were doing a line in the living room. Susan was there, too."

"What did y'all talk about?" Black said.

"Just stuff, mostly. Midge was always talking about how she hated Mr. Rathermore. She said that to everybody, so much that the kids just thought she was a crybaby. Nobody paid much attention to her."

Leslie paused. The only sounds were Curt Schlee's loud breathing and the scratching of Sharon's pen on her notepad. Leslie went on, "Midge was going on and on about how he made her do this and that, the way she always did, and the first thing you know this Chris dude goes, 'Well, if you hate your old man so much, why don't you just kill him?' "

Sharon felt a quick chill. Black exhaled through his nose before saying, "You're sure he said that to her?"

"I was right there," Leslie said.

"It's important the way it happened. You're sure Midge didn't come up with the idea first?"

Leslie wrinkled her nose. "Midge's elevator doesn't go all the way up, don't you know that?"

"We've spent time with her," Sharon said.

"Well, she never thought anything up on her own," Leslie said. "Do you know that the boys used to line up on her?"

Sharon swallowed bile as she nodded.

"Well, she wasn't hanging around asking them to. But Midge was so dumb, anything anybody told her to do . . . the guys would just go, 'Wouldn't you like to lay down in the backseat?' And Midge would do it like she was a trick dog or something. A guy told me one time, he was in one of those lineups, he told me that while they were, you know, doing it, that Midge was chewing gum and humming a tune."

More classic abused-child behavior, Sharon thought.

While it was happening, Midge would shut it all out by drifting away to fantasy land.

"When Chris asked her about killing her daddy," Black said, "what did Midge tell him?"

"Nothing, right then," Leslie said. "That was a couple of days later."

"You mean, when you kids were over at the Rathermores' another time?"

"Right. Me and this other girl had been in back with Mr. Rathermore." Leslie shot a guilty look at her father, who cringed. "We came out," she said, "and that time it was just the three of them, Midge and those two dudes. Chris did all the talking. He had a pad and pen, just like you." She nodded at Sharon, who quit taking notes and listened. Leslie was a pretty, perfectly groomed teenager, her posture trim and perfect as if she were discussing plans for the homecoming dance.

"Anyway," Leslie said, "Chris was asking Midge all kinds of stuff. Like, did she know how much money she'd get if Mr. Rathermore got wasted, stuff like that. He asked her for the code to the burglar alarm. She gave it to him and he wrote it down."

Black frowned. "Sharon, didn't the Leonard boy testify—?"

"That he got the information at a shopping mall," Sharon said. "Why would . . . ?"

"So we'd think there weren't any witnesses to Midge givin' out the alarm code." He returned his attention to Leslie. "This could be a problem, Leslie. If you testified, the prosecutor would ask you, if you heard all this, why didn't you tell somebody? Call the police or . . ." He trailed off.

Leslie rolled her eyes. "We didn't think they were serious. Besides, none of us liked Mr. Rathermore. He was just this horny old dude that gave us dope if we'd let him mess around. I don't think anybody cared if they did kill him." There was no apology whatsoever in the teenager's voice. If those other kids were going to commit murder, so what? What have we come to? Sharon thought.

Russ Black thoughtfully pinched his chin. "Leslie, one more time. You're sure it was the boys that gave Midge the idea? She never thought of it on her own?"

Leslie crossed her legs and rocked one foot up and

down. "No way. Midge was just going along with those dudes."

Sharon remembered a case she'd handled at the D.A.'s office and wrote herself a note. The case had to do with a group of teenage boys robbing a service station, and one kid's defense that the others had talked him into it. Sharon was pretty sure that just going along with the crowd didn't absolve Midge of guilt, but she was going to look it up. If nothing else, the fact that these two smart boys had talked dull-witted Midge into hiring them to kill her father should make some points with a jury.

Black now said, "So we'll be sure. These boys were sitting right there in front of you, and they were talking about murdering this man, and you never thought to tell anybody about it?"

Leslie seemed to think that one over. She wet her lips. "It sounds weird to older people, I guess. But you've got to understand, the kids we know talk about killing people all the time. It just wasn't any big deal."

Sharon exchanged nary a word with Russell Black as the two of them walked back to the car, strolling underneath fifty-foot elms and sycamores shading a hillside covered with dark green English ivy. The landscape below them descended to Lakeside Drive, and across the street an even steeper grade formed the eastern bank of Turtle Creek. The creek was swollen from the torrents of spring, which had ended the first week in June, the murky water running deep and silent on its way to the Trinity River. In late summer the flow would be down to the barest of trickles.

Sharon was so caught up in her thoughts that she barely noticed when Russ Black stepped up to open the car door for her. She sat in the passenger seat, swung her legs inside, and cringed slightly as her boss slammed the door with a solid thunk. Sharon pictured Leslie Schlee as she'd sat demurely between her parents and told of bloody murder. A second image flashed in Sharon's mind, this picture of Stan Green and Curt Schlee as they schemed to make the girl's story fit both of their needs. The detective needed a conviction, and Schlee wanted to keep his family name out of the paper. If the concocted story happened to be in Leslie's best interests, all the better. If not, so what?

The Buick rocked as Black got in behind the wheel. He reached around to insert the key in the steering column and turned the switch. Dash lights glowed red and the seat belt warning bell ding-dinged. Black paused with his thumb ready to turn the starter switch, and swiveled his head toward Sharon. His expression was grim.

"Over twenty years," he said, "I been tryin' cases against Dallas County. Every time they pull one of these shenanigans I think I've seen 'em all. Then they come up with a new one. Just dealin' with those people, sometimes I feel like I need a bath. All these mixed-up kids killin' people, that's bad enough. But it's really not the kids' fault. That homicide cop Green. Milton Breyer. Leslie's daddy, too. They're the ones that ought to be in jail."

Black started the engine and the Buick cruised down the drive into the street. Sharon turned her face to the window and swallowed a lump from her throat.

27

The American Airlines Boeing 727 carrying Anthony Gear in from Baltimore rolled to the gate under a blistering late June sun. The accordion walkway moved away from the building like a probe, clamping onto the airliner's side. Jet engines whined to a standstill.

Within the terminal, Sharon drummed her fingers on the railing, checked her watch, and paced back and forth. She'd been waiting—craning her neck to peer through the huge picture window overlooking the runway, going inside the gift shop to browse through the paperback novels, hustling down to the restaurant to give an estimated time or arrival report to an irritated Russell Black every fifteen minutes or so—for an hour and a half. Since they'd driven the competition out of business and assumed a virtual throat lock on interstate traffic at DFW Airport, American apparently saw no point in being on time.

Sharon walked over to stand at the head of the welcoming ramp. She had on the same clothes she'd worn to the office, brown spike heels and a beige summerweight business dress. Passengers deplaned, men in slacks and sports shirts or suits, some with carry-on luggage slung over their shoulders, and women in everything from shorts to business dress. One lady held a toddler by the hand. Sharon rose on the balls of her feet in anticipation. One man, a thirtyish guy with a narrow waist, tailored shirt and pants, and a mountain of brown hair sprayed into an immovable sculpture leered at her. She showed him an irritated smirk, then quickly looked away.

Gear was next to last to deplane, moving leisurely along behind a portly woman who was pulling a suitcase on rollers behind her. The detective's collar was undone, his yellow tie loosened to the third button on his shirt. A big brown satchel bumped the hem of his sports coat. He spotted Sharon, showed a crooked grin, raised a hand to shoulder level, and waggled his fingers. He stopped before her. "American sucks," he said.

"Tell me about it. Russ is in the coffee shop." She wasted no time, leading the way on padded red carpet toward the restaurant, sidestepping people who did column-rights into the rest rooms and baggage-claim area. A fiftyish woman hissed, "Well, I *never*," as Sharon dodged around her. Sharon showed the woman an apologetic smile, waved a come-on to Anthony Gear, and hurried on.

The restaurant was a serve-yourself, people lined up at the cash register carrying paper cups of iced-down soft drinks, doughnuts, wrapped sandwiches, hamburgers and hot dogs heated by microwave. Black was in a rear booth studying Sharon's child-abuse brief, trying for the millionth time to shoot holes in her argument. So far her theory had shown to be bulletproof.

Sharon and the detective went through the serving line; she filled a cup with ice and Coke while he poured himself steaming black coffee. He didn't offer to pay. An old government trick, Sharon thought. She handed a five over the counter, received a single and jingly change in return, and carried her drink over to slide into the booth beside Russ Black. Gear sank heavily across the table, blew on his coffee, and had a sip.

"I still can't find a damn thing wrong with this," Black said, rattling the pages of the brief.

"Trust me," Sharon said. "You won't."

"We got to hope the judge can't, either." Black looked at Gear. "Well?" He'd cautioned Sharon not to be overly friendly with Gear, and she'd noticed that Black's attitude toward the detective was somewhere between lukewarm and ice cold. They work better when you don't buddy around with 'em, Black had told Sharon. Let 'em know that their next check depends on performance, and if they screw around you'll cut 'em off quicker'n a minnow.

With Gear, she noted, the strategy seemed to work like a charm.

"That's my first trip to Baltimore," Gear said, settling back. "As different from Dallas as night from day."

Black scratched his nose. "What'd you find out?"

"Old," Gear said. "Little narrow streets, two cars can barely pass in opposite directions."

"They built them," Sharon said, "before there were any such things as automobiles. For horse-drawn carriages."

"Some of the houses," Gear said, "aren't five feet from the curb. Great seafood in that town. Fresh lobster and shrimp. It's kind of like ... you ever been to Boston? It's like Boston, only without all the graveyards."

"Revolutionary War cemeteries," Sharon said.

"That's real nice," Black said, testily rattling paper. "But today they got cars. What'd you find out?"

"They've got a new courthouse," Gear said to Sharon, "and you should see the old one. Got those thick stone walls."

"You're spendin' our client's money to go sightseein'," Black said.

Gear showed a peeved expression. "I never went sightseeing until after I finished working."

"Then you should have been on the seven o'clock flight yesterday evenin'," Black said. "What do you know about Linda Haymon that we didn't already know?"

"Harmon," Gear said.

"Harmon, Haymon. Dammit, what did you find out?"

Gear casually picked up his coffee cup. Visible beyond him through the restaurant entry, passengers dragged luggage along behind them as they moved up in the ticket-counter line. Gear sipped and swallowed. "Quite a bit," he said.

"Spare us the suspense, okay?" Black said.

Gear set his cup down and intertwined his fingers. "She did Little Theatre. Small productions. I got some clippings in here"—patting his satchel—"of reviews, from newspaper archives. The critics raved about her in *The Lighthouse*. It's a Walter Erskine play that never made it to the big show."

"I did that," Sharon said. "Old theater way down in SoHo that the fire marshal should have condemned. We did an el foldo after two nights."

"So great," Black said. "If we want to discredit her on the stand, we can say she was in a bad play."

"It wasn't *that* bad," Sharon said. "You need a few breaks is all."

Black sounded as if he might have a seizure. "Listen, get on to the—"

"I started looking up the reviews," Gear said, "after I checked up on her criminal record."

Black closed his mouth. He looked at Sharon. She looked back at him. Both lawyers returned their attention to Anthony Gear.

"No convictions," Gear said. "Two indictments, later consolidated into one and pled to. Maryland has a form of probation where if you keep your nose clean, your record gets expunged. That's why there's no conviction on her sheet."

"We've got that in Texas, too," Sharon said. "Deferred adjudicated probation."

"Which means," Black said, "that we can't cross-examine her on her record."

"We can't bring up the indictment," Sharon said. "But we can bring in outside testimony to attack her credibility. Somebody from Baltimore that knows her history can tell what she did without saying she was ever charged with a crime."

"The complainant in both criminal cases against Linda," Gear said, "was the same guy. Donald Weiss. I checked on him and found out he's chairman of the Baltimore Theatre League. Was then. Still is.

"Weiss," Gear said, "had a thing going with her. He was and is married. To the same woman. Thirty years. He gave me an afternoon on the condition that I wouldn't make any waves for him locally."

"Would he come down here to testify without a subpoena?" Black said.

"Probably. We're far enough from Baltimore that it wouldn't have to make the papers up there."

"Come on," Sharon cut in. "*Hard Copy, A Current Affair,* all the tabloids . . ."

"They'd cause him a problem," Gear said. "But I made sure he understood that the likelihood of his appearance in Dallas making Baltimore news was less than the likelihood of my getting his name in the papers up there if he *doesn't* testify for us."

"Sometimes you have to play a little rough," Black said.

Gear nodded. "I'll say one thing, the lady must give one helluva—" He glanced at Sharon. "Must be something in the bedroom," he finished. "Weiss was ready to pack up and move in with her. Give up everything."

"All you have to do is look at her," Sharon said.

"He moved her into a condo," Gear said, "in preparation for dropping the bombshell on his old lady. Even took out a life insurance policy, naming her."

"Naming Linda?" Sharon said.

"Right. Two hundred grand, and I couldn't get out of Weiss whether the policy was his idea or hers. I suspect the latter from what went on.

"Weiss had a son," Gear said, sipping more coffee, "that he used to bring around all the theater productions. Let the kid help out with the scenery, whatever. I bet you can guess what happens next."

"Christ," Black said. "Linda seduced the boy."

Gear pointed a finger. "You get an *A*."

"How old was Linda then?" Sharon said.

"Her Baltimore birth record says she was born in '51. This happened in '78, so that would make her twenty-seven. Weiss happened by the old condo one summer afternoon unannounced, and there Linda was with his kid in the old sackeroo. She'd just happened to offer the kid a lift after rehearsal, only they hadn't quite made it home yet.

"Weiss hit the ceiling, naturally," Gear said. "He decided, come hell or high water, he'd give Linda some grief over it, and filed a statutory rape complaint against her with the Maryland cops. That was the first indictment against our girl. According to Weiss, he nearly lost his wife when she found out, but they've patched things up over the years."

"And I suppose," Sharon said, "that they worked out a plea bargain for probation because Mr. and Mrs. Weiss didn't want their son to have to testify against her."

"Not exactly," Gear said. "Both parents were ready to throw the book at Linda. But they never prosecuted the first charge because of the second indictment against her."

Black favored Sharon with a confused scowl. She shrugged. Gear went on.

"The second case," Gear said, "was really a weirdo. In the middle of the investigation into the statutory rape charge, a detective found out in questioning the kid that he and Linda had actually been doing it on the sly for several months. The afternoon incident was a long way from being the first time. The kid breaks down and admits to the cop that Linda had talked to him about killing his father. The insurance policy, you know?"

"The boy doing it," Black said. "Not Linda herself."

"Right," Gear said. "Linda had even gone as far as buying a pistol and having the kid chart his old man's daily movements. Sound familiar to this case we're working on?"

"Sure sounds like a pattern," Sharon said. "I'm just wondering how much of this we could get into evidence."

"That's you lawyers' problem," Gear said. "That second indictment, conspiracy to commit murder, that's the one the parents didn't want the kid to testify to. The prosecutors had no case without the boy's testimony, of course, so had to agree to consolidate the charges and let Linda plead out. The boy had nine thousand yards of counseling after that, and according to Weiss he's okay now."

"Mr. Gear," Black said, "you've got a new assignment. Beginning now, I want to know what Linda Rathermore is doing twenty-four hours a day. If she has any contact with Chris Leonard or Troy Burdette, I want to know about it."

"That's already on my calendar," Gear said. "At my hourly rate."

"That certainly explains why she changed her name," Sharon said. "Sweet Jesus, she's got a thing for adolescents."

Gear drained the dregs from his coffee cup. "Well, at least she's upgraded some, if what we're all thinking turns out to be true. The kids in the Rathermore case are fifteen and seventeen. If you can believe this, the Weiss boy was thirteen years old at the time."

28

Sharon's walk showed brisk, all-business purpose as she approached the receptionist at Havenrest Sanitarium. She leaned over the counter and presented her business card. "This is Susan Rathermore's mother," Sharon said. "Here to see her daughter." She gestured toward Deborah North, who stood hesitantly just inside the entry.

The receptionist was a bleached blonde in a starched white uniform. Her dark roots showed and she was too heavy. She wore thick red lipstick. She looked the card over and laid it aside, then rattled computer keys and squinted at the monitor. "I don't have your name on Susan's visiting list."

"Well, I'd suggest you produce Susan," Sharon said. "Unless you'd like me to come back with a court order and a sheriff's deputy."

"I don't have the authority—"

"Then find someone who does," Sharon said.

"Oh, my," the receptionist said in a confused tone. "Listen, you'll have to wait a minute."

"A minute's about all I've got," Sharon said, "before I head for the courthouse."

The receptionist got up and carried Sharon's card through double doors to the rear. Her fat bottom wiggled. Sharon winked at Deb, looked furtively in all directions, then leaned over the counter to examine the still open computer screen. The numbers and characters were blue against a pale orange background. There were three names listed as authorized visitors for Susan Rathermore:

Linda Haymon Rathermore, Kathleen Fraterno, and Milton Breyer. According to the record, none of the three had yet visited the child. Sharon sighed in disgust. Any doubts she'd had about whether the prosecution knew that William Rathermore had been diddling his own daughter went flying out the window.

In less than a minute, the double doors parted and the receptionist poked her head out between them. "Come back here, please."

Sharon started around the counter with Deb following. The receptionist shook her head. "Just the attorney, if you don't mind." Deb had a seat on a low cloth divan in the corner. Sharon followed the receptionist down a hallway past a Mr. Coffee which hissed and dribbled hot brown liquid into a pot, and entered a small office. Having played escort, the receptionist left.

The woman seated behind the glass-topped desk was in her fifties. She was thin with bony forearms, and was on the phone. Her name plate identified her as MARJORIE PULLEN, OFFICE MANAGER. She placed her hand over the mouthpiece and said in a slightly hoarse voice, "Are you Ms. Hays?" She pronounced "Ms." as if it ended with a z. Sharon nodded. The woman offered the phone across the desk. "Our attorney wants to speak to you," she said.

Sharon hesitated, then said firmly into the receiver, "Sharon Hays."

"Orville Watts, Miss Hays. Watts and Gilmore. Is there something I can help you with?" Deep voice, Harvard smugness mixed with an educated Texas twang.

"You can help me, Mr. Watts, if you'll tell these nice ladies to let Susan's mother see her. Otherwise we don't have much to say to each other."

"I can't authorize such a . . . Susan's committed by order of the court, Miss Hays."

Sharon had just a second to reflect that none of these people, the receptionist, the office manager, or the lawyer, had to refer to any files when talking about Susan. Milton Breyer and his henchman had drilled every one of them. "I've been to the courthouse, Mr. Watts," Sharon said, "and reviewed Susan's case. The commitment order is signed by Linda Haymon Rathermore, who doesn't happen to be Susan's legal guardian. Her father's divorce decree gives him permanent custody, but there's no provision in the event of his death. Susan's mother has automatic custody now, and that's who wants to see her."

There was a pregnant pause, after which Watts said, "Look, let me call you back."

Sharon blinked and watched Marjorie Pullen. The office manager's mouth was slightly agape. Sharon said into the phone, "I don't have time to wait, Mr. Watts. Look, I'll help you out. Your instructions are to call Milton Breyer or Kathleen Fraterno if you have any questions about Susan, am I right?" She waited. Watts said nothing. Sharon went on, "Well, when you get ahold of them, they're going to tell you to stall me any way possible. That's not going to work. If you don't give this lady the green light for us to see Susan right now, I'm headed downtown. I'd have to review the law, but I think holding Susan here without the proper commitment order constitutes lawbreaking of some sort. Kidnapping or whatever. You're the sanitarium's attorney, Mr. Watts, so you probably know the law on that without looking it up. Tell me. What do the statutes say?"

Sharon listened to faint humming and crackling noises for a full fifteen seconds. Watts finally said, "I suppose we'd better let you see her."

"You know what?" Sharon said. "I think you had."

Sharon wished that she could hire Sheila Winston as a permanent adviser. Every crisis in the Rathermore case seemed to hinge on the best way to handle emotionally disturbed teenagers, and Sharon felt as if her decision-making process was nothing more than one coin flip after another. The afternoon visit to Havenrest was a good example. Much as she realized that Susan Rathermore needed quality time with her mother, Sharon understood as well that Susan knew things which were critical to Midge's defense, and that the time left before trial was running out in a hurry. So, friend Sheila, Sharon thought, when would be the best time to ask Susan a few questions? Sharon didn't have the slightest idea. She'd finally decided to let Deborah North visit with Susan alone, and mentally crossed her fingers in hope that she'd done the right thing. She checked her watch. Visiting hours ended in five minutes. She rose from the plush waiting room sofa and went to the window.

Rolling lawns and thick oak groves extended from the colonial-style porch to Forest Lane, a full half mile in the distance. On the other side of Forest Lane, mansion roof-tops loomed. There was a long, curving gravel drive leading from the street to Havenrest's main building; at the sanitarium entry stood a tall green archway. To the right of the archway was a bronze sign on which the name HAVENREST stood out in glistening bas relief. Late-afternoon sunlight filtered through the trees and cast shadows over the freshly mowed grass.

Deb North, clad in simple yellow slacks and blouse, sat beside Susan Rathermore on a white wrought-iron bench decorated with snowy oak leaves. Identical benches dotted the rest of the grounds, and visitors sat with patients on all but two or three. As Sharon watched, Deb and Susan exchanged timid smiles. Susan wore knee-length shorts and a plaid short-sleeve shirt. She had passed within five feet of Sharon as she'd walked with her mother through the sanitarium lobby, and Susan's wounds had caused Sharon to mentally wince. Recently healed scars crisscrossed Susan's arms from elbow to wrist, and more ugly raised welts showed on the backs of the teen-ager's legs.

The grief surging through Sharon's veins on seeing Susan heightened her compassion for Midge as well. Susan had the figure of a gymnast, tiny frame, square shoulders, and lithe muscular legs. Her face was a younger version of Deb's, slim, straight nose, delicate pointed chin. For any adolescent to be as obese as Midge Rathermore was cruelly unfair; for the same girl to have a sister—particularly a younger sister—as perfectly formed as Susan would make the older sibling's plight even more of a tragedy. Even in a normal family home, consisting of real parents with real love for their kids, Midge would have had severe inferiority problems. In the twisted Rather-more environment the problems would have multiplied a hundredfold. Christ, but these children had needed a solid father figure.

Which is exactly what you're trying to keep Melanie from having, Miss Lawyer Britches, a voice inside Sharon suddenly said.

Our circumstances are different, she thought.

Oh, yeah? Says who?

I'm not having this discussion, she thought.

Sure, toots. Just keep it all blotted out. I'm sure that's what Deborah North has done the past eight years, and look where it's gotten her. One of those visitors' benches will certainly fit your little fanny when you come to see Melanie in the sanitarium.

Sharon forced the voice out of her mind and concentrated on the scene outside the window. Susan and Midge Rathermore did have one thing in common. The haunted, vacant look on Susan's face matched Midge's permanent look exactly. Since she'd been having regular contact with her mom, Midge had been smiling more of late. Sharon hoped for the same for Susan.

And the same for Melanie? the voice inside Sharon said.

"Shut up!" she said aloud, then turned to face the lobby. The receptionist was staring at her. Her cheeks reddening, Sharon gazed once more onto the lawn.

The entire sanitarium bit caused Sharon to grind her teeth. Breyer and Fraterno had simply rushed Susan to the nuthouse in order to get her out of the way until after the trial, and Linda, lovely person that she was, would have considered having Midge's sister out of her hair a windfall. Not a single visit in all this time, Sharon thought.

She managed a tiny grin as she pictured Breyer and Fraterno once they learned that the defense knew Susan's whereabouts. The prosecutors (in between rolling in the hay together, Sharon thought) would run around the Crowley Courts Building like chickens with their heads cut off as they prepared a gang of phony psychologists to say that Susan wasn't competent to testify for the defense. Well, that suited Sharon to a *T* because the defense had no plans to use Susan as a witness, and Milt and Kathleen would be wasting their time. The defense now had Leslie Schlee, and she could provide all the child-abuse testimony needed to knock the prosecution for a loop. Assuming that the judge let them get into the abuse issue at all, which was far from a given. Sharon wrung her hands.

A bell pealed suddenly across the sanitarium grounds. Visitors and patients stood to embrace goodbyes. Deb and Susan walked up on the porch with their arms entwined, and Sharon went through the door to stand a few feet away. After the coolness inside the building, the heated shade of the porch felt even warmer than it was.

Deb brought Susan over. The former Mrs. William Rathermore's eyes were misty, but she was smiling. With an obvious catch in her voice Deb said, "Sharon Hays, I want you to meet my younger daughter. Susan, Sharon's the one responsible for my getting to see you."

Sharon extended her hand. "Hi, Susan."

Susan's grip was desperately firm. "Bring my mom back to see me. Please. I've been awful lonesome in here."

29

On Friday afternoon, eleven days before the Rathermore trial was scheduled to begin, Sharon swallowed her terror of firearms and bought a gun. It was a choice, she thought, between keeping some artillery close at hand and never getting another wink of sleep. Night after night she'd lain awake, picturing Bradford Brie creeping through her house, and made up her mind once and for all that her fear of guns could never match the trauma of being alone and unarmed through the night.

She selected one big kahuna of a .44 Bulldog with a coal black handle in a pawnshop. The Bulldog packed twice the kick as the .38 police special she'd borrowed to qualify once a year on the sheriff's firing range when she'd been a prosecutor—or had *failed* to qualify, actually, depending on the kindness of the instructor (who likely figured, What the hell, she's a woman and a lawyer and not likely to be called to duty anyhow) to let her slide by—and she chose the weapon because she wanted enough firepower to stop an elephant if necessary. Before she went to bed, she stowed the .44 in her nightstand drawer.

And spent still another night without sleep, tossing and turning as she pictured Melanie in one of her forays through mommy's bedroom in search of gum or candy, Melanie finding the pistol, squinching one eye closed as she peeked down the barrel and pulled the trigger with her thumb. By four in the morning, Sharon had had enough. She stalked into her den carrying a paperback edition of *The Firm* by John Grisham—which everyone else in the world had read two years ago, and which had rested unopened on Sharon's nightstand for eighteen months—flicked on a lamp, wriggled angrily into one corner of the Spanish-style sofa, and tried to read.

The reading went about the same as her attempts at dozing off had gone. Her mind wandered so that she went over the first paragraph four times without the slightest comprehension, and she finally tossed the paperback aside to stare bleary-eyed around the room. She was frustrated, angry, and totally exhausted.

Dawn found Sharon jamming panty hose and Jockey for Her cotton briefs into a stocking bag for loading into the washing machine. After measuring two capfuls of blue liquid All detergent into the washer, she dropped the bag inside. Then she set the dial on Gentle and the water temperature on Cold, and entertained herself by watching the water run until the tub was half full. Sharon returned to her bedroom, removed the gun from the nightstand, and dropped it on top of the covers, and stared at the cylinder and its loaded bullet chambers as if she could chase her fear of guns away by sheer will.

It was around seven when she finally decided, Bull. No way was she having a firearm in her home unless it was safely hidden. She got a coat hanger from her closet and bent the wire into a crude sling, and suspended the pistol inside her toilet tank. Now, she thought, when the wacko attacks me in my bedroom, I can talk him into letting me use the potty. The hiding place would have to do until she could think of something better.

All hope of rest abandoned, Sharon trudged down the sidewalk in early sunlight to bring in the newspaper. She'd finally found the time to mow her lawn on Thursday, and thick piles of clippings lay here and there on fresh-cut grass. The City of Dallas had decreed just that summer that no longer would the garbage folks handle grass clippings, and Sharon was going to have to rake her yard. If she could ever get her weary bones in gear, which was doubtful. She lugged the paper inside and sat on the couch to spread the first section open across her lap. She was halfway through the front-page story about the furor over Bill Clinton's proposed health-care plan when her fingers grew suddenly numb. The newspaper rattled as it drifted to the floor. Sharon's chin sank down to her breastbone. Her body sagged, and she was fast asleep.

Less than a half hour later, Melanie blasted her mom into groggy wakefulness. Sharon opened one eye to find the eleven-year-old, fully dressed in a print blouse and brand-new jeans, with one knee up on the sofa as she violently shook Sharon's arm. "Stores open at nine, Mom," Melanie bubbled. Her face was scrubbed, her hair brushed, and she smelled fresh as a daisy. Sharon felt as if she might actually die from lack of sleep.

God, Sharon thought, is this really happening? Every single other Saturday morning she could remember, it took nothing less than an A-bomb to get Melanie out of bed before ten. The den clock showed a quarter past eight. Sharon wondered how stiff the criminal charges would be for locking Melanie in a closet for a couple of days. She staggered to her feet and yawned. Shopping for camp day, that's what it was. This was the Saturday that Sharon, list in hand, was to trip gaily through the malls with Melanie in tow, in hot pursuit of new shorts, T-shirts, riding gear, and arts and crafts materials. To hell with camp, Sharon thought. To hell with everybody in this entire frigging world. She ignored Melanie, stumped into the kitchen, and sank two Eggo waffles into the pop-up toaster. "You can butter and syrup them on your own, dear," she said, then went into her bathroom and turned on the shower. She very nearly stepped in under the hissing waterfall without removing her underwear.

The shower should have refreshed her and made her zesty and zippy, but as she toweled off she merely felt like a cleaner zombie. Her hair dripping wet, she looked in the mirror and examined the bags under her eyes. No way can I go shopping, she thought. Absolutely no way. She'd have to put Melanie off until next week. Her mind made up, she stepped into shorts and an oversized T-shirt, and went into the kitchen to break the news. Melanie would wail and moan. Tough, Sharon thought, this is one day she's going to have to live with disappointment.

Melanie had drowned two thawed and heated waffles in syrup. Her fork lay beside her plate. Sharon said, "Melanie, I—" Then halted in mid-sentence to look closely at the child.

Melanie hadn't touched a bite of her breakfast. Her ex-

pression was vacant. She looked ... God, Sharon
thought, it's the identical look that the Rathermore kids
have. Well, not precisely, but plenty close enough for
concern. She sat across from Melanie and said gently,
"Penny."

Melanie started. She looked at her mother as if seeing
her for the first time in her life. "Nothing, Mom. Just
thinking about camp."

In a pig's eye, Sharon thought. In addition to her
eleven-year-old ways, Melanie sometimes showed a
strange maturity. A secrecy, actually, as if she wanted to
protect her mother from whatever sadness that Melanie
was feeling. Sharon was afraid that she sometimes didn't
notice Melanie's problems because she feared the knowledge of what was causing them. "It's something, Melanie," Sharon said. "You haven't touched your waffles."

As though trying to demonstrate, Hey, everything's
cool, Melanie used her fork to dissect a triangular wedge
of waffle and poked it, dripping with syrup, into her
mouth, and as though further trying to demonstrate, See
how much fun I'm having, she grinned as she chewed.
Acting is in the genes, Sharon thought.

"Sweetheart," she said, folding her hands on the table.
"something is bugging you. If you don't want to tell me
about it, I can't make you, but I'm going to worry about
it until you do."

Melanie laid her fork aside. "Can I have a glass of
milk?"

Sharon went to the refrigerator, pulled a half-gallon
carton of Oak Farms from the shelf, checked the label to
make sure of the spoilage date, and half filled a cup with
the cold white liquid. She set the cup in front of Melanie.
"This isn't going to change the subject, young lady,"
Sharon said.

"Mom," Melanie said hesitantly, then, more forcefully,
"Mom, am I ever going to meet my father?"

There was sudden weakness in Sharon's knees as she
resumed her seat. "Why do you ask?" It wasn't a good response and she knew it. Melanie's upper lip quivered.

"Just that some kids asked me," Melanie said.

"Asked you what, darling?"

"Well, this one kid, Connie. Her folks don't live together, but her dad's taking her to Sky Ranch. Trish gets to see her father sometimes."

Sweet Jesus, Sharon thought, now of all times. "Trish's father lives right here in Dallas, Melanie."

"Connie's daddy doesn't. He's way off in San Antonio."

Sharon considered ducking the issue by explaining how much closer San Antonio was than New York, but decided that the distance wasn't pertinent and wouldn't mean anything to Melanie anyway. "Let me ask you, sweetheart," Sharon said. "You've never said you wanted to see your father before."

"I didn't used to," Melanie said. "But I've been thinking about it."

"You've been wondering about him?"

"Yeah. Pretty much." Melanie drank some milk. Her gaze wasn't directly at Sharon; rather, the child was looking in the approximate direction of her mother's left shoulder. She's hiding something, Sharon thought. Something's rotten in Denmark here.

She felt a sudden surge of panic. Sternly she said, "Have you been in my bedroom again?"

Melanie's mouth twisted. She was on the verge of tears.

Don't attack her, you dumbass, Sharon thought. Something as big as this in a little girl's life, and her mother acting like a drill sergeant. Her tone now gentle and caring, she said, "It's all right if you found the letter, Melanie. I was going to show it to you." And felt she should run for president of the Liars' Club.

"It was on your dresser, Mom. I wasn't rummaging or anything." Her face screwed up with curiosity. "Is my daddy really on television?"

"He has been lately. If you read the letter, you know he's going to star in a show next fall."

"Can I tell people about it?" A sort of childlike anticipation now, wanting to get one-up on the other kids.

"If you like," Sharon said. Beans spilled, trying to make the most of the situation.

"Are you going to let me see him when he comes here?"

Of all the questions, Sharon thought, of all the frigging times for this to come up, and of all the questions for

Melanie to ask. Sharon's lack of sleep was now totally forgotten, her weariness replaced by an empty feeling in the pit of her stomach and an aching sensation where her heart labored like a sump pump. All these years of . . .

"It's something to think about," Sharon finally said. She forced a smile and winked. "Hey, what about shopping? Don't you think it's time we were getting a move on?"

30

On Monday morning, Sharon thought she'd found something which would knock her entire theory of Midge Rathermore's defense into a cocked hat. Her spirits sinking, she turned the page in the Federal Second. The decision she was reading had to do with a Boston housewife who'd shivved her husband with a steak knife as he sat at the dinner table. The Massachusetts court had ruled that since the stabbing had occurred forty-eight hours after the last time the husband had beaten hell out of his wife, she couldn't raise self-defense as an issue in her assault trial. Sharon continued to read. Aha, she finally thought, brightening. Since the federal appeals panel of judges had refused to hear the case on the grounds that no constitutional questions had been raised, the Massachusetts decision had no bearing on a Texas case. Nevertheless, Sharon had no doubt that Kathleen Fraterno would locate the Boston decision and try to use it in the Rathermore trial to muddy the water. Sharon notated the case on her legal pad, then moved the thick Federal Second volume aside and rubbed her eyes.

Russ Black came into the library and flopped down at the head of the conference table. The collar on his pale blue shirt was undone, and he'd loosened his tie. "We've got to go travelin' again," he said.

Sharon squeezed her right hand between her left thumb and fingers. She winced. "Where are we going?"

"We're gettin' the cook's tour of the crime scene."

"Oh?" Sharon continued to massage her palm. Her hand was tender as a boil.

Black frowned. "You hurt yourself?"

Sharon limpened her wrist and shook her fingers. "It's just sore. I've been taking some target practice with a pistol that doesn't like me very much. Wants to kick me. Like a sore backside when you first ride a horse."

"You need to learn to shoot. All single women should." Black propped his shin against the edge of the table and folded his hands around his knee. "How you holdin' up since the . . ."

Sharon pretended to scan a paragraph in the law book and did her damnedest to appear unconcerned. "As long as the guy's in jail, I'm all right," she said. "If I were to find out he's back on the street, though, I'd probably come down with the screaming meemies."

"How 'bout your little girl?"

"Slept through the whole thing, and I'm not about to tell her about it. She's fine," Sharon said. "When's the crime-scene tour?"

Black checked his watch. " 'Bout two hours from now. What's the word from Sam Spade? Our detective, Mr. Gear."

"His surveillance isn't working out all that wonderfully," Sharon said. "Linda's been living in the Rathermore lake house, up at Lake Tawokoni, ever since the murder. Mr. Gear shadows her wherever she goes, but so far the worst thing she's done is grocery shopping. I suspect Milt Breyer's told her that if she doesn't cool it until after the trial, he'll have her head."

"Damn. This time next Monday we'll be pickin' a jury." He dropped his knee from the table's edge. "Somethin' you should know about us goin' over the crime scene."

"Oh?" Sharon said.

"Yeah. Our guide on the walk-through is goin' to be your old friend Detective Green. That bother you any?"

Sharon's jaw dropped in dismay. "How did you . . . ?"

Black waved a hand as though batting mosquitoes. "Oh, hell, I knew about it before I hired you. I told you I keep up. And even if I hadn't of known, it looked sorta funny, him showin' up at your house in the middle of the night with that loony runnin' around in there."

Sharon pursed her lips. "Anything between me and Stan Green is over, Russ."

The corner of Black's mouth tugged sideways. "None of my business."

Her forehead tightened in concern. "Well, maybe it isn't. But I want you to know."

He shuffled his feet on the floor. "So consider that I know. Let's get goin', girl. I'll spring for breakfast on the way."

Sharon decided that the Rathermore home would have been safe from invasion during the Wild West days. The land sloped down and away from the house, a full quarter acre of perfectly groomed English ivy dipping down to Lakeside Drive, and any sort of Indian war party charging up the hillside would have been sitting ducks from the third-story bedroom window where Sharon now stood. Halfway down the hill was a flat asphalt parking area where Russ Black's Buick sat alongside a Dallas Police black-and-white cruiser. Behind the patrol car sat the unmarked Chevy four-door in which Stan Green had arrived. Across Lakeside Drive, Turtle Creek flowed deep and silent between twin columns of giant elms and sycamores. The view was absolutely breathtaking. The Rathermore Highland Park mansion was even grander than the Schlee home, two doors down the way. The serenity of it all made it easy to forget the bloody murder committed in this very bedroom. A shudder began in Sharon's spine and worked its way upward to her shoulder blades.

She turned. Russ Black was examining the wall panel which controlled the burglar alarm. Stan Green, slouching, one hand shoved casually deep inside his pocket, stood near the end of the four-poster bed. A squat uniformed cop leaned against the dresser. Other than curt nods and hellos, Sharon and Green hadn't spoken. The detective had responded to Black's questions with a series of noncommittal grunts; the prosecution hadn't wanted to show the crime scene to begin with, and any help Stan Green supplied would be purely accidental.

"So if somebody opened the front door," Black said, "the siren noise would come through this thing." He indicated the intercom speaker located below the ten-digit security panel.

Green hesitated before answering, obviously determined that the wily veteran lawyer wasn't going to trick him into anything. In a battle of wits against Russ Black, Sharon thought, old Stan is playing without any linebackers or defensive backs. She nearly giggled. Finally Green said, "Fifteen seconds after the downstairs door opens, or any window. The fifteen seconds gives time to reset the alarm in case it's somebody who belongs here."

"Okay," Black said, "and you can talk to somebody standing on the porch through this, too?" He frowned. The bumbling act was all a game; Russ and Sharon had gone over the workings of the Rathermore alarm system a thousand times. He was screwing around, trying to get the cop's guard down.

"Yeah," Green said. "It's an intercom."

Sharon left the window and walked slowly around the bed. The drapes on the four-poster king-size were dark red velvet with a satin draw cord. The side-by-side oil paintings of Linda and William Rathermore above the dresser looked like Dmitri Vails. Sharon narrowed her eyes to read the artist's signature. Yep, it was Vail's work, all right, and she suspected that the paintings had cost more than her annual income. Against the far wall was an early American vanity complete with pearl hand mirror and what must have been fifty spray bottles of perfume. Sharon wondered briefly if Linda had used one scent before bedding Rathermore alone, and another for the cluster fucks with the teenagers. On the Mexican tile floor between the bed and vanity, William Rathermore's body was still outlined in chalk, and there were dark stains here and there on the floor and on the walls. Sharon pictured the two nice-looking boys, their features wreathed in insanity as they bludgeoned Rathermore over and over with a steel lug wrench. She stepped carefully over the chalk lines. Excuse me, old pervert, Sharon thought.

"Has anybody checked this thing out," Black said, still hovering over the security panel, "to make sure it was working that night?"

Green now straightened defiantly. "You heard Mrs. Rathermore's testimony."

"I heard what she said. And that's not what I asked. We're wantin' to know if anybody from the police department verified with the security company that the alarm was workin' that night, or if we're just supposed to take Mrs. Rathermore's word for it."

Sharon wandered near the bathroom door and bent to examine the lock. The door was flimsy, hollow wood, thin as flypaper. The lock was a button apparatus like you'd buy in any hardware store. The floor beyond the bathroom entry was shiny pale blue tile. There was a sunken tub with fixtures in the shape of twin geese.

"Well, I don't know whether we checked it out or not," Green said. "I'll have to find out." When Stan Green lies, Sharon thought, his voice goes up a half octave.

Suddenly the uniformed cop broke in: "It was working two weeks earlier, because somebody turned an alarm in. It's on the Highland Park police records." The City of Highland Park had its own force, but had an arrangement whereby the Dallas Police could step into investigations when the H.P. cops felt they didn't have the manpower. Linda Rathermore's original call had gone to the Downtown Dallas Main Headquarters, and Sharon suspected that with the publicity potential of the case, the Dallas Police had simply muscled the H.P. boys out of the way.

Black coughed, and Sharon thought that the cough was to cover up the older lawyer's grin. He said, "There was an earlier break-in?"

The man in uniform was around twenty-five, with short hair and no sideburns. "Yes, sir," he said proudly. "I can give you a copy of the report if you'd like." He looked at Green as if to say, I guess I'm telling *them,* huh?"

Green looked as though he'd like to muzzle the uniformed guy. Black said, "Yeah, I'd like."

"Anything you give them," Green snapped, "clear it with me."

"He can clear it with you," Black said, standing away from the security panel, "or he can clear it with the judge. Gettin' a court order's a pain, but if we have to we have to."

"It's in here," Sharon broke in, bending over the bathroom door lock, "that she hid out from the boys, isn't it? Ran inside while they were beating her husband to death."

"That's what she said," Green said stiffly.

"Well, it occurs to me," Sharon said, "that those kids must be awfully weak if they couldn't break in to get to her. Either that, or they weren't trying very hard." She looked up and smiled. "What do you think, Detective?"

31

Sharon was never going to be able to concentrate on her phone conversation as long as Russell Black paced back and forth in front of her desk, mumbling under his breath, so she firmed her hand over the mouthpiece and said, "You're not helping any, boss. We're all on pins and needles, but stalking around glaring at me is counterproductive."

Black sank glumly into a chair in front of Sharon's desk. "Where the hell is he?" he said.

Sharon gave the older lawyer a tight but patient smile, then said into the phone, "Please tell him it's urgent." She hung up. "His beeper service has the message. So does his wife. I don't know anybody else to leave the message with, but if you've got any suggestions I'm open." She folded her arms.

Black snorted. "If you could buy these private detectives for what they're worth and sell 'em for what they *think* they're worth . . ."

"Stop flying off the handle. He got us Leslie Schlee, didn't he?" Sharon wondered how Black's wife had ever put up with his mood swings. She had the patience of Job, Sharon thought.

"Yep. And is gettin' all the mileage he can out of it. Now he's screwin' around."

The phone jangled. As Sharon reached to answer, Black jerked up the receiver and jammed it against his ear. "Yeah, lawyer's office," he said. Sharon sank resolutely back against her chair cushions and drummed her fingers. Russell Black on a tear was something else.

Black listened, scowling, then said, "Well, where in hell are you?" He rolled his eyes. "Dudn't sound to me like you're wanting to ..." then listened some more and finally said, "Don't move a muscle. We're on our way." He hung up. "Some detective you got, Sharon."

She sighed. "He must not be doing very well. When he got us Leslie Schlee, he was *your* detective."

"Whoever's detective he is," Black said, "he's jerkin' around out at some greasy motel. Come on. If Mr. Gear dudn't give a pretty good explanation for what he's doin', he's liable to get fired."

To say that the Windjammer Motel was off the beaten path was putting it mildly. The highway running in front of the place was riddled with asphalt-repaired cracks, and more crevices which no one had bothered to fix, through which browning grass grew. If a movie director needed a sleazy motel setting, Sharon thought, he need look no further. As Bogart told the German in *Casablanca,* she thought as she gazed over the dismal landscape, there are parts of East Dallas County you wouldn't want to invade, General. Across the highway was an auto graveyard, rusted hulks piled one on top of the other with one ancient winch against the skyline like a dinosaur skeleton.

The coffee shop windows were in the shape of portholes. Sharon thought that the round tinted glass surrounded by anchor chains would have been a jazzy idea in a seaside restaurant, but was simply ridiculous considering the stunning view of the wrecking yard. The anchor chains were dusty, the panes filthy. The adjoining motel building had once been white, but had last been painted sometime around the Battle of the Bulge; what paint was left on the walls clung in crusty gray flakes. Next door to the motel was a beer joint whose sign was missing some letters; it took some imagination on Sharon's part to translate -US-Y -AIL into "Rusty Nail," and also considered that the joint might really be called the Dusty Pail. Yo ho ho and a bottle of rum, Sharon thought. In the barroom parking lot were two ancient pickups and an old Oldsmobile with one fender bashed in. My Volvo would be right at home over there, Sharon thought. The motel parking area was deserted but for two vehicles, one a blue ten-year-old Dodge parked nose on to Room 12. The spotless yellow BMW two spaces down from the Dodge stood out like a nun at a hookers' convention.

Sharon and Russell Black sat in a booth across from Anthony Gear. There were two other customers in the restaurant, guys in a corner booth who wore skin-tight T-shirts, hadn't shaved, and looked as if they hadn't bathed in a week. The waitress—who doubled as the motel desk clerk—was easily in her seventies, walked with a limp, and was as stooped over as Rumpelstiltskin. Sort of a female Igor, Sharon thought. Her gaze fell alternately on the filthy wooden floor, on plastic-covered chairs with cotton stuffing poking out, and finally rested on one of the men in the corner booth. He sported two or three days' growth of mottled beard, and his front teeth were missing. Yolk dripped from his chin as he chowed down on two eggs fried sunny-side up. He grinned at her. She shuddered and looked away.

Russ Black said to Anthony Gear, "It's just the way it is. If my client's goin' to pay you, you need to keep in touch, and I shouldn't have to tell you." He sat between Sharon and the porthole window.

Sharon wondered if anything could bother Anthony Gear. The detective calmly dipped a doughy biscuit into thin cream gravy. He bit off a chunk and chewed. He wore the same plaid sports coat as always, but had changed to a green broadcloth shirt and light green tie. "When you finish bawling me out," Gear said, "I'll give you a report."

"Right now we don't need a report," Black said, fishing a piece of paper from his coat pocket. "What we need is for you to get on this. Pronto. Been callin' all over hell and gone lookin' for you."

Gear laid down his biscuit, took the paper, and unfolded it. "Get on what?"

"That's the name and phone number of the security company that handles the Rathermores' alarm system. I want you to meet with whoever's in charge of the outfit and see if they'll give us any information. If they won't, we'll have to subpoena their business records, and a copy of the subpoena will have to go to Milt Breyer. I'd just as soon he dudn't know we're talkin' to these people."

Gear produced a silver ballpoint and writing pad. "What are we trying to find out?"

Sharon leaned over and butted in in a hushed voice. "There was a disturbance about two weeks before the murder. We want to know what the security company did about it."

Gear raised untrimmed eyebrows. "Did pertaining to what?"

"Pertaining to the security code," Sharon said. "The usual practice is to change the code anytime someone turns in an alarm. If they changed it ... Well, our two young men testified that Midge gave them the code before Christmas vacation. Before the break-in. So how's come they had the new code, is what we're asking."

Gear scratched underneath his chin. "I'll be damned. You think Linda Rathermore gave it to them?"

"We're hoping," Sharon said.

"There's a problem," Gear said. "With the trial starting Monday, I can't do this until ..."

"Sure, while we're pickin' the jury," Black said. "Which wouldn't be a problem if you'd been keeping in touch like you're supposed to."

Gear's jaws clenched. He sopped his biscuit in gravy, keeping his head down as he said, "I can only be in one place at a time. You told me to watch Linda Rathermore."

"Which is what you're doin'," Black said, "sittin' around eatin' biscuits and gravy in this fleabag?"

Gear reached down and pulled up a small Canon camera by its carrying strap. "That's exactly what I'm doing."

Black cocked his head. "Huh?"

"She's a restless woman," Gear said. "Man, is she restless."

Black exchanged looks with Sharon.

"She just can't stay holed up in that lake house," Gear said. "Three or four times a day she goes into town, grocery store or whatever, but she didn't do anything that looks the least bit out of line until this morning."

Black stirred coffee the color of river mud. Sharon had taken one look at the half-washed empty cup before her and had told the waitress that she didn't care for anything. Russ's stomach, she thought, must be lined with stainless steel. Black set his cup into the saucer with a soft, glassy clink. "What'd she do today that's so different?"

Gear jerked a thumb toward the window. "That BMW out there is hers. She's been inside old unlucky Room 13 since, oh, about eleven." He checked his watch. "Six hours."

Five o'clock already, Sharon thought. Since the trip to the Rathermore mansion, the day had slipped completely away. Another evening for Melanie at Sheila's house. I'm neglecting my daughter, she thought, and once this frigging trial is over I'm going to change that. The blistering sun was still high over the roof; in July darkness didn't fall until nearly nine.

"Christ," Black said. "Who's she in there with?"

Gear washed down the biscuit with a swallow of milk. "Who knows? For all I know, Linda's in there by herself. But I sort of doubt it. I'm not budging from here until she comes out if it's a week." He hefted the camera once more and smiled. "So I do stay on the job, Russ, regardless of what you think."

"And we're goin' to see that you do," Black said. "Until Linda comes out of that room, you're goin' to have company."

Linda didn't come out in the open until almost eight, and in the interim Sharon was bored practically to tears. They'd left the restaurant around six, and for the past two hours had been seated across the street in Russ's Buick. Sharon was in the backseat with the two men in front. Her period was about to begin, and she was cramping. Every ten minutes or so, Black started the engine and turned the a.c. on to cool down the car's interior; even at eight o'clock it was over ninety degrees. Anthony Gear had a teeth-jarring habit of cracking his knuckles, which he did every quarter hour or so, and Sharon felt that if he cracked them one more time she was going to have a sobbing fit. She was thinking of a subtle way to tell Gear to stop when the door to the Windjammer Motel's Room 13 opened a crack, hesitated, then swung wide on its hinges.

"Geronimo," Gear said, sitting up.

Black bent over the steering wheel to peer around the detective toward the motel. Sharon draped an arm over the seat back and put her nose a quarter inch from the window.

It was Linda, all right. She moved cautiously toward the BMW, her head turning right and left in the building's shadow. She was dressed in snug white pants and a maroon knit blouse, her hair tousled as if she'd been in a wind tunnel. Linda was in one big hurry, and her expression was tense. She reached the BMW's driver's side, glanced around her a final time, then beckoned to someone still inside the room. A man came out and moved up to the car from the passenger side. Sharon put up a hand to shade her eyes.

Correction, Sharon thought, Linda's sweetie isn't quite a man. He was more of a boy, a good-looking teenager with thick sandy hair. As the youngster paused beside the car, Sharon had the same feeling she'd experienced when she'd first seen him in the courtroom. Most Likely to Succeed, hands down. The boy was Troy Burdette.

Gear said in a loud whisper, "Christ on a crutch."

Russ Black dug around on the floorboard under his feet, then lifted Gear's camera. He squinted through the viewfinder. "Where's the shutter button on this thing, boy?" he said. "Mr. Gear, you better not have forgotten to load the film. If you did, you're goin' to have me to answer to."

The old woman looked a thousand times more at ease in the motel office than she had in the restaurant. When she'd been wearing her waitress hat, her breathing had been like a cardiac patient's as she'd grumped from table to table, and she'd seemed in such a strain that Sharon had worried that the poor old thing might drop the coffeepot. In the office, however, the gray-haired lady could relax on a stool behind the counter and sneer with the best of them. A lit unfiltered Camel dangled from one corner of her mouth and her teeth were stained. Her vocal cords were sandpaper and there were big liver spots on the backs of her hands. "If you're the police, you got no call to come fucking with me," she said. Just a sweet old grandmama, Sharon thought.

"We're just the opposite, ma'am," Russ Black said. "We're lawyers defendin' a criminal client." He leaned his forearms on the counter in his best buddy-buddy posture while Sharon stood off to one side with her arms folded and her ankles crossed. Anthony Gear had left minutes earlier, following Linda Rathermore's BMW to wherever it was headed. Sharon thought that Gear's Land Rover was the most conspicuous surveillance vehicle she'd ever seen, but if Linda had suspected that she had a tail, she hadn't let on.

"Well, if you're a lawyer," the old lady said, "maybe I should let you talk to mine." Her black eyes reflected a million miles of bad road; lawyers impressed her zero, the police even less. Sharon thought fleetingly of the Ma Barker gang.

"I just want to know," Black said, "about that boy who just left outta Room 13 with the blond woman. He come here in a cab?"

"I don't know from nothing about people come here. If you want to know about cabs I'll call you one. Or you can leave in your car, mister, I don't give a shit." The cigarette wagged up and down between dry, wrinkled lips. Loose skin dangled from bony upper arms. "This ain't exactly no Hyatt Regency we can check out everybody's credentials. Somebody shows me American Express, I think they're pulling a fast one."

Black's nostrils flared. "It ain't exactly a home for runaways, either, lady. Let me ask you. You know what an accessory is?"

"Like, to a robbery? I ain't robbed shit."

Sharon took a step forward. "Like, to inducing a minor, ma'am. It's a felony."

"I ain't induced shit, neither." The lip curled in a sneer. She looked Sharon over with vulture eyes, and she didn't seem pleased with what she saw. "I just collect the rent." She coughed up phlegm.

Sharon wanted to stamp her foot. "Well, do you—"

"Hold it." Black's hand was on Sharon's arm. He winked at her, then laid a twenty-dollar bill on the counter. "That's the easy way, ma'am," he said to the old woman. "The hard way is for us to call the police and give them copies of some pictures we took. Of a forty-somethin'-year-old woman and a sixteen-year-old kid comin' out of Room 13. I don't think they'll find out she's the boy's mama, either."

The woman fingered one of her liver spots. Her cig had

burned down nearly to her lips; she squashed the soggy butt in an ashtray and fished for another. She thumbed a disposable lighter, lit, blew out smoke, and picked tobacco from between her teeth. Finally she pocketed the twenty and said, "Another kid brings him. The woman takes him home."

"They've been here before, then," Sharon said.

"A year or more they been coming. Used to be, oh, a couple of times a week, but I ain't seen 'em in a while. I never told you that, right? If anything comes back on me, I'll swear you two was shacked up here and tried to beat us for the rent." She showed Black an evil leer. "Old fart like you runnin' around with this young woman might not look so good, neither." Her gaze darted from Black to Sharon, then back again. "We got us an understanding, don't we?" the old woman said.

32

Sharon calmed her pretrial butterflies on the Saturday preceding the Fourth of July by taking Melanie shopping again. Actually, the mall excursion the week before had been a scam to take the eleven-year-old's mind off her father—and to give mommy additional time to make up her mind what to do about him—the result being that mother and daughter had spent a whole lot more time looking than buying, but now they shopped in earnest, knocking serious dents in Sharon's credit card limits. The buying donnybrook began at Sears Valley View (for hiking shoes, riding jeans, and three pairs of sensible khaki shorts which Sharon practically had to stuff Melanie into bodily, ignoring her daughter's loud protest that she'd be the *only kid in camp* wearing anything so dorky), continued on to J.C. Penney's Northpark (which had advertised knit shirts on sale, but, of course, happened to be out of the lower-priced knits in anything but sizes designed to fit a baby elephant, all of which caused Sharon to leave the store mumbling about false-advertising lawsuits even though she'd blown sixty bucks on shirts which *weren't* on sale), detoured to Lady Foot Locker (whose prices were a rip-off, Sharon thought, but which happened to be the only place in town carrying Nike Chug-Alongs, or whatever brand it was that Melanie *just had* to have to keep from dying from embarrassment), and finally ended at Morgan Boots, where mommy swallowed her Scottish instincts to spring for fifty-dollar western footwear. Three years earlier she had promised Melanie the boots (God, I must have been drunk, she thought as she forked over her MasterCard) if the child should ever make Roughrider in horsemanship at Sky Ranch. Melanie had passed the Roughrider test the previous summer, and the kid had the memory of an elephant when it came to mommy's promises. How Melanie could recall the boot promise—when the child could never remember where she'd tossed her underpants on the night before wash day—was a mystery to mommy. The shopping trip went on and on, and it was nearly ten before they got home. Day one of pretrial weekend survived.

On Sunday afternoon she took Melanie to the movies. Sharon had managed to duck the opening two weeks of *Jurassic Park*—even though Melanie was the *only kid in town* who hadn't seen the frigging picture—and still harbored misgivings about whether any movie starring dinosaurs ripping humans to shreds could possibly be suitable for an eleven-year-old. Nonetheless, mommy gave in, and was pleasantly surprised. There wasn't any actual blood or guts in the picture, and, thank God, nobody went to bed with anybody. Sharon had to admit that the raptors stole the show.

Melanie was so high on Sunday night that she was bouncing off the ceiling, and Sharon had to threaten bloody murder in order to get the child into bed. It was close to eleven before Sharon rescued the kid's pea green duffel bag in a tug of war with Commander, then stuffed the bag with camp paraphernalia while the shepherd lay nearby with his head cocked inquisitively. Around midnight, it was all that Sharon could do to crawl in between the sheets.

Exhausted as she was, she didn't sleep for almost an hour. She kept rehearsing her cross-examination of Linda Rathermore, and every time she closed her eyes an image of Linda popped into her mind. Then Linda would fade out, replaced by Midge Rathermore, the pitiful teenager expressionless as tears streamed down her cheeks.

Sharon had never been very religious, but before she finally drifted off she said a silent prayer. If it would help Midge's chances, Sharon supposed that she'd do most anything.

* * *

Monday the Fourth was no holiday for the two young women who took their daughters to camp. Sharon and Sheila wore themselves to a frazzle hauling boxes, duffel bags, and suitcases to load them in Sheila's Pontiac station wagon. By the time they pulled away from Sheila's, there was barely room for the women to sit in front while Melanie and Trish snuggled into the back with Commander in between them. Sheila had put up a tussle over taking the dog along, but the kids had won out. After all, they'd chorused, Commander wasn't going to have anyone to play with for *two whole weeks*.

The trip was an hour's drive, fifty miles on Interstate 20 watching barren countryside change into lush pine forest as they headed farther east, then a ten-mile jaunt on a two-lane blacktop road that was twisty as folded linguini. The journey's final leg took them through the sleepy little town of Van, Texas, then north to negotiate a one-lane dirt track leading over an earthen dam. Sky Ranch Camp lay behind a small man-made lake. The day was hot and windless, the lake still as mirrored glass. From the dam, the camp's swimming dock was visible across the way, and just off the end of the pier floated the Blob. This was a huge inflated rubber raft which was slick when wet, and off which squealing youngsters slipped and slid. Sharon had never been certain why the mere sight of the floating monstrosity sent the kids into orbit. As the station wagon labored across the dam, Trish and Melanie screamed, "There it *is*," as they giggled and pointed and pressed noses to the glass, and as Commander nearly tore the backseat to shreds, barking and leaping at the window. Sharon and Sheila locked exasperated gazes, then rolled their eyes.

It was nearly dark when, assisted by energetic college kids in shorts and Sky Ranch T-shirts, the mothers had the children moved finally into their cabin. Just as they did every year, Trish and Melanie had signed up on the buddy plan. They played "One potato, two potato" for choice of bunks. Melanie lost and glumly accepted the lower. The cabin counselor was a perky, tennis-anyone redhead named Nancy—a drama major at Stephen F. Austin U. in Nacogdoches, Sharon was interested to learn—who seemed mature and responsible. Four summers ago, the first time the girls had come to Sky Ranch, Sheila had fidgeted and fretted because Trish was the only black child in the entire camp. She needn't have worried; Trish and the white kids had become instantly thick as thieves. Now there were a number of black children scurrying about, and Trish thought that showing the new African-American kids the ropes were really big stuff.

After dark there was a fireworks display, where all joined hands and sang the "Star-Spangled Banner" while skyrockets exploded overhead and Commander whined and tugged at his leash. Firelight danced over Melanie's smiling features, and Sharon was in awe of how beautiful her little girl had become.

Finally it was time to leave. Melanie ran to her mother in the parking lot, threw her arms around Sharon's neck, and hugged for all she was worth. "I love you, Mom," she said.

Suddenly Sharon was in tears. She sniffled and buried her face in the side of Melanie's neck. "Me, too, precious," she said. "You have a good time, you hear?"

Luminous yellow highway stripes raced by the station wagon as it chugged on through the night. Headlight beams shone on a green overhead sign reading, in glistening reflector print, DALLAS 42, FT. WORTH 71. Sharon's feet were up on the dash. She snuggled into the corner formed by the seat back and passenger door, and hummed a silent tune. The trees were dark shapes against a blue-black background.

Sheila said, "What is it?" Exquisite chocolate-colored skin tinted red by the dash-light glow, both hands on the steering wheel. She had the cruise control on, her feet splayed out on either side of the gas and brake pedals.

Sharon said, "Hmm?"

"You haven't said a word in twenty miles."

Sharon propped her elbow on the armrest and laid her cheek against her palm. "Just thinking."

"About the trial?"

"What else?" Sharon said. From the backseat Commander gave a whiny yawn.

Sheila steered the Pontiac nearer to the median. "I'm surprised you haven't asked about my interviews with Midge and Susan Rathermore."

"I was getting around to it."

"You aren't worried that the prosecution's going to make a big deal of the fact that we're friends?"

"Sure they will," Sharon said. "They'll bring up our friendship the same way that we'll bring up the fact that Gregory Mathewson's testified ten zillion times for the state before. You've got all the credentials, Sheila. You've never testified in a criminal trial, and since you're waiving any fee, the jury's going to see that you've got nothing at stake. This is one case where our witness will outshine even old Gruntin' Greg."

"I hope so," Sheila said, then paused and said, "Susan has blocked it all out, by the way. The sexual abuse."

The a.c. fan was running on low; since sundown the car's interior had grown chillier and chillier. Sharon reached up to move the control switch from Norm to Vent. The air warmed instantly toward room temperature as goose bumps faded from Sharon's bare legs. "She won't talk about it at all?" she said.

"It makes a better case for abuse if she won't," Sheila said, "though how you get that across to the jury is up to you. It's not easy talking to her with those Havenrest people watching over my shoulder. I suppose you know the staff out there called and cleared it with the D.A.'s office before they'd let me see her."

"I expected them to. It's good they did, we want the other side to know we're talking to Susan. It might slow their horses a bit. How come you say it's a better case if Susan won't discuss the abuse?"

Sheila shifted in the seat, moving her left foot over to the right side of the gas pedal, crossing her ankles and stretching her legs. "Anytime the subject of her father comes up, she goes into another world. Won't react to any mention of his name. It's classically typical of sexually abused children, and to that I'll testify. If you want confirmation, check with someone from Harvard or any other brain factory. They'll all tell you the same thing, and the name that the kid blocks out is the pervert who's abused them. A hundred percent of the time."

Sharon rubbed her forehead. Wind rushed by outside the window in a whispered hiss. "God, I'd hate to have to put that poor child on the stand."

"Breaks your heart," Sheila said. "In the long run it'd be good for her to talk about it. It's likely the only chance she'll ever have for normalcy." Her voice softened, her tone more hesitant as she said, "Midge was a bit more of a problem."

"Did her mother go to the jail with you?"

"She was right there. Midge is more talkative than Susan, and I've got to tell you that I don't think Rathermore abused Midge. Per se."

Sharon sat up straighter. "Sheila . . ."

"Not physically. But I think he made her feel inferior to her little sister, which in ways is a more serious kind of abuse."

"Like, Susan was desirable but Midge was ugly?"

"Something like that," Sheila said.

The station wagon cruised underneath another luminous green sign, this one reading, DALLAS 36, FT. WORTH 65. Sharon said, "Sheila?"

"Uh-huh?"

"Does Midge really believe that she planned the murder with those boys?"

"I'm afraid she does. Why, what's your theory?"

"We think they used Midge as a stooge, and that Linda wooed the Burdette boy into love with her—"

"Into having this permanent hard-on, is what you mean."

"Right. I think Linda planned it all, had the boys talk Midge into thinking she was plotting a murder, and then threw Midge to the wolves. Linda gets the bulk of the estate, the lovesick little boy gets to do next to zero time, and Midge gets to spend years in prison. The Burdette kid probably thinks that when he gets out, Linda will be waiting with open arms."

"Is *he* in for a shock," Sheila said. "It's a bunch to prove, kid."

"That's why we're going ahead with the sexual-abuse defense. If we can't hang old Linda, then we've still got a chance of defending Midge based on the theory that she was only protecting herself from more abuse." Sharon sighed. "I hope I sound really confident. I'm afraid I don't feel that way." She fell silent, listening to the station wagon's radials *click-thud* over the highway expansion joints.

Sheila finally said, "On another subject."

Sharon lifted her eyebrows. "Yes?"

"Watched any TV this week?"

"Some."

"Seen the fall lineup?"

Sharon folded her hands in her lap. "I saw him. Super cop himself."

"You've got to admit," Sheila said, "that a starring role on CBS is a pretty big deal. What's the name of the show?"

"Minions of Justice." Sharon laughed in spite of herself. "He's the cop, another guy's the prosecutor. I guess I'm happy for Rob, though I'd have to think about it." The highway ahead was now dotted with a dozen or so pairs of red taillights, interstate traffic thickening as they drew nearer to Big D.

"I know you've told Melanie who he is," Sheila said.

Sharon started, then relaxed. "I suppose I knew she'd tell Trish. I didn't tell her voluntarily. She found Rob's letter in my bedroom."

"Well, you know the more publicity he gets, the harder it's going to be on her. He'll do interviews. He'll pop off to some reporter, and the next thing you know you'll be getting a call from the newspapers."

Sharon looked down at her knees. "All those years pretending he didn't exist . . ."

"As your personal psychologist," Sheila said, "I'm advising you to let him see her. He is her father, after all."

Sharon rubbed her eyes and swallowed a lump from her throat. "I've got to think of one thing at a time, Sheila. As soon as the trial's out of the way, I'll just have to figure out how to handle Melanie."

"Just don't let your own self-interest get in the way," Sheila said. "It's easy to do."

"I understand that." A slight testiness crept into Sharon's tone, and she felt instantly guilty.

"If you need backup," Sheila said, "just let me know."

Sharon leaned back, folded her arms, and regarded the ceiling. "I got myself into this. I suppose I'll just have to figure out how to dig myself out." She closed her eyes. "I'd as soon take a beating, tell you the truth."

33

Tuesday morning dawned. Preliminary fingers of pink touched the edges of wispy clouds, then the main-event sun appeared. The blinding circle of fire climbed slowly above the horizon, and by eight-thirty the thermometer hovered near ninety degrees.

Sharon Hays left the Volvo on the third parking level, then hurried onto the crosswalk leading to the Crowley Courts Building. Her high heels clicked a double-time march. A navy blue pleated skirt swirled around her calves and her bangs flipped testily. Her satchel was packed with motions and briefs, her lips firmed in a bring-'em-on, game-face expression.

So intent was Sharon with psyching herself up that she very nearly barged headlong into Cissy Breyer just outside the revolving courthouse entry door. Raven-haired Cissy had her own blinders on, head down, black Gucci shoes moving like piston heads, diamonds twinkling on fingers and earlobes. Sharon put on the brakes and smiled a timid greeting. During her final days as a prosecutor, when Milt Breyer had really been putting the pressure on her sexually, Sharon had dreaded running into Cissy, and encountering Breyer's oft-jilted wife still made her nervous. As Sharon opened her mouth to speak, Cissy swept past without a word and stalked into the Crowley Building. Sharon's mouth closed with an audible click.

Winthrop Stone, founding partner of Stone, Stone and Buckalew—law offices in Dallas, Austin, and Washington, finger in the state legislature's vagina and lips near the governor's ear—followed close on Cissy's heels. Stone was dressed in courtroom navy blue. He brandished a silver-headed walking stick, his satchel burnished leather, his black ferret's eyes moving rapidly from side to side. He favored Sharon with the curtest of nods. She said softly, "Hello."

Something brewing, she thought. She hadn't seen Cissy Breyer at the courthouse three times during her entire tenure with the D.A., and Winthrop Stone never personally appeared in court unless on behalf of the selectest of clients. Which Cissy's father definitely was, the selectest of the select, oil by the megabarrel and enough Texas land to form a state of his own, and then some. Big doings coming down, Sharon thought.

By the time she'd pushed through the revolving door and mounted the escalator toward the second level, she had dismissed Cissy Breyer and her high-powered lawyer from her mind. She had a client of her own to represent. Anticipation growing within her, Sharon turned her face upward toward the head of the escalator and drummed her fingers on the handrail.

The corridor outside Judge Sandy Griffin's courtroom was a madhouse, side benches jam-packed with humanity, reporters standing expectantly near the windows, men in short-sleeve shirts toting minicams. One TV camera aimed its lens in Sharon's direction as she came through the door leading from the foyer, and Andy Wade simultaneously flipped his steno pad as he said loudly, "Miss Hays. Got time for . . . ?" Sharon dodged around both newsman and cameraman and kept on truckin'. Just outside the court entry, Rayford Sly blocked her path. The movie second banana offered Sharon another of his business cards as he said, "If you should reconsider, Miss Hays . . ." Sharon ducked her head and pointedly ignored the guy. Sly turned and said something to the leggy on-the-scene *Hard Copy* reporter, who shrugged.

The courtroom was to have an extra bailiff for the Rathermore trial, in addition to the regular deputy who escorted prisoners in from the holding cell and ran errands for the judge. The reinforcement, a curly-haired jail guard whom Sharon had seen around, stood at attention in front of the entry. He'd traded his khaki deputy's uni-

form for a blue blazer which was too small along with
pleated gray slacks which were too baggy, and he was
taking tickets. Each district judge had their own system
for handling crowds during high-profile trials. In Sandy
Griffin's system the two front rows on the left-hand side
were reserved for the press while one front row, dead center before the bench, was for victims' relatives and sup-
porters of the defendant. The rest of the spectator section
was open seating. The bailiff had counted the available
seats and had an exact number of red pasteboard tickets
available. At eight o'clock courthouse hangers-on could
line up for the tickets on a first-come, first-serve basis,
and once the doors opened at eight-thirty only ticket hold-
ers got inside. No tickee, no laundry. The backup bailiff
showed Sharon a wink of recognition, opened the door,
and stood aside like a Broadway usher.

Sharon didn't waste any time in her trip down the aisle,
through the gate, and to the defense table, pausing only to
give Deborah North's shoulder an affectionate squeeze.
Deb was seated first-row aisle, and wore a blue pantsuit
with a white ruffled collar. Sandy Griffin was already on
the bench, accepting a plea from a chubby black youngster in jail garb, and Sharon had been right about the
makeup consultant. Judge Griffin had done wonders since
the examining trial, her lip rouge and cheek highlights
done in just the right pale shades. Only two prisoners
were handcuffed inside the jury box, a fat white man and
a skinny Hispanic guy with a mustache. On most morn-
ings a dozen or more repentants were dying to 'fess up
and take their medicine, but today Judge Griffin had arranged for a short docket call. The Rathermore trial
would be underway promptly at nine.

Ticket-holding spectators filled the pews end to end
and, Sharon knew, were about to be disappointed. As
soon as the plea bargains were over, the judge would
clear the room for jury selection. Then the panel from the
central jury room would file in, solid citizens, each with
an excuse not to serve in mind, and the process would begin. The panel members would recite the various spouse
fatalities and homes on fire which would make it impossible for them to be sworn in as jurors, and the judge
would deny all such attempts at begging off. From both
the defense and prosecution's viewpoint, agreeing on

twelve tried and true to stand in judgment over Midge
Rathermore wouldn't take too long; Sharon and Russ
Black would accept just about anybody who wasn't a
homicide cop or member of the district attorney's staff. If
Judge Griffin admitted the child-abuse evidence, a jury of
professional hangmen would be hard pressed to convict
Midge; but if Sandy Griffin excluded the abuse question,
the twelve apostles themselves wouldn't show much
mercy. The state had its druthers, of course, but a prospective juror being the parent of teenage children wasn't
proper cause for dismissal. It would suit Sharon if the
judge seated the first twelve citizens in the courtroom.

Russ Black had arrived early, and acknowledged
Sharon with a pat on the hand as she took her seat. Anthony Gear would be absent until the testimony kicked
off; the detective was hot on the trail of the burglar-alarm
company. Sharon hoisted her satchel up on the table,
looked to the front, and raised inquisitive eyebrows.
There seemed to be trouble in paradise among the prosecution team.

Milt Breyer and Kathleen Fraterno were seated in the
far end of the jury box, away from the handcuffed prisoners, and the two prosecutors were talking a mile a minute,
as if each were determined not to let the other get a word
in edgewise. Breyer wore a navy blue suit, crazy-quilt tie,
and terminally worried frown. Kathleen was dressed out
in a charcoal gray pantsuit which nicely hugged her
curves. There were dark circles under her eyes and her
makeup was streaked. Sharon squinted for a better look.
By golly, Kathleen *had* been crying; her eyelashes were
stuck together in a row of dark, wet points.

Sharon briefly pictured Cissy Breyer and her high-
dollar lawyer as they'd stalked into the courthouse, then
lifted and dropped her shoulders in a none-of-my-
business shrug. She unsnapped the catches on her satchel,
then stacked motions and briefs out on the table. She was
going to be here awhile.

Two days later, at two o'clock on Thursday afternoon,
to be exact, Russ Black said to prospective juror No. 42,
"You've never done any buddyin' around with old Milt
Breyer over there, have you?"

The panelist, a paunchy, balding man in slacks and

sports shirt, grinned and shook his head. If chosen, he would be the final juror. Those already seated consisted of four men and seven women. Three were blue-collar workers, one was a dentist. Additionally, both sides had approved five clerical people, one unemployed computer technician, and even one mortician. Once the selection of juror number twelve was complete, there would be two alternates left to pick. Jury selection was moving right along.

Judge Griffin sternly told the prospective juror, "Speak up, please. The court reporter can't record nods or head shakes."

To which the prospective juror replied, still grinning at Black, "No, ma'am, I've never met the prosecutor."

"And Miss Fraterno over there," Black said, pointing. "You and her don't have anything goin', do you?"

The man chuckled nervously. "No, sir."

If Sharon hadn't been so intent on going over her witness list, she might have applauded. Jury voir dire was one of Russ Black's specialties, the Deacon Andy Griffith act causing panelists to fall in love with him before the trial was underway. Sharon ran her finger down the column of names, paused, then leaned back and whispered to Anthony Gear, "This guy's with the security company, right?" Gear bent forward to read the name above Sharon's clear-lacquered nail, then nodded.

Satisfied, Sharon got up, went over, and laid the list in front of Kathleen Fraterno, then returned to her scat. The exchanging of proposed witnesses' names was mandatory for both sides before trial. Sharon had received the state's list on Monday. She had promised to reciprocate by lunchtime today, and was only a couple of hours late in delivering. She pretended to be absorbed in Russ Black's voir dire, but watched from the corner of her eye as Fraterno went over the defense witnesses. Kathleen, she knew, was about to come unglued.

"And Judge Griffin up there," Black said to the juror. "She ain't one of your fishin' or drinkin' buddies, is she?"

As Sharon pretended not to watch, Fraterno picked up the piece of paper and lazily scanned it. She stiffened. She laid the list on the table, yanked hard on Milt Breyer's sleeve, and pointed at something on the page.

Breyer leaned over to read, then regarded Fraterno with comically widened eyes. Sharon snickered to herself. The prosecution had just discovered that they'd be dealing with testimony from Leslie Schlee. How 'bout that, boys and girls? Sharon thought.

Russ Black leaned back and hooked his thumbs underneath his lapels, Jed Clampett style. "Your Honor, we accept this juror here."

Judge Griffin looked at the prosecution side. "Any objection?"

"None, Your Honor," Breyer said quickly. His gaze was firmly on the witness list, and he could have been approving Midge Rathermore's maiden aunt as a juror and never would have known the difference. He looked directly at Sharon as if he'd like to get his hands around her throat. She met his gaze with a what-me-worry grin.

Sharon left the courthouse that afternoon with her fingertips tingling in anticipation. The opening statements in the morning would be brief and to the point, and then Stan Green would testify. The detective wouldn't have much to say, and when he was finished, Linda Rathermore was scheduled for her stint on the stand. Before tomorrow was gone, Sharon would likely be halfway through with her cross-examination. She could hardly wait.

34

Just after midnight in the ninth-floor informants' wing of the Lew Sterrett Justice Center, Wilfred Donello tenderly stroked his personal punk. Man alive, Donello had never had it so good in lockup, lording it over a cell full of chickenshits, lying back and taking it easy while gutless informants made life a bowl of cherries for him. In the two weeks since he'd given up Bradford Brie—which sure didn't make Donello himself any snitch, dropping a dime on *that* insane prick, because the entire world was better off with Brie out of commission—Donello hadn't had to lift a finger. Not to mop. Not to scrub the toilet. Not to kowtow to a bunch of jail guards, either. He didn't even have to stir from his bunk to get his dinner; this gang of stoolies was so afraid of Wilfred Donello that they waited on him hand and foot. Why, if old Wilfred didn't feel like walking over to take a dump, this gang of weaklings would likely carry him over and set him up on the throne.

The punk whose backside and legs Donello was stroking at the moment was the pick of the litter. The sweetie-pie likely wasn't over eighteen, twenty at the most, and man-oh-man, did the boy ever have an ass on him. Shaved his butt and legs just like a woman, too, and knew just how to make the woman eyes over his shoulder, bent over Donello's bunk and waited for the big man to come and get it. Soft, moist mouth just like a girl's. You just wait, old punk, Donello thought, you just wait 'til old Wilfred gets him a good boner up and drives it home.

You'll think you're in heaven, old punk, just you wait and see.

The punk's name was Clarence, and the first time Donello had heard the name he'd gone, No shit, *Clarence?* You've got to be kidding me. Up until Donello had moved into the snitches' tank, Clarence had belonged to a big fat black guy named James. In fact, before Donello had come along, James had ruled the entire cell. Donello hadn't made his move right away. Stand-up experienced con that he was, Donello had bided his time.

The time had come four days after he had stowed his gear beneath the bottom bunk, third row in the twenty-four-man cell. James had been bent over the sink washing his face, big chocolate-colored gut touching the lavatory's rim, both hands cupped underneath the faucet. It hadn't taken much of a shove for Donello to ram James's head into the concrete wall, and the fight had been over before it started. James had been nearly unconscious when Donello had straddled him and beaten the slobbish black man into a bloody pulp for one and all to see. Ever since that moment the cell had belonged to Wilfred Donello, and James had been just another con in the jailhouse pecking order.

In the darkness of the cell, Donello's face flushed with excitement. His erect member throbbed. Spittle ran down his chin. "You ready? You ready for me?"

The punk turned his face to the mattress. "You bring it on, Big Daddy, you hear?"

And bring it on was exactly what Donello intended to do. He spread the punk's hot cheeks, closed his eyes, and moved in closer. It was going to be good. Jesus, it was going to be . . .

The movement behind Donello was nothing but a shadow, he thought, a shape moving among darker shapes. Likely, Donello thought, it was his own image cast by the dim lights outside in the corridor. As he returned his attention to the punk, a hand snaked around his neck and moved like lightning.

At first Donello thought that the stinging sensation at his left carotid artery was nothing but a scratch. Irritated more than angry, his hard-on wilting like time-lapse photography, Donello turned. Who in hell would have the nerve to . . . ?

Fat James was standing there, showing piano-key teeth in a grin. There was something in James's hand. Donello sneered. James was letting himself in for another good old-fashioned ass-whuppin'.

Donello stepped forward. "You want somethin' from me, nigger?" He balled his fist and swung a haymaker. James moved back a step. The punch landed on thin air. Donello staggered and righted himself. The first spurt of blood landed, thick and warm, on his forearm.

Puzzled, Donello touched his throat where James had scratched him from behind. Thick, hot liquid squirted over his fingertips and splashed on the floor. Christ, Donello thought. Jesus H. Christ, the fucking nigger's cut me bad.

Donello shook his head to clear his muddled brain, gritted his teeth, and threw another punch. His limbs had no strength all of a sudden, and the blow landed harmlessly on the black man's shoulder. James stepped forward to clamp a hand on Donello's wrist and forced the burly prisoner downward. Donello sank to his knees and screamed.

Suddenly the punk Clarence was there as well, grabbing Donello's other arm, Clarence and James working together as each pinned a muscular arm to the floor. Donello thrashed weakly and kicked his legs.

A red haze filtered over Wilfred Donello's vision. His chest was drenched with blood, and he was growing weaker and weaker. Jesus, was it possible? Was he going to ...?

As Donello sank into unconsciousness for the last time on this earth, the fat black man and the soft-bodied punk embraced in a lover's kiss. That was the last thing Wilfred Donello ever saw, two men touching their tongues together while the tough stand-up con beneath them wriggled convulsively and whimpered like a dying child.

35

Homicide detective Stan Green wore his best gray suit on Friday morning. As he answered Kathleen Fraterno's questions, he showed the jurors his standard, bland, protector-of-the-people expression, honing in on the twelve tried and true as if there were no one in the courtroom except him and them. One woman in the box, near the center of the second row, watched the detective with a look near pure rapture. Fraterno led Green through virtually the same testimony he'd given at Midge's adult-certification hearing, then passed the witness with a wave of her hand. From her vantage point on the defense side, Sharon saw that Andy Wade of the *News* wasn't even taking notes. Easier for him that way, she thought. The reporter could merely dig out his story about the cop's previous testimony, change a word here and there, and write the same things all over again.

Russ Black appeared to study a few tidbits he'd jotted down on a legal pad, but Sharon knew it was all for show. The veteran lawyer had a nearly photographic memory, and could recall every word the cop had said as easily as if he'd had a tape recorder. Black's pretended study of his nonexistent notes was designed to create a brief period of silence, to make the jurors wonder what was coming next. He played juries like a maestro with a fine cello.

Finally Black said thickly, "Detective Green, you said 'while ago that you were the officer in charge of the investigation. Could you tell the jury exactly what that means?"

Green cleared his throat and hesitated. It was a favorite trick of Black's to ask 'em what they least expected. The question was irrelevant, of course—but not far enough out in left field that Fraterno could object and have the objection sustained—and the sole purpose of asking it was to make the detective appear as though he was fumbling for an answer. Sharon reached out to pat Midge Rathermore's hand.

"Well, it means," Green finally said, "that any work that's done on the case is coordinated through me."

Black did a marvelous job of seeming puzzled. "Fine. You get the witnesses together, find out who knows what . . ."

"Yes, sir."

"Rehearse 'em on their testimony?"

"Objection." Fraterno didn't quite jump to her feet, but did grip the arms of her chair with white-knuckled hands.

Sandy Griffin yanked on an earlobe. "Sustained. Jury will disregard."

Twelve heads swiveled as one to look at Green, then Black, then the judge, and finally at the detective once more. The jury disregarded.

Black straightened some in his seat as he tossed the grenade. "Well, then, let me ask you this. How much money are you gettin' from these movie people? Round figures will do."

"Objection." Fraterno was more subdued. She tossed Milt Breyer a look of anguish. Breyer's neck seemed to shorten as he hunched down between his shoulders.

Black didn't give the judge a chance to rule on Fraterno's objection. "Judge," he said, "this line of questionin' goes to the motives of the witness. We think it's proper cross."

Judge Griffin rested her chin on her palm and thought it over. Sharon was familiar enough with Griffin's likes and dislikes to know that the judge didn't want to see law enforcement's dirty underwear trotted out in public, but Black's procedure was so right on target that no judge in captivity could cut him off at this point. Finally she said, "Objection overruled. Proceed with caution here, Counsel."

Milt Breyer rested his forehead on his clenched fist. He looked like the beginning of an Excedrin commercial.

"Detective Green," Black said, "do you know ... ?" He jerked a business card from his breast pocket and looked at it. "Do you know Rayford Sly?"

Green threw Fraterno a look that said, Help me. Kathleen's lips parted, then closed.

"He's right out there in the courtroom," Black said, turning in his chair to point at the rear. The movie guy was on his feet, headed lickety-split for the exit, but now halted in his tracks. "Looks like he was just leavin'," Black said. The courtroom exploded in laughter. The jurors smirked at one another. Sly quickly sat down. When the chuckles had died away, Black said, "My question was, Do you know Rayford Sly? I think it's a pretty easy question, Detective, don't you?"

Fraterno stiffened righteously. "Your *Honor*."

Judge Griffin pointed a finger. "Don't badger the witness, Mr. Black." Her tone said, however, that she definitely wanted to hear Detective Stan Green try to get out of this one.

"Sorry, Judge," Black said. "Detective Green, are you or are you not acquainted with a Mr. Rayford Sly?"

Green intertwined his fingers in his lap. "I've met him."

"You've met him." Black paused to let that one sink in. "He's with"—once more referring to the business card—"Aviton Productions, idn't he?"

"I believe he is."

"You believe he is. Okay, let me ask, have you made a deal with these TV movie people that you're to get paid for exclusive rights to your story on this case here?"

Green was trapped like a mouse, and Sharon was enjoying every second of it. Under normal circumstances the detective would merely lie, but these circumstances were far from normal. If Stan Green answered with a forked tongue, Black would slap the movie producer's fanny into the witness chair in a heartbeat, and Stan Green knew it. He wouldn't worry about committing perjury—because it was a given that the D.A.'s staff didn't indict their own witnesses for lying on the stand—but Rayford Sly's presence in the courtroom made the whole thing a horse of a different color. Sly didn't know that witnesses who aided the D.A.'s cause were immune from perjury charges, and would be petrified. Green looked down at his lap. "We may have talked about it."

"The same deal," Black said, pointing, "that the movie people may have talked over with Mr. Breyer, the prosecutor over there?"

"Objection." Fraterno sounded somewhat like Bette Davis in an old forties heavy drama. "Mr. Green can't possibly know the answer to that."

"Why?" Black's tone increased a few decibels. "Because they might be payin' the prosecutor more, and might not want the detective to think he's gettin' the short end of the stick?"

There was another explosion, the courtroom rocking in guffaws, a few spectators even doubling over and holding their midsections. Judge Griffin banged her gavel three times. "Order here. I'm sustaining the objection. And, Counsel, no more of this." The loud laughter ceased as if someone had turned off the radio.

"I apologize, Judge." Black rocked back and put his hands behind his head. "I got one more question, Detective. Idn't you gettin' paid for your story contingent on this little girl gettin' convicted?" He extended his hand behind Sharon to point at Midge. She seemed oblivious, doodling on the corner of Sharon's legal pad.

Green swallowed hard. For once Kathleen Fraterno didn't bother to come to the detective's aid with an objection; Black's question went directly to the motive of the witness and was as proper as a minister's daughter. "I don't remember," Green said carefully, "any arrangement like that."

"You don't?" Black's tone was incredulous. "Are you tellin' this court that you're makin' this deal without even knowin' the terms?"

"Objection. The witness has already answered." Fraterno's voice sounded faint and far away.

"Sustained." Sandy Griffin managed to sound impatient, but it likely took some effort on her part. The jurors were on the edges of their seats, which was exactly where Russell Black wanted them.

"Detective Green," Black said, "in your job, you're pretty much required to know the law, aren't you? What is and what idn't a crime?"

"I guess you could say that." Green's answer dripped

with chest-out importance. *Of course I know the law, buster, who do you think you're talking to?*

"Well, do you know," Black said, "that a public employee takin' money, personally, for tellin' things he learned through his employment, do you know that's called takin' a bribe?"

"*Objection.* The law is subject to interpretation, Judge."

"I'll ... withdraw the question," Black said contemptuously. He chewed on his lower lip and glared at the witness for a full fifteen seconds, giving the jury plenty of time to wonder what the hell other interpretation could be given to such a law. Finally Black said, "I got no more questions of this ... *witness.*"

Sheepishly Stan Green climbed down from the stand. A couple of jurors showed openly hostile looks as the detective went through the railing gate and exited to the rear. It was all Sharon could do to keep from jumping to her feet, clapping, and squealing like an adolescent at a Michael Jackson concert. All she did, however, was put her arm around Midge Rathermore and give the somber teenager an affectionate squeeze.

Felony prosecutor Edward Teeter didn't come into the office behind the 357th District Court until after noon on Friday, and almost failed to make it at all. The judge was playing golf, getting an early start on the weekend, and Teeter had spent the morning on the links himself—when the cat's away, and so forth. In fact, the only reason Teeter stopped by the office at all was that he'd hustled three bets a side from the misdemeanor prosecutor in one of the lower courts, and the pigeon had forgotten his wallet. Teeter had followed the loser downtown, had gone up to the misdemeanor court to collect his money, and now decided to check his office for messages. He sauntered in wearing brown knit slacks and a green Jack Nicklaus Golden Bear golf shirt. His right hand was tanned three shades darker than his left. He flopped down behind his desk, reached for a stack of call slips impaled on a chrome spike, then paused. A typewritten note lay dead center on his desk blotter. He picked up the note and read it, murmured, "Shit," under his breath, and picked up the phone. He punched in felony prosecutor Wendell Brat's extension and waited, listening to a series of buzzes on the line. There were so many felony prosecutors in the D.A.'s office that Teeter didn't know half of them, but he and Brat had gone to law school together and hired on as prosecutors at the same time. Brat was a superchief, specializing in high-profile prosecutions, and was a couple of steps up the ladder from his old college pal. Teeter secretly thought that Brat was an insufferable prick, but managed not to show it.

Brat clicked onto the line. "Brat."

Teeter allowed the note to drift down to his desk. "What killed the fucking guy?"

"Razor. He was trying to monkey with somebody else's monkey, is what the guards over at the jail say."

"What the hell's a guy doing with a razor in the county jail?"

"Thank the federal courts," Brat said. "They say the prisoner's entitled to shave. We give 'em nothing but Bic disposables, but they just light a match and melt the plastic from around the blade. Instant shank."

"What's that do to the Saw murder case against the Brie guy?"

"What murder case? Without Donello's testimony we've got nothing."

"I've got another charge to put on Mr. Brie," Teeter said. "Break-in and possibly attempted rape."

"I don't have any information on that," Brat said.

Teeter scratched his nose and moved the receiver from one ear to the other. "That's because we haven't filed on him. He was breaking in on a woman when he got busted. Before we talk dismissal of the Saw murder, give us a chance to go for the second indictment, huh?"

There was a pause, after which Brat said, "Too late, I've already sent the dismissal over to court."

Teeter clenched his left fist and examined his tan. "Kind of jumping the gun, aren't you?"

"Look," Brat said. "In the 342nd I got a guy on a capital. Three other guys blew a liquor store clerk away two weeks ago, and I just now got the file. I got cases out the ying-yang. If I can get rid of one, I get rid of it."

"Yeah, but . . . I don't think this Brie ought to be walking around. Crazy motherfucker. I think we should call over to the jail and put a hold on his release."

"Hold the phone." Brat clicked off the line.

Teeter snuggled the receiver between his shoulder and jaw, stood, and assumed his tee-off stance. Maybe he was a bit strong with the grip; he'd been hooking the ball like a maniac.

Brat came back on the line. "Too late again. Our Mr. Brie walked out on the street at ten past one."

Teeter sank into his chair. "Shit."

"How urgent do you think this is?" Brat said.

"Fuck," Teeter said. "Fuck, fuck, fuck. Hell, it's Friday afternoon. Tell you what, I'll get another indictment ready for Mr. Brie when the grand jury meets next Thursday. We know where the guy lives. He ought to keep for a week."

"Suits me," Brat said. "You have a nice weekend, you hear?"

"You, too," Teeter said. "I think I'll spend some time on the driving range."

36

At almost the exact instant when Bradford Brie emerged from the Lew Sterrett Justice Center—snugging up his sunglasses on his nose, ambling along down the walkway between the jail and the Frank Crowley Courts Building as he sucked in free air and pinched himself to make sure he wasn't dreaming—Sharon Hays had a sudden chill. It was the weirdest feeling she'd ever experienced. Not five minutes earlier some of the jurors had complained to the bailiff that it was hot as the blazes in the courtroom, yet all at once Sharon was freezing to death. She shuddered and hugged herself, and wondered if she might be coming down with something. The chill passed in a few seconds, and in just a few more seconds Sharon had completely forgotten about her brief discomfort. She had other things on her mind.

The trial's afternoon session had just begun. Linda Rathermore had had the jurors' undivided attention for the two hours before the lunch break. Particularly the male jurors had sat up and taken notice, with Linda in a deep purple skin-tight dress and snow-white open-toed pumps dominating the scene. Sharon would bet a week's pay that Kathleen Fraterno had had a conniption over the way her witness was dressed, but would have bet two weeks' pay that Linda, if pushed, would have thumbed her nose at the prosecutor and worn what she damn well pleased. Linda's horrified expression as she'd recalled the bludgeoning in her bedroom had been first-rate method acting, Sharon had thought. No wonder old Linda had received knock-out reviews up in Baltimore.

When Fraterno had finally passed the witness, Judge Griffin had delayed Sharon's cross-examination until one o'clock, and she had had a full hour and a half to become a bundle of nerves. The bailiff had brought her a chicken sandwich from the downstairs cafeteria, which she'd done her best to eat in the witness waiting room. She'd had one bite, washed it down with Coke, then had wadded the whole mess up in waxed paper and thrown it away. The butterflies in her stomach had beaten their wings like helicopter props ever since.

And now it was time. Sharon turned, winked, and smiled at Deborah North—who continued to hang on to her aisle seat, second row, for dear life in the jam-packed spectators' section—patted Midge's shoulder, acknowledged a go-get-'em nod from Russell Black, took a deep breath, and faced Linda Rathermore. She was posed in the witness box like a model in a Nothing Beats a Great Pair of L'Eggs commercial. A pin dropped in the courtroom at that moment would have shattered eardrums.

"Mrs. Rathermore," Sharon said, and was shocked at the strength of her voice, having been scared to death that all she'd be able to do was croak timidly at the witness, "you testified earlier that you and William Rathermore were married for seven years, is that right?"

"Yes." Linda's plucked right eyebrow lifted slightly; otherwise her expression didn't change.

"And that the two of you lived together before you married, and that you carried on an affair with him while he still lived with his first wife?" Sharon was only reaffirming what the jury had already heard; Fraterno had had the good sense to go into the affair in detail during her direct examination. *We've got nothing to hide, jury; what's a little intermarital screwing around got to do with this murder we're trying?*

"That's correct," Linda said.

"Mrs. Rathermore, during the time you and William Rathermore were married, was it your practice to have teenagers over to your house from time to time?"

There was just the slightest wavering in Linda's gaze. "Bill liked to have his kids' friends come by."

He certainly did, sweetie, Sharon thought. She reached

down and unsnapped the catches on her satchel, giving Midge an apologetic glance as she did. Midge was dressed in a denim skirt and white peasant blouse, neither of which fit very well. Deb North had done what she could, but shopping for Midge's clothes after the drastic weight reduction in jail was, at best, a guessing game. During Fraterno's direct examination Midge had acted as though she wasn't the slightest bit interested in what Linda had to say. Sharon would give anything if she could remove Midge from the courtroom before she started her next line of questioning, but that was impossible. Sharon extracted her brief file from the satchel and set it on the table. May as well get it ready, she thought. She looked once more at Linda Rathermore.

Sharon drew a shallow breath and forced herself to keep her tone on an even keel. "Mrs. Rathermore," she said, "how long after you and Mr. Rathermore were married did he begin to have sexual relations with his younger daughter, Susan?"

Sharon heard three distinct gasps, one from the jury box and another a couple of rows deep in the spectator section. The third came from the witness box as Linda put her hand over her mouth. Clothing rustled and panty hose whispered throughout the courtroom. Sharon waited for Fraterno's objection, but apparently the question had so rattled Kathleen that she was having trouble getting the word out of her mouth.

Finally Fraterno spoke. "Objection. Irrelevant, designed to be inflammatory. The deceased isn't on trial here."

Sandy Griffin's expression was a mixture of curiosity and judgelike concern. She toyed with a gold ballpoint.

Sharon rose. "May we approach?"

"I think you'd better, Counsel," Judge Griffin said.

Jurors frowned and twisted as Breyer and Fraterno came around the state's table and Sharon walked up from the defense side. Russ Black kept his seat, rocking back and looking slightly amused.

Sandy Griffin leaned over the bench and virtually hissed, "Exactly where are you going with this, Miss Hays?"

"That's what we'd like to know." Fraterno favored

Sharon with an icy stare. Milt Breyer looked frightened out of his wits.

Sharon folded her hands in front. "The fact that these kids were abused goes to the core of our entire case, Judge."

Griffin raised lightly penciled eyebrows. "Which is?"

"That she acted in self-defense," Sharon said.

Fraterno stared at Sharon as if she'd just grown a second head. Griffin said, "It's what?"

Sharon stood her ground. "Self-defense," she repeated.

"You're saying that your defense to murder-for-hire charges is that your client acted in self-defense?" Griffin rolled her eyes.

"I don't think I've ever heard anything so far out in left field, Your Honor," Fraterno said, but didn't sound convincing.

Sharon gestured toward the inch-thick stack of papers, held together by a rubber band, which lay near Russ Black's elbow. "We've prepared briefs, Judge."

Griffin squinted toward the defense table. "Miss Hays, if this is a delaying tactic . . ."

"It isn't, Your Honor," Sharon said.

Breyer looked as if he'd swallowed a frog.

Sandy Griffin sat back, composing herself. "I suppose I'd better deal with this in chambers."

"I thought you'd say that," Sharon said.

Judge Sandy Griffin was a no-frills operator when it came to office decor, which, Sharon thought, was unusual for a female. There were no potted plants, no richly upholstered leather furniture, no paintings or photos on the walls. The entire layout was government-issue stuff: a plain gray metal desk with a thin rubber covering on top, wooden slatted chairs for visitors, one coat tree in the corner on which hung the judge's charcoal gray blazer. As Judge Griffin sat down at her desk, she undid the top button on her robe to reveal a plain white blouse underneath. Behind her on the wall hung her sole decoration, a sign hung in between her framed bachelor's and law degrees. The sign read, in simple black letters, COST CUTTING BEGINS AT THE TOP. Sharon reminded herself that it was an election year.

Since the office contained only three visitors' chairs,

Russell Black had to borrow a seat from across the hall. Sharon sat down directly in front of Sandy Griffin while Fraterno and Breyer occupied chairs on either side of Sharon. Black placed his borrowed chair near the door and lounged, one arm hooked behind him and his legs crossed.

Sandy Griffin peered around Sharon to speak to Black. "What's your theory here, Russ?"

Black smiled blandly and pointed at Sharon. "Miss Hays came up with it. She can explain it better'n I can."

Griffin blinked. Fraterno and Breyer turned to stare in unison at Sharon. Like getting the third degree, Sharon thought.

"It's all in our brief, Judge," Sharon said. "It's a variation on the burning bed law, if that makes it clearer."

Fraterno stiffened visibly. "That statute doesn't apply here. It only applies to battered wives." She hadn't thawed toward Sharon since the flare-up at Joe Willie's Restaurant, and she apparently intended to keep things status quo. She ignored Sharon, directing her words to Judge Griffin.

Griffin picked up the brief, which Sharon had placed on the desk just moments ago. She'd also given a copy to Fraterno. Kathleen had yet to glance at her copy. The state was accustomed to having any defense motion automatically denied, particularly motions which required the judge to do any research. Where Sandy Griffin was concerned, Sharon was praying, the state might just be in for a surprise.

Griffin once more peered around Sharon as she pointed down at the file. "Have you looked this over, Russ?"

Sharon's hackles stirred. She expected to play second fiddle—that was part of her employment arrangement—but she was damned if anyone was going to treat her like a stick of furniture. She spoke up before Black had a chance to answer: "We've discussed it at length, Judge. Our theory is basically this. If our client did contract for her father's death—and we're certainly not prepared to concede that she did—but if the jury decides that our client hired those kids to kill Mr. Rathermore, she was entitled to do so. Same as a battered wife who can wait until her husband is asleep. Midge acted, if she did so, only to protect herself and her sister from sexual abuse by their father."

Fraterno leaned forward. "In all due respect, Your Honor, this is a waste of time. There's no precedent for this." Breyer kept silent, scowling in support of his assistant. Sharon would say this for the womanizing bastard, he knew when he was out of his element.

"It isn't a waste of anybody's time when charges this serious are brought against our client," Sharon said. She tried to emphasize the word *our* without being too obvious.

Griffin leaned sideways and spoke once more to Black. "You've read this, have you?" God, Sharon thought, she's going to get a crick in her neck.

He casually waved a hand. "Not only have I read it, Judge, I've tried six ways from Sunday to shoot holes in it for weeks. Miss Hays knows her stuff."

Griffin regarded Sharon with an expression of sudden respect. Russ Black was sort of the E.F. Hutton of the courthouse; when he spoke, people listened. Sharon felt like hugging the older lawyer and giving him a peck on the cheek.

"Judge," Fraterno said rather lamely, "I don't think we should string the trial out over something like this. Even if the theory held water, which I don't believe it does, the defendant was a minor child. She didn't have constitutional rights."

Sharon sat up straighter. "She does now. The state's seen it fit to certify her as an adult."

Griffin smiled curiously and ran a thumbnail across her upper lip. She picked up the brief in both hands as if weighing the pages. "I'm afraid she's got you there, Miss Fraterno. And as for how long the trial is delayed, that depends on how long it takes for the state to give me a responding brief on the issue. With all the law clerks you folks have got running around, that shouldn't take more than a couple of hours. I'm prepared to keep us overtime tonight if necessary, because I agree with the state's concern. I don't want to carry the trial on any longer than necessary." Griffin's eyes narrowed. "That *is* your concern, isn't it, Miss Fraterno? Not wasting the court's time?"

Now Milton Breyer spoke up. "Judge, we're not really prepared to—"

"Two hours, Mr. Breyer. Then I'll give my ruling. I'm going to spend the time in the law library myself, to see what I can come up with. I'll see you back in court at four o'clock, counselors." The corners of Griffin's eyes crinkled as she looked at Breyer, glanced at Sharon, then looked back. "It shouldn't be that much of a problem for you, Mr. Breyer. You've locked horns with Miss Hays before. At least that's my understanding." She grinned at Sharon. "I'm going to give your brief very careful attention, Miss Hays," Judge Griffin said.

They gathered on a hallway bench outside the courtroom, Sharon Hays, Russell Black, Anthony Gear, Deborah North. Newspeople milled about on all sides and did what newspeople do during breaks in trials—compared notes, groused about their salaries. They'd pretty well learned that any attempt to pry a statement from a member of the defense team was a waste of time, so aside from occasional glances toward the bench they left the foursome alone. Sharon made jittery small talk with Deborah North while Gear filled Russell Black in on his contact with the Rathermores' security company. Anything to break the tension.

Sharon had sat out jury deliberations by the score—so many, in fact, that waiting for verdicts had become old hat during her final days as a prosecutor. While the jury had voted in the Donello case, Sharon had returned to her office and taken a nap. This was much, much different. Judge Griffin's pending decision had Sharon wound up like the twine in the innards of a baseball.

"What's your gut feeling?" Deb said.

"Hmm?" Sharon fiddled with the hem of her skirt. "I can't say that I have any gut feeling, Deb. Honestly? We were tickled to death to draw Judge Griffin for this case because she'll at least consider what we have to say. But judges are politicians, and she's not that different from the rest. She wants to do two things: move her docket along and get convictions. Too many acquittals give the opposition ammunition for the election."

Deb lowered her lashes.

Sharon placed a hand on Deb's forearm. "It doesn't

mean she'll automatically deny us, Deb. But she'll grasp at any straw. I think my research is thorough enough that she'll have a hard time dodging around us."

"And if she denies you?"

"She does. We can still attack Linda with both barrels to hurt her credibility, but I'm afraid that any evidence about the sex abuse won't be allowed. Ballpark, I'd say an adverse ruling will hurt us about fifty percent." Sharon felt a twinge of conscience; she was putting Deb on. Fifty percent was conservative as hell. As Sharon glanced down the corridor, a clerk from the D.A.'s office hustled by carrying a stack of papers, did a hasty column right, and entered the courtroom. That would be the state's answer to Sharon's brief. She checked her slim gold watch. Three-thirty on the nose.

"How much longer do you think?" Deb said.

Sharon watched her lap. The tightness in her throat restricted her breathing.

"How much longer?" Deb said.

Sharon reached up and anxiously fluffed her bangs.

"Sharon?"

Sharon started, then turned on the bench. "I'm sorry, Deb. What did you say?"

Jurors in drawn-out trials eventually grow to function as a unit, trooping in and out of the box like robots, their faces impassive. When the bailiff led the Rathermore panel back into the courtroom at exactly four, Sharon read the signs that they'd conformed to the pattern. For the duration of the trial they were no longer individuals. They were a body. The jury, nothing more. Walked as one, sat as one.

The jurors seated, the bailiff stood at attention and bellowed, "Awl rise." Clothing rustled and throats cleared nervously as the ensemble stood, women smoothing their skirts behind them, men watching the judge's entry with impassively folded arms. The spectators and lawyers had lost their identities as well; for the time being they were as much a part of the courtroom as the walls and benches. Judge Griffin entered and ascended to her throne.

Sharon searched her face for a sign, any sign, a twitch of the eyelids, a change in the set of the judge's mouth. Griffin met Sharon's gaze, then looked quickly away. Oh, my God, Sharon thought, she's denying us. She's not going to let us ... Impulsively Sharon squeezed Midge Rathermore's limp, clammy hand.

"Please be seated," Judge Griffin said. The audience sat, as did the jury. Linda Rathermore crossed her legs in the witness box; her skirt rode up to reveal six inches of tanned and solid thigh.

All that work, Sharon thought. This poor retarded baby doesn't have a ghost of a ...

Judge Griffin stoically addressed the jurors. "I apologize for the inconvenience, ladies and gentlemen, but there are certain things that the law dictates the jury can't hear. And I'm afraid we're going to inconvenience you further, because it's unavoidable. We'll be in session today until after six."

The jury accepted this without emotion. Two days earlier, back when they'd all been people of flesh and blood, they would have bitched and moaned openly about dinners to be put off, husbands and wives to call. Now they were merely the jury, the arm of justice serving in silence.

The judge now let her gaze rest first on the defense side, then on the prosecution. She nodded imperceptibly at Kathleen Fraterno. Sharon thought, We're beaten. She lowered her lashes.

"The prosecution's objection," Judge Griffin said, "is overruled. You may proceed, Miss Hays."

And Sharon thought, Huh? She blinked. "I'm sorry?"

Griffin smiled. "I've overruled Miss Fraterno's objection, Miss Hays. You may go forward."

Kathleen Fraterno fidgeted in place. "Your Honor ..."

"Overruled, Miss Fraterno. The cross-examination of this witness will continue."

Sharon was weak in the knees, and very nearly flopped down into her seat in exhaustion. She took a firm grip on the edge of the table and looked at the witness. Linda Rathermore's eyes widened. Sharon permitted herself a tiny, grim smile. *Hang onto your panties, cutes. Little Sharon's about to rip them into shreds.* She took her seat at the defense table and hastily examined her notes. Russell Black triumphantly nudged her with his elbow. Elation made Sharon absolutely giddy.

She opened her mouth to speak, then paused. Get ahold

of yourself, Sharon Jenifer Hays, she thought. The adrenaline currently pumping could cause her to blow the whole thing if she wasn't careful. She gently closed her eyes, then regarded Linda with a look near total serenity. Linda's gaze darted nervously to one side.

"Mrs. Rathermore," Sharon finally said, "before the break I asked you, 'How long after you were married did William Rathermore begin to have sexual relations with his younger daughter?' "

Linda cleared her throat, looked down at her lap, darted a helpless glance in Kathleen Fraterno's direction. Finally she said, "I don't recall . . ." Then, as Fraterno offered no relief, suddenly interested in some lint on her sleeve, Linda stammered, "There wasn't any . . ."

"For the time being," Sharon said, "I'm going to withdraw the question, but—"

Linda sagged in relief.

"—I am reserving the right to bring the issue up at a later time."

Judge Griffin now had a curious tilt to her mouth, and Sharon didn't blame her. After all that folderol, the judge was likely thinking, Why isn't Hays pursuing the issue? Sharon pretended to read her file, calming her mind, getting over the shock of the judge's favorable ruling. Sharon had changed course because she really didn't expect Linda to answer—or expected her to lie if she did reply—and her sole purpose in raising the sex-abuse issue when she had was to get her brief and Midge's defense out in the open. Now that she had the court's permission to go ahead, Sharon wanted to approach the issue a little differently. Her plans firmed, she now smiled at the witness.

"Mrs. Rathermore, you testified that you were a television commentator, is that right?"

"A news anchor person. Yes, I did." Linda reverted to a programmed response; Sharon had touched briefly on Linda's past during the examining trial, so Fraterno would have had ample time to coach her witness on how to deal with her name changes.

"As Linda Haymon," Sharon said. "But Haymon isn't the name on your birth certificate, is it?"

"No. Harmon is," Linda said matter-of-factly. She now waited patiently for the question she was certain was coming next, the query as to why she'd changed her name. That wasn't the question Sharon had in mind, however. No way.

Sharon worked up saliva and prepared to toss a spitter. She examined her notes to find the name of the theater director up in Baltimore, then said, "Are you acquainted with a man named Donald Weiss?"

Linda's sharp gasp was audible to those in the back row, and probably to folks out in the corridor as well. Sharon wasn't watching the witness, though; she was checking Fraterno's reaction. At the mention of Weiss's name, Kathleen turned to Breyer and regarded the chief prosecutor with a puzzled frown. So they *don't* have any information on Weiss, Sharon thought. She wasn't surprised; in fact, it would have been shocking if Linda *had* owned up to that one. That her fling with a thirteen-year-old was news to the prosecution made things even better. Sharon squared her posture and prepared to take Linda Rathermore on a long and uncomfortable ride.

"Do you, Mrs. Rathermore?" Sharon said.

"Do I . . . ?" A ray of light glistened from Linda's slightly trembling lower lip.

"Do you know Donald Weiss?"

"It's been a long time."

"Yes, it has. Do you know Donald Weiss?"

"I believe I remember him." Linda accompanied her answer with a nervous laugh, and didn't do a half-bad job of regaining her composure. This chick took the wrong fork in the road someplace, Sharon thought. She could have been up for Oscars.

"Well, what do you remember about Mr. Weiss?" Sharon said.

"Up in Baltimore, he . . . was with the theater."

"He was *with* the theater? Mrs. Rathermore, wasn't Donald Weiss the chairman of the Baltimore Theatre League?"

Linda's eyes grew big and oh-I-remember-now round. "That's right, he was."

"While you were an actress, working up there?"

"Yes. He was of great assistance to me."

I'll just bet he was, sugar, Sharon thought. "Didn't you and Mr. Weiss work very closely together?" she said, letting a tad of sarcasm drip.

"Objection." Fraterno sounded unsure of herself. "Your Honor, unless counsel for the defense can tell us where she's going with this . . ."

"I was thinking the same thing, Miss Hays," Judge Griffin said.

Sharon swiveled her gaze to the bench. "It will be clear very shortly, Your Honor. If the court please."

"All right, Counsel, but we'd best see the fruits of this line very quickly."

"Certainly." Sharon stopped short of throwing the judge an open wink, and returned her attention to Linda. In the corner of her eye she watched Milt Breyer frantically search the defense's witness list, then nudge Fraterno and point out something on the page. They've located dear old Donald Weiss, Sharon thought. She repressed a grin. Sharon said to Linda, "Did Mr. Weiss's *great assistance* include the payment of rent on a condo where you lived?"

"Donald was a man of means. He helped a lot of actors." Fraterno's objection had given Linda time to prepare the answer, but it didn't come across quite as she'd obviously planned. A couple of the jurors smirked at one another. Still, her ability to keep from backing into a corner gave Sharon an odd sense of admiration for the woman.

"Well, during the time Mr. Weiss was *helping* you," Sharon said, "did you become acquainted with other members of his family?"

"Why, yes," Linda said without batting an eyelash, "Mrs. Weiss came to a lot of rehearsals."

"Mmm-hmm. And his children?"

Linda's gaze flickered. "His children? I don't . . ."

"His son, Mrs. Rathermore. His thirteen-year-old son." Now the jurors were on the edges of their seats.

"I seem to remember he had a son," Linda said.

Christ, Sharon thought, this could take weeks. Judge Griffin's face showed a scowl of impatience. Okay, Sharon thought, let 'em beat me up a bit. "Mrs. Rathermore," Sharon said, "are you aware that Mr. Donald Weiss is prepared to be a defense witness in this case?"

"Objection." Fraterno jumped up as if someone had yanked her chain. "Your Honor, this is *so* out of line."

Sandy Griffin said angrily, "It certainly is, Miss Hays,

and you should know it. Objection sustained, and you may consider this a warning, Counsel."

Sustain and warn away, toots, Sharon thought. She felt a twinge of conscience at pulling the stunt in Griffin's courtroom, but then had a fleeting glimpse of Midge from the corner of her eye, and her regret faded at once. The jurors exchanged astonished glances, and Linda's face rearranged itself like Play-Doh. Her mouth twisted and her eyes narrowed. Her teeth clenched in pure hatred. Ugly is as ugly does, Sharon thought. Linda's monster face dissolved in an instant, replaced by the serene Florence Nightingale expression, and Sharon had a sudden flashback to her own acting career.

She'd been doing a matinee performance of *The Peasants* in a moth-eaten old theater on 19th near Sixth Avenue when, in between acts, she'd made a backstage call to the doctor to learn that she was indeed pregnant. Act II had opened with Sharon's character alone by the hearth. The script had called for a loud knocking sound to come from the wings, and her line was supposed to have been "Hark, my darling. The king's men cometh." But the news of her rapidly approaching motherhood had totally rattled her, and when the sharp banging had sounded right on cue, Sharon had looked straight into the audience of two dozen or so and proclaimed in her finest stage voice, "What on earth was *that* noise?" She'd composed herself in seconds and gone right on with the performance as if nothing had happened, just as Linda Rathermore was doing right now. Embarrassing as it had been, Sharon considered the botched line and subsequent recovery to be her finest moment in show biz. Linda's cheeks, Sharon noticed, were a tad flushed, but otherwise the grieving widow had fallen right back into character. Break a leg, kid, Sharon thought.

"I'm sorry, Your Honor," Sharon said sheepishly, then firmly said to Linda, "If you recall that Mr. Weiss had a son, do you recall the boy's name?"

"I don't believe I do," Linda said.

Sharon thumbed testily through her notes. "Well, do you recall," she said, "an incident, specifically on July 19, 1978, when Donald Weiss came by the condo unannounced to find you—"

"*Objection.*"

"Sustained. Miss Hays . . ."

"—there in bed with his son?"

"The jury is instructed," Judge Griffin said, partially rising, her voice quavering, "to disregard that question in its entirety. One more time, Miss Hays . . ."

"Yes, ma'am." Sharon lowered her lashes, and decided she'd gotten about as far off on the wrong foot as she dared. She looked up. "I will rephrase the question, though, with the court's permission."

Griffin blinked impatiently. "Go ahead."

"In July of 1978," Sharon said to Linda, "do you recall a day when Mr. Weiss's son was doing some work at the theater, and you offered him a ride home?"

On Sharon's left, Russell Black drew a quick, shallow breath.

The witness regarded Sharon without the slightest hint of uncertainty. "That was years ago. I might've."

"Well, do you—?" Sharon began, then halted as Russ Black placed a hand on her forearm. She leaned over and he put his lips close to her ear.

"Let her go for now," he whispered. "She won't admit to a damned thing, and the jury's going to get bored with this."

Sharon frowned. "But I think—"

"Don't matter what you think, or what *I* think. What those people in the box think, that's all that's important." He winked. "let her go, Sharon. We can bring her back later. You got 'em chompin' at the bit to hear the rest of this. Let 'em wait."

Strong resentment flowed through her, followed quickly by uncertainty. Was she carrying this too far? The jury seemed mesmerized, all right, but the man on her left hadn't boxed the D.A.'s ears in the courtroom over and over without having a pretty good sense of when to charge ahead and when to back off. And more verbal sparring with Linda—which would elicit nothing from the witness but a series of denials—would likely turn the twelve tried and true completely off. Thank God for small favors and Russell Black, Sharon thought. She gave her boss a quick nod.

"After Leslie Schlee," Black said. "After Leslie, we'll bring her back."

Sharon faced the bench. "Your Honor, I have no further

questions at this time, but we will be recalling this witness during the defense's presentation."

Griffin's eyebrows lifted slightly in surprise, then she leaned forward and addressed the witness. "Do you understand that, Mrs. Rathermore?"

Linda started. "Do I . . . ?"

"It means," the judge said, "that you may go for now. But you are still under oath, and you are to remain on call. Is that clear?" Griffin hadn't missed the implication contained in Sharon's line of questioning, and the judge's tone of voice said that if the instructions *weren't* clear to Linda, she just might be spending some time as the guest of the sheriff.

Linda stepped confidently down and exited. As she passed the defense table her gaze met Sharon's, and her forehead tightened in a worried frown. The frown melted in less than a second, but it had been there, Sharon had seen it, and Linda had *known* that Sharon had seen it, which gave the two of them an understanding as to what was likely to come. One cool, conniving bitch, that one, Sharon thought.

Judge Griffin then made the jurors happy by calling it a day, a full hour earlier than the six o'clock she'd previously announced. Both teenage murderers had yet to testify, and Sharon suspected that there would be weekend meetings between the prosecution and young Messrs. Burdette and Leonard, with some fresh script material added to the rehearsals. And Fraterno would have some talks with Linda as well, and if Linda told the truth about Baltimore (which would be like pulling teeth, Sharon thought, getting *that* cold-blooded lady to 'fess up to anything), the prosecution would find itself in total chaos. Barring an earthquake, Sharon thought, we're going to win. We have to.

But earthquakes happen, she reminded herself.

It was going to be a long weekend.

37

Sharon bounced into her driveway just at sunset, having stopped off for a sliced beef sandwich at Coulter's Barbecue and having taken her time about eating. She sat for a moment and listened to the Volvo's motor tick and cool as loneliness flooded over her. Less than a week had dragged by, and already Sharon missed her little girl terribly. Sheila professed to be having a ball—Sharon had spend an envious half hour last evening listening to a telephone report of how Sheila had dined at Old Warsaw with her aerobics instructor, and had been dying to ask about the juicier part of the date but had restrained herself—but Sharon had noted a slight catch in Sheila's voice when the subject had turned to Trish away at camp. The truth was that all the big-talk, oh-boy-wait-'til-the-kids-are-in-camp discourse between Sharon and Sheila was just a bunch of hokey, and that the two of them were nothing but a couple of lonesome moms.

As for Sharon's two weeks of freedom, she'd been too caught up in the Rathermore case to even think about going out. On second thought, that wasn't quite true. She *had* been tied up in court, and she *hadn't* gone out at night, but her main reason for being such a couch potato was that she simply hadn't had the right offer. Her only invitations had been in the form of desperate answering-machine messages from Stan Green—whom she'd pointedly ignored each day in court—and she had made up her mind that if the lout of a homicide cop was the only pebble on the beach, then she was destined to a future alone with the old vibrator. But if the right guy should come along, she thought ... well, the poor unsuspecting man had best have plenty of staying power in the old sackeroo. Otherwise they were liable to find him stone-cold dead, stretched out on the mattress with a smile tattooed on his face. Sharon giggled softly as she alighted from the Volvo and started across the yard.

The sun was hidden behind the rooftops. Its final rays bathed low-flying clouds in pink and orange, and the porch was in deep twilight shade. Sharon checked her watch as she fumbled for her key. Ten to nine. There'd been a letter from Melanie in yesterday's mail, and Sharon had carefully set the envelope aside on her dining table for reading when she had plenty of time. She intended to get the letter and take it to her bedroom, and Melanie's letter was uppermost on her mind as she inserted the key, clicked the tumblers, and pushed the door open. She halted abruptly in the entry hall.

Uncertainty in her tone, she said loudly, "Commander?"

The house was silent as a tomb. There was no answering whimper, no joyous scratching of claws on carpet to signify that the shepherd was lumbering in her direction. No sound at all.

She called out, louder this time, *"Commander."*

Her heart was suddenly a lump of ice. It had taken weeks after the incident with the crazy man before she'd been able to walk into the house without being frightened out of her wits, but the terror had gradually subsided. Now the fear returned in a rush. The dog. Where was the freaking *dog*?

She relaxed as she thought, backyard. Sure, that was it. She recalled opening the door that morning just before she'd left, and Commander scrabbling across the deck to bound down and piss against the swing set. For weeks following the poisoned-meat incident she'd kept him imprisoned inside, but that fear had subsided eventually as well, helped along in no small part by the piles of poop she'd found on the carpet on two different occasions. Commander was nicely housebroken, but he wasn't Superdog, and eight or ten hours locked up in the house had proven too much for him. She suspected that the carpet soilings were a sign of resentment on his part as well, and for whatever reason she'd taken to putting him outside during the day. She laughed out loud at herself, went down the hall and halfway through the dining room, then screeched to a halt once more. The dread came back in a rush.

As she'd left her car and crossed the yard, the only sound she'd heard was the hissing of Mrs. Breedlove's lawn sprinklers across the street. There'd been the nagging sensation at the back of her mind that something was missing, but she'd been so intent with her thoughts of Melanie that the silence hadn't registered. Now it did.

Commander always raised a ruckus when she drove up, barking joyously and hurling himself against the side fence. In fact, he was so loud that some of the neighbors had complained, and Sharon had responded with half-hearted promises to do something about the noise. So why had there been total silence out back when she'd come home moments ago? Goose bumps raised on her arms and spiders paraded up and down her backbone.

You dummy, she told herself, the guy's in jail. Locked up. More than likely headed straight for death row. And of course, heh, heh, he's the only pervert in the entire city of Dallas, isn't he?

A knot at the point of her breastbone, every shadow in the house a monster poised to strike, Sharon forced her feet to move. She went into the den. From the kitchen on her right, the refrigerator motor hummed. The back door was closed. She jiggled the handle. Locked tight as a drum. Her fear subsided a bit.

But there was still no sign of Commander. The shepherd should have been right there, about to tear down the door.

Please be all right, you big dumb mutt, Sharon thought. She quickly undid the lock and went out on the deck. Commander lay on his side near the back fence, on the other side of the swing set. His nose was pointed away from her, and he wasn't moving.

Oh, my dear sweet God, she thought, he isn't moving.

A sob escaped from her throat as she half ran, half stumbled, across the deck. One of her spike heels wedged itself between the boards; her ankle twisted painfully and she fell headlong. Her pantyhose ripped up the side, and there was a numbing sensation in her hip where she'd jolted against the redwood. She ignored the needles of agony in her ankle, kicked out of her shoes, and scrambled to her feet. She limped across the yard with stiff Bermuda poking her soles at every step. She crouched beside the fallen shepherd and pressed her hand against the side of his neck. His flesh and fur were warm.

Commander whimpered. He raised his head to look at her with big, dark eyes. His tongue lolled downward. His great tail lifted, then thumped the ground.

"Oh. Oh, Commander, are you . . . ?" Tears streamed down Sharon's cheeks. She wiped them away, then felt the dog over with firm hands. When she pressed a spot near his collarbone, he yelped in pain.

She bent closer to the dog and gently moved the fur aside. At just the point where Commander's foreleg joined his shoulder was a small round hole. Blood oozed faintly from the wound. The shepherd tried to lick Sharon's hand, but the effort was too much. He went limp and snorted.

"Don't move," Sharon said. She rose, walked a few steps toward the house, then turned to the dog and extended her hand, palm out. "Just . . . don't move." She retreated quickly up on the deck and into the den. The vet's emergency number was jotted down in an index finder at her bedside. All but the wounded shepherd forgotten, Sharon climbed the two steps and entered her bedroom.

Her bureau drawers were pulled out. Her underwear—cotton Jockey for Her panties mostly, along with two pair of bikini briefs, one black and one maroon—were scattered at random on the floor. Her only black lace push-up bra lay wadded up in the center of the king-size. There was a dark, round wet spot on the spread alongside the bra.

She screamed at the top of her lungs, the sound tearing its way out of her throat and vibrating the walls. She placed both hands over her mouth and screamed a second time, backing in terror out of the bedroom and down the steps into the den. She sagged against the paneled wall.

Her gun. Where was her freaking *gun*? She forced herself to think. The toilet tank, that's where she'd suspended it, hanging there inside the tank in the small water closet beside her dressing area.

Which is exactly where the lunatic, if he was still around, was probably hiding.

Gritting her teeth, the image of the wounded dog firmly in her mind, she went back into the bedroom and crossed over to her dressing area. The bra and the wet spot on the bed leaped out at her. She paused to firm her resolve, then flung open the latticed door into her dressing room. No one there. She stared dully at her own reflection in the mirror.

Moments later, the pistol in her grasp, Sharon sat on her bed and called the vet. He agreed to meet her at the clinic. She hung up, grabbed a blanket from the linen closet, and returned to the yard. After she'd wrapped Commander in the blanket, she heaved him up in her arms and, staggering under the weight, bore him through the house and out to the car. As she laid him tenderly down in the backseat, Commander made another valiant effort to lick her hand.

Sharon sipped lukewarm coffee dregs heated in a microwave, and fixed her gaze on the veterinarian. "How long?" she said. She was seated on a high wooden stool near the counter separating the waiting room from the reception desk. On the wall were framed skeletal charts, cat and dog, and on the counter was a plaster of paris model of a dog's teeth. There was a faint odor of flea powder.

The vet's name was Bob Reasor. He was mid-thirties with coal black hair swept around to hang rakishly over one eye, and he wore yellow gym shorts and a maroon Texas A&M T-shirt. He was a friendly, even-tempered sort, but tended to become miffed if anyone referred to him as Dr. Bob. Reasor was a bachelor and, along with almost every veterinarian in the entire state of Texas, an Aggie. When Sharon had first brought Commander in for shots, just a month after Reasor had opened the clinic, he'd tried a couple of passes. She'd been flattered, but she'd had her schedule and he'd had his, and that had been that.

A shoulder-to-butt X ray of Commander's insides hung on a lighted rack, and Reasor indicated the hip joint with a pointer. "Next time I go to Vegas I'd like to take him along," Reasor said. "See that?"

Sharon squinted at a dark spot on the film. "How long, Bob?" she said.

"From here"—Reasor swung the tip of the pointer to touch the shoulder beside the entry wound—"to here"— then returned the indicator to the dark spot—"the bastard traveled, and didn't hit a thing. Couldn't have missed his heart by more than a centimeter, his left lung by even less. Odds of that happening . . ." He shook his head in wonder. "Phenomenal."

Sharon sipped more coffee. The stuff tasted terrible, but she barely noticed. It would help keep her awake. All weekend if necessary. "He's not in any danger, huh?" she said.

Reasor pursed thin lips. "Nah. Couple of days. You'd better trot out a blanket or put a pile of rags in the corner. He needs to stay quiet."

"Must have been a small-caliber, not to exit."

"Not necessarily," Reasor said.

Sharon cocked her head inquisitively.

"Commander weighs what, eighty pounds?" he said.

She nodded. "Close."

"I'd guess a .38 or even a .45," he said. "The impact knocks him back so that the slug remains in him. Anything smaller, say a .22, would tear right through. A human, anything over a hundred and twenty pounds, even a .38 will exit."

"You should try forensics," Sharon said. She was being overly cool and knew it. When she'd first come in she'd been almost hysterical, but now that she knew Commander wasn't on the critical list, she was overreacting on the opposite side of the emotional scale.

"I thought about it," Reasor said, laying the pointer aside. "I ever tell you I had a criminology minor?"

"Several times. Are you going to do surgery?"

He crossed his forearms on the counter. "I wouldn't advise it. If the bullet was going to interfere with his walk or pinch a nerve or something, yeah. This one I'd leave right where it is. If it shifts around we can operate later."

She stood and drained the remnants from her cup. "Can I see him before I go?"

"Sure. You know the way. I've got a couple of things to put up." Reasor knelt to slide the pointer into a drawer and flipped the switch to douse the light on the X-ray viewer.

Sharon went down a short corridor, passed through an examining room, and entered the clinic's boarding area.

She still was in her stocking feet, and stepped carefully around a puddle of urine on the concrete. She passed two cages which held kittens, then stopped to peer inside the open gate on the third cage at Commander. He lay on a small foam mattress. His tail thumped in greeting, though he made no effort to rise.

Sharon scratched the shepherd between the ears. "You take it easy, old-timer," she said. "You can't understand this, you big dumb mutt. But don't you dare die, you hear? I might not get over it, and I know Melanie wouldn't."

Sharon said emotionlessly into the phone, "I know you're at home, Mr. Teeter. That's why I called your house."

Assistant D.A. Ed Teeter assumed a suspicious tone. "How did you get my number?"

"It was tough, you know?" Sharon said. "You're not listed in the phone book." It was all the information she was going to give; she'd gotten Teeter's home number from her old friend Doris in D.A. personnel. Doris had been glad to help, and had even driven to the office to look the number up, but also had cautioned Sharon not to let the cat out of the bag. If anyone found out, Doris had said, heads would roll.

"That's right, miss, I'm not," Teeter said. "I don't want calls at eleven o'clock on Friday night."

Sharon was seated on her Spanish-style sofa, watching through her deck-side window while the smaller of two Dallas Police patrolmen inspected her back fence. His partner was up in the bedroom, looking around. Same two cops, she thought. Tall One and Shorty, Frick and Frack. Sharon had originally changed into an oversize T-shirt and jean cutoffs, but when the cops had driven up and had both given her the once-over, she'd gone in the back and put on loose-fitting western jeans. She said to Teeter, "Well, I do hate to bother you. But I don't like people shooting my dog and breaking in my house to fondle my underwear, either."

"Who is this?" Teeter spoke in a slightly boozy slur. Likely he'd been having a bedtime toddy.

"Sharon Hays."

There was a pregnant pause, after which Teeter said, "Oh."

"Oh," Sharon said back. "I've already checked at the jail, so I already know Mr. Brie is on the street. My only question is, what in hell is wrong with you people?"

"Hey, Miss Hays, I know it bothers you—"

"Ha."

"—for this to happen. There was sort of a mixup."

"Oh, really," Sharon said.

"Now we're going to ... I'll have an indictment whipped up the first of next week for the break-in at your house."

"To take to the grand jury on Thursday," Sharon said. "And if he's happened to have moved across the street, your people won't even pick him up. They'll put him on the computer and hope he gets arrested for something else. Maybe he'll trip over my body as he's leaving my house, huh? Then you might catch him."

"We don't take these things lightly," Teeter said.

"That's nice to know. You do read the paper, don't you?"

"Not much of it. The golf scores. I skip over the crime news—half the time the reporters get the facts all wrong. You should know that from being a prosecutor yourself."

"Well, one thing they do have right in today's editions," Sharon said, "is that we're having a trial. Right underneath your office, on the sixth floor."

"I know that," Teeter said. "The Rathermore trial. What I meant is, if you give them any interviews you're usually misquoted all to hell."

"What I'm leading up to," Sharon said, "is that both *Dallas Morning News* crime-beat people are covering the trial. And if I call the jail on Monday afternoon and find out that Mr. Brie's still not in custody, I'm going to call a press conference. Misquoted or not, I'm going to tell them the whole story about Mr. Brie, and that you people are sitting around on your collective butts and not doing anything to put him out of circulation."

Teeter breathed over the phone, not saying anything.

"I hope I'm making myself clear," Sharon said. "And in addition to telling them about Mr. Brie, I'm going to tell them about Mr. Breyer."

"Milton Breyer?"

"I don't mean the ice cream Breyers, Mr. Teeter."

Sharon paused as the tall patrolman came in and sat on the loveseat, clipboard in hand. Then she said, "I've got to go now. If you don't know what it is I might tell the press about Mr. Breyer, ask him. My broad hint is that it might have to do with what went on just before I quit the D.A. In the meantime, I'm going to see if I can stay alive until Monday. Goodbye, Mr. Teeter." She hung up and faced the policeman. As she did, Shorty came in the back door and sat beside his tall, thin partner.

The thin policeman licked his lips. "Looks like you've got a real weirdo here, Miss Hays."

Sharon had averted her gaze from the bra on her bed-spread every time she'd gone upstairs, once before she'd taken Commander to the vet and twice to change clothes. "You really think so?" she said.

"The crime-scene people are on their way," Skinny said. "In the meantime, if you're up to it ... Have you noticed anything missing?"

Sharon rolled her eyes. "Jesus Christ, the crime-scene people? As if we don't all know who did this."

"We've got to gather evidence, Miss Hays, you know that."

Sharon had a twinge of conscience. As opposed to the time they'd come by after the poisoned-meat incident, both cops now seemed attentive and concerned. "Sorry to be so bitchy," she said. "And, sure I'll—"

Her gaze was through the arched entry into the dining room, on the long, polished mahogany table. The letter she'd put there so carefully, the letter from Melanie, was gone.

Panic surged as Sharon looked the table over end to end. Could she be mistaken? No. She'd put Melanie's letter right there. The envelope had shown Melanie's return address at Sky Ranch. God, she thought, he's taken it. *The filthy bastard has taken Melanie's letter.*

The skinny cop sat forward on the loveseat. "Something wrong?"

Sharon lowered her lashes and examined her lap. She firmed up her mouth and raised her head. "Nothing's wrong," she said, "that wasn't already wrong. I'll be happy to make an inventory for you, but can it wait until Monday? I just remembered. I've got something to do."

38

Bradford Brie had never required much sleep to get by; in fact, he regarded time spent in bed as a waste of time unless he had a woman with him. Even in the Texas Department of Corrections—when the bosses had demanded that every man pick a hundred pounds of cotton between sunup and sunset, weighing each prisoner in at the end of the day and locking the slackers up in the hole on bread and water—Brie had never slept more than two or three hours a night even though he'd been so tired it was all he could do to crawl into his upper bunk. He'd spent most of the darkness hours just staring at the ceiling while Wilfred Donello snored and snorted just a couple of feet beneath him. As Donello dreamed on, Bradford Brie made plans. It was during one of those sleepless nights that he'd hatched his escape plot, and it had been the escape which bought him four whole days with the big-legged farmer woman. Those four days, Brie thought, had been the best ninety-six hours of his life, in complete control while the woman waited on him hand and foot and gave him sex whenever he wanted. Never before or since had Brie been so totally in control. A fucking king, that's what he'd been.

So at one o'clock in the morning, six hours after he'd returned home from Sharon Hays's house, Brie hadn't so much as thought of going to bed. He was too wired up to fall asleep even if he'd wanted to. What a victory, huh? He'd taken care of old Fido once and for all, then had left his calling card right there in her bedroom. Finding the letter from the little girl had been a bonus.

Brie lay on his sofa, reading the letter by the light of his one unshaded lamp. The sofa was green chintz with a tiny rose pattern, and one exposed spring kept poking him in the hip. He wore white cotton pants which were grimy around the cuffs, along with a loud Hawaiian shirt which had a dirty ring around the collar. His sunglasses lay on a nearby table with the earpieces sticking up. As he read, he scratched his big bent honker of a nose.

So the kid liked riding horses, huh? Well, old Bradford Brie had something for her to ride, and just thinking about the scrawny pipe-stem legs and bony little ass caused his pogo stick to come to life. He reached down to squeeze between his legs.

He glanced at the clock. Two hours at the most, he figured, maybe an hour to find this—he picked up the envelope and squinted to read the postmark—Van, Texas, burg, another hour to roust one of the local yokels who could point him to the camp. According to what the little girl had written to old mommy-cunt, the campers had some free time to walk back to their cabins after breakfast. That's when Brie was going to take the kid. He'd step casually out from behind a tree, and she'd look at him with trusting brown eyes. He'd tell her, I got a message from your mommy, sweetie, and then the kid would about piss in her pants to know what mommy had to say. Well, your fucking dog's dead, little girl, that's what he'd tell her then, and he'd let her have it, bam, right between the eyes. Then he'd carry her to his LeBaron convertible and away they'd go. Before she knew what hit her, they'd be tooling along some Florida beach, and she'd be his for as long as he wanted.

The kid would want to know about her dog, and Brie had taken a picture of the fallen German shepherd with just that in mind. *Here your fucking mutt is, little girl, and if you don't want to wind up just like him, you'll do as old Bradford Brie tells you.* She would likely begin to snivel at that point, but a good hard one right where it counted would get her in line in a hurry. Brie had experience with captives. At first the girl would be afraid just like the farmer woman had been. After a month or so on the road, however, she'd beg him to do her, because she'd understand that him doing her was better than the alternative.

From the moment he'd walked out of the Lew Sterrett Justice Center, Brie's number one goal—after his unfinished business with Sharon Hays, of course—had been to put at least a thousand miles between his own behind and Dallas County, Texas. He was no dummy. Maybe he'd never been too smart in school, he thought, but he had some education that school guys never dreamed about. Like many convicts, Brie knew the Code of Criminal Procedure backward and forward, and had a solid understanding of the manner in which assistant district attorneys conducted business. From the moment he'd learned of the murder indictment's dismissal, he had waited for the other shoe to fall. He was certain that the D.A. would now charge him with the break-in at the lawyer lady's house, and when he'd walked out of the jail and no one had been waiting with another warrant, he couldn't believe it. On the way home, he'd gotten the picture. Sure, he'd thought, it's Friday afternoon. What a break, huh? Any other day of the week they'd have had a second warrant before a man could say Jack Fucking Robinson. On Friday afternoon, the A.D.A. assigned to the break-in at Sharon Hays's house would either be fucking off on the golf course or drinking beer in some honky-tonk. Brie's best estimate was that the new charges wouldn't go to the grand jury until the following Thursday, but he wasn't taking any chances. By Monday morning he intended to be long gone. Along with the little girl.

Christ, but he'd always wanted to go to Florida, lie on the beach, and watch the women in their itty-bitty bikinis. He'd known a few Florida guys while in prison, and his mouth had watered as he'd listened to stories about palm trees by the millions and enough imported cocaine to keep a man in orbit for centuries. The most popular TV show in the Texas Department of Corrections had been *Miami Vice,* and Brie had never missed a single episode. On the Florida coast the living would be easy, and carrying his meal ticket along with him would insure that he'd never want for money. Anytime Brie ran short of cash, why, he'd just sprawl the little girl out in a motel room and snap a few pictures. He knew just where to sell the photos, too; no place in the world had as many old people's homes as southern Florida. Just give Bradford Brie a gang of horny old bastards with nothing to do but sit around and watch the sunset, and he would live off the fat of the land.

It was time to go. If he left right now he'd be in this—he picked up the envelope and checked the postmark once more—Van, Texas, by three in the morning. Brie folded the letter and crammed it into his hip pocket, then sat up to put on canvas tennis shoes. Adios, motherfuckers, was all he had to say to Dallas County, Texas. So long, see you later, I'm outta here.

He retrieved his wide-brimmed straw hat from the arm of the couch and put on his sunglasses. They were so dark that he could barely see at night, but that didn't matter. Appearances were what counted, and Brie considered that the shades made him look every bit as sexy as Newman in *Hud*. Softly humming the opening bars to "Ain't That a Shame," by Fats Domino, Brie went out on the porch and sucked in warm summer night air. His suitcase lay empty in the LeBaron's trunk; he'd go get his luggage and hurry to pack. And then, he thought, Florida here I come. He hop-skipped across the porch and stepped down on the weed-infested yard.

Jesus, with his sunglasses on he hadn't even noticed the woman. But suddenly there she stood, not five feet from him, her feet spread apart, right arm extended in his direction, left hand clamped on her wrist, holding a . . . He grinned slightly as he removed his sunglasses, then looked straight down the bore of one big fucking gun.

Bradford Brie spread his hands, palms out. His sunglasses dangled by an earpiece from his fingers. He said, "Now, look."

And Sharon Hays said calmly, "Back inside."

Sharon had called on her old friend Doris once more, this time to help her coax up Bradford Brie's address from computerized jail records. Even with the aid of a Mapsco, she'd had a terrible time finding the house. Oak Cliff was an endless succession of twisty, narrow avenues with broken, uneven pavement, all of which seemed to lead up one blind alley and down another. Streets changed names without rhyme or reason; Willow Avenue would become Tanner Boulevard, continue a few blocks under that title, then suddenly become Willow Avenue once more. Even when she was certain she'd located the right house, the numbers were missing from both curb and mailbox. She'd been about ready to throw up her hands when she'd spotted the car, the same old Chrysler LeBaron convertible as he'd driven on the night he'd broken into her house. The LeBaron sat in the drive on bald, dusty tires. A dead calm came over her as she parked a half block down the street, pulled on thin latex gloves she'd bought in an all-night drugstore, dug the .44 Bulldog out of her glove compartment, and walked up in the yard to wait.

And there she'd stood, gun in hand, for almost an hour, and four or five times she'd nearly lost her nerve. The police will eventually get him, she'd told herself, then had remembered that he'd already been safely in custody once and that Dallas County had let him slip away. If she'd only had herself to worry about, she very likely would have turned tail and run, but the scum had taken Melanie's letter. There was nothing Sharon wouldn't do to protect her little girl.

And all of a sudden—boom!—there he was, ambling across the porch wearing those dumb-looking sunglasses, gangly arms swinging at his sides. He was humming. The s.o.b. was *singing,* jolly old him, just hours after he'd shot her dog, gone into her bedroom, her most private and personal place in this entire world and . . . Sharon's heart turned instantly to flint. There was no doubt in her mind that she could shoot this man.

"Back inside," she said again.

He showed a look-at-me-I'm-harmless grin and put on his sunglasses. "Hey, now. You don't want to do nothing foolish, not to a man staying at home and minding his own business. Same as you ought to be doing, lady."

She didn't say a word. She eared back the hammer with two soft clicks.

He backed slowly up on the porch, his hands spread, his knees flexed, looking for an opening, any sign at all that her guard was down. He moved into the shadow of the overhang, only his feet in moonlight now, his big straw hat like headgear for the invisible man. "You got no idea what you're doing, you know?" he said.

"Open the fucking door and go inside," she said.

He hesitated, reaching behind him, and pulled the handle. The door creaked outward. He backed over the threshold. "Hey, no use to cuss a man. Nice lawyer lady like you, you never done anything like this. You know what, you might be even scareder that I am. You just might be, you know?"

She held the barrel of the .44 about two inches from his chin and followed him into the house. His grin was frozen on his face. The stench of grease-cooked meat assaulted her nostrils. "You have my daughter's letter," she said. "Where is it?"

His voice was a singsong chant, his manner taunting. "Well, now. What letter would you be talking about, lady? You come here to rob me or something? You got them gloves on, you must be one of them big bad criminal people. Scare a man to death, you know?"

She pointed the Bulldog at the floor between his feet and pulled the trigger, bracing herself just as she'd practiced. The gun blasted and slammed hard against her palm; the slug tore a fist-sized hole in the floor, ricocheted from the concrete foundation, and buried itself in the ceiling. The odor of burnt gunpowder obscured the meat smell.

"Goddamn, lady, you be careful with that thing." He dug the letter out, his tone now a frightened octave higher. "You hurt somebody, you're going to be in trouble."

"No need to cuss a woman, Mr. Brie," she said. "I want your gun now." She glanced at the page, recognized Melanie's handwriting, stowed the letter in her jeans, and steadied the Bulldog.

Slowly, walking on tiptoes, his chin moving up and down as his gaze roamed from the Bulldog to Sharon's face and back again, Brie went into the kitchen. Sharon followed two paces behind, tense and alert, watching his feet. *His feet will move first if he rushes me,* she thought. She hoped he did charge. Sharon had never in her life felt the kind of hatred for any human being which coursed through her at that moment. She fleetingly pictured Melanie in this creature's grasp, and very nearly pulled the trigger right then and there. She stepped on something sticky, lifted her foot, and placed it gingerly to one side.

He opened a cabinet drawer and reached in. She steadied the Bulldog. "By the barrel," she said.

"Sure, by the barrel. Old Brad Brie's no idiot, no, ma'am. Lady points a gun, I do what she says. Now, you be careful with that thing." Brie showed a broad grin as he lifted a .45 automatic from the drawer, holding the barrel between his thumb and forefinger.

Sharon stepped forward, took the .45 in her left hand, laid the Bulldog on the counter, and switched Brie's pistol to her right. "Go in there and sit on the sofa," she said.

He retreated into the grungy living room, backed up to the couch, and lowered himself slowly down, all the while keeping up the singsong banter. "I know what you're thinking, lady. But I'm out of jail legitimate. If you shoot me you've had it, you know? You can't do nothing to me. I'm just a citizen minding his own business." His look was uncertain, the chatter coming a mile a minute, the mouth slack with . . .

Fear. The man was scared out of his wits, and his terror surprised Sharon. That night at her house, when he'd waited for her outside her shower stall, he'd seemed so totally . . . so totally *evil* that she'd supposed nothing could make him afraid. His terrified babbling aroused a strange sense of pity in her in spite of herself. She shored up her determination. Pity? she thought. For him? She held the .45 in both hands, cocked the hammer, and squinted down the barrel. He knew what was coming; his mouth gaped open and his rapid speech dissolved at once into a whine. She steadied her aim, increased the pressure on the trigger, squeezing, squeezing, and . . .

And couldn't do it. Try as she might, she couldn't move her finger the final fraction of an inch required to blow the vermin into kingdom come. It was as if her hand was frozen. Shooting someone down in cold blood simply wasn't in her. Oh, my sweet Jesus Christ, she thought, *I cannot do it.*

She slowly lowered the pistol. Sharon Hays the avenger was suddenly Sharon Hays the lonely and frightened. The realization that Bradford Brie wasn't going to die after all brought her a strange sense of relief. He straightened on the sofa, and his plastic grin returned. He snugged up his sunglasses on his nose. "Now you're being smart," he said. "Come on, give me the gun and you can go on home."

She gestured with the pistol. "Don't you move a muscle or I *will* shoot you." Her words sounded more frightened than forceful. She swallowed. Christ, now what was she to do? Phone, she thought dully. Call Teeter, Mr. I-don't-like-people-calling-me-at-home Edward Teeter, and have the moron of an assistant D.A. send someone out here to arrest this guy. Breath escaped from between her lips in a rush as she glanced to her right. There was a black princess phone on the kitchen counter. "Don't move, do you understand me?" she said, and edged sideways toward the telephone.

And that's when Bradford Brie committed suicide.

The next three seconds would haunt Sharon for the rest of her life, and she would wonder over and over what went on in the lunatic's mind. Likely he thought a woman would never have the nerve. For whatever reason, his smile dissolved into a sneer and up he came, bounding from the sofa, taking one long stride in her direction, two, and . . .

Later she would be certain that she closed her eyes at the final instant. Her reaction, she would be sure, was pure reflex, the tightening of her hand on the pistol more an act of fear than anything else. The .45 erupted with a deafening blast which shook the walls. Sharon's hand jerked upward; she yanked the trigger to send a second bullet rocketing into the ceiling.

The first slug had caught him dead center in the left eye. Over he went, tumbling over the back of the couch with his arms flailing. As Sharon watched, the top portion of his head simply disappeared, his grin intact as he fell out of sight and thudded to the floor. The silence after the thud was louder to her than the gunshots had been. The wall behind the couch was spattered in red, garishly bright in the light from the one unshaded lamp.

Sharon stood frozen in place for long seconds, then let the pistol dangle beside her hip. Fearfully, each step an effort, she walked up to peer down over the back of the couch. Her feet were numb. Bradford Brie lay on his side with his neck oddly twisted, his one remaining eye staring at nothing. His sunglasses lay shattered amid fragments of bone and gray pieces of brain matter. Sharon whimpered, dropped the gun beside the corpse, staggered into the kitchen, bent over the sink, and turned the water on. She threw up over and over, retching until there was nothing left inside her, then dry-heaving as she crumpled to the floor.

She might have passed out for a few seconds; she wasn't sure. When her head cleared she was lying face-up on the linoleum. She struggled to rise, slipped and fell, and finally gripped the counter to hoist herself up. Go, she thought, I must go. Her .44 Bulldog lay on the counter. She picked it up and ran. The screen door banged the wall behind her as she charged across the porch, the wind whipping her hair and drying the inside of her mouth as her footsteps jarred across the uneven yard. When she finally made the half block to stand beside her Volvo, she leaned against the side of the car and retched. Then, her fingers trembling, her breath coming in tortured gasps, she fell in behind the wheel and drove away. It was an accident, she thought. *It had to be an accident.*

On the way home she narrowly avoided three separate collisions, fighting the steering wheel and fishtailing through intersections. After she'd parked in her driveway, she ran across her yard as if on fire, stumbled and fell on the porch and painfully scraped her palms. Once in her bedroom and safely beneath the covers, she pulled the sheets up around her throat, lay wide awake, and shivered violently until dawn. As the sun peeked over the rooftops, Sharon Hays slept a tortured sleep and dreamed of killing a man.

39

The insistent ringing of the telephone shocked her awake. She stared at the ceiling without comprehension, then rolled onto her side and recoiled from the blinding sunlight which streamed in through the window. She rose on one elbow to look around at the familiar things: her heavy wooden dresser, her vanity, little spray bottles lined up in a neat row. Her own bedroom, her safest place.

The phone vibrated the walls with an ear-splitting jangle. She yawned and reached, placed the receiver against her ear and said sleepily, "Yes?"

"I was about two minutes away from calling the police," Sheila Winston said. "Where have you—"

The police? Sharon thought. Why would anyone need the . . . ?

"—been all morning?"

Morning? she thought. Is it morning? "Right here," she managed. "I've been asleep."

"Well, you must have been—"

Sharon's gaze fell on the dresser once more, and on the big revolver lying there, the—

"—drugged. I've been calling every fifteen minutes since nine, and I—"

—.44 Bulldog she'd carried last night when she'd . . . *Oh, sweet Christ, I . . .*

"—thought you were dead or something. Do you realize it's after twelve?"

Dead? Sharon thought. No, I'm not dead, but the guy is, the man lying face-up with one eye missing, blood spattered on the wall and ... She cupped her hand over the mouthpiece, gagged, and swallowed bitter bile.

"Sharon?" Sheila said.

Sharon squinched her eyes tightly shut and forced herself to speak. "I was up late," she said.

Sheila's voice took on a teasing lilt. "Anyone I know?"

"No, I was ... working."

"That's what I'm calling about," Sheila said. "Are we getting together today?"

Through Sharon's nausea, realization dawned. Work. She'd told Sheila that they'd meet over the weekend and discuss the expert testimony Sheila was to give in the Rathermore case. Midge Rathermore, the pitiful teenager whom Sharon was defending, the case which yesterday had been the most important thing in her life, but which now ...

Sharon lowered her head. "Sheila, let me call you back, okay?"

"Does this mean we're not meeting?"

"No, it—" Sharon simply had to remove the panic from her tone. Had to. "Tomorrow, Sheil, okay? I've got some things I have to do."

Sheila sounded dubious. "Are you sure I shouldn't come over there?"

"No," Sharon said too urgently, then forced herself to speak more slowly and said, "Listen, I'll call you this afternoon. And thanks for checking on me, but I'm fine. Promise."

"You're sure."

"I'm sure, babe. Talk to you later, okay?" She hung up, hugged her knees to her chest, and hung her head.

Rationally, she had to think rationally. Had to make a decision. Well, okay, Rational Hays, she thought, do your stuff. She raised her gaze to stare at the bathroom door.

Bradford Brie, cruel lips curved into a grin, eyes hidden behind dark sunglasses, leaping from the couch, his body tensed, coming at her ...

She could call the police. No, not the police, but she could call A.D.A. Teeter, explain that she was over there to make a citizen's arrest, that the guy tried to rush her, and she ...

And *I shot him with his gun,* she thought with a bitter laugh, *and left his gun beside his body, all in an attempt* to make a citizen's arrest. And, oh, yeah, I was wearing latex gloves. Not to cover my fingerprints, of course, not at all. Those old Oak Cliff houses are disease-ridden, you know? A girl could catch AIDS or something.

She could call Edward Teeter, all right. Would the moron love it or what? A.D.A.'s had delirious orgasms over slam-dunk cases, and a murder charge against Sharon Hays at the moment would be as slam-dunk as they come. Teeter would figure the odds, realizing that the victim was somewhat less than pristine, and realizing as well that Brie being the same guy who'd attacked Sharon in her home would make an impact on the jury, so Teeter would make a plea-bargain offer. He'd start with ten years and be willing to cut it to five, and even drop the deadly weapon charge to make the guilty plea more attractive. And then it would be Sharon's turn to consider her chances, and in light of the fact that elimination of the deadly weapons charge would make her eligible for parole in something like eight months, she'd likely accept the offer. Case closed, on to the next wretched sinner.

Time to search the old soul, Sharon, she thought. If you turn yourself in, you're going to be looking at doing some time. No doubt about it. In Dallas County, Texas, murderers were prosecuted, and that was that. She pictured herself in a jailhouse smock, her wrists cuffed, waiting in line behind a string of whores for transfer to TDC. And pictured Melanie as a suddenly orphaned ward of the state. No, even worse than that, Rob would have custody. She pictured Melanie in Hollywood, living in a Beverly Hills mansion along with Rob and whatever female happened to have his fancy at the moment. She wondered if old Rob would bring Melanie down on visiting day. Fat chance, Sharon thought.

And if you'd consider pleading guilty, old Sharon, she thought, do you *feel* guilty? Of course not. Try as she might, she couldn't work up one smidgen of remorse over killing Bradford Brie. So it all boiled down to a simple matter of self-preservation. Would she be better off keeping her mouth shut, or calling the D.A.'s office and 'fessing up? The standard police line that "things will go easier on you," Sharon knew, was all a lot of bull. The truth was that confessions made things a whole lot easier for the police department, but the criminal was better off not saying a word. There were no fingerprints. I've got Melanie's letter, so there's nothing in the world to connect me to the crime. So, Sharon decided, I'll keep quiet and let the cards fall as they may.

And spend the rest of your life cringing in fear every time the phone rings or a car pulls up out front, the voice inside her said.

I'll have to live with that, Sharon thought.

Good luck, the voice inside her said.

She yanked the covers up over her head, rolled onto her stomach, and tried to go to sleep. An hour later, she was still awake, having twisted and turned until her sheets were damp pretzels of wilted cloth.

40

Somehow Sharon made it through the weekend. She trimmed rosebushes and pulled weeds like a maniac, and even went across the street late on Saturday afternoon to help Mrs. Breedlove paint her eaves. Anything, Sharon thought, anything to keep her mind occupied, and keeping busy did enable her to keep her head on straight during the day. But Saturday night was horrifying. Every time a car slowed in front of her house or the telephone rang, her heart practically stopped. She went over the newspaper with a fine-tooth comb, but if anyone had discovered what was left of Bradford Brie, the *News* didn't consider the event print-worthy.

During Sheila's visit on Sunday afternoon, Sharon got drunk on screwdrivers. Sheila had one drink to Sharon's five, remained sober, and halfway through the afternoon abandoned all hope of getting anything done in the way of discussing her testimony. Sheila sat quietly until nearly seven o'clock and watching her friend drink. To Sheila's credit she didn't pry, but knew good and well that something was wrong. Sharon would have given anything to open up to Sheila, but what could she say? *Boy, did I ever have fun while you and your hunk of an aerobics instructor were at the movies. I went over and killed this guy, isn't that the berries?* Before Sheila went home, she looked her friend over head to toe and sadly shook her head.

After what seemed like weeks, Monday morning arrived. As Sharon left Stemmons Freeway and drove alongside the Crowley Courts Building, the upper-level jail windows in the Sterrett Justice Center were visible over the parking garage roof. The barred openings were to Sharon like probing eyes, and each one drilled into her heart and soul. We want you, little lady, they seemed to say. She left the Volvo on the fourth level and negotiated the walkway to the courts building with a lump the size of a grapefruit beneath her breastbone. At the main entry to the Crowley Building a uniformed policeman—a broad-shouldered guy in his thirties with slim hips and a dimple on his chin—opened the door for her and stood aside. "Morning, miss," he said. Sharon almost panicked and ran at the mere sight of the uniform.

Her nerves had calmed somewhat by the time she exited the elevator outside Judge Griffin's courtroom, and her mind for the time being was back on the business at hand. One day at a time, Sharon thought, do what you have to do and go on with your life. Whatever was going to happen in connection with Bradford Brie's death was out of her control, but the Rathermore trial was something she could sink her teeth into. Putting on the blinders and concentrating on the trial would help her make it through one more day.

The young killers' testimony was scheduled, and while the hallway wasn't quite the madhouse it had been before Linda Rathermore's appearance, there was a good-sized crowd on hand. Sharon dodged around the reporters and hangers-on near the courtroom entry, then hustled down the aisle and through the gate toward the defense side. She gave a curt nod to Kathleen Fraterno as she went by. Fraterno ignored her. Sharon wore her all-business face, though her insides were doing panicky flip-flops.

As she sank down beside Russell Black, he leaned over and said, "We oughtta do all right today. Half their team is missing."

Sharon cocked her head. "Half their . . . ?"

"I'm bein' too generous," Black said. "It's only about ten percent of their team that's gone, ninety percent is still with us. But Milt Breyer's attendin' another hearin'."

Sharon glanced at Kathleen, who was studying her file, then said to Black, "Hmm. They must have changed the D.A.'s rules. Used to be, anyone who was in trial didn't attend hearings on other cases. They had a roving prosecutor to fill in for us in hearings that didn't concern the case at trial."

Black winked. "Well, it's not exactly a criminal matter he's tied up with."

Sharon frowned. "Milt Breyer doesn't handle any civil cases, Russ."

"He's not exactly handlin' this one. It's handlin' him. His wife filed divorce papers last week, and it's some kind of custody hearin'." He cut his eyes in Sharon's direction. "Rumor is Kathleen Fraterno's named as a respondent."

Sharon pictured Cissy Breyer, high-powered lawyer on her heels, as she'd swept grandly into the courthouse on the first day of trial. Serves the randy bastard right, Sharon thought, and hoped that Cissy left old Milt with nothing but his underwear. If that. She pitied Kathleen but only slightly. Fraterno was a big girl and had known just what she was getting into. Sharon said simply, "Christ."

"That all you've got to say?" Black said. " 'Christ'?"

"Christ. Yeah, Christ." She shrugged. "As in, Christ, they're getting a divorce, eh?"

"I thought you might be glad old Milt's sitting on the hot seat," Black said.

Sharon opened her satchel and removed a stack of files. "Whatever gave you that idea, boss?" she said.

Black and Fraterno stood before the bench, his bearlike shoulders towering above Kathleen's slight athletic frame. Fraterno handed a form over for Judge Griffin to read as a uniformed Dallas cop fidgeted in the witness chair. A couple of the jurors stifled yawns, and a good third of the spectators had left. As the main show, Burdette and Leonard, waited in the wings, the state was putting on chain-of-custody evidence with regard to the tire tool found in the Rathermores' flower bed. Tedious but necessary. Without evidence as to which cop had found the murder weapon and given it to whom, and where the weapon had been ever since, the tire tool and all the forensics testimony that went along with it—the bloodstains on the weapon itself, the comparisons in type between the stains and samples taken from William Rathermore—would be inadmissible. All probably a moot point since the killers themselves would tell how they'd used the tire tool to bludgeon Rathermore to death, and where they'd thrown the weapon after the crime, but if the chain of custody wasn't handled just so, the defense could score some points on appeal. Sharon checked her watch. After eleven. Her mind wandered from the proceedings as she looked to her right at Midge.

Midge's physical appearance hadn't improved; the rapid weight loss in the county jail had produced loose bags of flesh hanging below her jaw. She was clean and neat as a pin, however, today wearing a schoolgirl blue jumper, and the expression on her face spoke volumes. She was turned around in her chair, smiling into the audience at her mother. It had become a ritual during the trial, Midge showering Deborah North with loving glances as though the two of them were alone in the courtroom. At first the girl had clung to Sharon for dear life, as if her lawyer was all she had left in the world, but that was no longer true. Midge still was more attentive to Sharon than she was to Russell Black, but the mother-image feelings she'd had for her female lawyer had obviously been replaced by the real thing. If nothing else, Sharon thought, this terrible happening in Midge's life would restore the mother she'd lost, and mother-daughter relationships were powerful things.

And Sharon Hays, who only three days earlier had killed to protect her own daughter, brushed a tear from the corner of her eye. Please, Lord, Sharon prayed, don't let prison destroy what they now have together.

"Son, what you've said here is pretty serious." Russell Black, tilted back in his chair, his thumbs hooked into his lapels in his best folksy posture, honing in on young Troy Burdette like grandpa about to show the kid a brand-new fishin' lure.

"Objection," Kathleen Fraterno said. "Weight of the witness's testimony isn't something for the defense to speculate in front of the jury." The objection was off the wall but sharp nonetheless, and Sharon felt a sort of admiration for Fraterno. Kathleen was trying anything she could to break Russell Black's spell, both on the jury and on her witness. Burdette regarded the veteran lawyer with an expression near rapture.

"Sustained," Judge Griffin said, but sounded every bit as spellbound as the rest of the audience. Sharon felt a surge of hero worship and favored Russell Black with a grin. He responded by folding his hands over his midsection.

"This little girl over here," Black said, indicating Midge, "gave you the code for her folks' burglar alarm. That's somethin' that you're sure of."

"Yes, sir." Burdette's gaze flicked toward his father, who was seated dead center in the second row of the spectator section. "It's the only way I could have known it," he said.

"You couldn't have gotten the code anyplace else?"

"Not that I know of." Burdette wore a dove gray suit with tie to match, along with a maroon breast pocket hanky. His sandy hair was sprayed in place, his expression as earnest as Frank Gifford's.

"One more time, Troy," Black said.

"Your Honor." Fraterno tugged on the top button of her snow white blouse.

"Mr. Black," Judge Griffin said. "The witness has testified. Having him repeat things will only drag on and on." Sharon wondered about the exchange between the prosecution and the bench; Fraterno hadn't really objected, and Griffin hadn't really sustained. Odd, Sharon thought.

"But you're sure," Black said, not missing a beat, "that you got the code from Midge Rathermore just before Christmas, at her home?"

"Yes, sir. I couldn't forget something like that."

Black lowered his head, taking his time, appearing confused but, Sharon knew, not being confused one iota. He looked up. "Mr. Burdette, how well do you know Midge Rathermore's stepmama?"

Sharon watched the jury. A gray-haired lady in the top row had let her eyelids droop, but now sat up and took notice. Sharon glanced at Fraterno. She seemed curious but not particularly concerned.

Young Burdette, however, immediately lost his cool. His voice cracking like a pubescent thirteen-year-old's, he said, "You mean, Mrs. Rathermore?"

"That's Midge's stepmama, idn't it? How well do you know her?"

"I saw," Burdette said, then cleared his throat and said, "I used to see her around." Visible in the corner of Sharon's eye, Fraterno now sat bolt upright and made inquiring eye contact with her witness. Burdette looked quickly away from Kathleen and honed in on something at the rear of the courtroom.

Black opened his file and picked up a stack of photos. Sharon glanced at the top picture, the best one, the face-on shot of Troy and Linda beside her car just outside the motel room. "Lemme ask you, Mr. Burdette," Black said. "You got any idea where the Windjammer Motel is?"

Fraterno's lips twitched. She obviously didn't know whether to object or go blind.

"I," Burdette said. "I'm not . . ."

Black stood, ambled bearlike over to the prosecution side, and dropped the top photo in front of Fraterno. It was standard procedure prior to the introduction of evidence, but Russell Black made the gesture seem like the climax scene in a gunfighter movie. He stood grandly back while Fraterno examined the picture. Her eyes widened. She drew in a breath. She favored her witness with a glare that might easily wilt roses. Fraterno stood. "Objection. This isn't on their list of physical evidence. The rules of procedure—"

"Your Honor." Black stepped toward the bench and spread his hands, palms up. "This is rebuttal evidence I got here. The witness has testified that he barely knows this woman."

Griffin motioned, and Black and Fraterno did double-time marches to stand before the bench. Fraterno handed the picture to the judge, whose eyes widened as she looked the photo over. One juror, a dark-haired man in a plaid shirt, nearly fell out of the box in his effort to see what was in Judge Griffin's hand. She murmured something which only Black and Fraterno could hear, then said loudly, "Your objection is overruled, Miss Fraterno." She handed the picture to Black. Sharon breathed an audible sigh, which brought her a sharp look from the judge.

Black now handed the picture to the court reporter, who applied an evidence sticker as Black put hands on hips and showed Troy Burdette a broad smile. Burdette squirmed like a four-year-old in church. Judge Griffin admitted the photo and handed it over to the bailiff for passing around in the jury box. Some of the jurors frowned as they looked. One young woman giggled. The matronly gray-haired lady who'd nearly fallen asleep earlier now glared at Burdette as if she'd like to spank his bottom.

When Black finally got his hands back on the photo, he smiled at the judge. "Your Honor, can I approach the witness?"

Griffin nodded. "Proceed."

Black laid the picture on the rail in front of Burdette, then leaned over in a buddy-buddy attitude. "Mr. Burdette, you recognize anybody in there?" he said. He glanced at the court reporter. "For the record, that's Defense Exhibit Four." The court reporter dutifully rattled the keys on the shorthand typewriter.

Burdette picked up, then dropped the picture like a hot potato. "I . . . She was giving me a ride."

Black snorted. "You mean, she just got *through* givin' you a ride."

Laughter rocked the courtroom. Two of the jurors doubled over in glee, and even the bailiff laughed out loud. Burdette glumly regarded the floor as Fraterno testily folded her arms. As Sharon glanced over her shoulder, Troy Burdette's father looked about to choke. Griffin banged her gavel, obviously repressing a grin of her own. "Mr. Black," she said in the same tone she'd likely use in saying, "Oh, what a kidder you are."

"I apologize, Judge." Black's eyebrows moved closer together in a scowl. "She was givin' you a ride from where to where, Mr. Burdette?"

"She was . . ." Total panic now, Burdette's gaze whipping back and forth between Kathleen Fraterno and his father. Sharon wondered briefly which of the two Burdettes was the most concerned over the question. Finally the witness said, "To school."

Black smiled from ear to ear. *Just you and ol' Russ Black, son.* He pointed at the photo. "To school. Well, tell me, Mr. Burdette. And the jury. Just what is it you were learnin' inside that motel room?"

As whoops and giggles from the spectator section shook the rafters and Sandy Griffin's gavel banged like gunfire, Sharon reached out and patted Midge Rather-more's hand. She then turned in her chair, looked toward the aisle seat, second row, and showed Deborah North an undisguised thumbs-up sign.

Sharon peeked out into the corridor to find out if her witness had arrived. She thought, Oh, God, she's here.

And there she was, all right, the desk clerk from the Windjammer Motel in all her splendor, wearing a shape-less print dress which resembled a dressing gown, her gray hair like a rat's nest, puffing on a Camel while sit-ting beneath the no-smoking sign, hacking up phlegm in between exhaling clouds of smoke. She was the only oc-cupant of the bench, and passersby gave her a wide berth while wrinkling their noses. In making up her witness list, Sharon had had to call the Windjammer to ask the wom-an's name. Gertrude Reems. Just perfect, Sharon thought. She waggled her fingers at Gertrude and smiled. Gertrude sneered at her.

Sharon retreated down the aisle and through the gate. She said to Russell Black as she sat, "We're in luck. She made it."

He was examining his file, having just finished work-ing Troy Burdette over and now preparing to do the same to Christopher Leonard. "Has the old crone bathed?" Black said.

"I wasn't close enough to smell her," Sharon said, "but I doubt it."

"Well, hopefully," Black said, "Mr. Leonard will 'fess up that he took his buddy out to that motel, and we won't have to use the dear old lady after all."

"I've got my fingers crossed," Sharon said. "If we do have to put her on, she's your witness, boss."

The bailiff had escorted Midge out to the toilet during the break, and now returned her to her seat. Judge Griffin called order. On the prosecution side, Kathleen Fraterno half rose. Her gaze locked with Sharon's for an instant, and Sharon detected a distinct smirk in her expression. What's going on? Sharon thought.

She wasn't long in finding out. Fraterno faced the bench. "The state calls," she said, "Dr. Gregory Mathew-son."

And Sharon thought, What the hell . . . ? She looked to Black, who shrugged helplessly.

Of course, Sharon thought. Kathleen had just reared back and tossed another curveball, breaking perfectly into the corner of the strike zone. Whatever Kathleen had stooped to in her personal life, she was still one bitchin' lawyer. During the break Fraterno would have grilled both Leonard and Burdette, found out the real skinny on the motel trysts with Linda Rathermore, and made the decision that she didn't want to throw Leonard out for Russell Black to dissect until the young witness had plenty of coaching. Gruntin' Gregory Mathewson would take up the balance of the day, and tonight there'd be yet another rehearsal. They've got more on-set script changes than most movies, Sharon thought.

Mathewson, his paunch even bigger than Sharon remembered from Midge's certification hearing, pretty well repeated his testimony from that proceeding. Several times. His testimony went on and on. Midge, according to Gruntin' Greg, was a bright, mature sixteen-year-old who well understood the difference between right and wrong. If there was ever a girl who knew murder was wrong, Mathewson said, that girl was Midge. Sharon waived cross-examination, partly because she was afraid she'd fly off the handle with the phony psychologist, but mainly because she didn't feel any need to shoot holes in his testimony. Sheila Winston would do that when she took the stand as the defense expert. Mathewson registered surprise that no one took him on cross, then regained his composure, such as it was, and waddled from the courtroom.

So it was that at just before five o'clock in the afternoon, Griffin dismissed the jury for the day. Kathleen had bought her rehearsal time, though Sharon doubted that the extra evening would do the state's cause much good. Unless Fraterno somehow pulled a rabbit out of a hat, Midge was going to win. As Sharon gathered her things up to leave, she impulsively leaned over and kissed her client on the cheek. Midge smiled fleetingly at her lawyer, then returned her total attention to her mom.

So charged up was Sharon over the way the trial was going that when she told Gertrude Reems she'd have to come back tomorrow, and that the defense wasn't certain whether her testimony would be needed or not, and Gertrude, Camel bouncing up and down in one corner of her mouth, said, "You assholes are putting me to one fucking helluva lot of trouble," she smiled sweetly and slipped the old crone twenty bucks out of her own pocket for her trouble.

Sharon's elation lasted about two minutes, long enough for her and Russell Black to exit the courtroom and make it halfway down the hall to the elevators. She was high as a kite, her heels beating a merry tattoo on corridor tile. It was likely, Sharon thought, that her current heady feeling was in part overreaction to her personal problems—which really weren't all that weighty, she thought, only a dead guy and a few little murder charges to worry about—but she was so happy that she didn't care. She even smiled at Andy Wade as the reporter went by, then regretted her friendliness as he turned around and followed her, begging for an interview. She told him over her shoulder that he'd have to wait until the verdict was in.

She even gave Russell Black's chain a small tug. "I don't get it, boss," she said. "You're in there mowing 'em down and you look like you just lost your only friend in the world."

Black kept pace with her, head down. "Whatever can go wrong in one of these trials," he said, "will go wrong. Count on it, Sharon."

As if on cue, the elevator doors opened and Anthony Gear emerged. He was in a hurry, one arm swinging, his sports coat folded over his other arm. His expression was drawn. Russell Black said, "He don't look good. What'd I tell you?"

Gear halted in front of the two lawyers, glanced past them down the corridor, and motioned. "Come on over here. We can't let them hear this."

Sharon glanced behind her. "Them" was Kathleen Fraterno and Milt Breyer, who stood in animated chatter twenty feet away. Kathleen was reading Breyer a riot act of some sort, her eyes blazing, her backside twitching as she stood first on one foot and then the other. I'll bet they're not discussing the trial, Sharon thought. She followed Gear and Black to a spot beside the windows. Visible on the other side of Stemmons Freeway, the glistening green ball atop Reunion Tower was shrouded in haze.

Black folded his arms and regarded his feet. "Have we got trouble, Mr. Gear?"

Gear looked from Black to Sharon and back again. He lowered his eyes. "The worst," the detective said. "It's Leslie Schlee. She's not going to testify."

41

Sharon's bangs drooped. Her ankles ached. She removed her spike-heeled shoes and rubbed her feet. She closed the *Southwestern Reporter* in disgust, padded in stocking feet across the hall to Russell Black's office, and sank dejectedly into a visitors' chair. "There's no way out," she announced to the room at large. "Midge is going to have criminal responsibility unless we can come up with some evidence of abuse."

Russ Black mumbled something under his breath and drummed his fingers on his desktop. Anthony Gear sat forward on the sofa, undid the top button on his shirt, and rolled his eyes. Deborah North sat on the other end of the couch with her legs drawn up beneath her. She adjusted her position and put both feet on the floor, and sipped black coffee from a Styrofoam cup. Misty-eyed, she said, "You'll have to spell that out for me. From where I sat in the courtroom it looked like y'all were kicking ass." Visible over her shoulder through the window, the sky was midnight black. Street people shuffled along here and there on Jackson Street, peering down into the gutter in search of anything useful.

Sharon expelled air from her lungs and massaged her forehead. "We're all going to have to take our heads out of the clouds, Deb. Here's the law. We're pretty sure that we're going to prove Linda gave the boys the new security code without Midge knowing about it, and that Linda was in on her husband's murder. That's going to put Linda's fanny on the burner, but it's not going to get

Midge out of the fire. Midge did contract with those little hellions, and the fact that Linda was behind it doesn't matter. A murder-for-hire conviction doesn't hinge on whether the deed was done successfully, and all the state really has to prove is that Midge tried to have it done.

"Our only legal defense," Sharon said, "is that Midge was only protecting herself and Susan from further abuse. The judge has already ruled that we can get into that, and she'll instruct the jury that if they find abuse, they've got to vote for acquittal. Getting that point across was only half the hurdle; now we've got to produce *evidence* of the abuse. And the burden of proof is on us. Unless we put on evidence, the judge won't give the instruction." She smoothed her skirt. "Without Leslie Schlee we're dead in the water. Absolutely . . . dead."

Deb's eyes were glassy. "Good God."

Black's ankles were crossed on one corner of his desk. He sipped Coke through a straw from a Whataburger cup. "By the numbers, Mr. Gear, one more time. And don't leave anything out. You never know what's gonna be important."

Gear carried his coffee cup to the small refrigerator inside Black's credenza, squatted on his haunches, and poured a ribbon of Half 'n' Half from a pint carton. He stood and refilled his cup from the Mr. Coffee. "It'll take awhile," he said.

Black removed the plastic top from his cup and crunched on ice. "I don't think any of us are gonna be sleepin' much tonight, anyhow."

Gear took a paper napkin from a stack and carried his coffee back to the sofa. "I called in some accounts to get this, guys still with the Bureau that owe me. We can't get any of them involved."

"We wouldn't waste the time," Black said. "FBI agents are the only people in the world immune from subpoena. Not legally, but you just try hauling one of 'em into court. Take an act of Congress."

Deborah North stared off into space, her expression vacant. There was a painful lump in Sharon's throat which she couldn't quite swallow away.

Gear sat down and crossed his legs. "I smelled a rat when I was calling our witnesses this afternoon, you know, to make sure they were going to appear and whatnot, and every time I'd call the Schlee house and I'd get the maid and the runaround. In that order. Only information she'd give was that Leslie was out of town, and neither Mr. nor Mrs. Schlee would call me back. That's when I started checking around.

"Back when I first started on this case," he said, "there were some hot and heavy rumors floating around about Curtis Schlee, Leslie's father. Once we'd made contact and Leslie'd agreed to testify for us, I didn't see any real point in following up, but now I did."

Gear blew on the surface of his coffee, sipped, and made a face. "This guy at the Bureau I called, one time I helped him track a guy one of my clients was looking for. He verified on the q.t. that the FBI's had Curtis Schlee under investigation for months. He's the lawyer for"—Gear stroked the edge of his cup with his thumb—"three savings and loans. *Used* to be savings and loans before the FSLIC moved in and took them over, what, '89? Two or three years. The auditors turned up a few things, some of which landed the presidents of all three S&L's in federal prison camps. One discrepancy was, Curtis Schlee wasn't getting any legal fees for representing those fine institutions. Since Brother Schlee isn't exactly known as a charitable guy, this made the FBI sort of curious.

"What Schlee was doing," Gear said, "he was taking loans in *lieu* of fees. Big tickets, three and four million at a pop, developing land in Plano. Ever hear of Crosscreek Country Club?"

Black frowned and shook his head, and Sharon permitted herself a small grin. If it wasn't on the sports or crime pages, Russ Black didn't know about it. She said, "I've heard of it. Typical development, homes a half-million and up. If you buy a house you get a country club membership to boot. Wasn't there some talk about moving the Byron Nelson Classic to Crosscreek at one time?"

"Bullshit talk," Gear said, "instigated by the developers as a come-on. They filed for bankruptcy and left a bunch of homeowners holding the bag with unpaid liens from subcontractors. Big-time bankruptcy. Curtis Schlee was the prime owner, along with a couple of guys who, coincidentally, happened to be on the boards of all three bogus savings and loans."

Black scratched the back of his hand. "That's all federal stuff. What's it got to do with us?"

"I'm getting there," Gear said. "It takes time, like I told you. I don't have to tell you lawyers that what Schlee was doing was illegal as hell, both from the standpoint of having the S&L officers involved in his development and forgoing his legal fee in return for getting the loans. It took the feds a few years, like everything else they do, but they were just getting ready to drop the hammer on him. The city police and county D.A., they knew about all this. My buddy at the FBI says there was a meeting four nights ago."

"After the first day of the Rathermore trial," Black said, glancing at Sharon. "The day we gave the prosecution our witness list."

Deb North stared at her cup, started as if just realizing she held it, and took a sip of coffee. Sharon had invited Deb to the meeting under the pretext that it was her money paying for the defense, but the real reason was to get Deb's mind off her little girl down in the jail. Don't suppose we're helping her state of mind, Sharon thought. Deb had confessed to Sharon that she hadn't slept a wink in three nights. She certainly looked the part, dark circles under her eyes, her movements wooden as she produced a Virginia Slim, looked around the room, then poked the cigarette back in the pack to nestle beside its brothers and sisters.

"The witness list featuring Leslie Schlee," Sharon said.

"Right on," Gear said.

Black raised a cautioning hand. "Hold on. If you're tryin' to say the feds and the state cut some kind of deal to keep Leslie from testifyin', you're sayin' a mouthful. The feds don't usually care what happens in state cases. They browbeat county D.A.'s for information on people that the FBI's interested in, but it dudn't work the other way around."

"You're right, in ninety-nine cases out of a hundred," Gear said. "But this one's got a hook to it. There's a federal snitch, a black guy in South Dallas name of Roscoe Blade. Now, old Roscoe's a lovely dude. He's a pimp and a dope dealer, has been for years, we used him even back when I worked for the Bureau. He told us a lot of things . . . well, you name it, nothing went down in South Dallas that Roscoe didn't know about. In return for his cooperation he get anonymity, a few bucks, and, the main thing, he's got no sweat on getting busted as long as the information keeps flowing.

"Now, Roscoe," Gear said, "made himself a big mistake a couple of months ago. He shot a street dealer, blew the guy away because the guy shorted him two twenty-five-dollar papers of coke. His major mistake was that he did it at a party in front of about two dozen witnesses, and his minor mistake was that murder's a state and not a federal crime. If it had been their jurisdiction, the feds would have hushed the killing up."

Sharon's forehead tightened. She'd just been considering pouring herself a cup of coffee, but now dismissed the idea. "And it just so happens," she said, "that Stan Green is a homicide detective."

Gear pointed a finger. "You get an A, Miss Hays. The deal—and this is strictly on the q.t. from my buddy in the Bureau—the deal is that if Leslie stays off the witness stand, the county drops the murder indictment against Roscoe Blade, and the feds in turn leave Leslie's father alone. The feds consider Roscoe Blade a lot more important to their operations than another developer to prosecute. Lord knows, they've got hundreds of those guys."

"You're saying," Deborah North said with a catch in her voice, then cleared her throat and said more firmly, "You're saying that they're willing to let a murderer and dope peddler go free, not to mention a savings and loan thief, just to put my little girl in prison?"

Sharon looked at Deb. "I know. It makes me ashamed to have ever worked for the D.A.'s office."

"Christ," Black said, then sighed and said again, more softly, "Christ. Well, there's the movie deal to think about. Without Midge getting convicted there's no movie money, and I 'spect Milt Breyer sort of had that in mind when he was wheelin' and dealin' with the FBI."

"God," Sharon said.

Black leaned back and scratched his forehead. "Well, if the feds are involved, we're wastin' our time tryin' to find Leslie. Uncle Sam's got places to hide 'em we never even dreamed of." He folded his hands. "So. Where do we go from here? Without Leslie Schlee we've got no abuse evidence. Milt Breyer will laugh us out of the courtroom—if he's able to laugh after his wife gets through with him. Any suggestions?"

Gear regarded the floor. "Don't look at me. I pass."

"There might be one answer," Deborah North said.

Three gazes shifted as one to look at her.

"Susan," Deb said. "My other daughter."

Sharon felt pity like a knife through the heart. "She's not capable of that, Deb. According to Sheila Winston, she's blocked the abuse out of her mind."

"If I talked to her . . ." Deb trailed off, then said, "I think she's got guilt feelings about the way Midge was treated in that house. For her big sister she might . . ."

There was a moment of silence. Finally Sharon drew in a deep breath. "It's a long shot, Russ. But I may have an idea."

Black regarded her with ice blue eyes. As daylight had faded and the room had darkened, the older lawyer's wrinkles had disappeared as if by magic. As he must have looked twenty years ago, Sharon thought.

"I'd be surprised if you didn't have an idea, young lady," Black finally said. "What do you think I hired you for?"

42

The mansions stood along Lakeside Drive like Camelot after sunset, shapeless hulks against a blue-black sky, majestic trees lining the street like leafy sentries. To the west, where the land sloped off to form the bank of Turtle Creek, frogs jumped in shock as the tiny white Volvo chugged along, as though even the frogs recognized it as an invader for the lowlands.

Sharon applied the brakes at the entry to the circular drive ascending from the street up to the Schlee home. She sat and thought a minute, then ground the lever into reverse and backed up to park parallel to the curb. She got out, then halted in her tracks. The curb where she'd stopped was painted yellow, so she got in and backed even farther down the hill. Three nights ago you killed a guy, she thought, so why risk a parking ticket to boot?

She walked cautiously up the drive with English ivy above and below, balconies overhead like gun turrets. She'd stopped by her house to change into thigh-length baggy shorts, navy cotton shirt with a Lakewood CC emblem on the sleeve, and white Reebok sneakers. She carried nothing in her hands, no briefcase, no legal documents. She wasn't paying this visit as a lawyer.

The front of the house was dark, no lights in any of the windows. A pale BMW convertible was parked beside the front porch, and was the only auto in sight. The license plate was personalized: VSCHLEE. That would be the lady of the house, and Sharon was counting on Mrs. Curtis Schlee being at home. Her husband might take his daugh-

ter and head for the hills, but no one—not the feds, not
the district attorney, not even the Lord himself—was going to remove Virginia Schlee from her Highland Park
mansion; if Sharon had Virginia pegged correctly, she'd
figure that enduring a marriage to someone like old Curtis had earned her the right to do exactly as she pleased.
Sharon hop-skipped up on the porch, raised the brass
knocker, and let it fall. The banging noise echoed around
inside the house like a series of drumbeats.

Sharon waited. There was no response; no lights came
on, no approaching footsteps sounded from within. She
knocked again and waited a few more minutes. Still no
answer.

She went down the two steps to stand on the drive and
look the BMW over. Moonlight reflected from polished
fenders. She glanced both ways; up and down Lakeside
Drive, the mansions stood quiet as rugged mountains.
Across the road by the creek, frogs *chirruped* and crickets
whirred.

Sharon broke into a trot and circled the southern edge of
the house, then climbed the ivy-covered hillside. Water-
softened dirt gave beneath her feet. A head-high stone wall
blocked her path at the top of the rise; by standing on tiptoes
she could peer inside the grounds. There were patches of
mowed and clipped lawn back there, and stone pathways
winding here and there through the garden. There were tall
white flowers, their petals closed in the darkness like folded
bells. Beyond the garden a light glowed; in the distance water splashed. Sharon thought fleetingly of dancing class as
she high-kicked over her head and hooked her ankle on top
of the wall. She took a deep breath and then vaulted over,
hanging in midair for an instant before her feet thudded into
spongy grass. Her breathing quickened as she took the nearest pathway and headed toward the light at the back of the
grounds.

The artificial glow grew brighter as she moved through
the trees, and the splashing noises grew louder. She
passed a gazebo, more rows of tall white flowers, and two
sculpted nude maidens whose arms were about each other's waists, and whose free arms pointed longingly in opposite directions. The mansion towered on her left,
climbing ivy covering its walls. The odor of honeysuckle

wafted into her nostrils. A mosquito whined hungrily past her throat; she slapped the insect away.

She finally emerged from the grove and stood overlooking a swimming pool. It lay in a valley of mowed lawn, and was half the size of a football field. A high diving platform stood at one end like a scaffold. Lights beamed beneath shimmering surface ripples. Wavering blue-green shadows danced on treated concrete, and on lounges, tables, and chairs made of cedar planks.

A strong, supple, and graceful swimmer moved through the water. One brown arm moved upward to bend and pose as the face turned to breathe. Then the face disappeared beneath the surface as the arm descended in a powerful stroke. A fluffy beach towel was piled on one of the end pool-side tables. Sharon trotted down the grassy slope and sat in a chair. She crossed her legs, folded her arms, and waited.

Virginia Schlee reached the bank, grasped its edges, raised herself out of the water, and braced her foot to shove off on another lap. She wore no bathing cap; dripping honey blond hair clung to her shoulders. Her gaze fell on Sharon; she gasped and froze in place. As if in a trance, she let her legs slide down into the water. Then she pulled herself up and rested her elbows on the bank.

The two women watched each other.

Finally Virginia said, "Hand me that towel." It was more of a command than a request.

Sharon didn't stand, but snatched the towel and tossed it over on the bank. Virginia showed a disdainful smirk, then climbed athletically out of the water and toweled her hair. She had a gymnast's body, supple arm muscles rippling as she massaged her head with terry cloth. Sharon glanced at the slim, taut legs and wiry shoulders and, in spite of herself, felt twitches of envy.

Virginia draped the towel limply across her shoulder. Her French-cut one-piece swimsuit was alternate shades of pink and gold. "I could call the police," she said.

"I know," Sharon said. "I'm Sharon Hays, Mrs. Schlee. I was here with—"

"I know who you are. I heard your knock. Don't you know there's no one home?"

Sharon uncrossed and recrossed her legs. "I'm going to talk to you, Virginia."

"Like hell you are. What do I have to do, put a sign in front?" Virginia sat on the bank, drew her legs up Indian-style, and folded her arms around her knees. "Go away and leave me alone."

Sharon tugged the hem of her shorts. "To tell you the truth, I expected the bum's rush from one of your servants."

"Curt gave them the week off. Didn't you hear me, Miss Hays? Goodbye." Virginia stretched her legs out, crossed her ankles, and leaned back on her hands. A smooth thigh muscle tautened, then relaxed. She adjusted the elastic at her hip with a soggy pop. Sharon wondered how old Virginia was. At their first meeting Sharon had suspected cosmetic surgery, but the body was too supple and the face too smooth. Leslie was sixteen. Her mother could be under thirty-five, Sharon's own age. Curtis Schlee was over fifty.

"I want you to know," Sharon said, "what Leslie's backing out on testifying for us is going to cause."

Virginia pointed a finger. "I want you to know what your staying here is going to cause. It's going to cause a police car to arrive, and you to go to jail."

"The last time I was here," Sharon said, "you seemed to be on our side."

Virginia vacantly stroked her thigh. "Well, let's just say I changed my mind. That was then and this is now."

Sharon slowly shook her head. "We know about the FBI and your husband. The savings and loans?"

Virginia's mouth softened. One plucked eyebrow lifted. Red-nailed fingers played with the top of the bathing suit.

Sharon felt slightly guilty for bringing up the issue, but wasn't about to stop at that. "There's nothing funny about a federal investigation. I know that. And I'd be lying if I tried to tell you the feds can't take all your assets away and put your husband in jail. But the type of pressure that's being put on ... for you to succumb won't help Leslie a bit."

Virginia petulantly ran her fingers through hair damp with chlorinated water. "What would you know about Leslie?"

Sharon steadied her gaze. "I know what any mother would know. Leslie needs to face what happened."

Virginia looked away again. "I have my daughter's well-being in mind, thank you."

Sharon almost repressed the surge of anger which coursed through her, but not quite. "Her well-being? Or yours?"

Virginia's mouth slackened. To the faint choral accompaniment of lapping water, she said, "Why, one goes with the other."

Sharon's jaws clenched. "I'd like to have the time to prove to you that the two are millions of miles apart, but I don't."

"Then why don't you leave?"

"Dammit. Dammit to hell," Sharon said. "Why are there people who think that money's the answer to everything?"

Virginia's head swiveled until she was looking at Sharon head-on. "Well, isn't it?" she said.

Sharon's jaw dropped. She didn't say anything.

"Well, isn't it?" Virginia said again.

Sharon lowered her eyes. "If that's what you think, then maybe I *am* wasting both of our times."

Virginia's gaze roamed, first falling on the pool, then on the huge house in the background, the second-floor landing with its white molded stone railing. "Do you have any inkling of how hard I've worked for all this, Miss Hays?"

Sharon looked up. Virginia had said, "How hard *I've* worked," as if Curtis Schlee hadn't lifted a finger. "I suppose you have made a few sacrifices," Sharon said. "But I'd be careful that I wasn't sacrificing my child."

"That's the most off-the-wall thing I've ever heard. Without all this Leslie would have nothing."

"Unless," Sharon said steadily, "she still had your love."

"She does have that, and a whole lot more," Virginia said. Her eyes relaxed in a faraway look. "I was seventeen when I met Curt, and working as a cocktail waitress down on Greenville Avenue. You were supposed to be eighteen to serve liquor at the time, and I had to come up with phony ID to get the job. Do you have any idea what it's like to be seventeen and on your own, with no one to help you?"

"Well, not at seventeen," Sharon said. "But I did wait

tables to get through law school, and I had a baby to support at the time." She wanted to add that she hadn't taken some rich older guy up on his proposition, either, but she stopped herself.

"If you know what's happening with the FBI," Virginia said, "then you'll know what we'd be risking if Leslie testified for you. Everything we have, including this house, is tied up with those loans."

"I agree that you could lose every dime, but you might not lose your daughter, Virginia. The way you're going about it, you can forget Leslie."

Virginia looked down at her lap. A drop of water fell from the tip of her nose onto a bare leg.

Sharon flipped her bangs away from her forehead with the back of her hand. "Let me tell you a story about a mother I know. Midge Rathermore's. She gave up her children for money, some time ago. Maybe you should ask her if it was worth it. She's dying to have her little girls back, but one's in a crazy house and the other one's going to prison. At least she is unless I can talk some sense into you."

Virginia firmed up her mouth. "What do you mean, talk some sense into me? My daughter's not going to prison, remember? And neither is my husband, and no one is going to touch our assets unless I do what you're suggesting."

Sharon felt reason slipping away, mentally tried to relax but couldn't. "Your *assets*? Your child is a bit more than an asset, Virginia. My daughter and I don't have very much, but we've damn sure got each other. What's Leslie got as it is? A mother who looks like an Olympic athlete and a father who is in with the politicians, both of whom, when Leslie wants something, throw some money at their child and tell her not to bother them? Oh, yes, I forgot. Leslie had some real nice playmates. The Rathermores."

Virginia Schlee straightened her posture. "Don't you dare talk to me that way. The Rathermore thing was a mistake that won't happen again."

"Oh?" Sharon said. "How can you be sure of that? God, Virginia, one of Leslie's classmates had a friend whose father gave Leslie dope and took her to bed. So what are you going to do? Buy her more friends?"

Virginia extended a finger toward the garden. "You get out of here the same way you came."

"So now," Sharon said, "Leslie's own father's afraid of going to jail, which he likely deserves, and Leslie's mother's afraid she might lose her big house and servants and whatnot. So the solution is to tell Leslie to hide. If she has to leave one fancy private school behind, no problem, just whip out the old checkbook and send her off to another."

Through her anger Sharon watched Virginia Schlee, searched for some sign that she was getting through to the woman. Virginia's posture slumped some, but her expression was stone. Sharon caught her breath and went on.

"Well, I'll tell you something, Virginia. If you don't make Leslie face facts and tell what happened to her at the Rathermores', you're going to lose her. If you haven't already. You've got a sixteen-year-old addict on your hands as it is, and if you don't change something you might wake up and find a couple of kids in *your* bedroom with a gun or tire tool. I won't lie to you and say the feds are bluffing, because if Leslie does testify they'll very likely send your husband to jail. But if it saves Leslie, it'll be worth it to both of you."

Virginia opened her mouth in shock. "My God, how can you . . . *Worth* it to us? You . . . just don't understand. I'm truly sorry about Midge Rathermore, but it's a tough world. You have to protect yourself." She lowered her gaze. "Goodbye, Miss Hays."

Sharon stood, her body trembling. "All right, it's your choice. I've got my little girl. If you don't want to try to save yours, it's your business. You can catch the rest of the trial on TV or in the newspapers. If Midge goes to prison, I hope you think all . . ." She looked toward the house, gesturing. "I hope you think all *this* makes up for that. To Leslie *and* to Midge."

She walked away without another word, up the grassy slope with blue-green shadows dancing on all sides. Just before she entered the tree grove, she paused and turned. Virginia Schlee hadn't moved, her shoulders hunched over her knees as she sat on the concrete, her body perfect, her gaze steadily on her own sun-browned feet. Sharon felt no pity for the woman. She resumed her brisk pace, wanting out of there, wanting familiar surroundings.

On her way to climb the wall, she passed the sculpted maidens. They seemed lost and very lonely.

Sharon drove the Volvo out of the rich man's neighborhood, headed for East Dallas at nearly breakneck speed. Once inside her own little house, she took a picture of Melanie down from the mantel. The photo was two years old: Melanie, leggy as a colt, smiling on tiptoes in her pink ballet costume. Sharon carried the picture into her bedroom, set it on the dresser, and stared at the likeness of her daughter for a long, long time before she finally went to bed.

43

Sharon entered the Crowley Courts Building in the depths of despair the following morning, head down, shoulders sagging. She dreaded giving Russell Black the news that she'd failed miserably with Virginia Schlee, and even more she dreaded facing Deborah North. She didn't know how she was going to look at Midge. The pitiful teenager wouldn't understand what was happening to her. Not yet, anyway. Morosely Sharon mounted the escalator, grasped the handrail, and rode upward with her satchel resting against her hip.

She'd slept barely a wink, staring into the darkness of her bedroom and racking her brain. Regardless of the picture of Linda Rathermore painted for the jury's benefit, without evidence that Midge and Susan had been abused, Midge's defense was dead. As she reached the head of the escalator and crossed the lobby toward the elevators, Sharon's feeling of defeat had already progressed to the point that she was mentally rehearsing arguments in mitigation of Midge's punishment.

As Sharon pressed the Up button and stood back to wait, assistant district attorney Edward Teeter passed her line of vision. Teeter was engaged in conversation with a uniformed sheriff's deputy, and he didn't look in Sharon's direction as he followed the officer onto the escalator headed down.

So intent had Sharon been on the Rathermore case, Bradford Brie had been shoved into the far reaches of her mind. But the sight of the persecutor brought Brie's image back into sharp focus, his ugly sneer as he rose from the couch and rushed toward her. As she entered the elevator car, her body shook with a violent tremor of fear.

"So I'm afraid that's it, folks," Sharon said. "Leslie's not going to be available." She sat on a pew in the spectator section with Deborah North on her left and Anthony Gear on her other side. Russell Black was one row forward, directly in front of Sharon. He was turned around with his arm draped over the seat back. It was a half hour before court was to convene, and the bailiffs hadn't admitted any spectators yet. Up beyond the rail at the state table, Kathleen Fraterno and Milt Breyer went over some documents as Stan Green watched intently over the prosecutors' shoulders. At the sight of the trio Sharon's lip curled.

Deb North wore pressed green slacks and a tan blouse. "Tonight we can visit Susan. Maybe . . ."

"I think we should," Sharon said. "But don't get your hopes up. Sheila says that Susan's blocked out everything having to do with the abuse, and this is one time I wish Sheila wasn't such a crackerjack psychologist. She's rarely wrong, Deb."

"I'm not for throwin' in the towel," Black said, "until we've tried everything. Mr. Gear, I still want you to take a shot at locatin' Leslie. We can subpoena her if we have to."

"And have her suddenly remember zero when she does testify?" Sharon said.

"I didn't say it was much," Black said, "but it's all we got. Two days, I figure, for the state to put on the Leonard kid and whoever else they're goin' to. Our expert witness and the guy from the security company can take up another day. I think you got three days to come up with her, Mr. Gear."

Gear shrugged, his expression hopeless. "Sure, I'll do what I can."

He left the courtroom double-time, and the two defense lawyers left Deborah North seated alone and proceeded down the aisle and through the gate. Sharon had made it halfway from the gate to the defense side when a firm hand wrapped around her forearm. She turned with inquisitive raised eyebrows.

Stan Green's chin was on a level with her nose. The

detective wore an iridescent gray suit which was far too flashy for the courtroom. On him, Sharon thought, any suit would look cheap to me.

"Look," Green said, "when this is over, you think we could—"

Sharon's eyes flashed sudden fire. "Hi, Stan. You know someone named Roscoe Blade?"

"Do I . . . ?" The corners of his mouth twitched.

"How about someone from the FBI who might be interested in Leslie Schlee's father, Stan? You know somebody like that?"

Green folded his hands in front and smirked his best policeman's smirk.

Sharon rose on the balls of her feet and got in the detective's face. She was livid. "Fuck you, Stan. You hear me? If you ever even speak to me again, I'll knock your teeth out." She stepped back and blinked. "You can call my bluff if you want to, you big, strong man," she said.

As the bailiff called the courtroom to attention for Judge Griffin's ascension to her throne, Sharon stood alongside Midge Rathermore with her emotions firmly tied in knots. She'd done her best to smile encouragement as Midge's keeper had led the puffy teenager into the courtroom, but Sharon was afraid her smile hadn't showed much conviction. Judge Griffin instructed all present to sit. Sharon sank into her chair and examined her notes, Midge's breathing loud in her ear.

We've got about three days, Sharon thought, to try to get Leslie Schlee into court. In the meantime, she told herself, you're not going to help anything by going around in a trance. *Concentrate,* Sharon. Christopher Leonard's upcoming testimony had to be uppermost in her mind, and she had to do anything she could to help Russell Black turn the kid into mush during cross-examination. She steeled herself to take down everything the Leonard boy had to say, and to find every single hole in his testimony that she could.

And listened to the voice inside her say, Sure, kid. Just forget that your star witness has disappeared, and that the poor child on your right is going to jail no matter what you do.

She is not! Sharon said under her breath. *I won't let her.*

Oh yeah, the voice told her, and try not to think about the guy you murdered the other night. Just put it out of your mind.

And Sharon whispered fiercely, *"Shut up!"* Black turned to look at her with his mouth agape. She said sheepishly, "Nothing. Just talking to myself."

Judge Griffin folded her hands and said, "The state will call its next witness."

Sharon bent fiercely over her legal pad, pen clutched tightly.

Kathleen Fraterno stood and faced the bench. "Your Honor," she said firmly, "the state rests."

And Sharon thought, Huh?

Judge Griffin's eyebrows lifted. "Am I hearing you correctly, Miss Fraterno?"

"You are, Your Honor," Fraterno said. "The state rests. We have no more witnesses to call."

As Fraterno resumed her seat and Milt Breyer watched the defense table with an obvious smirk on his face, Russell Black expelled air through his nose. Sharon turned and gave Deborah North a helpless shrug. Deb looked terrified. Sharon didn't blame her.

They know, Sharon thought, alternating her gaze between Kathleen Fraterno and Milt Breyer. As long as we don't have Leslie Schlee to testify, they simply don't need any more evidence. They might have to go through the motions of indicting Linda Rathermore at a later date, but with no evidence of abuse, Midge would be convicted.

Russ Black now stood. "Your Honor, this was sort of unexpected. We need some time to get our folks together."

"Your witnesses," Judge Griffin said.

"Yes, ma'am."

"Assuming your case is already prepared," Judge Griffin said, "that should take only a few phone calls." She checked her watch. "I'll give you until after lunch, Counsel."

Black opened his mouth as if to say that until after lunch wasn't nearly long enough, then closed his mouth and finally said, "Okay, Judge." Arguing, Sharon understood, would be pointless. Anthony Gear's three days to find Leslie Schlee had dwindled in seconds to a great deal less time than that. Something less than twenty-four hours, Sharon thought.

44

Sharon thought that Sheila Winston, pretty features attentive, wearing a brown business dress along with light tan flats, had made about as good a witness as the defense could hope for. As she neared the end of Sheila's direct examination, the question of race entered Sharon's mind for the first time. Only three of the jurors were black: a schoolteacher, a computer-equipment salesman, and an airplane mechanic. Gregory Mathewson, the state's hired gun, was white. Sharon herself seldom noticed Sheila's race anymore, but this was Dallas County, Texas. There was an infamous story which had been repeated around the courthouse for years. The story concerned Joe Brown, the judge who thirty years earlier had presided over the Jack Ruby trial, and who'd been dead himself for going on twenty years. It was said that Judge Brown used to delight in giving wet-eared, fresh-out-of-moot-court attorneys the jurist's sagest advice. "Son, you show me a nigger," the old judge used to say, "an' I'll show you a sumbitch that's fixin' to steal somethin'." The unwritten Joe Brown law had ruled Dallas County for years, and was still in force even though no one would own up to it. So as Sheila waited for the next question, Sharon glanced toward the jury box. She was pleased to note that Sheila seemed to have the jurors wrapped around her little finger, especially the men. That Sheila was beautiful didn't hurt her credibility one iota.

As Sharon pretended to study her notes, she glanced at her watch. She and Sheila had done their jobs not only in presenting the psychologist's testimony as to Midge's mental capacities, but in stringing Sheila's stint on the stand into sort of a filibuster as well. It was almost five. Sharon could now bring the direct examination to a close, give Fraterno time for a brief cross, and go home knowing she'd bought Anthony Gear one more day. Not that it's going to be enough, she thought with a lump in her throat.

Sharon pushed her notes aside and prepared to sum up. "So, Dr. Winston, in your professional opinion, do Midge Rathermore and her sister, Susan, exhibit the characteristics of sexually abused children?"

"Most definitely," Sheila said. Her Phi Beta Kappa key shone on her breast pocket. In her warm-up testimony her educational and experience credentials had exceeded Gregory Mathewson's a hundred to one.

"And Dr. Winston," Sharon said, "once more in your professional opinion, what would Midge's reaction to her father be?"

"She was deathly afraid of him. Neither Midge nor her sister would resist him because they were terrified."

Sharon folded her hands. "Physically terrified?"

"Yes," Sheila said.

"And also in your professional opinion, given your extensive examination of Midge Rathermore, under what circumstances would Midge kill?"

"Only to protect herself and her sister. Or if she *believed* she was protecting herself and Susan from further abuse."

"In self-defense?" Sharon said.

"Yes." Sheila's answer was calm.

"And if she was going to kill, say, her father," Sharon said, "what method would she use?"

"She'd be too afraid to confront her father. She'd either sneak up on him from behind, or possibly try to have someone do it for her."

Sharon coughed daintily into her cupped hand, then said, "And she wouldn't do it for profit? To, say, gain her inheritance?"

Sheila looked directly at the jury box. "Midge has dull-normal intelligence. Given her age as well, money means nothing to her."

"And is that your professional opinion, Doctor?"

"It is," Sheila said.

Sheila, if your new boyfriend doesn't kiss you, I might, Sharon thought. "Pass the witness," she said. In addition to watching the jury, she had been observing Kathleen Fraterno's reaction out of the corner of her eye. Kathleen hadn't taken a single note, really offbeat behavior for a prosecutor during expert-witness testimony.

Fraterno sat up straight in her chair. "Dr. Winston," she said, "where do you live?"

Sheila recited her East Dallas address.

"And where," Fraterno said, pointing, "does Miss Hays, the defense attorney, reside?"

"I don't know her exact address."

Fraterno uncrossed and recrossed her legs. "Well, approximately."

"It's right down the street from me, if that's what you're asking." Sheila appeared slightly miffed. Bad show, Sheila, Sharon thought, don't blow your cool.

"Right down the street from you," Fraterno said. "Dr. Winston, is your first name Sheila?"

"I've already testified that it is."

"True. You have. Doesn't Miss Hays, the defense attorney, normally call you by your first name?"

Sheila permitted herself an irritated blink. "That's right."

"Dr. Winston," Fraterno said, "do you have a daughter?"

"I do," Sheila said. Sharon tried to make eye contact with Sheila, tried to give Sheila a cool-it look, but Sheila's gaze was testily on Kathleen Fraterno.

"Please tell the jury," Fraterno said, "how does your daughter get to school?"

Sheila now glanced at Sharon. I can't help you here, old pal, Sharon thought, Fraterno's question is right in line. Sheila lifted, then dropped her shoulders. "Sharon takes them in the morning. I pick them up."

"Sharon?" Fraterno said. "That's the defense attorney, Miss Hays?"

"It is."

Fraterno assumed a skeptical tone. "You and the defense attorney car-pool?"

"Yes, we do."

"Well, in view of that," Fraterno said, "is it fair to say

that you and Sharon Hays are more than passing acquaintances?"

"You could say that."

"In fact," Fraterno said, "you are best friends, aren't you?"

"I suppose," Sheila said.

Fraterno pretended to mull over Sheila's answer, then shot a knowing glance in the direction of the jury box. "Pass the witness," she said.

Sharon chewed her lower lip. To hell with it, she thought, I have to. She leaned forward. "Your Honor, I have redirect."

Judge Griffin lifted her eyebrows. It was the first redirect of the trial. "Proceed, Counsel," she finally said.

"Sheila," Sharon said, then grinned like an imp and said, "Now that we're exposed, you can call me Sharon, okay?" the jury twittered. Surprisingly, Fraterno didn't object. Griffin gave Sharon a sharp look but kept quiet. "Sheila," Sharon said, "have you ever testified in a criminal trial before?"

"No, I haven't."

"With your credentials, no one has ever asked you to appear as an expert witness in the past?"

"I didn't say that," Sheila said proudly. "I get calls all the time."

"Then why haven't you agreed to appear before?" Sharon said.

"I have an aversion to being an expert witness for a fee. The fee compromises one's opinion." She spoke modestly but with confidence. A couple of the jurors exchanged surprised glances, as if it was news to them that expert witnesses received money for their testimony to begin with.

"And are you receiving a fee for testifying in this case?" Sharon said.

"Certainly not."

"Unlike," Sharon said pointedly, "Dr. Mathewson, who testified for the prosecution?"

"Objection." Fraterno practically came out of her chair.

"Sustained," Judge Griffin said.

"Pass the—" Sharon said, then did a double-take and said, "Oh. One final question."

Sheila sat attentively.

"Sheila," Sharon said, "inasmuch as we're friends, have I ever used your professional services?"

Sheila brightened. "Once."

"And what did that occasion have to do with?"

"You were concerned about your daughter, Melanie. She was born out ..." Sheila paused and looked concerned.

"Go ahead," Sharon said. "We want to be open here."

Sheila cleared her throat. "Your daughter was born out of wedlock. You were worried about her reaction to that, and what you should do about her questions pertaining to her father."

A couple of the female jurors appeared stunned. One male juror looked at Sharon and grinned. Sort of a hungry grin, she thought, like, Come wid me to ze casbah.

"Sheila," Sharon said, "what was your advice to me?"

"I told you she should see her father, and the sooner the better. I said you should make every effort to contact him."

"Exactly the way I remember it," Sharon said. Fraterno sat up as if to object, then relaxed. "Did I take your advice, Sheila?" Sharon said.

"You certainly didn't," Sheila said. "In fact, you quit speaking to me for a week."

"And why didn't I take your advice?"

Sheila frowned. "You want my opinion, or the reason you gave me?"

Sharon smiled and made a grand gesture. "You're the expert witness, Doctor. Your opinion, by all means."

"Well, all right," Sheila said. "I think you were rationalizing because you didn't want to have anything to do with the guy. What you *said* was that I wasn't giving an unbiased opinion because I was too close to the subject. Shssh." She rolled her eyes.

"And, Sheila, if you recall," Sharon said, "what did I tell you about using your services in the future?"

Sheila got it. She grinned. "You said that the only way you'd ever use me again," Sheila said, "was on a case where I wasn't personally involved."

"Where your opinion wouldn't be prejudiced?"

"That's right, as I remember it," Sheila said.

Sharon restrained a giggle. "Pass the witness," she said.

* * *

All elation Sharon had felt over Sheila's testimony flowed out of her, leaving in its wake a soggy lump of despair as she sat outside in the garden at Havenrest Sanitarium and listened to Sheila's conversation with Susan Rathermore. Sheila, bent forward from the waist in a listening attitude, occupied one end of a bench with Deborah North on the opposite end and Susan, pretty in a baby blue school dress, in between the two women. Sharon and Russell Black sat about ten feet away from the trio and exchanged worried looks. The session wasn't going well. It was after eight o'clock, the hot summertime sun dipping below the treetops as dusk settled.

"Susan, did your daddy spend a lot of time with you?" Sheila said.

Susan twisted her hands in her lap. "Oh, yes. He took me to a lot of places and bought me things."

Deb North caught Sharon's eye and imperceptibly shook her head. According to Deb, William Rathermore had virtually ignored both Midge and Susan up until the divorce.

"You mean, when you were little?" Sheila said.

"Yes, ma'am. I remember we went to Six Flags and rode all the rides."

"And how did you feel about that?"

"I loved it. Loved my daddy." Susan closed her eyes and smiled like a four-year-old. Her voice went up a decibel.

"And when you were older?" Sheila said.

The grin dissolved into an expression of hopeless confusion. "When I was . . . ?"

Sheila threw Sharon an exasperated glance, then said to Susan, "Let's say, when you were twelve. How did your daddy treat you then?"

Susan's eyes narrowed and her mouth drew up in a pout. "My daddy's gone."

"Gone where, Susan?"

The pout became at once a cunning grin. "Just away. He went away."

Sheila sighed in frustration. "Susan, what is the last thing you remember about your father?"

Susan looked far away, down the path in the direction of the highway. She raised her arm and pointed. "Can we go down there? Sometimes just at sunset you can see robins. Oh, can we?"

Sharon sniffled, lifted her hand, and brushed away tears.

"To try to have Susan testify," Sheila said, "would be a total disaster. First of all, she'd tell you nothing about the abuse. You saw her reaction. Her mental state right now is such that I don't know if she'd ever recover from the trauma of facing all those people."

The four now stood on Havenrest's front porch, in between two majestic white pillars. It was dark; behind them lights shone through the lobby windows, and in the parking lot a spotlight beamed down to illuminate the roofs of autos. Just moments earlier, Susan had gone in for the night, had stopped in the foyer and desperately hugged her mom.

"And what about using Midge?" Sharon said. She was certain the question was hopeless, but . . .

"I think that would be even worse for you." Sheila fiddled with the strap on her shoulder bag. "First of all, Midge actually believes she had her father killed. You're the lawyer, but I don't think you're going to get her to say anything different on the stand. Midge has come a long way emotionally, but she still thinks that hiring those kids to commit murder makes her somehow more acceptable in the eyes of her peers. As for the abuse . . . Well, you told me what she said the first time you talked to her, that her father liked . . . you know. Midge simply won't be of much help in that regard. She'll refuse to relate specific instances."

Russell Black cleared his throat and shuffled his feet. "Any word from our detective?"

"He left a message," Sharon said. "Says he's running into a series of stone walls. Even his buddy from the FBI won't talk to him about Leslie Schlee's whereabouts." She folded her arms and looked down. "I'm afraid we're out of luck there."

"Damn," Deborah North said suddenly. "Damn, damn, *damn* you lawyers and all your bullshit. We're talking about my child."

Sheila hugged herself. Sharon and Black looked in silence at Deb for a moment, then Sharon said, "We're doing what we can."

"You've already brought out that that ... *woman* was going to bed with teenage boys. Why can't you ... ?"

"I know this is hard for you to understand, Deb," Sharon said. "Criminy, the law is hard enough for lawyers to understand at times. But nothing we've brought out lets Midge off the hook. She did promise to share her inheritance with those kids if they'd kill her father, and regardless of what happened unbeknownst to her afterward, that makes her guilty of solicitation of capital murder. Our only defense is that she did it out of fear for her own and her sister's safety.

"But what we've done by raising the abuse issue," Sharon said, "is shift the burden of proof. It's up to the state to show that Midge solicited those other kids for purposes of committing murder, and they've presented evidence to that effect. It's now up to us to prove the abuse. If we don't, the judge won't even instruct the jury that if they believe the kids were abused, they have to acquit." She moved in close and put her arm around Deb's shoulders. "I wouldn't blame you for hating us right now, Deb. Just please believe we're doing everything we can."

Deb started to say something, but her words dissolved into a sob. Sharon grimaced hopelessly, first at Sheila, then at Black.

Black cleared his throat. "Seems like our Mr. Gear finding Leslie is about our last straw."

"Looks that way to me," Sharon said.

45

Exhausted from yet another sleepless night, Sharon sat morosely beside Midge Rathermore the following morning and waited for Russell Black to conduct another filibuster. They'd agreed before the trial had convened to give Anthony Gear as much time as possible. Try as she might, Sharon couldn't shake the feeling that all the time in the world wouldn't help.

Black stood at the defense table wearing a slightly rumpled gray pinstripe, cleared his throat, and said loudly, "The defense calls Steven Gallagher."

Through the dreary fog in her head, Sharon got a small lift from the apprehensive rustling in the courtroom and the quick, hushed confab between Kathleen Fraterno and Milton Breyer. Steven Gallagher's name had never appeared in the newspapers; when Gallagher had shown up on the defense's witness list, with no address, Andy Wade of the *News* had asked both Black and Sharon umpteen times who Gallagher was, but they'd stonewalled the reporter. Sharon had suspected that the prosecution would have a bitch of a time getting a line on the mystery witness, and she'd been right. Fraterno's and Breyer's expressions told her that they hadn't a clue. Sharon turned just as Gallagher came in from the corridor and headed down the aisle. Her gaze fell instantly on Rayford Sly, the second-banana movie guy. Sly was seated near the center of the second row from the back, and his eyes were wide with curiosity. Sharon wondered briefly whether Gallagher could make it to the witness stand before Sly offered him a movie deal. Surely not right in the middle of the trial, she thought. She'd bet a month's pay, however, that as soon as the session was over, Sly would wait in the corridor with pen and business card ready.

The packed house found out about Steven Gallagher in a hurry. He was around fifty, with a few sparse hairs sprouting from the top of his head, and the cords in his neck sagged like those of someone in his seventies. Gallagher wore a dark blue suit and sported a middle-aged potbelly. He raised his hand for swearing in, assumed his seat in the witness chair, and gave his full name with an address in Kansas City. Kansas, not Missouri, he emphasized.

"Tell us if you will," Black said, "what it is you do for a livin'."

"President," Gallagher said. "Securico Companies." The man was a study in contrasts. While his sagging throat made him appear much older than he was, the strong and forceful voice was that of a man in his thirties.

"That's a ..." Black said. "That's a security company, idn't it?"

Fraterno straightened in her chair. Milt Breyer's gaze was on the back wall, as if he wasn't listening. Wifey on his mind, Sharon thought.

"Yes, it is," Gallagher said.

"Burglar alarms?"

"The best." Gallagher practically strutted in the sitting position.

"I'm sure they are," Black said, "but I'm not in the market right now." Titters rippled through the audience. When they had subsided, Black said, "Mr. Gallagher, did y'all install a burglar alarm at 3517 Lakeside Drive, here in Dallas, out in Highland Park?" There was no phony referring to notes now; Black was honing in, all humor gone from his tone.

"That's right," the witness said.

"Do you people ... ? If there's an alarm turned in to the police under your system, are your people notified?"

Gallagher chuckled. "We're notified before the police. The alarm goes into us, over the phone lines, and we forward it electronically to the authorities."

Sharon watched Fraterno. Stan Green would have told

Kathleen about the pointed questions concerning the
alarm system during the defense's crime-scene examination, and she would first have given the cops instructions
against letting the cat out of the bag, then would have sat
and wondered why the defense hadn't subpoenaed any
police records. Now she knew why, but it was too late for
her to do anything about it. She twisted nervously in her
chair.

"Okay," Black said. "Do your records show that there
was a break-in at the Rathermore house on December 21
of last year?"

"There was an alarm turned in," Gallagher said. "Our
records don't reflect whether or not it was an actual
break-in. You'd have to go to the police for—"

"Right," Black said. "Uh, that was about a week after
school let out for Christmas, wadn't it?"

Gallagher seemed puzzled. "I live in Kansas City, sir.
I don't have any idea when Texans break for Christmas."

Sharon repressed a grin. Vintage Russell Black, honing
the jury in on the date when the killers had supposedly
gotten the code from Midge, but at the same time seeming to have asked a bumbling question.

Grinning apologetically, Black now gave the throng another tad of humor. "Or San Jacinto day, either, I guess,"
then waited like a pro for the subsequent laughter to die
down and said, "After an alarm goes in, Mr. Gallagher,
what's your policy then?"

"You mean, in regard to the security system?"

"Yes, sir. The alarm."

Gallagher cleared his throat. "We tell the customer
we're changing their security code."

"Now that's," Black said, looking confused, "that's the
numbers you punch into the panel to shut the thing on
and off, idn't it?"

"Right," Gallagher said.

"You *tell* the customer?" Black said. "Or you ask 'em."

"Well," Gallagher said, "the system comes with certain
warranties. If they refuse to change the code it voids the
warranty."

"Okay," Black said. "Do your records show that you
changed the code at 3517 Lakeside Drive after the December 21 break-in? Excuse me, you already said you

don't know if there was a break-in or not. After the *alarm* was turned in on that date."

"Alarm, yes," Gallagher said. "And yes, we did."

"Now, Mr. Gallagher," Black said, scratching his nose, "how do you go about changin' the code?"

"We make the adjustments in our office, then forthwith deliver the new code to the customer."

"Forthwith," Black said. "You mail it to 'em?"

"Oh, no," Gallagher said. "We're security professionals."

"Glad to hear it, but I ain't buyin'," Black said, then waited for his laughs, got them, and then said, "Okay, forthwith, how do you deliver the new code?"

"In person. By our own messenger. The customer signs for the new code."

"The customer. That mean just anybody that's home? Like this little girl over here?" Black indicated Midge, who exhibited a shy smile.

"No. The recipient must show identification. *Picture* ID," Gallagher said.

"Okay," Black said. He raised his voice. "Tell the jury, please, sir. Who signed for this new code?"

"Our records state," Gallagher said. "Mrs. Linda Rathermore."

"Nobody else?"

Gallagher produced a small white card form his breast pocket and looked at it. "We compare the signature, sir. No mistakes. That's why we've been in business these past thirty years."

Silence. Testimony sinking in, jurors looking at one another, getting the point. "Come to think about it," Black finally said, "maybe we should talk. My security folks don't go to all that much trouble." He grinned. "No further questions, Judge."

Sharon felt a surge of elation and turned in her seat to give Deborah North a knowing wink. She froze. Anthony Gear stood just inside the back courtroom door, his expression grim. He zeroed in on Sharon, shook his head, and spread his hands. "I can't find her," he mouthed silently.

She bent over the table, picked up the yellow pencil which lay on her legal pad, and broke the pencil in two.

Fraterno waived the opportunity to cross-examine Steven Gallagher, which brought some puzzled looks to jurors' faces and a sinking feeling in the pit of Sharon's stomach. Kathleen knew exactly what she was doing. She wasn't likely to do much in the way of tearing the security man's story down, but that wasn't the main reason she didn't have any questions. The glances which she exchanged with Milt Breyer spoke volumes. They knew of the race to locate Leslie Schlee, and wanted the trial over with.

Russell Black fiddled with his notes as he said to Sharon out of the side of his mouth, "Want to have another go at the lady?"

"You notice Mr. Gear back there?" Sharon said.

"I saw him," Black said. "We need Linda back on no matter what. We can do enough damage with her so's the jury might not give Midge much of a sentence even if they convict her."

Sharon shrugged. "Bring her on, then."

Black nodded and stood. "Defense recalls Linda Rathermore." His heavy basso carried to the back and shocked the spectator section into dead silence.

Fraterno popped up at the defense table. "Your Honor, may we approach?"

Griffin's plucked eyebrows lifted in surprise. "Come ahead."

"Linda's your witness, Sharon," Black whispered. "You better get in on this."

Sharon gave Midge's arm an affectionate squeeze, pushed her chair back, got up, and followed the older lawyer to stand alongside Kathleen Fraterno before the judge. Sharon noted that there were dark circles under Kathleen's eyes.

Fraterno folded her arms and placed one foot slightly before the other. "Judge, Linda Rathermore's disappeared. We've had people looking for her for two days."

Sharon started, swiveled her head to study Fraterno. She wasn't lying. So old Linda had seen the way the trial was going and headed for the hills. Sharon softly closed her eyes. Christ, she thought.

Black expelled air through his nose. "Well, just how hard have these people been lookin'?"

Fraterno stared helplessly at the bench and didn't answer.

The corners of Sandy Griffin's mouth turned downward. "I don't understand. I instructed the witness to be available."

"So did we, Judge," Fraterno said. "She's simply gone. Her luggage is gone, a bunch of her clothes—"

"Judge, I'm wonderin'," Black said, "how tough she'd be to find if it was the state wantin' to talk to her."

"I think Mr. Black is out of line with that remark," Fraterno said, squaring her shoulders.

"I think the state is out of line not keepin' track of their witness," Black said.

"Be that as it may," the judge said, "what would you have me do? The court can't make Mrs. Rathermore appear out of a bottle."

"Well, I'm askin' for a recess," Black said, "until the witness can be located."

Fraterno drew herself up to her full height. "We'd oppose that, Your Honor. It would cause unnecessary delay."

Black glared at Fraterno in a manner that shocked Sharon to the balls of her feet. She'd never seen her boss go toe to toe with a female before. "Unnecessary, hell," he said. He looked at the judge. "They've let this witness slip away from them, and we're entitled to more time."

"I'll remind the court," Fraterno said, "that the witness is no longer ours. I don't say we've done the best job of keeping up with Mrs. Rathermore, Judge, but it was the defense who wanted to recall her. Not us. Keeping up with a recall witness is the recaller's responsibility."

Griffin looked at her watch, used a thumb and forefinger to wind the stem. One corner of her mouth tugged to one side as she canted her head. "I'm afraid she's got you there, Mr. Black. Why didn't the defense have someone watching her?"

For once Black was stumped. He lowered his head. "Our investigator's been busy elsewhere."

Griffin said, almost tenderly, "I'm afraid that's not the court's problem, Mr. Black. The trial has to go on."

Black looked up at the ceiling. He bent sideways and whispered to Sharon, "Any ideas?"

Abject despair caused her to look toward the defense

table. Midge was turned around, once more shooting loving glances at her mom. Sharon turned back to the older lawyer. "See if we can get enough time to have a go at Midge."

"Christ, Sharon," Black said, "your psychologist has already told you . . ."

Sharon steadied her gaze. "I know that, boss. We've got to try."

Black sighed. "Yeah, I guess we do." He looked at the judge. "Judge Griffin, can we have fifteen minutes to talk to our client?"

"I can grant that," Griffin said, then raised a warning finger. "But no longer than a quarter hour, Mr. Black, under any circumstances."

"We understand, Judge," Black said dejectedly.

As Griffin advised the jury of the delay, the lawyers headed for their respective tables. Halfway to her seat, Sharon did a sudden column-right and headed directly for the prosecution side. Black followed, gripped her arm, and said, "Where you goin'?" Sharon shook the hand off and continued grimly on her way.

Fraterno and Milt Breyer were standing near the rail, talking in whispers. Sharon confronted the pair and said, "Kathleen, you've got to come off of this."

Fraterno arched an eyebrow. "What's 'this'?"

"You know what I'm talking about," Sharon said. "That woman arranged the whole thing with those kids and you know it. Let Midge up, Kathleen. Drop the charges."

Milt Breyer stepped between the women. He wore his best man-for-the-people charcoal suit, spotless white shirt, and pale blue tie. His hair was sprayed as if sculpted in place. "You're just a bit out of school talking to us like that, Miss Hays. Have you lost your mind?"

Sharon was suddenly so angry that her buttocks twitched. Her eyes flashed fire. "You shut up, Milt, or I'll kick your balls right here and now." She backed up a half step, like a field goal kicker preparing to launch one.

"Jesus, I—" Breyer said, then looked at Sharon closely. His complexion paled. "You're asking for trouble if you do something like that," he said. Sharon thought for an instant that the prosecutor was going to defensively cover his crotch, but he merely folded his hands in front and stepped out of the line of fire.

"Keep out of this, then," Sharon said, then faced Fraterno. "This is between you and me, Kathleen. It has nothing to do with legal bullshit, movie deals, or anything else in this case that's gotten in the way of justice. Midge didn't do this, Kathleen. This poor, overweight, abused little girl didn't any more cause Rathermore's death than you did. Now, let her go."

Fraterno's features softened for just an instant, and a tear formed in one corner of her eye. Then she firmed up her mouth. "No go, Sharon. You having problems or something?"

Sharon's fists clenched at her sides. "It's on your conscience, dear," she said, "and I wouldn't trade places with you for all the tea in China." Without another word she spun on her heel and stalked away. She'd been within an inch of attacking Kathleen Fraterno right there and doing her best to pound the prosecutor into a pulp. The only thing that had stopped her was a fleeting image of Midge superimposed over a picture of Melanie in her ballet costume, and a glimpse over Kathleen's shoulder at Rayford Sly, grinning at her from the spectator section. Would that have been a great scene in the picture or what? Sharon thought.

Midge was handcuffed to a chair in the conference room adjacent to the holding cell, her round shoulders slumped, eyeing her lawyers with moist but uncaring eyes. "I hated Daddy," she said in a monotone. Loose flesh sagged beneath her chin.

"Baby," Sharon said. "Oh, God, baby, listen to me. We know how you felt about him, and no one's going to blame you. But you've got to tell what went on between him and Susan and those other kids."

The teenager's face twisted into a pout. "I don't want to tell anything about that fucking Susan. I hate her, too."

The hallway door opened, then closed. Sharon turned. Sheila Winston stood nearby, her pretty face drawn in concern. Sharon swiveled her head and said to Midge, "If you don't help us, we can't help you. Midge, don't you know that Linda planted the whole idea in those boys'

minds? It was someone else's doing, not yours. *Please,*
sweetheart . . ."

"Was not. It was *not* that stupid Linda's idea. I hate
her, too. Hate them all." Midge folded her arms and
pursed her lips. "I don't want to talk anymore."

Russell Black sat nearby, stone-faced and helpless.
Sheila sank into a chair on Sharon's right.

"Midge, Leslie Schlee told us those boys were first to
bring up killing him," Sharon said.

"Did not. Leslie knows better. It *was* me." Midge's upper lip curled. "I don't think I like you anymore. Go
away."

"Good *God,* Midge." Sharon buried her face in the
palms of her hands. She wept.

Sheila's touch was tender but firm on Sharon's arm.
"I've got to tell you, sister, you're hurting more than
you're helping. Sessions like this will only make her re-
gress."

Sharon angrily raised her head. Her makeup streaked,
she said, "Dammit, Sheila, I have to . . ." Her words
trailed off. Sheila's expression showed as much feeling
for Sharon as it did for Midge, if not more. Sheila
squeezed Sharon's hand and lowered her gaze.

"I don't know anything about the legal aspects," Sheila
said. "But you're not going to get her off dead center, and
any progress she's made, this can take her right back to
ground zero. She's simply not going to be any help, period." Midge now stared at a point in the far corner as
though she were alone in the room. If Sheila's words had
any effect on the teenager, it didn't show.

Sharon sniffled and dug in her purse for a handkerchief. "It means we're beaten, Sheila. It means we don't
have a chance to save this child."

Her insides mush, her posture the epitome of abject despair, Sharon stood off to one side and let Russell Black
handle the bench conference. She glanced at Fraterno,
caught an almost indiscernible quiver in Kathleen's lower
lip. Milt Breyer looked pompous and pleased with himself.

"We'll talk about it in the jury instruction conference,
Mr. Black," Sandy Griffin said with understanding, "and
I'll even go over transcripts of the testimony if you'd

like. But I don't recall a single piece of evidence that either Miss Rathermore or her sister suffered any abuse, sexual or emotional, and lacking such evidence, I'm powerless to so instruct the jury. I need to dismiss the jury now, for the remainder of the day, and we'll go into chambers for the conference."

"How 'bout Linda Rathermore's testimony, Judge?" Black said. "I think somebody would *infer* abuse from—"

"Inference isn't evidence, Mr. Black. I've issued a bench warrant for the woman, and that's all I can do. I can't *force* the district attorney's office to press charges against Mrs. Rathermore"—here she shot a nasty glance at Fraterno and Breyer, who simultaneously bowed their heads—"but I can assure you that if they don't, I can make things uncomfortable for them. Now, as for the conference—"

There was a loud disturbance at the rear of the spectator section. Griffin interrupted her speech and glared. Woodenly Sharon turned toward the noise.

"Bailiff," Judge Griffin said loudly and sternly, "I've told you over and over not to admit anyone once this trial is in session, other than witnesses. Now tell those people the courtroom is full, and that they're to wait outside in the—"

Sharon's dull gaze fell on the bailiff, who stood just inside the entry with his hands spread apologetically, then shifted to the wiry, honey blond woman on the bailiff's right. The woman, erect in posture, athletic of build, was Virginia Schlee.

Sharon's heart stopped and her stomach jumped into her throat.

And the bailiff said, "I'm sorry, Judge, but they say they've got to see—"

As Sharon looked even farther to her right at Leslie Schlee, Leslie demure and coed-like in a navy blue dress with a sailor collar, holding hands with—

"—Miss Hays. Say they're supposed to be witnesses or something. I *told* them about your rules, but they—"

—Curtis Schlee, all arrogance gone from his bearing, Curtis Schlee alongside his daughter in a plain blue suit, his gaze on the floor. He looked up, locked gazes with Sharon, and mouthed silently, "Put her on."

"—just wouldn't listen," the bailiff finished.

"I'll deal with this in a minute," Judge Griffin said, then whispered, "Sorry, Mr. Black. What were we saying?"

So intent was Black on his argument that he hadn't even glanced to the rear. Kathleen Fraterno had, however, and her jaw dropped nearly to the floor. Black said, "Judge, I think we need to be afforded every chance to—"

Sharon stepped up and yanked on Black's sleeve so hard that she jerked him off balance. Black righted himself, his features twisted in surprise. Sharon said fervently, pointing, "Back there, boss. Look back there."

Now Black turned, surveyed the rear of the courtroom, gaped in shock, then practically gave himself whiplash as he whirled to face the bench. "It ain't over, Judge. We got another witness to call."

"Objection, Your Honor," Kathleen Fraterno said. "This is irregular as it can be."

46

Leslie Schlee faced a spellbound jury and an equally mesmerized, jam-packed seating section as if the crowd
wasn't even there. She sat demurely in the witness chair,
her knees together schoolgirl style, her fingers intertwined in her lap, and paid heed to only three people:
Sharon Hays, who tenderly conducted Leslie's direct examination from her chair at the defense table, and Leslie's
mother and dad, wedged in alongside Deborah North on
the second-row aisle. The pretty adolescent answered
Sharon's questions in a bell-clear voice, and after each response glanced toward her parents for approval. Sharon
took a break, poured herself a cup of water from a
chrome carafe set before her, and glanced over her shoulder. Virginia and Curtis Schlee were holding hands.
Sometimes things work out, Sharon thought.

She returned her attention to the witness. "As best you
recall, Leslie, how long did these activities continue?"

"I beg your pardon?" A polite tone, reflecting upbring-
ing.

"These sessions over at the Rathermores' house."

"You mean, the sexual stuff?"

Visible in the periphery of Sharon's vision, one female
juror winced. Sharon didn't blame her. The story Leslie
had related was excruciating to hear. "Yes," Sharon said.

"I guess it was . . . my first time over there, I was fourteen. All the kids at school, they'd been talking about it
for a long time. I went over there until Mr. Rathermore
got . . . you know. About a year and a half."

"Until Mr. Rathermore got killed?"

"Yes, ma'am."

"And during that entire time," Sharon said, "the only member of his own family that Mr. Rathermore took to bed was his younger daughter, Susan?"

"That's right," Leslie said.

"Never Midge?" On Sharon's right, Midge had buried her face in her crossed forearms.

"Midge, no. She tried, even tried to get in on it a few times, but he wouldn't let her."

"Oh? And why was that."

Fraterno offered a lame objection. "The witness cannot know Mr. Rathermore's reason for—"

"I'll withdraw and rephrase the question," Sharon said rather testily. "Why did Mr. Rathermore *say* he didn't want sex with Midge?"

"He told us," Leslie said, her eyes down, "that she was too fat."

"And did he say so in front of her?"

"All the time. He called her piglet and made her wait on the rest of us. Bring us dope and stuff."

"And as for Susan," Sharon said, "was she a willing participant?"

"In the . . . ?"

"Yes, Leslie. In the sex."

"She didn't fight it or anything," Leslie said. "Sometimes she'd cry, but he'd just laugh at her. The other kids, they'd laugh at Susan, too. We were high all the time, most of us."

Sharon glanced at her watch. Leslie had been on the stand for nearly two hours. The story was pretty well told, but Sharon had one point to reaffirm. "One last time, Leslie. You're positive, absolutely certain, that when the discussion of killing Mr. Rathermore came up in the living room, it was Troy Burdette who first mentioned it."

"Oh, yes, ma'am. I couldn't be mistaken about that."

"And Midge didn't draw him into the conversation, or . . . ?"

"Troy. It was all troy," Leslie said.

"Thank you, Leslie. I know this has been as difficult for you to tell as it was for us to hear. Pass the witness, Your Honor," Sharon said.

There was pin-drop silence. Judge Griffin bit down on the end of a ballpoint, her eyes glazed. The jurors seemed limp. Sharon herself was weak as a kitten.

On the prosecution side, Fraterno and Breyer were bent close to each other, whispering. She vigorously shook her head. He held up a hand, palm out, in her direction, then said to the judge, "I'll cross-examine this witness, Your Honor." Fraterno pointedly closed her file and stared off into space.

Griffin looked stunned. "Be my guest, Mr. Breyer."

He sat with his back straight as a ramrod and pyramided his fingers beneath his chin. "Miss Schlee, don't you think it's pretty convenient for you to have this sudden recollection after all this time?"

Leslie gave him a coquettish look of contempt. "It's the same thing I've always said."

"Oh?" he said. "Said to whom, Miss Schlee?"

Sharon tightly crossed her fingers. Breyer was a bumbling idiot in the courtroom, but just the kind of bumbling idiot to intimidate the dickens out of this child.

"I told my daddy," Leslie said. "I also told the policeman you—"

"Your . . . daddy. Miss Schlee, have you had any contact with Midge Rathermore since she's been in jail?"

Leslie's gaze shifted slightly. "Yes."

Sharon tensed. Black inhaled loudly.

"She calls you, right?"

"Sometimes."

"And during these phone calls, have the two of you discussed the testimony you've just given?"

"No, I—"

"Or more to the point," Breyer said, "has Miss Rathermore promised you any rewards for what you were going to say? Midge Rathermore is good at promising rewards, Miss Schlee, isn't she?"

Sharon rose to object. Black stopped her with a hand on her forearm. "Let him hang himself," Black murmured.

"I wouldn't know about that," Leslie said stiffly.

"Well, Miss Schlee," Breyer said. "Please tell the court. And the jury. Exactly what did you and Miss Rathermore discuss?"

Leslie licked her lips, her eyes darting from side to side. "I ... we ..."

"What did you discuss, Miss Schlee?"

At that instant Midge looked up. Leslie watched the overweight girl for a second, then showered Midge with a tender smile. "I told Midge that if she needed a friend, I'd be there. Midge never had any friends. A girl like her needs them."

Breyer's face appeared frozen, and for an instant Sharon wondered if old Milt might be having a stroke. He looked at Fraterno. She ignored him, her head down, her cheeks the color of ripe plums. Two jurors—the gray-haired woman and a motherly type in her thirties—favored Leslie with looks of sympathetic nuns. Breyer thumbed furiously through his notes. Air escaped his lungs and his chest fell like a deflating tire. "No further questions," Milton Breyer finally said.

Leslie stepped down, and Virginia and Curtis Schlee followed their daughter outside, mother, father, and child with hands firmly joined. Russell Black rested the case for the defense; Sandy Griffin dismissed the jury for the day, then told the lawyers that in the morning they'd have closing arguments: thirty minutes for the prosecution, an hour for the defense, then an additional half hour for the prosecution's rebuttal if the D.A.'s felt they needed the time. Sharon was drained, and even glad her courtroom work on the trial was finished. Russell Black would do the closing argument, of course. He was the best there was.

The two left the courtroom amid a hail of newspeople's questions from all sides, minicams trained on the pair, Sharon smiling and shaking her head as she issued one no-comment after another. As she excuse-me'd her way around Andy Wade, she paused and narrowed her eyes.

Stan Green had Curtis Schlee cornered near the elevators, his chin just inches from Schlee's nose, his jaw working nonstop, his face the picture of angry animation. Virginia and Leslie stood nearby in silence, Virginia's arm protectively around her daughter's shoulders. As Sharon quickened her pace and moved in the direction of the arguing men, Green waved a finger in Curtis Schlee's face.

Russell Black beat Sharon to the punch. His long legs covered the distance in four strides, and the veteran lawyer moved up to shove the detective roughly aside. Green stood his ground and pointed at Curtis Schlee, Schlee cowering against the wall, his face pale through his tennis tan. "I was talking to him," Green said.

"Maybe you were," Black said, his fists clenched, "but now you're talking to me."

"I've got no business with you," Green said.

"Well, you might have," Black said. "I can't stop you from getting together with the feds to railroad this man, but two things. Number one." He held up a finger. "I guarantee you that if Curtis Schlee's indicted over that savings and loan bullshit, I'm callin' my first press conference in twenty years and tellin' the newspapers exactly what you people did to try to keep his daughter off that witness stand. And number two," he said, lowering his hand to his side, "in any federal charge Curtis Schlee's got himself a free lawyer if he wants it." He turned to Schlee. "I don't know if you'd want me or not, Curt. But the offer stands if you're interested."

On her drive home, Sharon came somberly down from her feeling of being high. The ghost of Bradford Brie still haunted her—though she'd managed to shove his death and the cloud it had left hanging to the back of her mind—but that wasn't her problem. It was the trial itself, and the deep-set notion that things had simply gone too easily. Far too easily. By the time she parked in her driveway, she had convinced herself that something was about to go wrong.

47

The something which was about to go wrong jumped up and slapped Sharon's face the following morning as the bailiff brought Midge in from the holding cell. Or if *slap* wasn't the proper word for it, the sensation was certainly more than a gentle nudge.

As Midge timidly took her seat, Sharon's insides sagged in pity. All through the trial Midge's appearance had improved on a day-to-day basis. The teenager was never going to be pretty; the years of obesity had left too much loose skin on her body for her to ever have a model's figure, but during her comings and goings in the courtroom, her grooming had gone from good to better to marvelous. Just yesterday, when the man from Kansas City had taken the stand, Midge's hair had been soft as silk and combed into luxuriant waves. Now, though, as she came into court for final arguments, her appearance had gone to hell in a hand basket.

Sharon couldn't believe that Midge had gone so far downhill in one twelve-hour period, but she had. All of the wave was gone from her hair, which fell over her collar in limp, greasy strings. On the teenager's chin was the ugly red beginning of a pimple. She wore the same blue dress as she'd had on the day before, and the cloth was wrinkled as though she slept in her clothes. As Midge sat down, Sharon did her best to hide her shock and patted the teenager's hand. Sharon risked one glance over her shoulder; from her aisle seat in the spectator section,

Deborah North regarded her daughter as if she were watching a horror movie.

Judge Griffin assumed her place promptly at nine. She'd announced yesterday that she was setting her docket off for final arguments, so there'd be none of the usual preliminary plea bargains or arraignments. Griffin motioned to the bailiff, and the audience stood in anticipation of the jury's arrival. As they did, Milt Breyer stood on the prosecution side. Judge Griffin called out to the bailiff, who halted in his tracks.

"Judge," Breyer said, "the state wishes to offer a rebuttal witness."

Kathleen Fraterno turned in her chair to catch Sharon's eye. "I'm sorry," Kathleen mouthed silently, then lowered her gaze while surreptitiously pointing at Breyer. The feeling of something about to go wrong froze at once into a lump the size of a basketball and plopped into Sharon's stomach. She stared at Fraterno. Lie down with dogs, Kathleen, Sharon thought.

Russell Black popped to his feet. "They've already rested their case, Judge."

Breyer put clenched fists on his waist. "We rested our *case-in-chief*, Your Honor. We're entitled to rebuttal. The witness isn't on our list, by the way. As rebuttal, she doesn't have to be."

Griffin beckoned and both sides approached. As Sharon stood alongside Russell Black, her feet tingled in anticipation. Fraterno wore a curve-hugging black pantsuit which Sharon thought made her lean look cheap, the girl of Milt Breyer's dreams. For the first time Sharon noted that Judge Griffin had abandoned the makeup altogether and gone back to her old pale-faced self. Sandy's makeup lady must have gone the same place as Midge's hair stylist, Sharon thought.

"Mr. Breyer, the district attorney's office should know better than this," Griffin said, leaning forward. "The defense rested yesterday afternoon, and if you'd wanted a rebuttal you should have said so."

"We didn't specifically waive rebuttal, Judge," Breyer said. Fraterno continued to watch the floor.

"Same as," Griffin said. "You kept your mouths shut and agreed to closing arguments this morning."

"We weren't aware of this witness until last night," Breyer said.

Bullshit, Sharon thought. It was last night before you finally decided, To hell with what Kathleen wants to do, you pompous ass. Damn ethics, full speed ahead, is Marvelous Milton's motto.

"We've already wrapped up, Judge," Black said, "and our witnesses are scattered to hell and gone. What if we have to rebut the rebuttal?"

"While it's highly irregular," Judge Griffin said, pinching the bridge of her nose, "and while I'm fully aware that Mr. Breyer is being an absolute horse's ass about this ... the statutes allow the state broad latitude at the trial level." She showed Black a look of apology. "I'm afraid I have to let him get away with this, Mr. Black." She glared at Breyer, who smirked as though nothing turned him on like an insult. Griffin raised her voice. "Bailiff, summon the jury."

The body trooped in, men and women in sync as though trained by a drill instructor. The jury sat. While Sandy Griffin explained to them that there was one more witness to present, Sharon shuffled through her notes. Every person connected with the case was accounted for. Most had testified. Linda Rathermore, check. Troy Burdette, check. Chris Leonard hadn't testified, but Sharon was dead certain the state wouldn't have the nerve to put Leonard on, not with Linda's motel trysts hanging over their heads. Besides, Milt Breyer had said that *she* wasn't on the state's list. Leslie Schlee? Sharon was suddenly cold.

Christ, Sharon thought, what if their witness is Leslie? What if they'd applied enough pressure on Curtis Schlee to get her to change her story? Could they?

"Call your witness, Mr. Breyer," Judge Griffin said.

Breyer half stood and turned toward the spectator section.

"State calls," he said, "Sonya Brown."

Sharon and Black stared at each other. *Who?*

She looked at the back of the room. The courtroom door remained closed. There was no sign of Stan Green, who'd ushered all of the state's witnesses in and out. What is this, Sharon thought, a joke? Then there was movement in front of and to the right of the defense table, and a guard brought Sonya Brown in from the holding cell.

Midge Rathermore murmured softly, "Sonya."

Sharon stared at the teenager's messy hair.

Sonya Brown was thin as a whippet, and even in the plain jailhouse smock her walk was unmistakable, straight from Oakland Avenue, shoulders back, hips swaying in perpetual bumps and grinds. *Hey, baby, want a date?* Her skin was the color of buttered rum, taut over throat and cheekbones. She raised her hand for swearing in, then flowed into the witness chair and crossed her legs. There were bruises on both bony shins.

My God, Sharon thought, have they sunk this low? Have they really gotten this freaking desperate?

"Please state your full name for the record," Breyer said to the witness.

"Sonya Brown." A female baritone, a South Dallas rolling of the letter *r*.

"And where do you now reside, Miss Brown?"

"I been over in the county four monts." Sonya showed no embarrassment whatsoever, as if being in jail was like staying with her sister while looking for a new apartment.

"That's the Lew Sterrett Justice Center," Breyer said. "The county jail?"

"Yes, sir." Sonya had big, loose lips which remained parted when she finished speaking, and teeth like curb stones. Light reflected from a gold inlay.

"Miss Brown, are you acquainted with the defendant in this case, Midge Rathermore?"

Sonya's gaze shifted slightly, directed at nothing. "We cells togethah."

"Is she seated here in the courtroom?"

"Right there." Sonya's pointing finger wasn't precise in its aim, and for an instant Sharon thought the witness was pointing at her.

"During the time the two of you have shared quarters," Breyer said, "have you become well acquainted?"

"I does Midge's hair evah day. I couldn't this mornin'."

"Because you weren't in the cell?"

"No, sir. They brung me ovah here around five-thirty." As if for emphasis, Sonya yawned.

Sharon watched the jury. Surprise jailhouse witnesses

were common foils of the D.A.'s office, but the jurors
didn't know that. They seemed spellbound. Take a path-
ological liar, Sharon thought, hang a "state's witness"
sign around their neck, and suddenly they were Abraham
Lincoln. The knot in Sharon's stomach seemed to double
at once in size. That Sonya did Midge's hair would give
the witness instant credibility with the women on the jury.
The hairdresser knows all.

"During the time you've known her," Breyer said,
"have you had occasion to discuss Midge's knowledge of
the death of her father?"

"Oh, yes, sir. She told me she done it."

Sharon wondered briefly whether Breyer had bothered
to tell Sonya that Midge was alleged to have *hired* the
killing done rather than doing it herself. It wouldn't have
mattered to Sonya. If the testimony hadn't had such drastic potential consequences, Sharon would have laughed
out loud.

"You mean, that she *paid* someone to kill her father,"
Breyer corrected.

"Yes, sir." Sonya's expression was moronically dull.

"Miss Brown . . ." Breyer went through the charade of
examining notes. "Miss Brown, when was the last time
you talked to Midge Rathermore?"

"Last night after supper. We was talkin' about me
fixin' her hair today."

"During that discussion, did the subject of this trial
come up? Specifically, Miss Brown, did you discuss the
testimony of a Mr. Steven Gallagher?"

"The dude from outta town?"

"Yes, Miss Brown," Breyer said. "The gentleman from
Kansas City."

"Yeah. Midge said after they changed the burglar
alarm, she give the new code to this boy was gonna kill
her daddy."

"You mean, the code for disarming the security system?"

"Sure do."

"And you're sure," Breyer said, practically preening in
place, "that Midge Rathermore told you that after the
code was changed, she got the new code and gave it to a
boy."

"Yes, sir. Ain't no doubt about that."

"A boy who intended to kill Midge's father?"

"That's what she said."

"Continuing with the conversation of last evening," Breyer said, "did Midge Rathermore also mention Leslie Schlee?"

"Sure did, sir."

"And what did she tell you in regard to Leslie?"

Sonya drew up to her full seated height. "She said Leslie was her friend, and that her and Leslie made up this stuff about her daddy messin' with teenage kids. Said Leslie was gonna lie to get Midge outta trouble."

One juror, a black woman in her forties, was looking at Midge. Heretofore Sharon had seen the same juror gazing upon the defendant with a sort of motherly tenderness, but now the woman appeared uncertain and even a little angry. the juror realized that Sharon was watching and quickly looked away. Sharon lowered her head and doodled on her legal pad. Her vision was so blurred that she didn't have the slightest idea what she was writing down.

On cross, Russell Black did his best with what he had to work with. "Miz Brown, what is it you're in jail for?"

"Objection." Breyer's hands were folded, his shoulders hunched slightly over the table. "The witness hasn't been convicted, Judge."

"Sustained," Sandy Griffin said, almost reluctantly.

"Okay," Black said. "Miz Brown, what have you ever been *convicted* of?"

"Prostitooshon. Jist once." Sonya managed to sound as though whoring was as innocent as baking cookies.

"Well, lemme ask you, Miz Brown. What reward has the state promised you for giving this testimony?" Black said. A warning bell sounded in Sharon's head. Should have asked the question differently, boss, she thought.

Sonya's eyes grew round as Whoopi Goldberg's. Her mouth slackened. "You mean, they's a *rewahd*?"

Black looked down as laughter erupted. The question had backfired big time, and Sharon suspected that Russell Black got caught with his pants down in the courtroom about once in every century. Black waited until Sandy Griffin's banging gavel had restored order, then cleared his throat.

"Not a money reward, Miz Brown. I'm askin' you

what kind of a deal they made you for gettin' up here and tellin' this ... story."

Now Sonya seemed indignant. "They didn' promise me nothin'."

Sharon leaned back to glare at Fraterno. She wouldn't turn her head in Sharon's direction, though her face reddened even more. Of course they hadn't given poor little Sonya a written snitch agreement. The deal with the state went like this: you do us good, we talk about it. Shortly after the trial, whatever misdemeanor beef had been filed against Sonya Brown would disappear, and no one would be any the wiser. Within months, even weeks perhaps, Sonya would return to jail on new charges. The Sonya Browns of the world always did.

"And you're not *expectin'* anything, I guess," Black said, "after you finish this testifyin'."

Sonya put on the same face she'd probably used when the cop had propositioned her, paid her, then had hauled her downtown after she'd assumed the sock-it-to-me position. *Who, Me?* "I wouldn' know nothin' about that, sir," she said.

Black inhaled, then exhaled slowly through his nose. He gave Sharon a look that was every bit as helpless as she felt at the moment. Finally he said, "Pass this woman. This ... *witness*. No further questions, Judge."

Sonya sauntered out just as she'd come in, hips swinging, all but snapping her fingers. As she pranced by the defense table, Midge showed her hairdresser a vacant, happy smile.

48

"Dammit," Sharon said, looking out the corridor window. The sky over downtown Dallas was a hazy blue; smoggy haloes blurred the outlines of the glistening ball atop Reunion Tower and the Renaissance Plaza spire. "Dammit," she said again. "If only we could've had one more shot at Linda."

"Or maybe," Anthony Gear said, "we should've used the old woman from the Windjammer Motel." He was seated on the front edge of the bench with his forearms resting on his thighs and his tie hanging straight down between his legs. Deborah North sat alone across the hall, staring at nothing. Up and down the corridor, courthouse gossips gossiped and newspeople newsed.

"I tell ya," Russell Black said, bending low on the bench to scratch his ankle, "and I been doin' this for twenty-five years. There's never been a trial where you don't feel like you've left somethin' out you should have put in. Usually you're right, too, but think. We already beat Linda up as much as we could, and showed she was havin' relationships with those kids. And the old woman? She'd scare Godzilla to death, not to mention the jury. We put on what we put on, and did a damn good job of it. If the jury wants to believe that whore on the end, well, there's not much we can do about that." He glanced at his watch, then at Gear. "How long they been out already?"

The detective checked his own watch. "Hour thirty-seven. The longer the better, huh?"

Dallas Morning News reporter Andy Wade came close,

and opened his mouth as if to speak. Black vigorously shook his head. Wade shrugged, did an about-face, and headed for Breyer and Fraterno. The prosecutors were about a hundred feet down the hall, talking in whispers.

"Most people believe a jury out a long time is good for the defense," Black said, "but that's not always true. I got an acquittal once in forty minutes. Another time I remember, they were out four days and went ahead and hung my guy."

Sharon nervously smoothed her skirt, wanting to comfort Deb North but not having the slightest idea what to say, wanting to do anything to ease the tension. Russ's final argument had been perfect as always, just the right blend of fact and heart-bending emotion. Kathleen's closing statement had been . . . well, merely adequate, Sharon thought, but she'd honed in sharply on Sonya Brown's testimony, which was about the only ammunition left to her. Sharon had to hand it to Fraterno; if Sharon herself had just been named a respondent in someone's divorce, she doubted she could find her way to the courthouse. Breyer had shown good sense in letting Kathleen do the honors, Sharon thought. Midge's fate was in the hands of the jury. Or God, Sharon thought, if there's any difference between the almighty and twelve tried and true. We should win, she thought. We put on the best evidence. But anyone who believed that juries decided cases on the facts alone simply had their head in the clouds.

She said softly, "I know there are exceptions, boss, but it's usually true. If they stay out a long time they're undecided."

"Or just dumb," Black said, then looked guardedly around. "Christ, don't let any of those reporters hear me sayin' that. Headlines'll be, 'Black Calls Jury Dumb.' "

Sharon laughed nervously, so did Anthony Gear, and Black finally joined in the merriment, three people on pins and needles, grasping at anything to keep from screaming in agony. Sharon suddenly had to go to the bathroom. She excused herself and headed up the corridor.

And stopped in her tracks as assistant D.A. Edward Teeter emerged from the elevators, accompanied by two uniformed county deputies. All three men showed grim faces.

Oh, my sweet God, Sharon thought, not now of all times. They've found him. They've found that filthy pervert Bradford Brie lying in a pool of his own blood, and they've somehow traced him to me. Not now, she thought helplessly. Not until Midge's verdict is in, until I can prepare Melanie for . . .

As the men approached, it was all Sharon could do to keep from sagging limply to the floor. They stood before her, Teeter in the center, flanked by the two lawmen. One deputy was big with truck-sized shoulders, the other a squat redheaded fireplug.

She looked at them.

"We need to see you, Miss Hays," Teeter said.

Christ, oh, Christ. "I'm waiting on a verdict," Sharon said, her speech rapid, her voice up an octave.

"We heard," Teeter said. "But this won't keep. Tell her, Wilson."

The big deputy had stubble on his chin. "We just come from that fella Brie's place. The grand jury returned a true bill and we just got a warrant this morning."

"Brie?" Sharon smiled, even though her lips felt like they might crack.

"Yeah, you know. Somebody killed that guy, Miss Hays. Shot him in his living room with his own gun." Wilson narrowed his eyes.

"Oh, how . . ." Words stuck in Sharon's throat. "Awful," she finished weakly.

"Anyway," Teeter said, "we thought you ought to be one of the first to know about it. The guy won't be bothering you anymore."

Sharon was about ready to extend her wrists to receive the handcuffs. "Any idea who . . . ?"

"None," Teeter said. "To tell you the truth, that's a file not likely to be closed anytime soon. Maybe years from now some guy already in prison will get a sudden urge to tell, but we've got too much else on the burner to waste a lot of time on a case like that. Anybody could be the suspect, killing that guy. Guess you wish it could've been you, huh?"

Sharon's lips twisted. "Could have been . . . ?"

Wilson's hard-bitten features relaxed in a grin. "What I think it'll be, Miss Hays," he said, "is one of those misdemeanor murders they're always talking about. You've heard that one, haven't you? A misdemeanor murder is where somebody killed the guy, but who cares?"

The other deputy broke up, laughing and holding his sides. "New one on me. Pretty good."

"Anyway, because we sort of dropped the ball," Teeter said, "I wanted to tell you in person. You should rest easier knowing Mr. Brie is handled without the aid of the system. Have a nice day, Miss Hays."

The three turned to go, then Teeter stopped and said, "Oh, and Miss Hays. Good luck on your verdict. We've been hearing things about the Rathermore case, and just want you to know the whole D.A.'s office doesn't side with Milt Breyer on this one." He took two more steps toward the elevator, then said over his shoulder, "That's not for publication, Miss Hays. I'll deny saying that if it ever comes back to me." He left with the two cops in tow.

Sharon was able to stand until Teeter and the deputies had boarded the elevator and the doors had closed. As soon as the men disappeared from view, she staggered to one side and leaned against the corridor wall to support herself.

Sharon came out of the ladies' room with her makeup on straight and her knee joints twin masses of jelly. Mentally she was pinching herself. God, had it really happened? Was she really and truly going to get away with murder? Wait a minute, she told herself, it wasn't really *murder*. It was an accident, plain and simple. Besides, killing Bradford Brie didn't bother her conscience; to protect Melanie, she'd kill the bastard a second time. As she neared Judge Griffin's court, Sharon did her best to put Bradford Brie out of her mind, steeling herself for the agonizing wait until the jury's return.

The corridor was wall-to-wall activity, rapid movement everywhere, spectators and newspeople alike jockeying for entrance into the courtroom. As Sharon watched, Deborah North, her movements wooden, walked past the head of the line and went inside. Sharon's heart came up in her mouth.

Russell Black approached, his expression worried, took Sharon's arm to spin her around and head her toward the entry. "They're comin' in already, girl," he said. "Didn't take 'em long, huh?"

* * *

Sharon was too nervous to remain seated but too limp with worry to stand. During her final days as a prosecutor, waiting for juries had been old hat to her, but now her flesh crawled. She thought this had to be the most awful moment of her life—even worse, in fact, than the instant when Bradford Brie had rushed her in his filthy living room. Her action at that time had been impulse fueled by self-preservation instinct, and the enormity of what had happened hadn't struck home until much later. This was different. This was total agony.

Sharon glanced at Midge. She still was impassive, the dull-witted teenager acting as if the events unfolding were a movie and she was the watcher, and that once it was over she'd simply get up and go home. Sharon swiveled her head to look at the prosecution side; Kathleen Fraterno sat with her chin resting on intertwined fingers as Milt Breyer pretended to read the newspaper. Anthony Gear reached up to give Sharon's shoulder an encouraging squeeze; she turned and smiled as the detective winked at her. Russell Black's expression was stoic, almost resigned. Impulsively Sharon gave Midge a little hug. As she did, the bailiff ordered the courtroom to its feet and the jury returned.

They didn't smile and they didn't frown. Juries never showed emotion. Never, as if their secret was too terrible for them to share. Christ, jury, tell me *something* by your look, Sharon thought. Frown at me. Giggle at me. Anything, just don't . . .

All sat, jurors, judge, and spectators. At the rear of the courtroom a man coughed.

"Has the jury reached a verdict?" Sandy Griffin said.

The foreman stood, a thin man with an Adam's apple the size of an eight-ball. "We have, Your Honor."

Sharon's toes curled up inside her shoes.

The bailiff adjusted the knot on his tie, took the slip of paper from the foreman, and carried it up to hand over the bench. Judge Griffin unfolded the slip with a papery rattle. She read silently. "Defendant will rise," she said.

Midge was suddenly in tears, sobbing hopelessly, her heavy legs buckling as she tried to hoist herself out of her chair. Sharon braced her client with helping hands. Finally Midge faced the bench. Except for her loud sniffling, there was total silence.

Judge Griffin read without emotion, "In Cause Number 114708, County of Dallas, on the charge of murder, we the jury—"

Sharon softly closed her eyes.

"—find the defendant—"

And leaned toward Midge.

"—not—"

Oh, God, oh, God, oh, sweet word not. And reached for the child,

"—guilty."

and hugged the daylights out of her before the words were completely out of Griffin's mouth. Sharon stood among the growing crescendo of voices and held Midge's head buried in the hollow of her shoulder, Midge's body heaving with sobs, the jurors smiling now, even the judge's mask cracking as the corners of her mouth turned upward.

"What'd I tell you, huh?" Russell Black said, grinning from ear to ear. "Never a doubt, girl."

Sharon laughed long and heartily as she hugged the sobbing teenager even harder and cried her own tears of happiness. "So *now* you're going to cry," she whispered in Midge's ear.

Sharon stood off to one side and let Russell Black have the interview to himself because he deserved it. It was his show and that was all there was to it, spotlights on and minicams whirring. She relaxed, folded her arms, and leaned her back against the corridor wall, enjoying the performance along with the rest of Black's fans, the weathered, knowing face smiling like a politician's, some humor in each of his answers, his meaning deadly serious. He's a star, Sharon thought. He ought to be.

She wistfully left her place and strolled along the corridor, passing the jabbering knots of people, pretending not to notice the glances of recognition which came her way. Melanie would be home in a couple of days. Sharon hadn't made up her mind what to do about Rob. Before she reached her final decision, she was certain that she'd argue with Sheila several more times.

Deborah North was waiting in the courtroom on pins

and needles, and Sharon had left her alone. Judge Griffin had ordered the bailiff to bring Midge's things from the jail, then to release the teenager to her mother. Sharon would like to see the reunion, but the moment was for Midge and Deb and no one else. With enough love they'll make it, Sharon thought.

As she neared the elevators, she softly hummed under her breath the opening bars to "Help Me Make It Through the Night," the old Crystal Gale tune. On the way home she was going to treat herself to the latest Garth Brooks CD at the music store, a bottle of Cutty from A&A Liquors, get on the phone and invite Sheila over. She pressed the Down button, leaned against the wall, and crossed her ankles.

Less than twenty feet from where she stood, Milt Breyer was in an animated conference with the two movie guys. As she watched, Breyer held his hands out in a pleading attitude. Rayford Sly vigorously shook his head. The elevator opened and Sharon stepped inside the car. The doors began to close, but she stopped them. She looked again as Breyer wagged his finger at the movie guys and continued to plead his case.

Sharon hesitated. What the hell, she thought, I've earned it. She laughed out loud. Breyer and the movie men turned as one to look at her. She released her hold on the elevator doors and they started to close.

"Lights. Action," Sharon Hays said. Then the sliding doors cut the men and their puzzled frowns off from her view.

49

After all the nail-biting, dreaded anticipation and grinding of teeth, Sharon thought that the sight of Rob in the flesh was a bit of a letdown and, yes, somewhat unreal. As though a cutout of someone she used to know was pasted over the face of a statue.

She sat beside Melanie in a darkened corner of a Channel 8 sound stage and watched the interview, and had to admit that the whole thing was mesmerizing. Rob, his sun-lamp tan bronze under the spotlight, relaxed in an easy chair and fielded questions from—what the hell is her name? Sharon thought—the Channel 8 entertainment-review specialist, a perfect-haired blonde whose sun-lamp tan was even darker than Rob's. When Sharon had lived with him, he had had a gap between his two front teeth; now the gap was gone, replaced by a row of unstained porcelain which positively glinted when he smiled. Twice they held up the session, minicams off, while both Rob and the interviewer went over the allegedly spontaneous interview questions and made a few changes.

Now the interviewer said, "What is it that made you want to do this character?"

And Rob, elbows on armrests, spread his hands, palms up, to say, "This isn't just another cop, that I didn't want to do. Detective Ragan has some depth to him. There's his commitment to the job, and his struggle to keep the violence separated from his family life. I've got a child of my own, and believe me that's important."

Barf, barf, Sharon thought. Earlier, Rob's response to

that identical question had been that he liked the action, the tough-guy image of the role, and the detective's unwavering commitment to right a dog-eat-dog society. The change had been Rob's agent's suggestion, an oily-looking bald guy in pressed Dockers and a knit shirt who sat just off camera. In the darkness, Melanie tugged Sharon's sleeve. She bent her head to lend her daughter an ear.

"Was he always this much of a show-off, Mom?" Melanie was wearing a starched blue dress which had put serious dents in Sharon's credit line at Lord and Taylor's, and Sharon was already wondering if her conscience would let her fudge a bit on the department store's return policy. Like his agent, Rob wore Dockers along with a lime green knit polo, both guys looking as though they were in a hurry to make their tee time.

"Was he, Mom?" Melanie whispered urgently.

In her best Sunday tailored navy blue suit and spike heels, having blown fifty-six bucks for a shampoo, blow-dry, styling job, and manicure at Neiman's (telling herself it was all for Melanie, but knowing deep down that she wanted her ex-lover to see that Sharon Hays could still turn a few heads when she wanted), she felt both overdressed and dumb. I won't do it, she thought. I will not put Melanie's father down to her. Apparently Rob was going to be with them for life now, one way or the other, and any opinions Melanie formed simply had to be her own.

"Was he a show-off, Mom?" Melanie said.

"Let's just say," Sharon said, "that he used to be a bit more reserved, sweetheart."

The unmistakable odor of pancake makeup wafted up Sharon's nostrils as Rob near-kissed her, first just missing one cheek, then the other. "*Muf*-fin. Hey, you're looking great," he said.

Sharon blinked. "Hi, Rob. You look great, too."

"And is this . . . ? *Is it*?" Rob down in a crouch now, grinning at Melanie, the smile straight from acting class. "She's your absolute image, Muffin. Give Daddy a kiss, sweetheart."

My God, Sharon thought, she's eleven years old, not two. Rob looked up at Sharon as if he expected her to say, Say hello to your father, dear, something like that, but Sharon merely rolled her eyes.

Melanie stepped forward and offered her cheek. "Hi, Dad." For just an instant Sharon thought the child would burst into giggles.

"Hey, Harry, will you *look at her*?" Rob standing, grasping his agent's upper arm, his other hand palm up in Melanie's direction.

"Got you a real little princess here, Rob-oh," Harry said. He looked at his watch. "Don't forget the radio guys."

"Oh, hey ..." Rob snapping his fingers, his gaze on Sharon, the classic acting-class look of apology. "You understand, Muffin, huh? Listen, tomorrow I'll make more time."

A pang of regret shot through Sharon as she looked at Melanie, her daughter not showing much emotion, Sharon despising whatever lunatic notion had prompted her to take Rob up on the invitation to visit the studio and hear the interview. Which had come by mail, through the agent.

Sharon locked gazes with Rob and forced a smile. "Sure, we understand, Rob. Break a leg, will you?"

Sharon drove halfway home before she could think of anything to say, Melanie gazing out the window at asphalt pavement, fast-food restaurants along Lemmon Avenue, the Burger King, KFC with Colonel Sanders himself grinning from the sign. Melanie's expression was vacant as—God, Sharon thought—Midge Rathermore's had been the first time Sharon had met her in the holding cell. *If that's all there is, then let's keep dancing.* If I've screwed up by taking her to see him, Sharon thought, I'm never going to get over it.

She stopped at a red light behind a Dodge minivan, screwed up her courage, and said, "Well, what did you think?"

Melanie watched her mother with moist brown eyes. "About my father?" Until now she'd referred to Rob as "my daddy."

"Yes, him," Sharon said.

"Oh, he's cool, I guess. Can we get something to eat?"

"Just 'he's cool'? How did he make you feel?"

"I don't know," Melanie said. "Kind of the same way as when I found out the guy on television was my dad. Just that the guy on television is someone my mom used to know. Not really like he's my father or anything. I guess I've always had you, Mom, and we don't really need anybody else." She seemed to Sharon to be a decade older than she was, the little girl growing up to see what life was all about.

Sharon gripped the wheel with both hands. "Well, maybe tomorrow, if he's got time . . . would you like that, possibly get to know him better?"

Melanie seemed thoughtful. She stretched out on the seat and put her head in Sharon's lap. "If you want me to, it's cool, Mom. I'd rather just do something with you, though. Hey, you think we could go to the movies together?"

A tear ran suddenly down Sharon's cheek, and she swallowed a painful lump from her throat. The light changed to green and the minivan moved on. She reached down and touched Melanie's cheek. "I love you, sweetheart," Sharon said.

"I love you, too, Mom. Could we get something to eat now?"